From *Max & Jane*

"I want you to help transform me, a superplain Jane, into the kind of girl that you and your friends would go for. . . ."

"But, Jane, you look fine the way you are," Max told me when he got a chance to slide a word in edgewise. "You don't need to change."

I laughed. "Listen, Max," I said to him, staring straight into his eyes. "Would *you* go for me?"

From *Justin & Nicole*

"For your information," I told Madison and Rose, aka Snob Central, "I *am* going to the prom. And I'm wearing *this* dress."

Rose snorted. "Who's your date? Your cousin? Or maybe an older brother?"

I looked wildly around the dress shop, searching my brain for the name of a guy—any guy. And then my gaze landed on *him*. Mr. Made-to-be-Naomi-Campbell's-dream-guy . . .

From *Jake & Christy*

All signs of fatigue gone, my mother's eyes shone at the thought of seeing me in my floor-length gown. As I said, she has a thing about the prom.

"You and Jake are going to have a wonderful time," she mused. "It means the world to me that you two are going together."

"Uh . . . yeah. It'll be a blast," I agreed.

How could I have even *considered* getting out of the date with Jake? There was no way I could let her down. . . .

**ALSO AVAILABLE FROM
LAUREL-LEAF BOOKS**

BEING BINDY, *Alyssa Brugman*

CODE ORANGE, *Caroline B. Cooney*

HOME IS EAST, *Many Ly*

I IS SOMEONE ELSE, *Patrick Cooper*

LADY ELENA: THE WAY OF THE
WARRIOR, *Patricia Malone*

QUEEN B, *Laura Peyton Roberts*

Prom Season

Three Novels

Elizabeth Craft

Published by Laurel-Leaf
an imprint of Random House Children's Books
a division of Random House, Inc.
New York

This omnibus was originally published
by Bantam Books in separate volumes under the titles:
Love Stories Prom Trilogy 1: Max & Jane
© 2000 by 17th Street Productions
Love Stories Prom Trilogy 2: Justin & Nicole
© 2000 by 17th Street Productions
Love Stories Prom Trilogy 3: Jake & Christy
© 2000 by 17th Street Productions

Laurel-Leaf and colophon are registered trademarks of
Random House, Inc.

ALLOYENTERTAINMENT   Produced by Alloy Entertainment
                      151 West 26th Street
                      New York, NY 10001

www.randomhouse.com/teens

Educators and librarians, for a variety of teaching tools, visit us at
www.randomhouse.com/teachers

RL: 6.0
ISBN: 978-0-375-84074-6
March 2007
Printed in the United States of America
10 9 8 7 6 5 4 3 2 1

Contents

Max & Jane

One

Jane

*H*OPELESS. *ABSOLUTELY HOPELESS.* I stared at myself in the tarnished mirror that hung over the sink in the girls' bathroom. And I didn't like what I was seeing. There might as well have been a sign hanging over my head that read Jane Smith, the Queen of Blah.

"Mirror, mirror, on the wall, who's the dullest of them all?" I whispered to my reflection.

"You are," I answered myself without a moment's hesitation.

I wasn't disfigured or anything. But my looks had the overall personality of a paper towel. Straight, dirty-blond hair, boring blue eyes, and distinctly *un*kissable lips. As for fashion . . . Let's just say that my idea of dressing up was wearing my "good" blue jeans and a T-shirt sans ketchup stains. All in all,

Plain Jane Smith was no one to get excited about.

I am the last girl in this school who Charlie Simpson would ask out on a date, I mused as I inspected my teeth in the mirror for signs of renegade poppy seeds from the bagel I had eaten this morning.

Charlie Simpson. Even *thinking* his name made a tingle travel from the tips of my toes to the top of my spine. Charlie was, for lack of a better term, my dream guy. Yes, he was tall, dark, and handsome. He was also one of the most popular guys in school. I doubted there was a girl in all of Union High who wouldn't be psyched to have Charlie slip his leather varsity letterman's jacket around her shoulders on a chilly fall evening.

I leaned close to the mirror, peering at several blackheads that were the current bane of my existence. What would it be like if my skin were as soft and smooth as one of those *CosmoGirl* magazine cover model's? Or if I had the kind of beauty and style that made guys stop and stare as I walked down a crowded hallway?

The bell rang for third period. I breezed into Mr. Atkison's classroom, giggling with a couple of cheerleaders. As I slid into my seat, I sensed a pair of electric blue eyes staring at me.

"Hi, Charlie," I greeted him, batting my foot-long black lashes. "How's it going?"

He ambled toward me, then perched on top of my desk. He was so close that I could smell the sandalwood soap he used in the shower. "Things would be a whole lot better if you would agree to

2

accompany me to our senior prom," he answered.

"I would love to go with you," I told him, batting my eyelashes again.

Yeah, right! And I would love to be checked into a mental hospital too. I had been doing my own lame version of batting my eyelashes at Charlie every chance I'd had for the last four years. Ever since I had first seen him, the summer before my freshman year in high school, I'd had an enormous crush on him.

It had been one of the hottest days of August, and I was baby-sitting the Janson twins for what seemed like the thousandth time that summer. To get out of playing yet another hot, sweaty game of kick the can, I took Simon and Ethan to an indoor ice-skating rink. I thought I had found the perfect way to spend the afternoon—until Ethan fell down. He was sprawled out on the ice, wailing and crying.

And then it happened. From the other side of the rink I saw *him* skating toward our little group in strong, smooth glides. The first thing I noticed was his size. He was tall, making the twins and me seem like miniatures in comparison. When he looked at me, his blue eyes twinkled.

He crouched next to Ethan. "What's wrong, Chief?" he asked. "Did you and the ice have a nasty encounter?"

Ethan looked up at this stranger. "Yeah . . ." He was half wailing, half interested in what this guy was going to say next.

The guy looked at me, then at the twins. "I'm

3

Charlie Simpson," he said. "And I've fallen down on this ice so many times that you'll find imprints of my butt all over this place."

Simon giggled. I giggled. A moment later Ethan's tears stopped, and *he* giggled. "I've only fallen once," he informed Charlie.

Charlie raised his eyebrows. "Once? That's nothing! My kid brother, Bobby, has fallen so many times that I'm beginning to wonder if he knows which way is up!"

A moment later Ethan pushed himself up off the ice. "Let's go, Simon!" he said, the tears gone as suddenly as they had come.

I'm in love. It was the first thought that came into my mind. *Charlie isn't only gorgeous, he's a hero.*

"Looks like the little guy is going to live," Charlie commented.

I felt my face turn bright red. This was it. My big moment to flirt with a totally cute guy. "Uh . . . yeah—th-thanks," I stammered.

I wanted to say something witty, something inspired. Instead I stared at my hands and scraped the ice with the tip of my skate blade. *Anything. Say anything,* I ordered myself. *Don't let this opportunity pass you by.*

Suddenly my blade stuck in the ice. "Ahh . . ." I started to pitch forward.

In a flash a pair of strong, warm hands encircled my waist. "Gotcha." Charlie's voice was delightfully low and husky and close to my ear. Instantly most of my body was covered with goose bumps.

4

"Thanks," I murmured, trying to catch my breath. He had touched me—voluntarily! *Yes!*

Now what? Was I supposed to ask him if he would like to skate around the rink with me? Or maybe I could suggest casually that we gather our charges together and take a hot-chocolate break.

Yeah, right. I was usually too shy to ask a stranger what time it was. There was no way I was going to have the guts to ask a perfectly formed member of the male half of the species to join me at the snack bar.

Charlie looked restless. He opened his mouth, and I knew the end of our conversation was at hand. I had to do something drastic. "I'll see you—," he began.

"So, do you, uh, go to Union?" I interrupted before Charlie could make his exit.

He smiled. "I will as of next week. I'm going to be a freshman," he informed me. "You?"

"Same," I answered.

I racked my brain for another question. But the inside of my mouth felt like a cotton ball, and my heart was beating a million beats a minute from having worked up the nerve to ask the *first* question.

In the distance Simon waved at me. "Come *on,* Jane!" he yelled. "Ethan wants to try to skate backward!"

I rolled my eyes. So much for my first attempt at flirting. Duty called. "See you," I said to Charlie.

"Bye, Jane." He turned and skated toward Bobby.

As I headed toward Simon and Ethan, I couldn't help grinning. Okay, so basic shyness had prevented

5

me from getting into a free-flowing conversation with Charlie. At least he knew my name now. There would be plenty of time to work on my flirting skills for future use. After all, I had four years of high school ahead of me!

"Four absolutely *wasted* years," I informed my reflection.

Sure, I had seen Charlie once school had started freshman year. But the first time I caught sight of him, he was standing with a bunch of popular guys that I recognized from junior high. When I walked by the group, Charlie didn't seem to remember me.

That morning I hadn't had the guts to go up and say hi to him. And, four years later, I *still* didn't have the nerve. As far as Charlie Simpson was concerned, the girl from the skating rink didn't exist.

If only he would notice me, I thought now, gazing into my boring blue eyes. Where were the fairy godmothers when a girl really needed one? If only some fluttering, floating Tinkerbell type would wave a magic wand and make Charlie fall head over heels for me.

Abracadabra. I would walk into English class, and the air would crackle with electricity. From across the crowded room Charlie would stare at me, his eyes smoldering with passion.

"Jane Smith," he would murmur. "I never realized that *you* are the girl from the skating rink. For four years I've dreamed of this day. . . ."

And then he would ask me to the prom. My fantasy was so real that I found myself smiling into the mirror. I flipped my ponytail and fluttered my eyelashes.

"I would *love* to go to the prom," I murmured softly.

Behind me I heard someone clear her throat. Oh no! My stomach sank to my feet. I bit my lip and spun away from the mirror.

"Excuse *us,* Jane," Rose McNeal announced. "We didn't mean to interrupt."

Rose, along with Madison Embry and Shana Stevens, was standing next to the door of the girls' bathroom. Great! Three of the most popular (and least nice) girls in the senior class had witnessed me being a complete idiot!

I had crashed back into reality in the worst imaginable way. Public humiliation! "Uh . . . gotta go," I mumbled.

A moment later I was out of the bathroom, but I could still hear the girls' giggles as I headed down the hallway. So far this had the makings of one of the worst days of my life!

"I'm aware that some of you enjoyed and understood the subtle themes running through William Faulkner's *As I Lay Dying* more than others," Mr. Atkison commented to our English class forty minutes later. "Luckily for those of you who don't find Mr. Faulkner's writing as easy to digest as an MTV video, you'll have plenty of choices for the topic of your final papers."

I sat up a little straighter in my chair, snapping to attention. I was one of those made-to-order students who obsess about homework, deadlines, and bibli-ographies. The words *term* and *paper* switched on my note-taking autopilot.

I carefully wrote down the names of American authors we could choose to research for our papers as Mr. Atkison rattled them off. Ernest Hemingway, Nathaniel Hawthorne, Flannery O'Connor. The list went on and on.

When Mr. Atkison stopped talking to take a breath, I shook out my hand and flexed my fingers. Two rows ahead of me, one desk to the right, Charlie Simpson was sketching on an otherwise blank piece of notebook paper. Even from my van-tage point I could see that the drawing was a carica-ture of Mr. Atkison—his mouth oversized and a huge piece of chalk in his hand.

I smiled. Charlie wasn't only drop-dead gor-geous, he was funny. As Charlie passed the sketch to Jack Lacey, I imagined a different life for myself. One in which Charlie passed his drawing to *me*. I would smile, giggle a little, then gently admonish him for being a tad insensitive.

Later we would discuss our English-paper topics in a quiet corner of the library. And then our eyes would meet over a copy of *The Sun Also Rises*. Charlie would lean toward me. . . . *I closed my eyes. A moment later I felt the soft touch of his warm lips against mine. The kiss deepened, and the library around us faded into nothing. . . .*

I sighed, imagining that same kiss under the strobe light at the prom. The thought of walking into the senior prom on Charlie Simpson's arm made me ache. *But that will never happen,* I reminded myself. *Not unless I experience a miracle.*

"The deadline is *not* flexible, folks," Mr. Atkison announced. "I know I've been soft in the past, but I'm serious this time."

Well, one thing was certain. I would have absolutely no trouble getting my paper done on time. Girl-without-a-life Jane Smith had nothing better to do than pore over research books and run spell checks.

As the bell rang, I took a last look at Charlie and resigned myself to the obvious truth: I was hopeless.

TWO

Jane

"ICE BLUE IS definitely the 'in' color this spring," Nicole Gilmore commented over a plate of limp green salad. "Practically every prom dress advertised in *Teen People* is silk, strapless, and blue."

I was sitting with Nicole and Christy Redmond, my two best friends, at our usual lunch table. At the moment we were complaining about magazine models and the stuff that passed for food in the Union High cafeteria.

Christy peered over Nicole's shoulder and glanced at the magazine spread. "Do you think that model has breast implants?" she wondered aloud. "Her chest looks like a flotation device."

I glanced down at my own terminally flat chest. Nope. No plastics in this seventeen-year-old torso.

I was as flat as the proverbial pancake.

Nicole handed the *Teen People* to Christy and flipped open what was by now a well-worn copy of *Seventeen*. "Then again, there's a lot of shocking pink featured in *Seventeen*," she commented. "Maybe we have more fashion options than I originally thought."

I speared a piece of macaroni and popped it into my mouth. Ugh. Why couldn't every day be pizza day?

Nicole turned the page and pointed at yet another dress (this one pale lavender with spaghetti straps). "Now, *that's* pretty," she declared.

I didn't bother commenting. Prom dresses. Corsages. Boutonnieres. And then there were this year's most popular prom themes—an evening in Paris, Mardi Gras, a cruise down the Nile. The editors of this month's slew of magazines seemed to have one-track minds. And all of it was making me slightly sick to my stomach.

"Isn't there anything *useful* in those magazines?" I asked my best friends. "Something along the lines of 'Ten Great Ways to Spend Prom Night—Alone!'"

Christy groaned. This wasn't the first time during the last hour that I had referred to my always dateless status. But hey, I wasn't afraid to admit that I had the wallflower market cornered.

"Jane, why don't you just *ask* him to go to the prom with you?" Christy asked.

"Ask who?" I squeaked. Blood immediately rushed to my face.

Nicole set the magazine onto the grimy table. "Duh. Charlie Simpson, your one and only."

Unfortunately I couldn't will the blush on my face away. There was no point in denying my crush on Charlie. Nicole and Christy knew better than anyone else that I had fallen hard for the guy. How many times had I bored them with the ice-skating-rink story?

"Oh, right," I answered. "I'll just walk up to one of the most popular, best-looking guys in the school and calmly beg him to accompany me to his senior prom."

"No one said anything about *begging*," Nicole insisted. "We just suggested that you *ask* him."

I pushed the plate of macaroni as far away from me as I could. My appetite was gone. "We all know that's not going to happen," I told my friends. "If I asked Charlie Simpson to the prom and the news got around school, I would be in for some major humiliation."

Christy leaned over and squeezed my hand. "Well, maybe someone else will ask you to the prom. Then you can dance with Charlie while you're there."

"Forget it. I plan to stay home on prom night and watch a *Laguna Beach* marathon on MTV." This conversation was seriously bumming me out. With every sentence I uttered, I became even more ex-cruciatingly aware that I had no chance with Charlie.

Nicole took a long swallow from her can of diet Coke, then looked thoughtful for a moment. "Personally, I don't understand what all the fuss over prom is about. The whole thing is like New Year's Eve—pure, overwhelming pressure to get a date and have a good time." She wrinkled her nose. "Who needs it?"

Nicole sounded sincere. But I couldn't help wondering if she would change her mind about going to the prom if some cute guy asked her.

"What about you, Christy?" I asked our other friend. "Do you think Nathan is going to pop the *p* question?"

Christy and Nathan Evert had gone out a few times, but every time we asked her if he was potential boyfriend material, she would shrug noncommittally. At this point it was sort of hard to picture the two of them slow dancing cheek to cheek and gazing into each other's eyes.

"I *hope* Nathan comes through with the invite," Christy replied. "My mom has dreamed about seeing me in a prom dress since I was, like, three years old. I know it would mean a lot to her to have the chance to see her dream become a reality."

A heavy silence fell over the table as the three of us thought about Christy's words. Mrs. Redmond had been sick for a long time now. Although Christy refused to talk about her mother's illness, Nicole and I knew that the fear of her mom's possible death was never far from Christy's mind.

"All of this talk about the prom and slinky, let-it-all-hang-out prom *dresses* is making me want to eat one of those mondo pieces of chocolate cake that the lunch ladies have prepared for our dining pleasure," Nicole said finally, breaking the silence. "Are you two going to join me?"

"Definitely," I declared. "And I want ice cream with mine."

I smiled at my friends. So what if Charlie Simpson didn't know I was alive? I had two of the best friends in the world, and that counted way more than some prom date. At least, that's what I tried to tell myself. . . .

Halfway through my seventh-period study hall I had narrowed down the possible authors to research for my English term paper to Flannery O'Connor and Zora Neale Hurston. As I wrote down notes on a fresh sheet of paper, I felt a familiar tingle of excitement. Grade-A nerd that I was, I actually enjoyed schoolwork.

I was sitting in my favorite corner of the library, a sunny spot next to a huge picture window. I could feel the afternoon sun on the back of my shoulders, and I loved the pervasive smell of hardback books. The truth was that there was no place in all of Union High that I felt more comfortable in than the library.

"Hey, Jane." The greeting had come from somewhere behind my left shoulder.

For a split second my heart leaped into my mouth. A low, husky voice—just like the one from my daydream—had whispered into my ear. I glanced up from my book . . . and crashed back into reality for the umpteenth time that day.

"Oh. Hi, Max." I smiled weakly at Max Ziff, feeling like a total fool.

He raised an eyebrow. "Don't sound so excited to see me."

"Sorry . . . I was, uh, pretty engrossed in my work." *And for a moment I allowed myself to believe that you were Charlie Simpson,* I added silently.

"Good. For a second there I thought I smelled bad." Max pulled up a straight-back wooden chair and sat down across from me.

I grinned. Max Ziff wasn't the type of guy who walked the halls of Union High smelling bad. With dark, curly hair and hazel eyes, Max was one of the most popular guys in school. He was also the *only* popular guy (popular *person*, actually) that I managed to converse with in a fairly normal fashion.

Max and I had gone to junior high together, and since we both took a lot of advanced-placement classes in high school, we usually ended up in English, history, and math together. Exchange enough homework assignments with a guy, and eventually he seems more or less like an actual person—not just a popular jock. I just wished that Charlie would talk to me about tests and papers the way that Max did.

Max pulled a notebook from his backpack and opened it to a blank page. "I missed English because I was talking to a college-baseball recruiter," he informed me. "Any chance you'll fill me in on the term-paper topics?"

I shrugged. "Sure."

On a normal day I would have simply handed him my copious notes from English class and left Max to his own devices. But today I had a one-track

15

mind. I *had* to say Charlie's name aloud.

"But why don't you just get the assignment from Charlie Simpson?" I asked, trying to keep the nervous squeak out of my voice. "He's in our class."

Max snorted. "Charlie is an awesome guy, but paying attention in class isn't his forte."

I already knew this information, having watched Charlie sketch Mr. Atkison for fifteen minutes. But I was half hoping that once Max started talking about his friend, he would keep going. Instead Max just looked at me with an expectant expression on his face.

Oh, right. The assignment. I pushed my notes in Max's direction. "Here you go. One prime set of notes, coming up."

"Thanks, Jane. You're the best." He uncapped his pen and bent over the page of notes.

Yep. That was me. Good ol' reliable Jane. I was the girl with the killer test scores and the irresistible school-supply organizer. Too bad there wasn't a course for transforming oneself from the ugly duckling to the cool, beautiful, much-sought-after swan. An A in that class could guarantee a date with Charlie.

Max yawned. "Man, I've been exhausted lately," he said, rubbing his eyes. "Between baseball, Shana, and classes, I'm totally overwhelmed."

"Yeah, I know what you mean," I replied. Which was a lie. I had plenty of time for school—too much time, in fact.

Max bit his lip, studying the paper topic. "Wow.

16

This baby is going to be a major pain in the butt," he commented. "Between this and that ten-page history paper we've got to write for Mrs. Renfrow, I don't know how I'm going to manage."

"You'll do fine," I assured Max. "You always ace your classes."

"Yeah, but sometimes I wish I were a geek," he mused. "Then I could whip out papers without being distracted by baseball practice and a girlfriend."

"Even geeks have distractions," I pointed out. "Jocks don't have the market cornered."

Max looked up from the notes. "Oh, sorry . . . I didn't mean—"

I could have finished his sentence for him. *I didn't mean to offend you, Plain Jane Smith, geek of all geeks.* The fact that Max thought I fit into the untouchable geek category was written all over his face.

Great! My negative self-image was officially *not* all in my head. Obviously others had me labeled as a nerd as well.

"Uh . . ." How was I supposed to respond? *Gee, don't think twice about it, Max. I love being called a geek. It's the thing that gets me out of bed in the morning.*

"Anyway, thanks for the info, Jane." He flipped his notebook shut and practically leaped out of his chair. "I'll see you later."

"See you. . . ." My voice trailed off as I watched Max's retreating back.

Part of me wanted to chase after Max and beg him to tell me what I could do to transform myself from geek to nongeek. After all, he was popular. He probably had the magic recipe that separated the prom queens from the wallflowers.

I could just imagine Max's reaction to *that* request. He would run screaming from the library. *Wouldn't he?*

Some of Max's statements replayed in my mind. He was busy. Extremely busy. And he was clearly anxious to get a baseball scholarship to a good college. Which meant that he would do whatever it took to keep his grades up.

My heart sped up as a completely insane idea began to form in my mind. *Do it, Jane,* I told myself. *Take a chance.* What was the worst thing that could happen? *More public humiliation.* Well . . . so what?

I had only one life to live. There was no reason to hold back. In a couple of months I would be a high-school graduate, and I would probably never see any of these people again.

Go for it! I told myself, jumping out of my chair. I had to act *now,* or I knew I would wimp out in a major way.

"Max!" I called out in a loud whisper. "Wait up! I've got to talk to you."

I took a deep breath and closed the distance between us. This was it. My own personal moment of truth . . .

Three

Jane

*A*M I COMPLETELY *insane?* I asked myself two seconds later. The answer came quickly. *Yes.*

Max stood in the door of the library, waiting politely for me to say whatever it was I had to say.

"Never mind . . . I, uh, thought you forgot your pen."

Max held up his blue ballpoint pen. "Nope. I've got it right here."

I knew I should turn around, hang my head, and go back to my safe, private table in the corner of the library. But my feet seemed rooted to their spot on the stain-resistant gray carpet that covered the library floor.

"Hold on," I exclaimed as Max turned to leave. "I have a proposition for you."

I was acutely aware of the carpet, a hangnail on my

thumb, the chipped paint on the wall next to me. I was also acutely aware of the expression on Max's face.

He looked confused—really, *really* confused. "Uh . . . a proposition?"

I nodded. I couldn't believe the words that were about to come out of my mouth, but I knew there was no going back now.

"I'll write your English paper *and* your history paper for you," I told him. "On one condition."

Max was staring at me, his mouth slightly agape. "Why would you do that?" he asked. "I don't get it."

I cleared my throat, preparing myself to make a reasoned, logical argument that would convince Max to go along with my plan. "Well, as I understand it, doing these papers is going to seriously interfere with some vital parts of your life."

He nodded. "Yeah . . . so?"

"*So*, I'll write the papers for you—if you do something for me." I laced my fingers together and cracked my knuckles.

"Uh . . . what do you want me to do?" Max asked, obviously uncomfortable with the way our conversation was going.

"I want you to help me transform *me*, a super–plain Jane, into the kind of girl that you and your friends would go for."

Max's mouth had been agape before. Now his jaw was practically on the floor. "*Transform* you?"

"Yes," I said firmly. "I'm tired of being a geek. I want to be that *other* kind of girl—the kind that could theoretically be popular."

Max smiled. Then he frowned. Then he smiled again. "Jane, don't you think you should ask a girl to help you with this . . . transformation? I mean, I don't know anything about . . . feminine . . . stuff."

I shook my head. "No way. I need a guy's point of view. Like, I need to know what kind of clothes *attract* a guy. And what kind of hair." I was really warming up now. "I want a guy to tell me about music and body language, the laugh, the walk, the talk—everything."

"But Jane, you look fine the way you are," Max told me when he got a chance to slide a word in edgewise. "You don't need to change."

I laughed. Max sounded so earnest. "Listen, Max," I said to him, staring straight into his eyes. "Would *you* go for me?"

He shrugged. "I don't notice any girl besides Shana."

Shana Stevens. Long blond hair, round blue eyes, cherry red lips. She walked around like she owned the school—in exactly the manner that I wished I could.

"That's my point, Max," I insisted. "I want you to help me become a girl like Shana—a girl who gets a guy's attention and *keeps* it."

For what seemed like an hour (but was probably around twenty seconds) Max didn't say anything. "Even if I agreed to help you with this, uh, project, you writing my papers would be cheating."

I had anticipated that Max might say something along these lines. But I was ready with an answer.

"Max, you're a straight-A student. If you had time, you could write the papers yourself."

"True . . ." He seemed tempted. Who wouldn't be?

"The important thing is learning, right?" I asked. He nodded. "Well, once I finish the papers, you can read them. Then you'll have learned something significant about the subject matter."

He sighed. I imagined a cartoon devil sitting on his left shoulder, a cartoon angel sitting on his right shoulder. Each was telling him to give me a different answer.

"Please, Max," I said simply. "This means a lot to me."

Finally Max grinned and stuck out his hand. "It's a deal."

"Thanks." I felt like throwing my arms around him. Instead I reached out and shook his hand.

Watch out, Charlie Simpson, I exclaimed silently. *Here comes non-plain-Jane Smith!*

Three. Eleven. Fourteen. I spun the combination on my locker, and it popped open. I started pulling out books at random and stuffing them into my backpack. Now that I had two extra papers to write, I was going to have to be more efficient with my schoolwork than ever.

I was also going to be busier than ever. Max and I were enacting Operation Plain Jane (my name for it, not his) right after school. I almost felt like I had an actual date.

Nicole materialized at my side, carrying a backpack

that was noticeably less weighted down than mine was. "Jane, there's a basket of curly fries with your name written on it at the food court."

"We're going to fill ourselves up with junk food and then try to charm the guy at the movie theater to let us in for free," Christy added. She had appeared beside Nicole.

"Sorry, guys, I'm busy." I zipped up my backpack and slammed the door of my locker shut.

"Busy?" Nicole asked. "Don't tell me you need to get a jump start on next week's calculus assignment."

"Actually, I'm about to embark on a major project," I informed my friends. "And it has nothing to do with homework."

Christy wiggled her eyebrows. "Do tell, do tell."

I glanced in either direction down the corridor. The coast was, as they say, clear. "I'm about to enact a plan to try to attract none other than *the* Charlie Simpson," I told them.

Nicole's eyebrows shot up to her forehead. "How? What's the plan?"

I gulped. I loved my friends—and I trusted them—but I wasn't about to tell them the whole truth of my strategy. I didn't need the standard lecture on what a great person I was and how I didn't need to change.

"I can't tell you two the details—yet." I smiled mysteriously and swung my backpack over my shoulder. "But you'll be the first to know if I manage to snag a date with Charlie."

Nicole and Christy looked at each other, then at

23

me. Finally they grinned. "Just don't do anything we wouldn't do," Christy said.

"And don't get arrested," Nicole added.

"But good luck, Jane," Christy told me, reaching out to squeeze my arm. "If you ask me, Charlie would have to be blind and deaf not to want to go out with you."

"Ditto for me on that sentiment," Nicole added.

"Thanks, *chicas,*" I told my friends.

I waited for them to get halfway down the hall before I headed toward Max's locker. Those girls were supportive—but they were also snoopy.

From two locker banks away I saw that Max wasn't alone. He and Shana Stevens were sharing a knee-melting kiss at Max's locker. I paused next to the water fountain to wait for the kiss to end. Max had promised to keep our deal a secret, and I had no intention of announcing my plan of action to his less-than-friendly girlfriend.

Finally the happy couple broke apart. I watched as Shana sauntered down the corridor, her head held high. *That's how I want to feel,* I thought wistfully. *Confident. In love. On top of the world.*

I felt a surge of excitement as I abandoned my post at the water fountain and walked toward Max's locker. If he was half as good a tutor as I hoped he would be, I would be a whole new girl after I got Max's help with my hair, clothes, and banter skills.

Who knew? Maybe I really did still have a shot at getting a date with Charlie. After all, I lived in a world where a small underdog indie film like *Crash* had won the Best Picture Oscar. That was proof that something seemingly impossible *could* happen. Even if I didn't get Charlie to ask me to the prom, at least I was taking matters into my own hands (actually, Max's hands). It was worth a try. I knew deep down in the innermost recesses of my geek soul that I wouldn't be able to live with myself if I didn't at least give love a chance.

I didn't want to graduate from high school with an unfulfilled sensation—as if I had been too afraid to go after my deepest wish. And I definitely didn't want to embark on my college career being haunted by what I *didn't* do in high school!

"Jane Smith," Max called out as I neared. "Ready to begin the first afternoon of the rest of your life?"

I laughed. "Reporting for transformation, sir." And with that statement I began my metamorphosis.

Half an hour later I slid into a booth at Jon's Pizza. The cozy restaurant was far enough away from school that Max and I didn't think we would see anyone we knew. The last thing I wanted was for a group of mindless jocks to overhear my "cool" lesson.

Now, watching Max take a seat across from me, I realized that I was already starting to feel slightly transformed. Maybe I wasn't Madison Embry or Shana Stevens . . . but hey, I *was* about to share a pizza with one of the cutest guys in school. The fact that he already had a girlfriend didn't seem terribly important at the moment.

"Jane, can I ask you something before we start

all of this?" Max asked suddenly, his voice serious.

I sipped my glass of ice water, stalling for time. I had a feeling Max was about to attempt some amateur psychoanalysis, and I wasn't sure I was up to it. Then again, if this plan was going to have any kind of success, we had to be able to trust each other. "Sure," I told him. "Ask me anything."

"Can you explain *why* you want this transformation so badly?" he inquired. "I wasn't kidding when I said that I don't think you need to change."

It was a fair question. But putting four years' worth of living in a social vacuum into a speech of twenty-five words or less was more or less impossible. For a couple of seconds I stared at the ice melting in my glass and thought about how to explain being *me* to Max.

"I'm tired of being invisible," I said finally. "Just one time I want to be noticed at Union High."

"What do you mean by invisible?" he asked. "You've got lots of friends; everybody knows who you are."

I shook my head. "Sure, some people know my name because they've asked if they can copy my homework now and then. But they don't *know* me."

Max leaned back against the side of the booth and looked thoughtful. "There are over two thousand people in our school. . . . Who, exactly, are *they?*"

"You know, the popular crowd—the cheerleaders, jocks, the kings and queens of high school." I took a deep breath. *It's about trust,* I reminded myself, determined not to let my own embarrassment stand in the way of making Max understand.

"It's *your* crowd that makes me feel invisible," I continued, looking Max straight in the eyes. "Around you guys I feel about an inch tall. And I'm sick of it. I want to stand out."

"But you *do* stand out," Max insisted. "You stand out in all of your classes. I mean, you're one of the smartest girls in the entire high school."

I rolled my eyes. "Being noticed for my GPA isn't what I have in mind," I told Max. "I want to look and act like the kind of girl that you and your friends would ask to the prom."

There. I had said the *p* word. The seed was planted, and if the universe wanted to respond, I was going to make sure I was prepared when opportunity knocked at my door. I just hoped that Max didn't back out of our deal. He seemed to be wavering.

"I don't understand why you would want to be someone you're not," Max said after a long pause. "Okay, so you're not the most glamorous-looking girl at Union. . . . Who cares? That's just not your personal style."

Easy for him to say. Max had probably had a date every Saturday night since he was a freshman in high school. I doubted that he would be willing to give up being captain of the baseball team in order to join the chess club.

"Look, Max, we shook on this deal," I said firmly. "I appreciate your concern, but I think I know what's best for me."

At that moment a waitress stopped beside our

table. "Are you two ready to order?" she asked.

Max looked at me. "Jane?"

I shrugged. "You order for me," I told him. "It's your first assignment."

"We'll share a large pizza with pepperoni, mushrooms, and olives," he told the waitress. "And we'd like a pitcher of Coke."

"Phew, I thought you were going to order me a salad with dressing on the side," I said to Max after the waitress had left our table. "It seems like most of the popular girls exist solely on yogurt and rice cakes."

"Aha!" Max exclaimed. "This is one of those moments when you *are* lucky to be getting the input of a guy. You see, Jane, most girls think that we males like it when they eat next to nothing and stare longingly at our cheeseburgers and fries."

"But . . . ?" I leaned forward, hanging on his every word.

"*But* we actually hate that. It's much cooler when a girl eats like a normal person. She seems a lot more confident about who she is."

Interesting. I was learning already. "Thanks for the tip."

I unzipped my backpack and pulled out a fresh notebook. At the top of the first page I wrote *Transformation 101.* Underneath I carefully listed my first instruction: *1. Eat like a normal person.*

Max laughed. "Jane, your second is this: *Relax!*"

"Huh?" I looked up from the page.

He pointed at my notebook. "You're not

studying for a *test*. You're trying to create a new image for yourself."

"Right," I answered. "And I don't want to miss a word of advice that comes from your mouth. This is way too important."

Again Max laughed. "As your *teacher,* I'm ordering you to put away those notes, Jane Smith. And that's final."

Well, when he put it like that, I didn't have much choice. I flipped the notebook shut and returned it to my backpack. But without the pen and paper in my hand, I felt more nervous than ever.

"Okay. I'm ready." I folded my hands on top of the worn table and waited for Max to begin enlightening me.

"We'll start with the basics," Max said in a professorial tone. "Above all else, the kind of girl that, quote, 'my friends would go for,' unquote, always comes across as relaxed, cool, and casual."

I nodded. "Relaxed. Cool. Casual." I was itching to write it down, but I didn't dare make a move toward my notebook. "Got it."

Max looked a little skeptical. I guessed my clenched fists and ramrod-straight back didn't seem free and easy enough for him. With an effort I forced myself to ease back into the booth and stop white-knuckling the table.

"Here's the tough part," Max continued. "Although you have to come off as relaxed and casual, you must *also* make it clear to the people around you that you're really busy. You have tons of social demands and several interesting activities that consume much of your precious time."

Luckily the waitress returned with our pizza and Coke at just that moment. I was starting to feel a small amount of panic. If these were the basics, what kind of information was I going to have to process when we got to the advanced material?

"I'm getting a little confused," I admitted to Max as I covered a slice of pizza with grated Parmesan cheese.

"Let's say you stop to say hi to someone in the hall," Max began. "Be totally casual about saying hello, and then leave quickly because you've got someplace you have to be." He paused.

I swallowed another bite of pizza, hoping that none of the sauce was dripping onto my chin. "But what if I *want* to hang out with that particular person, no matter how busy I am?" I asked. "Or what if I'm not really all that busy?"

Max stared at me as if I were an alien. I felt like I had an E.T., Phone Home sign on my forehead. "What . . . what did I say?" *Great. Thirty minutes into the transformation he's already labeled me as beyond help.*

Max set down his slice of pizza. A sure sign he was about to say something of great significance. "Jane, you've got to remember that this is all about image. You're not being yourself—you're being a *version* of yourself."

Slowly I was starting to get the picture. What was going on inside me didn't matter. What *did* matter was what I projected to the world at large. If I could get down the right walk, the right talk, and the right laugh, nobody needed to know that I spent some evenings alphabetizing my bookshelves.

I glanced at my watch. "I should probably get going," I told Max. "I have a yoga class in an hour."

Max looked surprised. "You do? Cool!"

I laughed. "No, I don't. But I guess I'm starting to get the hang of this."

"A gold star for my pupil!" Max announced with a grin. "I think there's hope for her after all."

I took an imaginary bow, pleased with myself. Only one lesson and I was already bantering with one of the coolest guys in school. *Of course, Max is different,* I reminded myself. *He's easy to be around.*

Yep. I might be managing to feel relaxed around Max Ziff. But I was still a long way from getting a prom date with Charlie Simpson.

Four

Jane

BY NINE O'CLOCK that night I had spent at least an hour staring at my history textbook. Now that I was signed up for four term papers, it was essential that I devote double the time every night to schoolwork.

On a normal night I would have been absorbed in this chapter about Watergate, the scandal that led to Richard Nixon's resignation as president of the United States. But I couldn't concentrate tonight. So far I had read the same five paragraphs about thirty times.

Pizza with Max had been a decidedly auspicious beginning to my process of transformation. *So far, so good,* I assured myself. By the time Max and I paid the bill, I had made him laugh no less than three times. Not bad for a geek.

"If only I could be as comfortable with Charlie as I am with Max," I said aloud. *Ha!*

I couldn't see *that* happening. Last week Charlie had asked if he could borrow a pen from me at the beginning of English class. I had handed him the pen wordlessly, positive that if I uttered even one word, my head would explode. His gorgeous smile had practically blinded me.

For half of the class I had practiced what I would say when Charlie gave the pen back. *Keep it,* I would tell him. *And think of me every time you flick your Bic.* But when the moment arrived, I was struck dumb yet again.

"Uh . . . keep it," I had mumbled finally. "I don't like that pen anyway. I mean, I like it. . . . I wouldn't have given you a bad pen. But I'm kind of tired of it. . . ." In two seconds I had gone from mute to bumbling idiot.

Charlie hadn't responded directly to my mumbles. But he *had* given me another warm smile. And possibly a wink. I still hadn't decided whether the movement I sensed in his eye was a twitch or a wink. Either way, he had given me back the pen—but with a heartfelt "thank you." Not a "thank you, *Jane,*" but still, it was something.

I sighed deeply. Charlie's face was burned into my brain. That face . . . that body . . . that warm laugh. *If only he would notice me, really notice me . . .* I was one hundred percent sure that if he gave me even half a chance, he would like me. We were definitely meant to be together—just not necessarily in this lifetime.

I was so deep into my detailed analysis of my five-second exchange with Charlie that I didn't notice at first that the phone was ringing. At about the fourth ring the vision of Charlie's face evaporated and I tuned back into reality.

I picked up the receiver of my Mickey Mouse phone (probably the least-hip telephone ever manufactured). "Hello?"

"Hey, girl," Nicole greeted me. "It's me."

"Actually, it's *us,*" Christy added. "But you've got to speak up because Nicole is hogging the receiver."

"Hi, guys." I turned down my stereo and flopped onto my bed. "What's up?"

I could picture the two of them in Nicole's bedroom, having a mini tug-of-war as they both tried to listen to the conversation. I could also imagine the exchange that precipitated this phone call in the first place. If my instincts were correct, my best friends were about to grill me on my whereabouts this afternoon.

"We want to know what's up with *you,*" Nicole declared, right on schedule. "Christy and I spent most of the afternoon speculating about this mysterious plan to snare the elusive Charlie Simpson."

I laughed. Nicole has a flair for the dramatic—probably because she faithfully records her favorite soap operas every day for later viewing. Part of me was dying to open my mouth and pour out every detail of my afternoon with Max. I knew my friends would be fascinated by my project.

But Max and I both made a pact to keep our

deal a secret, I reminded myself. Aside from the avalanche of humiliation I could experience if the wrong people found out about my transformation project, Max and I both realized that the faculty at Union High wouldn't view my "helping" Max write his papers with much enthusiasm.

"I'm giving myself a total makeover," I informed my friends. Not exactly the truth, but not a lie either. "I'm going to do everything in my power to turn myself into the kind of girl that would make Charlie Simpson's tongue hang out of his mouth."

"Like, you're going to start wearing eyeliner and lip gloss?" Christy asked. "And maybe get your hair highlighted?"

"Yes, yes, and maybe," I responded to Christy's rapid-fire questions. "But this is about a lot more than a cosmetic overhaul. I'm going to create a whole new *image* for myself."

Nicole whistled. "Sounds like a pretty major undertaking, Jane. What was your inspiration?"

I hesitated. Nicole was, if anything, perceptive. I could sense in her voice that she didn't think I was giving them the whole story.

"I, uh, found an article in a magazine about how to 'snag your crush,'" I told my friends. "I'm going to follow the steps and see if I get anywhere with you-know-who."

"What magazine?" Nicole asked.

"It was in . . ." Darn. I didn't want to tell an outright lie. But telling the outright truth wasn't an option either.

At that moment the doorbell rang downstairs. It was probably just an enterprising encyclopedia salesman, but said salesman couldn't have arrived at a better time. "Gotta go, guys," I said quickly. "There's an ax murderer at the door."

I hung up the phone and trotted downstairs. Since Mom and Dad were at their bimonthly potluck-dinner-slash-book-club night, I peeked through the curtains before I went to the door.

"Max!" I exclaimed.

I couldn't have been more surprised to see somebody if a perfect stranger had been standing on our front stoop with a Publisher's Clearing House check in his hand. And I immediately expected the worst.

I bolted to the front door and threw it open. "Hey, what's going on?" I asked. "Is there a problem? Did someone find out about our deal? Are you calling it off?"

Max took off the white baseball cap he was wearing and waved it in the air. "Truce! Truce!" he called. "Please, counsel, stop badgering the witness."

I giggled, stepping away from the door to let him inside. "Sorry . . . I guess I got a little nervous when I saw you standing out there."

Max laughed. "So much for relaxed and casual. I think we're going to have to do today's lesson all over again."

Oops. The guy had a point. I had totally blown my first opportunity to practice my new modus operandi.

"Let's start over," I suggested. Pause. "Hi, Max. How's it going?"

He grinned. "It's going great. What are you up to, Jane?"

I still wasn't sure what he was doing here, but this was definitely great "cool" practice. I shrugged nonchalantly. "I'm studying—suddenly I find myself with a lot more homework than usual."

He raised his eyebrows. "What *else* are you up to?"

Uh . . . I had no idea where he was going with this. "Let's see. . . . Well, I also have my stereo on," I informed him. "So I guess I'm listening to music."

"Much better," Max approved. "See, you're listening to music and doing a little homework."

I was getting more confused by the second. "Yeah, that's what I just said. I'm studying." Was there an echo in the living room?

Max shook his head in a way that was quickly becoming very familiar to me. "Jane, if a popular girl is home to answer the door, she'll never announce that she's spent the evening up in her room with her nose in the books."

"What does she say?" I asked. I resisted the urge to start pacing, realizing right away that walking back and forth across the living-room carpet wasn't the best way to project "relaxed."

"She'll tell you that she's giving herself a pedicure, listening to a new CD, talking to a friend on the phone," he explained. "And then, like an afterthought, she might say, 'And I'm doing a few of those trig problems.'"

37

"Oh." I felt stupid. And boring. I *never* polished my toenails. "I just study all the time." I sank onto our worn sofa and stuck a pillow over my head.

I felt Max sit down beside me. A moment later he plucked the pillow away from my eyes.

"You can still study, Jane," he assured me with a gentle smile. "Just call it something else—if anyone ever asks."

"Okay. I'll make a mental note." *I'll make a mental note to declare myself insane for thinking I could ever fit in with the popular crowd.*

"Now, what kind of music were you listening to as you painted your fingernails and gave yourself a new hairdo?" Max asked.

I sensed this was a test. And I was pretty sure I was going to fail. "Um . . . an opera," I confessed. "My dad has gotten really into opera lately, and I guess it, like, rubbed off on me."

Even *I* knew that opera wasn't cool. But since I didn't know what music *was* cool, I had no tools for lying to Max at my immediate disposal.

Predictably Max gave me his patented head shake. "No, no, no. Opera is no good." He paused. "I'll tell you what. Pick me up for school tomorrow morning. I'll give you a list of cool bands and bring along some tapes to play for the ride."

"It's a deal," I told him. Then I realized I still had no idea why Max had gone out of his way to come over here and quiz me on my evening. "Why are you here anyway?" I asked.

He grinned. "I wanted to check up on my favorite

pupil. Something told me this surprise visit would be a great opportunity for learning."

Suddenly I felt exponentially better than I had five minutes ago. If Max thought I was a lost cause, there was no way he would be wasting his time like this. Obviously he thought I had potential.

I just need to realize that potential, I thought. And now that I had Max, there was hope. Jeez. It was no surprise that I was known as Plain Jane Smith. Up until now I had been doing everything wrong.

But that's going to change! I promised myself. *As of right now.*

Five

Max

I WAS STILL stuffing tapes into my backpack when I heard Jane honking for me on Tuesday morning. I glanced at the digital clock on my nightstand and smiled. Jane was five minutes early—exactly as I should have known she would be.

I raced downstairs and ran out of the house. Jane was trusting me with her image—I didn't want to blow my own image by seeming like a lazy slob who couldn't get out of the house in the morning.

"Morning," I greeted Jane, sliding into the front seat of her VW Bug.

"Hey, Professor," she said with a big smile. "I can't wait for this morning's lecture."

I watched Jane as she revved the engine. It was funny. Until I was sitting across from her at Jon's Pizza the day before, I had never noticed how pretty she was. I mean, I had talked to Jane dozens of times over the years about tests and papers and homework assignments.

But I had never really *looked* at her. I had never noticed how her blue eyes sparkled when she was excited. And I had never realized that her blond hair was sort of a honey color. *Probably because she's always got it pulled back in a ponytail,* I added to myself.

Even now, at eight o'clock in the morning, Jane looked as fresh as . . . well, as fresh as a daisy. Her smooth skin glowed with a sort of natural light. And even though she wasn't wearing any makeup, Jane's lips were a deep, rosy red. *She's got the kind of prettiness that the experts are always calling "natural,"* I realized.

Shana looked totally gorgeous all the time. But she wore a ton of makeup to come off looking as natural as Jane! And I knew that for a fact. Her purse was usually loaded down with half a dozen of those little compacts. How many times had I given her a hug—and then discovered a virtual painter's palette on my crisp white T-shirt? Plus if I ever arrived early to pick her up for a date, Shana would stay in her room for an extra fifteen minutes, perfecting her hair and makeup.

Jane put the VW in gear, and the little car shot down the road. "I'm waiting, Professor," she told me. "Every second you're not talking, I'm not learning." She turned to me and shot me a warm grin.

I grinned back. Every time Jane gave me one of those dazzling smiles, I felt like laughing. She radiated

41

vibrancy and passion and excitement—especially for this so-called project.

I still thought the whole endeavor was pretty weird, but I couldn't help being drawn in by Jane's enthusiasm. I was really trying to understand why getting noticed by the popular crowd was so important to her . . . but so far I hadn't been able to see why the lives of the "in" crowd were so much better than Jane's.

I picked up a shoe box full of CDs that was on the passenger-side floor of the Bug. Pavarotti. Mozart. Puccini.

"Jane, I hate to break it to you, but you've got a shoe box full of nerd music." I waved the box under her nose to emphasize my point. "Classical and opera are *not* the kinds of music that makes guys crazy."

Jane frowned. "But I *like* that music. Listening to a whole opera is an *experience*. The music is so dramatic and emotional. . . . It carries me away."

I shook my head. Wow. I could see that I was really going to have to work on Jane if I wanted her musical tastes to evolve into the twentieth century. I selected a CD labeled *La Bohème* and popped it into the car stereo. I planned to explain as we listened to the music why it belonged under the subheading Dullsville.

The music started, filling the car with what sounded like a hundred-piece orchestra. I glanced over at Jane. Her gaze was fixed on the road, but I saw a faraway look in her eyes. It was almost as if the opera music had transported her to a whole other world.

"Jane, you're spacing out on me," I said, nudging her arm.

"Let's just wait one minute. There's a great section coming up. A climactic scene in the opera."

"One minute," I agreed.

Leaning my head against the back of the black vinyl seat, I let my eyes drift shut. I had to admit that there was something pretty far-out about this music. The woman singing sounded like her guts were being ripped straight out of her body. It was heart wrenching!

"What's happening?" I asked Jane. "Is someone murdering her?"

Jane reached over and patted me on the shoulder. "Don't worry, Max. She's not dying—yet." She shifted the car into neutral, and we coasted to a stop in front of a red light. "Right now she thinks she's never going to see her lover again."

"Heavy." I knew that we had been listening to the opera for a lot more than a minute, but Jane seemed so entranced that I didn't have the heart to eject the tape so that we could get to the cool music.

Besides, I was kind of interested in hearing what was going to happen next. If the diva sounded like a wounded cow (a wounded cow with an amazing voice, of course), what was she going to pull out from her vocal cords when things got worse? I closed my eyes and listened.

"We're here." It seemed like only a second had passed when Jane's gentle voice interrupted the sound of the music.

"But . . . what happened?" I asked, opening my eyes and blinking several times into the light coming in through the windshield.

Jane grinned, then popped out the CD. "I'll tell you what. Why don't you borrow this? You can listen to the whole thing tonight."

I frowned. "I still won't know what happened," I pointed out. "They're all singing in, like, Italian. Or French. Or something."

"Italian," Jane informed me with a laugh. "And don't worry about understanding the words. Listen to the *music*."

I took the CD from Jane's outstretched hand, slightly agog at the fact that I was volunteering to listen to an opera. *If anybody finds out about this, I'll be laughed off the baseball team,* I thought wryly.

But I was intrigued. Not only by the music, but by Jane's obvious knowledge of a subject so foreign to high schoolers across America. *But I'm supposed to be the teacher,* I reminded myself as Jane switched off the ignition.

"Hey, take this list of hip bands," I said, holding out the carefully typed list I had made last night. "And you'd better borrow a few of my CDs. From now on you can listen to *these* on the way to school."

I unzipped my backpack and pulled out a few tapes. I was sorry I wasn't going to get to see the expression on Jane's face as she listened to actual teenager music for maybe the first time ever.

Jane transferred the tapes to her overflowing shoe box. "I'll listen to them tonight," she promised.

"While I'm talking on the phone and perfecting my do-it-yourself manicuring techniques."

"And the homework?" I asked.

She shrugged, flipping her ponytail over one shoulder. "Oh, I don't know. . . . Maybe I'll try to get in a little reading for Atkison's class."

I felt like giving my A student a rousing cheer. "Good job, Jane. I think you're getting the hang of this stuff."

"I'd better be," Jane responded. "There are only a few more weeks of school, and I want to eradicate my geek status by graduation—if not sooner." She checked her watch. "Speaking of sooner, we'd better hurry. In two minutes we'll both be officially late to homeroom."

As I slid out of the car, I tried to identify the surge of emotion that was washing over me. And then I got it. A big ball of protectiveness had welled up inside me.

Jane was so sweet, and she was trying so hard. I hated the idea that people in school—some of them friends of mine—had made her feel invisible for the past four years. How could someone so adorable feel so undateable?

As we walked side by side toward the main building, both of us were quiet. I considered taking this opportunity to suggest to Jane that she didn't have to wear Levi's to school *every* day. But I decided against it. There would be plenty of time for constructive hints in the days to come.

Really, it's too bad she wants to change, I

mused. *Jane is quirky and interesting just the way she is.* I couldn't imagine that anyone who spent more than fifteen minutes talking to Jane Smith would call her "plain."

"See you later, Professor," Jane called out as we entered the building and headed to our separate homerooms.

"Adiós," I called back. "That's Spanish."

I could still hear Jane's soft laughter in my mind when I opened the door to my homeroom. Then I realized I could hear something else. It was me. And I was humming a tune from *La Bohème.*

I laughed out loud. *Who is changing who?* I wondered.

"Where were you this morning?" Shana Stevens, my girlfriend, asked me as I sat down in the chair next to hers at our regular lunch table. "I waited by your locker, but you never showed up."

I slipped my arm around Shana's shoulders and squeezed her tight. "I got really into this album I was listening to," I explained (which was more or less the truth). "By the time I got to school, I had to go straight to homeroom."

"Well, I missed you." Shana turned toward me and leaned in close.

I inhaled the clean scent of her shampoo as I bent my head and touched her lips with mine. As always, I tasted Shana's lipstick as I kissed her. *Just once I would like to lock lips with my girlfriend and not feel like I'm snacking on a cosmetics factory,* I thought.

"I missed you too," I murmured, giving her another squeeze. "You look beautiful today."

And she did. In a short black miniskirt and a skintight white T-shirt, Shana looked like she had stepped off the pages of a fashion magazine. Her long, shapely legs were smooth and tanned, the toenails peeking out from her platform sandals expertly polished. *Picture-perfect*, I thought. *That's my girlfriend.*

"Are you two going to make out or eat?" Rose McNeal asked from across the table.

"Eating. Now, there's an appetizing notion," I commented, staring at the hideous mess (supposedly macaroni 'n' cheese) that covered my plate.

"That's why I bring a salad from Anderson's Market every day for lunch," Shana reminded me. "I wouldn't touch the so-called food they serve in this cafeteria with a three-foot lacrosse stick."

"According to Max, there are a lot of things you won't touch with a three-foot lacrosse stick," Charlie Simpson joked.

Madison Embry scooped into her mouth a spoonful of the vanilla nonfat yogurt she brought every day. "All I know is that one plate of mac 'n' cheese has more fat grams than I want to consume in a month."

"If only the rest of the cretins that inhabit these hallowed halls would join us in a revolt," Shana said. "Then maybe we could convince the administration to start serving sushi and tofu."

"I wouldn't want to unite with certain Union High students for *any* cause," Rose countered. "We might catch their inherent lameness."

I stuck a fork into my fat-filled mac 'n' cheese and tuned out the girls' conversation. Every lunch hour followed basically the same pattern. We all sat down at our table. Charlie, Scott, and I discussed our plans for baseball practice, then lapsed into silence while the girls competed to see who could come up with the nastiest sidebar.

"Speaking of lame, check out the revenge of the nerdettes over there," Shana said to the group. Her gaze traveled disdainfully from Jane to her two friends. "They're studying those fashion magazines like they were cramming for one of their advanced-placement chemistry classes."

"It's so pathetic," Madison announced, as if she were the ultimate arbiter of what was and was not pathetic in this world. "I mean, they're drooling over photos of prom dresses like they were actually going to get the chance to *wear* one."

Usually I barely even registered the girls' constant barrage of criticism. But today I found myself unable to ignore them. Hearing Shana, Madison, and Rose put down Jane and her friends was making me feel slightly sick to my stomach.

Then again, an objective opinion on Jane's looks might give me a better idea about how to direct her in this transformation process, I reasoned. *This could be totally valuable.* Even if it was also totally annoying.

"I don't get it," I said, interrupting the insult parade. "Why are those particular girls losers?"

Shana stared at me as if I had just grown another

head. "I'll assume that's a rhetorical question," she declared.

I shook my head. "Seriously. I mean, they're all nice and attractive and smart. . . . So why don't they have it? Why are they social outcasts?"

Shana wrinkled her nose. "Attractive? Under what dictionary do those three stooges qualify as *attractive?*"

"I think someone messed with his lemonade," Rose commented. "Either that or it's time for Max to take a trip to the eye doctor."

"Please. Just take a look at their geeky, blah clothes," Shana told me. "Notice their stupid pony-tails." She was really getting into it now. "They don't even know that any decent, self-respecting girl doesn't go out in public without makeup. Have they ever heard the word *attitude?*"

"They look like they came to the cafeteria straight from gym class!" Madison added. "Ugh."

I kept nodding as Shana, Madison, and Rose continued to list reasons why Jane and her friends were losers. But inside, I disagreed. Would a loser make me laugh every time I had a conversation with her? Would a loser be able to light up a dark pizza place with her bright smile?

Nonetheless, I knew that Shana knew of what she spoke. As one of the most popular girls in school, she had a full understanding of what made a girl special in the eyes of her peers.

"Are you saying that with different hair and new clothes, one of those girls could have your look?" I asked. "I mean, if it's all about ponytails and blush brushes, any one of them should be able to elevate herself to your status."

"*My* status?" Shana asked, shooting me a warning glance.

"Well, she would never be as beautiful as you are," I added quickly. "But do you think an average girl could, you know, make herself stand out with the right changes?"

Shana shrugged. "Theoretically—but it'll never happen. Not one of those girls has the slightest sense of style."

I shoved another bite of macaroni into my mouth, pondering Shana's words. At the very back of my mind I was starting to contemplate a slightly bizarre idea.

The truth was that I *knew* what attracted me, at least physically, to a girl—it was sitting right next to me, hand on my knee. But I had no idea how to go about making Jane look like Shana and her friends.

That kind of makeover was a challenge meant for a self-possessed, stylish girl. And Shana was nothing if not stylish.

Yeah, right, I thought. *I can just imagine asking Shana to give Jane some pointers on the subject.*

Bad idea.

Six

Jane

"OH, HI, CHARLIE," I chirped casually. "How's it hanging?" Scratch that. "How's it going?"

It's going great, Jane, I answered myself. *I'm totally psyched that you've decided to come out of your shell. I've wanted to ask you out for the past four years, but I was always too intimidated by your brains to start a conversation.*

"Hey, a girl can have a fantasy now and then," I told my reflection in the mirror that hung in our front hallway.

But I had done enough talking into mirrors lately. Tonight I was going to have a shot at real-life, person-to-person, flirtatious banter. And I was so nervous that my mouth felt as if it were filled with saltwater taffy.

I paced across the living room, trying to work off some of the excess energy that had been building up inside me ever since Max suggested we hang out tonight for another lesson. I felt like I had downed a double espresso and a pound of chocolate.

Chill out, Jane, I ordered myself. There was no reason to be so jittery. After all, it was just this morning that I had felt so free and easy with Max, lecturing him on opera as we drove to school.

Outside, a horn beeped twice. *He's here!* I raced to the kitchen and grabbed my keys and my backpack off the table.

"Bye, Mom! Bye, Dad!" I yelled up the stairs.

"Bye, honey! Have a good time," Mom called from her bedroom.

One of the advantages of being a chronic good girl was that my parents never badgered me with the Great Inquisition before I left the house. Since they knew there was zero chance I'd be brought home by a police officer, they trusted me to make my own decisions. Thank goodness! I was *not* anxious to announce to my parents that I was going out with a guy on a *non*date in order to improve my heretofore *non*existent flirting skills.

I ran out the front door, slamming it shut behind me. By the time I got to Max's car and opened the passenger-side door, I was breathless from my forty-five-second sprint.

"Hi!" I panted. "Let's go."

I smiled at Max, taking in his freshly scrubbed face and carefully combed hair. In jeans and a crisp white button-down shirt, my nondate was definitely looking adorable.

"Wrong, Jane. This is all wrong." He gave me the head shake. "But I have to admit that your enthusiasm *is* a refreshing change of pace."

"Wrong?" I echoed. "I've already done something wrong? I just got here!"

"The thing is, the type of girl you're aspiring to be would never fly out of the house as soon as a guy honked his horn. She would wait for the guy to come to the door."

"Then why did you honk?" I demanded. "Now I feel like an idiot."

"Don't worry about it, Jane," Max said in his most teacherlike voice. "This was just a little pop quiz—next time I'm sure you'll pass." He paused. "But just to make sure, let's do it again."

I suppressed a wave of humiliation as I got out of the car. *This is exactly the kind of detail I'm aiming to absorb,* I told myself. No need to be ashamed. Besides, I had learned in the past few days that the faster I forced myself to move on from my endless social gaffes, the faster I made real improvements.

I slipped into the house and shut the door behind me. Inhale. Exhale. Inhale. Exhale.

"I'm back, Mom and Dad," I yelled upstairs. "But I'll be leaving again in a minute."

My breathing had slowed to a normal rate. Several seconds passed. And by the time the doorbell rang a minute later, I was totally composed.

Answering the door at the exact moment the

bell sounded probably wasn't much cooler than bar-reling out of the house on hearing the honk of a horn. *One, one thousand. Two, two thousand.*

In my mind I fast-forwarded time three weeks. I imagined myself wearing a slinky black prom dress and five-inch heels. On this side of the door I took a deep breath, at peace with myself and the world. Then—still in my head—I slowly opened the door. And saw Charlie Simpson, my date to the senior prom, looking absolutely gorgeous in a black tuxedo. Of course, he held the most beauti-ful corsage I had ever seen in his outstretched hand. . . .

I was so involved in the fantasy that I was actu-ally disappointed to open the door—for real—and see Max Ziff standing there.

"Good evening, Max," I greeted him. "How nice to see you."

"Hi, Jane," Max answered with a grin. "You're looking lovely tonight."

My disappointment was quickly replaced with a small thrill from the compliment. Sure, Max only said I looked pretty because he was playing a part. But it was still nice to hear.

And I understood now why Max had insisted that I go back inside to start our nondate the right way. Running out to the car, I had felt like Max's buddy, his pal. But now, looking at him on my front doorstep, I felt like . . . well, like a *girl*.

And I liked it. I liked it a lot.

*   *   *

"So we've established that we can't go to the mall. Or to Wednesday's Café. Or to any of the other places where I usually hang out." Max tapped his fingers on the steering wheel, then turned to me. "Any ideas?"

Max and I had been driving aimlessly for fifteen minutes. But we still hadn't decided on a destination. First Max had suggested we go to the mall. Unfortunately there was a high probability that a bunch of Max's crowd would *also* be at the mall. And a sighting of Max Ziff with Plain Jane Smith would definitely cause a stir. Ditto every other place Max had suggested.

Our goal for tonight was clear. I was supposed to practice being witty and fun yet incredibly desirable and cool. I was supposed to be open but retain an air of mystery. The task was daunting enough without the threat of being spied on by a bunch of overly critical, nosy jocks.

"We need to go someplace where none of your friends would venture," I reasoned. "A place where we can be free to work on my transformation without the slightest fear of anyone discovering that I'm ghostwriting two of your term papers."

"I know that's what we need. But I'm out of ideas—"

"Turn left!" I interrupted. "I just had a flash of brilliance."

Obediently Max switched on his blinker and turned left. "Tell me."

"We'll go to King Louie's bowling alley," I

announced. "Nicole and Christy and I go there all the time. It's a blast, and the only people we ever see there are bald middle-aged men."

Max looked skeptical. "Bowling?" He paused. "Well . . . we definitely won't run into any of my friends at King Louie's. But Jane, bowling isn't cool."

I shrugged. "Do you have a better idea?"

"Nope." Max pressed on the gas and sped toward Route 2, which led to the bowling alley. "I guess it's fine for tonight. As long as you realize that someone like Shana would *never* think that knocking down pins in rented shoes was a fun way to pass an evening."

"I'll hang up my bowling shirt after tonight," I promised.

Twenty minutes later I was attempting to show Max how to choose the right bowling ball. He hadn't been joking when he told me that he had never bowled before.

"How about this one?" Max asked, holding up a small, pink bowling ball for my inspection.

I giggled. "Uh, that would be the perfect ball— for an eighty-year-old lady." I picked up a large, black bowling ball and handed it to Max. "Try that one."

Max took the bowling ball in his right hand, flung back his arm, then lurched toward the lane. I watched as he dropped the ball with a thud. It rolled slowly toward the pins.

"Yes!" Max shouted. "I think it's gonna be a strike!"

The ball veered left and dropped into the gutter.

"Or not," I commented wryly. I picked up a ball for myself. "Watch and learn."

I held the ball in my right hand, balancing it with my left. Then I used my best bowling form to take three steps forward as I swung my right arm behind me. When I at last released the ball, it sped straight down the center of the lane. A moment later all ten pins clattered to the floor.

"Now, *that's* a strike!" I jumped up and down, and Max slapped me a high five.

"Wow!" he exclaimed. "That was, like, art."

I laughed. "It's not all that hard, Max. By the end of tonight I personally guarantee you'll get at least one strike."

"If I get a strike, will you buy me one of the embroidered polyester King Louie Lanes bowling shirts?" he asked, wiggling his eyebrows.

I groaned. "Even *I* know that a King Louie customized button-down isn't the fashion statement anyone in their right mind would make," I retorted. "But the shoes *are* pretty cool."

For a moment Max looked horrified. Then he laughed. "That was a joke. Right?"

I shrugged nonchalantly. "Maybe. Maybe not."

For the next hour I coached Max on the finer points of amateur bowling. I had never thought of myself as an athlete (and I still doubted that bowling qualified as an actual sport), but it felt good to be better than an established jock at *any* game involving a ball.

"Are we still keeping score?" Max asked finally.

"Unfortunately for you, yes," I answered. Glancing at the scorecard, I couldn't help but laugh. "You're up to fifty," I informed him. "I, on the other hand, have bowled one hundred and twenty so far."

Suddenly Max dropped to the floor and did ten push-ups. Around us, families turned to watch.

"Max, what are you doing?" I hissed. "Everybody is *looking* at you—and not in a good way."

He jumped up with a grin. "That's my good-luck ritual," Max explained. "I do ten push-ups before every baseball game—and right now I need all the help I can get." He turned and waved to the people who were watching. "Thanks, folks. The show's over!"

I wasn't sure whether I should be embarrassed or delighted. I wasn't used to drawing attention to myself, but part of me loved Max's carefree self-confidence. Not for the first time this evening, I realized I had never had such a good time with someone of the male persuasion.

I've never had so much fun with anyone, for that matter. Talk about bizarre! In a million years I wouldn't have guessed that I could feel so comfortable around a guy like Max.

"I'm having an extrasensory moment," I told Max. "I predict a strike in your very near future."

He held the bowling ball in both hands and gave it a big kiss. "From your mouth to the bowling gods' ears."

"Position!" I cried out. "Remember to position your feet!"

Max stood directly in front of the lane and stared at the pins for several seconds. Then he took three steps, just as I had shown him. At the same time he pulled his right arm back in a full, fluid motion. A moment later the ball rolled down the lane. . . .

"Strike!" I screamed. "Strike!" So much for not wanting to bring attention to myself.

"Yes!" Max shouted. "I did it!"

He sprinted toward me, then grabbed me in his arms and swung me around. "Strike!" I repeated.

I didn't know what else to say. For the first time in my life a guy other than my grandfather or father had swept me up in a spontaneous hug. It was a big event—even if the guy was Max.

He set me down. "Uh . . . sorry about that. I guess I got a little overexcited."

Great. My first hug, and he wished he could take it back. *Max is probably thinking about how stupid he would feel if any of his friends had seen that,* I thought.

"No problem," I told him.

He grinned. "What the heck . . ." He pulled me close again, squeezing me tight. "Thanks, Jane," Max said as he let me go. "I haven't felt this kind of adrenaline rush since I hit my first home run in Little League. Who knew bowling was such a blast?"

"I did," I pointed out. "It was *my* suggestion."

"Touché."

I glanced at my watch. Oops. It was getting pretty late, and so far Max and I hadn't worked on my witty/fun/flirtatious/mysterious/desirable lesson at all.

"We'd better get started on tonight's curriculum, Professor," I announced. "Can I buy you some nachos at the snack bar while you tutor me?"

Max gave me that you're-an-alien glance. Uh-oh. What had I messed up now? Were nachos inherently uncool? Was the mention of the words *snack* and *bar* the kiss of death?

"Jane, we've been conducting our lesson since we got here," he declared. "And you did very well, I'd like to add."

I was stunned. "But . . . but I was just being myself the whole time!" I exclaimed. "I didn't know it was a test!"

Max shrugged. "I guess this means you're a natural at being cool and fun, Jane Smith."

Now I was the one who wanted to throw *my* arms around Max. This had to feel ten times better than getting a strike. Max Ziff had just informed me that I had spent a whole evening in a mode he described as both "fun" and "cool." And I hadn't even been trying!

"We're really getting somewhere," I said excitedly. "Max, thank you so much!"

"You're welcome." He sat down and untied his bowling shoes. "Jane, I think we're done. Tonight proves that you're the kind of girl my friends would go for."

Yeah, right! I thought angrily. *I'm sure Charlie Simpson would jump at the chance to take me bowling!*

"That's nice of you to say," I replied, my voice icy. "But we both know it's not true."

"Jane—," Max started.

I held up one hand to stop him from continuing. Anything he said would just make it worse. "I don't look anything like Shana and her friends!" I cried, furious that I even had to humiliate myself by pointing out such an obvious (not to mention painful) fact. "If anything, you and your friends might deign to play a game of basketball with me or something."

"But that's not what I mean. . . ." His voice trailed off, and he gave me a sort of woeful puppy-dog stare.

"Are you getting bored of this whole project?" I blurted out. "Is that why you're trying to convince me that we're through?"

"No, Jane . . . I . . ." He stopped talking, then slipped off the bowling shoes and pushed his feet into his brown loafers. "Listen, we should probably get going."

"Yeah, we probably should." The enthusiasm had completely gone out of my voice as I spoke.

I can't believe Max is letting me down. If he had his way, Max's part of our bargain was finis. And I was still Plain Jane Smith. I was upset about the prospect of not completing my transformation.

But worse than that . . . I was disappointed in Max. And yes, I was hurt. So hurt that all I wanted to do was get home, crawl into bed, and cry.

Seven

Max

JANE HADN'T SAID more than two words since we left the bowling alley. I felt a tight knot in the pit of my stomach as I remembered the cold way she'd stared at me when I told her that I thought her metamorphosis was complete. She was the last person in the world I wanted to hurt . . . and yet I didn't know how to *help*.

"Well, we're here!" I said brightly as I pulled up in front of the Smiths' house. "Home, sweet home."

She didn't say anything. And she didn't make a move to get out of the car. *Good going, Ziff. You've made the girl so upset, she's catatonic.*

"Uh, Jane? We're here."

"I realize that," she said stiffly. "I'm waiting for you to get out and open my door for me. Isn't that what *Shana* would do?"

I smiled at Jane's valiant attempt to stay a step ahead of The Rules. "Actually, none of the girls do that—they just go ahead and get out."

"Oh, okay." Jane's face was so sad that I was afraid she about to burst into tears.

Once again I felt a huge wave of protectiveness toward my so-called pupil. The thought of Jane crying made me feel horrible. As she started to open the car door, I put my hand on her arm to stop her.

"Wait a second—we need to talk." Jane frowned, but she leaned back into her seat and looked at me, her eyes questioning. "I'm not bored with our project at all," I continued. "But I'm worried that I can't help you with all of the girlier stuff in your metamorphosis. I mean, what do I know about hair and makeup?"

"You know more than I do," Jane insisted. "I know zilch, zero, nada."

"The point is . . . You've made it clear tonight that what you want most of all is to look different."

"I won't argue with that thesis statement," Jane agreed in her typically quirky, endearing way. "Basically I want to *not* recognize myself in the mirror."

I stared at Jane's face, unable to comprehend why she would want to transform herself into someone else. "But you're so—"

"So *what?*" she snapped, interrupting me.

Beautiful as it is, I finished silently.

"So plain and ordinary that I couldn't look like Shana or her friends no matter what I tried?"

The girl had no confidence! If I hadn't witnessed her low self-esteem in the looks department myself, I would have thought she was faking this. And I knew Jane didn't play mind games.

"I was *about* to say, 'But you're so cute as is,'" I informed her.

Cute *is a better word than* beautiful, I told myself. *Beautiful* would have been . . . well, not entirely appropriate. Under the circumstances.

Jane smiled, but the smile didn't reach her eyes. "Thanks for the vote of confidence," she said softly. "But I know what I look like. And to prove how plain I am, I haven't had a single date all through high school."

"Jane . . ." Tears welled up in her eyes. She blinked them away, the small drops making her deep blue eyes even darker.

"All I've ever really wanted was to go to the prom," she admitted. "I wanted to go with someone I really liked so I could have just one incredible night of feeling special, pretty . . . wanted."

"Is that what this whole turn-Jane-into-a-popular-girl-look-alike project is all about?" I asked. "Are you doing this to get a date to the prom?"

She nodded, staring at her hands, which were folded in her lap. "I must sound pretty stupid," Jane commented, her voice barely above a whisper. "Now that I'm saying this stuff out loud . . . well, I don't know what I was thinking."

My heart ached for Jane. She was so sweet, so vulnerable, so *Jane*. I hated to hear her sound so defeated. Especially because I knew that she was dead wrong. Any guy would be lucky to have her as a date to his senior prom. With Jane the night would be one to remember.

I can't let her down, I realized. I had to find a way to help her. Period.

"First of all, you're not stupid," I said firmly. "I admire you. Not very many people have the guts to go after something they really want."

"Yeah, well . . . a lot of good it's done me." She clenched and unclenched her fists, then turned her head and looked straight into my eyes. "Thanks for everything you've done, Max. But I know when it's time to quit."

"Listen, I have an idea. A foolproof way to turn you into a glamour girl—practically overnight."

"You do?" Jane's eyes brightened.

I nodded. "Yep. But we'd have to include someone else in our project." I paused to let her absorb what I had said. "So . . . are you up for it?"

"I don't know—who's this other person?" Jane sounded wary but hopeful.

"I can't tell you yet," I responded. "But I promise that it's someone you can trust."

I held my breath as I waited for Jane to tell me whether or not she would go along with plan B. *Say yes,* I urged silently.

"Okay, I'll do it," she announced finally. "No guts, no glory."

Jane flashed me one of her dazzling smiles, and I instantly felt better. Somehow I had managed to salvage the evening after putting not only my foot but my fist as well into my mouth.

Now all I have to do is set the plan into action, I thought. And that might not be as easy as I hoped.

At seven o'clock the next morning I was sitting in my girlfriend's living room, gearing up for a possibly major begging session. If I knew Shana Stevens, the caffé latte and almond croissant I had brought along would go a long way toward putting her in the mood to say yes to the favor I was about to ask.

"Shana will be right down, Max," Mrs. Stevens told me. "But watch out for yourself. She's not at her sunniest this early in the morning."

I grinned. "Thanks, Mrs. Stevens."

A full five minutes later, Shana stomped into the living room. And she wasn't smiling.

"Max, what are you doing here?" she demanded. "I just woke up! I haven't even taken a shower, much less put on my makeup or curled my hair."

"Good morning to you too," I greeted her. Then I held out the breakfast I had brought. "A peace offering for dragging you into the public eye so early in the morning."

What was it with girls and hair? They seemed to think they weren't actual human beings until they had sprayed, curled, or teased.

Shana seemed to warm up to me as she peered into the bag. "Thank you, sweetie," she said. "I don't mean to be a jerk. . . . I just want to look good for you."

I took a couple of steps toward Shana and

enfolded her in my arms—caffé latte and almond croissant included. "You look gorgeous exactly the way you are."

And I meant it. I preferred to see Shana the way she looked now, without all of her carefully applied makeup. With her hair falling around her shoulders and her face fresh and clean, Shana was natural and soft . . . feminine.

Like Jane. The thought had come from out of nowhere. But it was true. Since I had been hanging out with Jane, I had been thinking about girls in a whole new way. Essentially I had discovered that girls were people too.

Shana and I had been going out for six months, and our relationship was solid. But had we really gotten to know each other yet? I loved her because she was beautiful, and because we were in the same crowd, and because we did all of the same things on weekends.

But those couldn't be the *only* reasons I loved Shana. There had to be more. Deep down, Shana and I obviously had some kind of connection. Right?

Then again, I've never really thought about it before, I mused. We got along; we were attracted to each other. . . . Until now it had seemed that those were the only important elements in a relationship.

"He*llooo?*" Shana snapped her fingers in front of my nose. "Max? Are you in there?"

I blinked. "I was thinking about how lucky I am to have you for a girlfriend," I said, which was sort of true. "Now, what did you ask me?"

67

Shana gave me a smile and fluffed her hair. "I wanted to know why you felt it necessary to come over here so early."

Ah, yes. Back to the issue at hand. Turning Jane into an "it" girl. I clasped Shana's hand and led her to the Stevens's overstuffed, floral-print sofa. She sat down and looked at me skeptically.

"Is this bad news?" she asked. "Because I don't deal with bad news before eleven o'clock."

"No bad news," I assured her. "Actually, I want to ask you for a favor. It's going to sound pretty strange at first—but it's important to me."

Shana raised an eyebrow. "Go on."

"You know Jane Smith, right?" I asked. I realized that I was standing in front of Shana, sort of looming over her. Quickly I sat down beside her.

"Plain Jane Smith," Shana responded, her voice laced with contempt. "What about her?"

My jaw tightened slightly at Shana's dismissive acknowledgment of Jane. But I forced myself to smile pleasantly.

I cleared my throat, feeling more nervous by the second at the prospect of revealing the bargain that Jane and I had made to Shana. "She's helping me out with something," I explained. "And in return, I'm helping *her* out."

"I don't get it." Shana sipped her caffé latte and gave me a blank stare.

"I'm really busy right now," I said, circling around the issue. "And I have these two huge term papers to write."

68

"Uh-huh . . ." Shana sounded bored. She was probably irritated that this conversation was cutting into her primping time.

I had to cut to the heart of the matter. "Basically, Jane Smith is writing my term papers for me," I told Shana. "And in exchange, I'm helping her transform herself."

"Transform herself? What does that mean?"

"Jane wants to fit in with our crowd," I explained. "She wants to be like you and Rose and Madison. . . . You know, the kind of girl that guys really go for."

"You've got to be joking," Shana declared. "Plain Jane couldn't be like me and my friends if she spent the rest of her *life* trying. The raw material simply isn't there."

Not the response I was hoping for. But I wasn't exactly shocked that Shana's initial reaction was so negative. She had offered more or less the same opinion about Jane's potential when I had brought it up indirectly at lunch yesterday.

"If you really *look* at Jane, you'll see that she does have what it takes," I insisted. "I mean, she's got pretty blue eyes, a great smile, and totally smooth skin." I envisioned Jane as I spoke, remembering the way that smile had filled me with warmth when we were bowling last night. "And her hair—"

"I get the picture," Shana interrupted. "Although you're the *only* one who can see it—Plain Jane Smith is, in reality, Kate Moss in hiding."

Oops. I had been waxing a little too poetic about another girl. And it didn't help that the girl in question was someone that Shana thought was on the bottom of the high-school-cliques food chain.

But it was hard *not* to say great things about Jane. In the past few days I had discovered that Jane was the kind of person *I* would like to be. Open. Honest. Smart. Brave. *But Shana doesn't need to know all of that,* I reasoned. *Once she gets to know Jane, she'll see those qualities herself.* Hopefully.

All of these thoughts came one after the other, overlapping and mixing in my brain. Only a second had passed when I spoke.

"Obviously Jane can never be as beautiful as you are," I told Shana. "And you're ten times more interesting and dynamic than Jane is."

But I don't believe that, I thought. *It's a lie.* Jane was different from Shana—but she wasn't *less*. In her own unique way Jane was simply awesome. Still, the words seemed to have a soothing effect on Shana. Her face brightened.

"Can't we help her out?" I asked, not letting the question die. "Think about how good you would feel if you made another girl realize her potential."

Shana sighed. "Okay. I'll do it."

I knew I was beaming as I put my arms around Shana and hugged her tight. "Thank you, thank you, thank you."

"You're welcome," she responded. "But don't expect any miracles."

I grinned. Jane didn't *need* a miracle. All she needed were a few fashion tips and some makeup lessons. I couldn't wait to tell her the good news.

Eight

Jane

I HOPE I *won't regret this,* I thought as I slammed the door of my locker shut on Wednesday afternoon. Max had promised we were going to begin the most important part of my metamorphosis today. I was to turn from caterpillar into butterfly with the help of the right clothes, the right hair, and the right makeup.

But I still didn't know the identity of the mystery person Max had enlisted to help us. Which was why my heart was pounding so hard in my chest.

I strode down the corridor, attempting to have that I'm-cool-and-confident-don't-mess-with-me air. I hesitated when I saw that Shana was standing next to Max at his locker. As comfortable as I felt around Max, I still didn't have the nerve to approach him when Shana Stevens was within a five-classroom vicinity.

Max caught sight of me. "Jane, over here!" he called.

So much for avoiding Miss Popularity. I ambled toward the happy couple, mentally preparing myself for a painfully awkward exchange of pleasantries.

"Hey, Max," I greeted him.

He gave me a warm, encouraging smile. "Jane, do you know my girlfriend, Shana?"

I nodded. "Hi, Shana." Okay, so we didn't officially *know* each other. But I knew who she was.

"Hello, Jane." Shana smiled in a friendly way, but I couldn't help but notice that she was appraising me from head to toe with her icy blue eyes.

I felt about two feet tall as I glanced toward Max. *What's the deal?* I asked silently.

Max seemed to read my mind. "Shana is the person who is going to lead you down the glamour path," he explained. "I've filled her in on what we've been doing, and she's totally psyched to help out."

I gulped. Shana Stevens, the most popular girl in school, was going to take time out of her busy social life for *me?* It seemed impossible. But here she was, nodding while Max informed me of this new development. *Who did you think he was going to enlist for the project?* I asked myself. *Tyra Banks?*

"Thanks, Shana," I said softly. "I really appreciate it."

She shrugged. "Don't worry about it. One trip to the mall and I'll have you looking like . . . well, looking a whole lot better." She paused. "No offense."

"Great!" Max clapped. "Ladies, let's proceed to

72

the parking lot. Your chariot—or at least my parents' Saturn—awaits."

I laughed at Max's joke, but Shana merely rolled her eyes. As I followed Max and Shana down the hall, I was all too aware that my gait was neither cool nor confident. But I was willing to endure a few hours of discomfort if it meant getting Shana's expert advice.

Who knew? Maybe by the end of the afternoon Shana would realize that I had a lot more to offer than she ever could have guessed. After all, Max seemed to like me. Was it such a crazy notion that his girlfriend could like me too?

I thought of the many times I had seen Shana and her friends sneering at me. Not once had any of them picked me for a team in gym class or offered me a seat in the cafeteria. For that matter, in four years none of them had ever addressed me in an even semicordial manner.

But they were reacting to the old Plain Jane Smith, I reminded myself. The remodeled version of me might be just the kind of girl that Shana would want to hang out with on a Friday night. . . .

"We're definitely going to have to do something about her clothes," I heard Shana say to Max. "She looks like she robbed an army-supply store."

. . . Okay, so maybe it was going to take some time for Shana to see that there was a cool person behind this baggy shirt and these faded jeans. *I'll just hope for the best,* I decided. *And expect the worst!*

★   ★   ★

"The fifteen square feet surrounding us should be every young woman's Mecca," Shana informed me twenty minutes later.

As soon as we had entered the mall, Max had left us (abandoned us, in my opinion) in order to participate in an air-hockey tournament at the arcade with his baseball teammates. Think of Shana as your fairy godmother, Max had told me.

I *had* been wishing for exactly that. A fairy godmother, complete with delicate wings and glitter-dusted hair. But in my mind, my Glinda the Good Witch was slightly less intimidating. As friendly as I could tell Shana was trying to be, she obviously wasn't used to conversing with someone of my social nonstanding.

We stood in front of the Lancôme counter in Macy's cosmetic department, where I was faced with an overwhelming display of eye shadows, lipsticks, powders, blushes, perfumes, and creams. I had walked by similar displays dozens of times in the past, but I had never really absorbed the sheer number of products that a girl could use to "enhance" her so-called natural beauty. As far as I could tell, there was nothing *natural* about it.

"Are you armed to charge?" Shana asked, spritzing herself with something she had referred to as "body mist."

"Uh . . . what?" I had noticed that Shana, unlike Max, spoke in a particular lingo that I was finding difficult to decode.

"A credit card. Do you have a credit card?" She

grabbed another of the tiny, pastel-colored sample bottles and held it to her nose.

"Oh yeah. I mean, yes, I have a credit card."

Thanks to years of responsible baby-sitting, I was one of the few teenagers in America who had my own (not my parents') credit card. Up until now I had barely used it. But I had a feeling that was about to change—in a very expensive way.

"Good. You're going to need it," Shana responded. "If you want to look like the kind of girl that Max and his friends would go for, you want to look like me and my friends, right?"

I nodded. "Yes, definitely."

"Well, a little pink lip gloss isn't enough," she informed me. "You're going to need a *total* makeup makeover."

"Whatever you say, Shana. I'm in your hands."

She turned to the saleswoman. "Consider the girl's face a blank canvas," she said to the lady. "She needs a new look, from moisturizer to lip liner."

The petite woman's face lit up. "Yes, of course. We'll bring out the cheekbones . . . and contour the lines around her nose. And then we'll give her eyebrows an actual *shape*."

Shana was nodding vigorously. "She needs major plucking. Right now she's more or less sporting a unibrow."

I tried to follow the rapid-fire conversation between the saleswoman and Shana, but they were speaking in what sounded like a foreign language. Somewhere between the mention of under-eye concealer and eyelash curlers, I decided I'd sit back and let the experts try to make me pretty—by any means necessary.

For a full thirty minutes the saleswoman, who introduced herself as Tiffany (Tiff, for short), worked on my face. As she brushed, blushed, and lipsticked, I listened to her endless, instructive monologue. Not for the first time during my entire transformation process, I wished Max hadn't banned my notebook.

"Don't worry, Jane," Shana said. "We'll buy you a copy of Kevyn Aucoin's *Face Forward* so you can practice doing all of this stuff on your own."

Apparently my face was an easy read. I wondered if Shana could also read the anticipation that was building up inside me. Tiffany kept murmuring about my "splendid cheekbones" and "ripe lips." I was starting to believe that with enough pounds of powder on my face, there was actual hope for me.

At last Tiffany set down her eyebrow pencil and sighed contentedly. "Voilà!" she exclaimed. "I have created a masterpiece."

"You look great, Jane," Shana said, her voice warmer than it had been all afternoon.

I was almost afraid to look when Tiffany handed me a small mirror to hold up to my face. What if I had purple eye shadow up to my hairline? Or bright pink lipstick that made me look like a relative of one of the Teletubbies?

I lifted the mirror and gazed into my brand-new reflection. "Wow . . ."

The person staring back at me bore a faint

resemblance to Plain Jane Smith. But we were distant cousins, at most. My usually boring blue eyes practically popped out of my head, and I could actually *see* those cheekbones that Tiffany had kept commenting on. Even my skin looked different. . . . It sort of glowed from within.

Sure, I was wearing the same old pair of jeans and blah shirt. But my face—my face looked like the kind of face that went on dates and ate lunch at the popular table and laughed in the hallways at school with good-looking guys. The uncool clothes and dorky ponytail still needed to go. But hey, one step at a time—I was making progress. Amazing, unbelievable, awe-inspiring progress.

"Thanks, Shana." I hopped off the high stool I was sitting on, and before I could think twice, I threw my arms around her. "This is so great of you."

Shana patted me on the back. "Don't worry about it."

As Tiffany happily began to ring up my dozen purchases, I stared at Shana, who was applying a shade of deep rose lipstick. She still looked like the ultimate ice queen, with her nose stuck in the air, every hair in place, and her designer clothes. But clearly she was a lot more than a seventeen-year-old fashion plate. She had done me an enormous favor.

"Why are you doing this?" I asked, unable to help myself.

Shana blotted her lips with a Kleenex, contemplating the question. "Well, it's always struck me as a waste when girls walk around looking horrendous when they could look good if they tried." She smiled. "No offense."

Huh. I knew I hadn't exactly been a model look-alike before now, but I had never thought of myself as *horrendous.* Frankenstein's monster was horrendous. I was merely plain and ordinary and nothing to notice in a crowded room.

But I wasn't about to point out all of that to Shana. What was the saying? *Don't look a gift horse in the mouth.* Shana had helped me out, and I was grateful. That was the important thing.

Shana glanced at the slim gold watch that encircled her slim, perfect wrist. "We'd better get going," she announced. "Max promised to take me out to dinner in exchange for . . . uh, well, he promised to take me out to dinner."

I signed the receipt Tiffany handed me without allowing myself to fully comprehend the amount I had just spent on cosmetic products. I would have to log dozens of hours with the Moellers' toddler to pay for my brand-new face. But if I got a date with Charlie Simpson, every minute spent splashing in the kiddie pool would be well worth it.

As I followed Shana out of the department store, I kept turning my head to glance at myself in the endless row of mirrors. Each time I was surprised to see the face that gazed back at me. I couldn't wait to see Max's face. Would he believe that the girl who'd introduced him to the joys of opera and bowling could be the same girl who he was about to meet?

"There he is," Shana announced as we left the

store and headed toward the mall's enormous food court. Max was standing, as instructed, next to the giant, neon, first-floor map of the mall.

"If Max has eaten an order of chili fries, I'm going to kill him," Shana continued. "I don't want to be the only one at dinner who's hungry—I'll have to get by on a small dinner salad and a couple of rolls."

I wasn't quite grasping the connection between an order of chili fries and Max and Shana's romantic dinner (I assumed it had something to do with a girly girl not eating more than her boyfriend at mealtime), but at the moment I didn't care. More pressing concerns were consuming the sum total of my brainpower. Such as . . . how was Max going to respond to my makeover?

"Drumroll, please!" Shana cried when we were within earshot of Max. "I present Jane—my newest creation!"

Actually, I'm Tiffany's creation, I thought. But so what? I took a deep breath and stared at Max, waiting for a reaction.

At first he just blinked. Then his mouth dropped open just a little and his eyebrows went up into his forehead. "Whoa . . ."

"What do you think?" I asked, my voice cracking. *Please say I look great. Or even good. Or even fine.*

"You look amazing," Max said slowly, as if he still wasn't sure he was looking at the same Plain Jane Smith he had sent off to the makeup counter with Shana a little less than an hour ago. "Truly . . . amazing."

I gulped. "Thanks." I absorbed Max's compliment,

his words echoing over and over in my mind.

My knees began to feel wobbly. In a Jane Austen novel I would have been described as about to "swoon." Sure, Max had said nice things to me before. But this was something new. His eyes were locked to my face, staring, staring, staring.

"Let's go, Max," Shana announced, her voice slightly shrill. "I made reservations at Café Bouche." She turned to me. "You can get back to your car from here, right, Jane?"

"Yes, of course," I answered automatically. Shana's tone didn't leave much room for argument.

Besides, I wasn't ready to leave the mall yet. I hadn't been poring over *Vogue* and *Elle* for the past week for no reason. I had every intention of going on a minor shopping spree.

"Are you sure?" Max asked. He glanced at Shana, then back at me.

"Yes!" I insisted. "Go!"

As I watched Max take Shana's hand and lead her toward the escalator, I felt an annoying pang of envy. It wasn't that I was jealous of Shana and Max per se. But I wished *I* were the one heading off to a romantic, candlelit dinner with a great guy.

Don't despair, I commanded myself. The look in Max's eyes had assured me that yes, I was turning into the kind of girl Max and his friends would go for.

I have the look now, and I've had the lessons in how to act, I reminded myself. *Now all I've got to do is find a way to make Charlie Simpson notice!*

★　　★　　★

"Don't just sit there!" I begged Nicole and Christy a couple of hours later. "Tell me if you like it!"

I was standing in the Gilmores' basement, blocking my two best friends' view of the television set. Every Wednesday night, in what had become something of a sacred ritual, they got together for their own must-see TV. (I usually stayed away since when I watched television I spent most of the time pointing out stupid dialogue and wondering how anyone ever sat through the commercials.)

But I couldn't contain my excitement about my new look, and I had burst into Nicole's house to show off my makeover for my small (but intensely supportive) fan club. Both Nicole and Christy appeared to be speechless—a rare event that I took as a good sign.

"You look awesome!" Nicole finally exclaimed. "But . . . what happened?"

"Did you go on one of Oprah Winfrey's makeover shows without telling us?" Christy asked. "Or did you get all of this from a magazine?"

"Max did it!" I burst out. I couldn't keep my secret from my friends a moment longer. "Actually, Tiffany, the cosmetics saleswoman, did it. But it's all because of Max."

Nicole pushed the mute button on her remote control. "Max? As in Max Ziff? How did he get involved in your self-improvement plan?"

Christy grinned. "Are you and Max . . . you know . . . an item?"

I shook my head vigorously. "Of course not!

He's totally in love with Shana." I paused, unsure of how to explain our deal without breaking my promise to Max that I wouldn't tell anyone I was writing his term papers.

"Don't stall!" Nicole insisted. "We want to know everything!"

At last I took a deep breath. Then in the most vague terms possible I explained to my friends that Max and I had agreed to trade favors.

"And as his favor to me, Max is helping me become the type of girl he and his friends would go for," I finished.

"In other words, the kind of girl that Charlie Simpson would ask to the prom," Christy commented.

I felt myself blushing, but I nodded. "Exactly."

"Well, all I can say is that Tiffany-the-blush-girl really knows her stuff," Nicole declared. "You look like a cover girl."

Talk about magic words! I basked in Nicole's compliment as if I had just been crowned Miss America. Shallow? Yes. But I had spent the past four years being deep and thoughtful. Right now all I wanted was to be hip and pretty.

"I can't wait to try out the new me at school tomorrow," I said with a sigh. "I just hope Max's reaction is everything I'm hoping it will be."

Christy frowned. "Max? Uh, don't you mean *Charlie?*"

I nodded. "Right. I mean, Charlie." I paused, flustered. "Did I say 'Max'?"

"You said 'Max,'" Nicole confirmed.

That was weird. I had been thinking about Charlie, but Max's name had accidentally slipped out.

"Anyway, I can't wait to get to school tomorrow," I said cheerfully.

"Jane, you do look great," Christy said, her voice a bit too tentative for my liking. "But don't you think the Cindy Crawford makeup job might be a little much for everyday wear?"

I shrugged. "You're just not used to it," I responded confidently.

It took time for people to adjust to a new look. And I had no doubt that within a week, Nicole and Christy would be as enthusiastic as I was. Besides, as much as I loved my friends, they weren't my target audience. Charlie was.

Nine

Jane

"MIND IF I sit down?" a soft voice whispered in my ear the next afternoon.

Despite the fact that he was whispering, I recognized Max's voice immediately. "Sure," I whispered back, glancing away from the pile of notes in front of me to give him a smile.

It was the last period of the day, and I had retreated to the library to take full advantage of my Thursday-afternoon study hall.

Max slid into a chair and placed a book on the table. "It's about John Kennedy," he informed me, pointing to the book.

I gestured toward a stack of books—all about President Kennedy—at the end of the table. I had checked them out in order to research Max's history paper. "I think I'm covered," I told him.

He nodded. "Just the same, I want to help you out. What if the teacher grills me about my paper? I'd better be ready to answer questions."

I handed him a neat stack of blank index cards. "In that case, I would be much obliged if you'd start writing down relevant quotes."

Hey, working on his paper—even the research part—wasn't something Max had to do according to the terms of our agreement. But I wasn't about to say so. Between my personal mission and the awe-inspiring number of pages I had to write before the end of the semester, I was in way over my head.

After a few minutes I almost forgot that Max was sitting beside me, carefully copying quotes about JFK onto my note cards. We worked silently, totally absorbed in our research. I had never felt so comfortable with a guy that I could be just inches away from him yet not be totally self-conscious.

Finally I set down my pen and shook out a cramp in my hand. "Wow, it's almost last bell," I commented, catching sight of my watch.

Max looked up from his textbook. "Hooray." He shut the book and leaned back in his chair. "By the way . . . I, uh, like what you've done with your new look. I mean, you know, going kind of lighter on the makeup."

"Um . . . thank you." I don't know why we both seemed tongue-tied all of a sudden. Maybe because members of the opposite sex didn't usually sit around a library table gabbing about rouge.

"I mean, you looked awesome yesterday.

Really glamorous. But it was sort of over the top." He paused. "That didn't come out right. What I meant to say is that you don't need a lot of makeup to look great."

Max was right. I was wearing a lot less makeup than I had been immediately post-Tiffany. But not by choice. Truthfully, I had done and redone my base, blush, and liner so many times this morning that I had finally had to go with a curtailed version of the new me. Still, I had been getting compliments all day. And I loved it.

"Thank you, Max," I whispered, feeling shy all of a sudden for no apparent reason.

He grinned. "Now do you believe I'd go for you?" His hazel eyes sparkled as he waited for my answer.

"Maybe." I still wasn't convinced.

Even though people had been flattering me all day, Charlie Simpson hadn't seemed to notice the radical change in my appearance. He had barely glanced my way during English class, even though I had made sure to walk right by him on the way to my desk.

"Are you at least going to thank me for getting Shana involved?" Max asked. "She's way more help than I ever could have been."

"Shana's great," I agreed. And I was still anxious to get her help in the hair and wardrobe department.

But I loved spending time with Max. *He* was the one who had given me the confidence that allowed me to talk to Shana like she was a regular person instead of feeling totally out of her league.

Being around Max, I felt not only completely comfortable, but also one hundred percent alive. I had shared my deepest fears with a guy for the first time, and now I wasn't ready for my partnership with Max to end. Not yet.

"You know, I still know nothing about sports," I reminded Max. "Maybe you could fill me in on the basics of football and baseball. Then I'd always have something to talk about with . . . you know . . . a guy like you."

Max slapped his forehead. "Sports!" he exclaimed. "How could I have neglected such crucial territory?"

I shrugged. "I guess I have to think of everything."

"Tell you what," he suggested with a laugh. "I'll tell you everything you'll ever need to know about football and basketball over a basket of chili fries."

"Deal." On the outside, I was calm and cool, just as Max had taught me to be. But inside, I was totally excited. An afternoon with Max sounded like the perfect way to continue one of the most eventful weeks of my life.

"You did *not* eat thirteen corn dogs in one sitting," Max exclaimed. "Nobody your size could accomplish that kind of feat."

We were sitting at one of the dozens of wrought-iron tables in the middle of the mall's infamous food court. Now that Shana knew the truth, Max and I had decided that we no longer needed to go to great lengths not to be seen together. If anyone asked, we would simply say that I was "helping" Max study for a test.

I laughed. "Please—don't dare me to do it again. I felt sick for three days."

Max shook his head (I was used to the gesture by now) and gave me what I would label a "bemused" smile. "You're a constant surprise, you know that, Jane?"

I batted my eyelashes. "*Moi?* A surprise? Professor, you flatter me." I stuck another chili fry into my mouth and chewed it quickly. "Then again, I doubt Shana or Rose would do something as gauche as eating thirteen corn dogs."

"Jane, to be cool, you don't have to be like everyone else," Max informed me. "In fact, I would say just the opposite." He paused. "Anyone who can eat that much processed beef is all right with me."

I felt a warm glow. Who knew that stuffing my face with junk food on a dare from Nicole at the state fair would win me such high praise? Life was, if anything, unpredictable.

"Still, I'd rather be a cheerleader," I announced to Max. "I've never seen a pom-pom girl with no prom date."

Max rolled his eyes. "You'll have a date to the prom, Janie. Who could resist that ponytail?"

Janie. Nobody but my grandmother had ever called me Janie before. Wow. In Max's mind, I was worthy of an actual nickname. That, more than anything, made me realize how much progress I had made this week.

"Hey, the guys are here," Max declared, gazing over my shoulder. "Jane, this is a perfect opportunity for you to try flirting."

I barely heard what Max said after the words *guys* and *here* sank in. Every hair on the back of my neck stood up, and I couldn't breathe. I knew, I just *knew,* that Charlie Simpson was heading our way. This was it. Charlie was going to notice me, talk to me, think, Hey where's she been hiding for the past four years?

I used every ounce of my considerable willpower to restrain myself from turning around to confirm whether or not Charlie was one of the "guys" Max had spotted.

"Yo, Max," Brett Richmond called. "What's up?"

"Not much," Max answered. "Jane and I are chillin' with some chili fries."

Three, two, one. The guys reached our table. Brett Richmond. Jason Frango. Pitter-pat. Pitter-pat. *Charlie Simpson.*

"Hi, Jane," Brett greeted me. His voice was friendly . . . but confused. There was no doubt about it.

"Jane and I are brainstorming for one of our classes," Max explained. "And hanging out," he added, ever mindful that I not think of myself as just a study dork.

"Hi, guys." *Did those words actually come out?* I wondered. I was so nervous that my throat was totally constricted.

"Hey." Jason clearly had no idea who I was. But

I *did* notice (unless I was temporarily insane) that his eyes lingered on my face for a few more seconds than necessary. Score!

But Jason wasn't the guy who was making me feel like the laws of gravity had gone by the wayside. I looked at Charlie, willing him to talk to me.

Ideally he would pop the prom question right now, on the spot. If that didn't happen, I would have settled for a request for a date. Or a how-are-you. Or hello. *Okay, I'll settle for a nod and smile.*

"Hey," Charlie said, nodding at me.

My heart skipped several beats as all the blood in my body rushed straight to my cheeks. *You're cool. You're confident. Yet you're also flirtatious.* "Hi, Charlie."

I waited for him to say something else. *Anything.* Instead his eyes sort of glazed over and he turned to Max. "You watching the game tonight?" he asked.

"Maybe," Max answered. "I'll call you later."

Oh, to be able to casually announce one's intentions to pick up the phone and dial Charlie's number. It would be heaven! *555-6174.* I had memorized the digits almost four years ago, hoping that someday I would have a reason to use it.

"Have fun, you two," Brett said.

As the guys moved away from the table, I felt oddly deflated. Here I was, sitting with one of the most popular guys in school. And I had been acknowledged by his friends as more or less an actual person. But Charlie didn't even notice me! I might as well have been wallpaper.

The more I thought about the way Charlie's eyes had skimmed over me, the worse I felt. Even Jason hadn't really been looking at me, now that I went back over the sequence of events. He had probably been reading the big printed menu over my head.

I was, in a word, crushed. If Charlie hadn't paid any special attention to me now, he never would. The transformation was a big, fat failure.

Max probably knows I'm hopeless, I decided. He'd been flattering me for one reason and one reason only. He wanted to spare my feelings.

And why *wouldn't* he want to be nice to me? After all, I was the girl who was freeing up his time by writing two huge term papers for him. In theory, Max was helping transform me. In reality—he was just humoring me.

I blinked back tears. This experiment had been a joke. And I was a fool.

Ten

Max

SOMETHING WAS WRONG with Jane. I didn't claim to know much about girls, but I did know how to discern if a girl was trying to hold back tears. Jane's bright blue eyes glistened, and she was blinking rapidly. She was also biting her lip and avoiding my gaze.

"Jane?" I called her name softly. "What's wrong?"

She shook her head. Uh-oh. Tears were definitely imminent. I was at a total loss. Shana cried a lot (she could start gushing at the first sign that a carefully shed tear might get her what she wanted). But I knew that if Jane was about to sob, something was seriously amiss.

"Um . . . let's go take a seat on that inviting bench next to the plastic potted palm," I suggested, trying to lighten the atmosphere. "We can pretend this is Paris

92

and we're watching the tourists stroll by."

Jane attempted a smile. "Sure. Whatever."

We left our junk-food-littered table and walked to the small, vinyl-covered bench. It wasn't exactly private, but at least it was out of the way. I took a deep breath and prepared to grill.

"Spill it," I said. "I know something is up."

"I . . . I . . ." A single tear slid down her cheek. "Never mind. It's stupid."

The sight of Jane so upset was making me queasy. I was used to her smile, her laugh. This was terrible.

"Please, Jane, tell me what's wrong. I promise I won't think it's stupid." I paused, searching for the words that would make my new friend open up to me. "And I'll do anything I can to make you feel better."

"Charlie." That was it. One word. Charlie.

Is she speaking in code? I wondered. I definitely needed more to go on if I was going to solve Jane's problem.

"You're not referring to Charlie Simpson for some reason, are you?" I asked hesitantly.

She nodded, her face a study in abject misery. "Yeessss." It was sort of a half wail, half sob.

"I don't understand, Janie," I said softly, hopefully maintaining a soothing, patient tone of voice. "Are you crying because we ran into Charlie? I mean, I know he's not the friendliest guy in the world. But once you get to know him, you'll like him—"

"I *do* like him," Jane interrupted. "*That's* the problem."

"You have a crush on Charlie," I stated matter-of-factly. Finally I was getting the picture. Unfortunately the queasy feeling didn't go away. If anything, it was worse.

Jane nodded. "I've had a crush on Charlie Simpson for the past four years. That's why . . ." Her voice trailed off.

"Why what?" I demanded. I sensed that I knew how Jane was going to finish the sentence. But I wanted to hear it from her lips.

"Charlie is the whole reason I wanted to do this dumb transformation," Jane admitted. "I thought that if you helped me turn into the kind of girl Charlie would be interested in . . . Well, I thought maybe he would ask me out."

Whoa. I was stunned . . . and numb. For the first time I understood Jane's determination. She wasn't embarking on this metamorphosis because of some abstract wish to fit in with the so-called cool crowd. She had a single-minded purpose.

I couldn't believe that she had gone to all of this trouble in order to *maybe* get a date with Charlie. What was so special about Charlie? Yeah, he was a good guy. And girls thought he was cute. But I had thought Jane was deeper than that. A lot deeper.

"And it's obvious that I have zero hope with him," Jane continued when I didn't say anything. "He barely even glanced in my direction when he stopped by our table! If he didn't notice me then, he's *never* going to."

"Jane . . ." But I didn't know what to say. She was so distraught.

"Thanks for all of your help, Max. Really. But this whole thing was a total mistake."

I wanted to reassure Jane. But I was still stuck on the fact that she had been pining for Charlie since, apparently, the dawn of time. I just couldn't believe it. *What am I feeling?* It was a combination of nausea, shock, and something that felt a lot like anger. Or at least irritation.

Could I be jealous? The thought popped into my head before I could stop it. But no. That was impossible. I had a girlfriend. I was madly in love with Shana. So it didn't make any sense that I could be jealous of Jane's feelings for Charlie.

I was surprised. That was all. And okay, I was feeling a little protective about Jane. I didn't like to see her hurting this way. And indirectly at least, Charlie was responsible for the tears that had rolled down her cheeks.

"This hasn't been for nothing," I insisted. "You know it hasn't. And I'm sure that Charlie *will* notice you. Give him a little time."

Suddenly Jane sat up ramrod straight. "Max, you have to *swear* that you won't tell anyone that I have a crush on Charlie. *Nobody.* Not even Shana."

Obviously getting a date with Charlie meant more to Jane than almost anything else in the world. I was her friend, and it was my duty to do whatever I could to make her dream come true.

It was the least I could do for a person who had,

somehow, done a lot to open up my world in ways I never would have guessed even a week ago. She'd given me opera and bowling. *And I'll deliver Charlie Simpson.*

"I won't tell a soul," I promised. "But I do have a great idea about how to get Charlie to notice you."

"I don't know. . . ." Jane stared off into the distance, contemplating my words.

"Do you trust me?" I asked. "If you do, you'll let me help you."

She gave me the kind of half smile I had come to recognize meant Jane was nervous but hopeful. "Okay," she announced.

And with that simple statement, I had a mission.

I was still thinking about my conversation with Jane when the doorbell rang at my house at ten o'clock that night. But all thoughts of Jane flew out of my head when I saw Shana's angry face. Something was up—and all signs suggested that whatever it was had to do with me.

"Hi, sweetie," I greeted her. "It's so awesome to see you." I held out my arms and silently prayed that Shana would walk right into them.

She didn't. "Mind if I come in?" she asked, her voice icy cold. "Or do you have company?"

I opened the door even wider. "Of course. I mean, no, I don't have anyone here." Being confronted by a girl's anger always turns me into a blithering idiot. "Come inside."

Shana breezed past me and stalked toward the

living room. "Cut the act, Max," she commanded. "Madison saw you."

"Saw me?" I asked. "Saw me . . . *what?*"

Shana perched at the edge of the sofa, but she looked like a tightly wound coil, ready to spring at any moment. "You were spotted at the mall with another girl this afternoon." If her tone was ominous, her eyes were outright stormy.

I laughed. "That was Jane," I assured her. "We went to the mall to talk sports. You know, working on the project."

Shana raised one eyebrow. "According to Madison, you two looked *very* friendly."

This day had been crazy. First I found out that Jane's whole reason for *being* was to go on a date with Charlie Simpson. Now Shana was going postal due to an innocent sighting of Jane and me at the mall. This was insane.

There was nothing going on between Jane and me. Nothing. And it was annoying that Shana would even *suggest* otherwise.

"Of course we looked friendly," I told her. "We've become *friends.*"

My tone had sounded a lot more hostile than I intended. I was practically shouting. *De Nile ain't just a river in Egypt, Max,* I said to myself. But despite the emotions that were whirling inside me, I had to stay focused on the facts. I had a girlfriend. And Jane had a major crush on one of my best friends.

I shook my head, clearing out the confusing, conflicting messages that my heart was sending to my brain. Clearly I had spent too much time in the company of girls this week. I was getting *way* analytical.

"Max, I think you're wasting entirely too much time on your little charity case," Shana snapped. "It's . . . well, it's pathetic."

A sharp pang of irritation caused most of the muscles in my body to tense up. "Shana, Jane is *not* pathetic. And neither am I."

"Whatever." She gave me a tight smile that was anything but sincere. "From now on, I'll take over your loser friend's attempt at being a real person."

I had been prepared to grovel. I had been prepared to soothe Shana's hurt feelings. But there was no chance that I was going to sit here and listen to her bad-mouth Jane. Maybe Shana didn't see Jane for who she really was, but *I* did. And I was going to make sure that Charlie did too.

"Jane is *not* a charity case," I stated (hopefully for the last time). "She's a really cool person, and she's a friend." I paused. "In fact, I was thinking . . . well, that we should set up Jane on a date."

Shana flopped onto the couch and sighed dramatically. "With whom, might I ask?"

"With Charlie," I suggested. "He's single, she's single. . . . It's a perfect match." Silently I willed Shana to agree with me.

She snorted. "Face facts, Max. There is no way that Charlie would be interested in Jane—even if she does look better, thanks to my help."

I stared at my girlfriend's beautiful face. Usually the moment I looked into her eyes, I caved. She wanted to see a chick flick? Fine with me. She wanted me to order a vegetarian soy burger instead of the baby-back ribs? Fine with me. She needed a ride to school at six-thirty in the morning for an emergency cheerleading practice? Fine with me.

But at this moment I knew that no amount of hugs, kisses, or cajoling was going to deter me from my goal. "Charlie *will* like Jane," I insisted. "And I'll prove it to you—we'll all go on a double date, and you can see for yourself."

"This should be interesting," Shana responded, flipping her hair. "Sort of like watching a train wreck."

I sat down beside Shana and put my arm around her. "We'll have a blast," I assured her. "We can all go bowling and eat nachos and play Foosball."

Shana turned her head. She gave me a you-are-crazier-than-I-ever-dreamed-possible look. *"Bowling?"*

Oops. *I forgot that bowling isn't cool.* But *why* wasn't bowling cool? It was fun, harmless, and a lot cheaper than dinner at La Fondue or some other stuffy, overheated restaurant.

Actually, a lot of things that were considered un-cool were really fun. Chess, for instance. I had been a member of the chess club freshman year, and I had loved it. And then varsity football and baseball had come along . . . and everybody told me that it was dorky for a jock to be in the chess club. I had dutifully quit . . . but why? *Not because I don't like to play chess anymore,* I realized.

Huh. For the first time in a long time I was thinking about what I *really* enjoyed and what I had

99

been *told* to enjoy. Was it possible that I had lost a sense of myself to the degree that I didn't even know my own tastes?

I'm going to change that, I decided. From now on I was going to listen to my own heart—not to other people's heads!

Eleven

Jane

"JANE, I'VE BEEN wanting to do this for a long time." He put his hands on my waist, drawing me closer and closer to his broad chest.

It was late at night, and we were all alone in the Union High library. The only light came from a small lamp on one of the study tables. Aside from our voices and the sound of our breathing, the room was bathed in silence.

"I don't know . . . ," I whispered softly. But I was powerless to resist as his full, red lips neared mine.

I wanted this kiss. I wanted it more than anything in the whole world. I closed my eyes as his lips touched mine. Electric sparks traveled up and down my spine, leaving me breathless. After what was either forever or only a brief second, he pulled away.

"Jane, put your hair up in that cute ponytail and

scrub off all the makeup that's hiding your beautiful face," he whispered. "And then tell me you'll go to the prom with me. . . . Please, say yes."

"Yes, Max . . . yes . . ."

My eyes popped open, and I found myself staring into the dark. I had been dreaming about . . . Max. *Max!* I sat straight up in bed, my heart pounding. The sheets were twisted around my body, and the comforter had fallen to the floor. But I was clutching my pillow tightly to my chest.

Remembering the image of Max's face from my dream sent flutters dancing up and down my nerve endings. It was exactly the same sensation that I felt every time I encountered Charlie in the hallway at school. Or in English class. Or in the cafeteria.

But I hadn't been dreaming about Charlie. It had been Max who was kissing me. And Max who I had dreamed of asking me to the prom. *Why is this happening?*

Max wasn't the guy I longed for. Charlie was. Just today at the mall I had felt that uncontrollable flutter when Charlie approached our table.

Hadn't I? Second by second, I replayed in my mind the entire encounter. Max had said that the guys were there. My heart had stopped (basically). My palms had started to sweat. But . . . but . . . what I felt was . . . anxiety. And nerves. And fear. *Not* The Flutter.

My eyes were beginning to adjust to the darkness, but as I looked around my room, it was as if I were seeing everything for the first time. And it wasn't just the dresser and the nightstand and my old teddy bear that looked new to me. It was *me*. And my entire life.

I thought about how upset I had been when Charlie hadn't noticed me the way I had hoped he would. Had the tears I shed been for *Charlie?* Or had the tears been for the failure of my transformation? That's what Charlie's lack of flirting represented to me, I realized. That even transformed, I still wasn't the kind of girl a guy like Max would go for.

Somewhere along the way I had stopped caring quite so much whether or not Charlie asked me to the prom. Sure, I still told myself that I cared. But it wasn't the same all-consuming desire that had forced me to approach Max that day in the library.

Instead I had become consumed with the idea of transforming myself. Of becoming the *kind* of girl who guys like Max and Charlie would go for. I had wanted to accomplish something concrete with my metamorphosis. I had wanted to gain something I could hold on to, now and in the future.

The fact that Charlie's eyes hadn't rested on me for more than the requisite half second had confirmed my worst fears—that Plain Jane Smith could never be anything more. Even trying my hardest, I had been unable to attract the kind of guy who would make me feel special, who would make me stand out.

At least before, when I had been my boring, inconspicuous self, I could dream of the day when things would be different. I had been a bundle of potential, believing that I always had a chance at being an "it" girl.

Now I had tried. And I had failed. No matter what, I would never be the kind of girl who Max or Charlie would ask to the prom . . . or anywhere else that mattered. It wasn't just about this week or next week.

I had a long life of *not* standing out to look forward to. In college . . . after college . . . my life would be a series of boring nonadventures, designed to highlight me as the reliable, straight-A student who nobody felt inspired to invite to a party.

I slumped back into my pillows and pulled the covers up over my head. Hot tears forced their way out of my eyes. All I wanted to do was hide from the world forever, safe inside my cocoon, where I could cry in peace.

As far as I could tell, I had nothing—and no one—to look forward to.

"I never thought I'd like working at Cherie's," Nicole commented. "But the pay isn't bad, and the dresses are gorgeous. It's too bad I'm not going to the prom—I get a twenty percent employee discount."

Nicole had recently started to work at the most expensive dress shop in the mall. She was determined to save enough money in the next four months to buy herself a used car to take to college.

"You should see these girls, shopping for prom dresses." Nicole said, shaking her head. "You'd think that since the day they were born, the only thing they've been waiting to do is shop for a strapless taffeta sheath." She paused. "Speaking of taffeta, you should come take a look around the shop, Jane. You've got to be ready when Charlie pops the big question."

"I'll pass," I told Nicole, unwrapping the cellophane from what was passing for my lunch.

"How can you eat that stuff?" Christy asked, wrinkling her nose as she surveyed my nutrition-free selection.

I had bypassed the limp green salad, chicken à la king, and strawberry Jell-O that the cafeteria was offering for lunch on Friday. Instead I was digging into a pack of overly processed cupcakes I had bought from the vending machine. My mood called for junk food. Period.

"For the next two days I will eat only potato chips and chocolate products," I informed Christy. "I'm declaring a moratorium on healthy living."

Nicole frowned at the piece of gray chicken that she was about to put into her mouth. "This can't be a part of Operation Glam Girl. I figured from now on you'd be eating tofu burgers and soy shakes."

I stuffed another bite of cupcake into my mouth, shaking my head. "Nope. I'm abandoning the transformation end of my deal with Max. It's hopeless."

"But Jane, you were so excited. I mean, just yesterday you said you had found your 'inner homecoming queen,'" Christy pointed out.

I felt like cringing. How could I have said something so stupid?

"I'm Plain Jane Smith, and I always will be," I announced to my friends. "The Maxes of this world are not there for my taking."

Nicole raised her eyebrows. "*Maxes*?" she asked. "I thought you wanted *Charlie*."

"Uh . . . did I say Max?" I felt my face turn bright red. Jeez. I had been embarrassed so many times this week that my face was a perma-tomato. "I meant Charlie. Definitely Charlie."

I didn't bother to add that I'd had a more-than-friendly dream about none other than Max Ziff just last night. I had bared my soul enough for one week. Enough for a lifetime. From now on, I was going to keep my pathetic fantasy life to myself.

"Charlie is an idiot if doesn't notice you," Christy stated firmly. "He should consider himself the luckiest guy at Union High that you've got a crush on him."

I shrugged, sick to death of the entire subject. "Can we drop it?" I asked. "I just want to be me for a while."

Nicole pushed aside her plate of chicken and grabbed one of my cupcakes. "Well, I, for one, am not sorry to see you letting go of this whole makeover extravaganza."

"Yeah, Jane," Christy added. "We like you just the way you are—were—thank you very much."

I smiled at my friends, despite the sadness inside me. Nicole and Christy loved me unconditionally—and for now, that would have to do. Actually, I didn't really mind giving up my dreams of buying an all-new wardrobe and spending half an hour a day doing my hair and makeup.

But . . . but something was bumming me out in a major way. *It's Max,* I realized. I had gotten used to hanging out with him. And I was going to miss it. I was going to miss it more than I ever would have imagined.

"Janie, I've been looking all over for you!" Max's exuberant voice broke into my thoughts as I walked toward my sixth-period precalculus class.

"Hey, Max." I had been more or less avoiding him all day. After my bizarre dream I needed to get my head together.

He was grinning and apparently oblivious to my less-than-enthusiastic greeting. "Tell me you're free tomorrow night." He paused. "No, that's not right. I'm telling *you* that you've got to be free tomorrow night. If you have plans, you *must* cancel them."

"Uh . . . why?" I had never seen him so excited. "What's going on?"

Max looked ready to burst. "You have a date. Actually, it's a double date, with me and Shana . . . and Charlie Simpson!"

My jaw dropped. I tried to ignore the ringing in my ears and focus on what Max had just said. This couldn't be happening! But the look on Max's face assured me that I wasn't hallucinating. He had managed the impossible.

So much for abandoning my project. There was no way I could turn Max down. Not when he looked this excited and had done me a huge "favor."

"Oh!" What else was there to say?

"And tomorrow, Shana wants to take you shopping for some date-worthy clothes." He reached out and squeezed my shoulder. "So is this great, or is this great?"

I nodded. "It's great," I echoed. But more than anything, I felt shocked and afraid. Uncomfortable.

"Listen, if Charlie doesn't fall for you on Saturday night, then there's something seriously wrong with him," Max said softly.

As I watched him walk away, I leaned against a bank of lockers and pressed my cheek against the cool metal. What was wrong with me? Just yesterday I had been completely depressed because I was convinced that the transformation hadn't been effective.

Now I had received the supposed best news of my life, but all I could think about was Max. And he was the person who had told me again and again that he liked the way I looked *before* I started my metamorphosis. At least, that's what he'd claimed.

But this is good, I told myself. I had gotten what I wanted. A date with Charlie Simpson. This was the culmination of everything Max and I had been working for.

So I was going to get psyched about my date— and force myself to quit thinking about Max. He was off-limits. Max had a girlfriend—one who had been incredibly helpful to me. Guilt washed over me as I remembered the dream I'd had the night before.

"Charlie is the one I want," I whispered aloud. "Charlie."

Twelve

Jane

"GIVE HER SOME highlights, Jamie," Shana instructed my hairdresser on Saturday afternoon. "We've got to do something about that dishwater-blond hair."

Jamie—whose hair was a beautiful, curly, red mane that any girl would have envied—studied my face. "Yes, we need to lighten you up," she declared. "We'll bring out the eyes and the cheekbones with some layers around your face."

I opened my mouth to respond. Did I *want* highlights and layers? "I don't know—"

"You'll love it," Jamie assured me. "An hour and a half from now you'll walk out of here looking like a supermodel."

Before I could say another word, she tipped back my chair. A moment later I felt warm water running over my head, drowning out the sound of everything else going on around me.

For the first time all day I began to feel relaxed. Ever since I'd met Shana in front of the mall two hours ago, I'd been plunged into a whirlwind of activity. Shana had taken me from store to store, giving me piles of clothes to try on in each one.

With a simple thumbs-up or thumbs-down, she would declare whether or not my outfit was worthy of purchase. Seven shops, one Wonderbra, and five credit card purchases later, I was ready not only for my date tonight but for dates well into my twenties.

Adrenaline had pumped through my veins as we left the last shop and headed toward the salon. Spending a lot of money on amazing clothes had made me feel, for the first time, like a normal, healthy teenager. And I had loved every second of it.

If Shana thinks I need highlights, I need highlights, I decided as Jamie massaged shampoo into my thin hair. I trusted Shana's instincts implicitly.

Jamie turned off the water and tilted my chair upright. As she toweled my hair dry, I smiled at Shana in the huge mirror that lined one wall of the salon.

"Good-bye, dishwater blond," I said to Shana.

She grinned. "Jamie does wonders," she informed me. "*Everyone* comes here to get their hair done."

"Thanks again for doing all of this for me, Shana," I said as Jamie pulled a comb through my hair. "I never could have prepared for this date without you."

"No problem." Shana smiled at me from her chair. "Speaking of the date, Max never got a

110

chance to fill me in on the details. I mean, how did this thing even come together?"

"I'm not sure," I answered honestly. Thursday afternoon Max had promised that he would get Charlie to notice me, and less than twenty-four hours later he had arranged the date. I hadn't bothered to ask who, what, when, why, where, or how.

"Well, whose idea was it?" Shana asked. "Did you suggest it? Or did Max?"

"Um . . ." I didn't know how to respond.

The idea of admitting my long-standing crush on Charlie Simpson wasn't exactly appealing. Enough people—well, me and three others—knew that I had harbored a thing for him. I didn't want to advertise my abiding desire to sit across from him during a dinner date.

"Come on, Jane," Shana pressed. "You can tell me. We're friends."

How can I argue with that? I wondered. Shana had gone out of her way to help me with Girl 101. I owed her my trust. And my friendship. So what if she hadn't been nice in the past? Now that Shana had gotten to know me, she realized that I was a cool person after all.

I smiled sheepishly, and once again I was positive that the dreaded blush had crept into my cheeks. "Well . . . I guess the date with Charlie was *my* idea—indirectly."

"What do you mean?" Shana asked. "I want to hear the whole story—and don't leave out any of the gory details."

As Jamie tipped my head and slathered my hair with something that looked like wet concrete, I searched for the right words with which to explain my feelings for Charlie.

"Well . . . the other day I confessed to Max that I've had a crush on Charlie since the summer after eighth grade," I said, going straight to the point. "I didn't want to tell him, but Max sort of pried the secret out of me."

"Hmmm . . . interesting." Shana nodded. "So what did Max say when you told him?"

I smiled, remembering the moment. "He was totally understanding. He said Charlie would be crazy not to want to date me, and then he said he had an idea about how to get us together." I paused. "But I never thought it would actually happen."

"Wow. You and Max have gotten close," Shana commented. "It sounds like you two tell each other everything."

I nodded. "You must feel like the luckiest girl in the world to have Max as your boyfriend," I commented. "He's probably the nicest guy I've ever met."

"I am lucky," Shana agreed. "And so are you." She flipped the magazine she was reading shut and stared right at me. "I mean, it wasn't easy for Max to convince Charlie to go on this date," Shana said. "But Max believes in his 'cause' so much that he managed to do it."

"Uh . . . oh." My heart was sinking straight to my feet. Had Max really had to twist Charlie's arm to make him go out with me? That was more humiliating than if I had never gotten the chance to go out with him at all!

Either way Shana had insulted me. Hadn't she?

"You know, this haircut is going to look so amazing!" Shana trilled, as if she hadn't one second ago said something that she knew would hurt my feelings. "I can't wait to see how it looks after Jamie does the blow-dry!"

Huh. Shana sounded so friendly, so sincerely excited about tonight. Maybe I had heard her wrong before. Yes. That must have been it. Shana wasn't the *most* sensitive person in the world. But I knew she would never say anything to deliberately hurt me. If she didn't like me, she wouldn't have involved herself in my transformation in the first place.

I pushed the uneasy feeling away and concentrated on tonight. With my new clothes, my new makeup, my new hair, and my new form-enhancing Wonderbra, Charlie Simpson was finally going to see Plain Jane Smith in a whole new light.

I just hoped I didn't trip over my chair or spill soup in my lap!

"Which earrings should I wear? The silver hoops or the rhinestone studs?" I held up one of each pair of earrings for Nicole and Christy to inspect.

"The hoops," Nicole declared. "They're sexy yet casual."

I had called my friends an hour and a half ago and begged them to come over for an emergency pep-talk session. So far, they had managed to keep me calm enough that I hadn't thrown up.

"Does my mascara look okay?" I asked. "I don't want to get that raccoon thing happening."

Christy laughed. "Jane, you look beautiful! Just relax."

"It's kind of hard to relax in this dress," I admitted to my friends. "It's so tight that I feel like I'm wearing a dress-sized rubber band."

"You could always change into jeans and a T-shirt," Nicole suggested.

"Ha!" I responded. "I'd rather spend the next few hours holding my breath than discard my new image."

Because the outfit looked good. Actually, it looked great. Pink, tight, and sleeveless, the dress fell to just below my knees. I had added a pair of high, silver, strappy sandals that made me at least three inches taller. So what if it felt like I was walking on stilts? My legs looked awesome!

Nicole glanced at her watch. "Uh-oh. Christy and I had better get out of here. Unless you want your two ugly stepsisters hanging around when Prince Charming shows up."

"Thanks for helping me out," I told my friends. "I don't think I could have gotten through the last two hours of powdering, puffing, and primping without you two."

"I hope Charlie knows how lucky he is," Christy said, giving me a warm hug. "You deserve the best."

"Be sure not to chew with your mouth open, and you'll be fine," Nicole advised me, grinning.

"Got it." I hugged her close, wishing I could take

Nicole and Christy along on the date for moral support.

A moment later my friends were gone, and I was left alone with my sweaty palms and nervous stomach. The clock was ticking. There was no way I could back out of the date now even if I wanted to.

I stood in front of the full-length mirror in my room. My makeup was perfect. My hair looked great (I loved the way Jamie had framed my face with subtle layers). The jewelry was right. And the dress . . . Well, I practically felt naked. Which was probably a good sign.

I don't look exactly like Shana and her friends, I thought, studying myself from every angle. There was some inherent, intangible element missing from my appearance. But I definitely looked cool and sophisticated—a whole new me.

I wonder if Max will like this dress, I thought, tugging on the hem. And then I froze. Max. Max. Max. Everything always came back to him.

"Stop it, Jane," I ordered myself. "Stop thinking about you-know-who."

I picked up my brand-new blush brush to do a final touch-up. But the doorbell rang before I could apply any more makeup.

"I can do this, I can do this, I can do this." I repeated the phrase like a mantra as I grabbed my purse and raced down the stairs.

I stopped in front of the door, pasted on a smile, and took a long, deep breath. *Good luck, Jane,* I told myself. And then I opened the door.

Standing in front of me were Max, Shana . . . and

Charlie. Until this second I hadn't been one hundred percent convinced that Charlie would actually show. But he had. Clad in pressed khakis and a light blue shirt that brought out the color of his eyes, Charlie looked as gorgeous as I had ever seen him.

My heart pounded as I realized that this was *it*. Tonight I would find out once and for all if I had what it took to attract a guy like Charlie Simpson.

I froze again, for just a second, as I realized that Charlie had gone from dream guy to the embodiment of everything I didn't think I could ever really have, transformed or not.

After tonight I would know one way or the other. Either way—bad or good—I would have my answer.

Everything would be okay . . . as long as I remembered to breathe!

Thirteen

Max

"WE'RE HERE," I announced, pulling into the parking lot of C & O Trattoria, one of the nicest Italian restaurants in town.

I glanced into the rearview mirror for the tenth time, trying to gauge how things were going between Jane and Charlie. He was sitting *really* close to her. They barely knew each other, but Charlie wasn't wasting any time. He was cracking one (unfunny) joke after another, trying to impress Jane with his charm.

But that was good. Right? Right. I wanted Jane to be happy, to get what she wanted. But . . . but . . . what? *Why am I having a problem with this?* I asked myself.

"I assume you made reservations," Shana proclaimed, climbing out of the car. "This place is always packed on Saturday night."

"Uh . . ." Oops. I had neglected that small detail.

"Don't worry about it, Max," Jane told me, slamming the car door shut. "We can hang out and talk while we wait for a table."

"This guy. You can't take him anywhere." Charlie pounded me on the back. Then he slung an arm around me and bent his head close to mine. "Dude, she's pretty hot," he whispered loudly.

"Yeah. I know." For some reason I wasn't in a Saturday-night kind of mood as we walked en masse into the fancy restaurant.

"Ziff. Party of four," Shana informed the tuxedoed maitre d'. "And we would like a table by the window. I don't want to be stuck next to the kitchen like I was the last time I was here."

The maitre d' bowed. "Of course, miss." But I noticed a pained expression on his face as he wrote my name down on a small white tablet.

"We'd better not have to wait more than fifteen minutes," Shana declared. "Otherwise I'm going straight to the manager."

I didn't bother to respond. I had learned from past experience that once Shana had started to complain about restaurant conditions, the safest thing to do was to let her ramble until she got what she wanted.

While Shana was frowning and wrinkling her nose, Jane was positively beaming. She looked around the restaurant as if she were seeing the Sistine Chapel for the first time.

"I love these stained-glass windows," she said to

118

Charlie. "I feel like I'm actually in Italy." She became totally still for a moment, then cupped a hand around her ear. "Max, they're playing *La Bohème*!"

"La *what?*" Charlie asked, looking bewildered.

"Oh . . . never mind," Jane responded quickly. "It's just this dumb opera that Max and I were laughing about the other day."

I knew Jane was lying. She *loved* opera. But how could I fault her? She was only acting the way *I* had taught her to.

"Max, will you get me a diet Coke from the bar?" Shana more commanded than asked. "The air is so dry in here that I'm absolutely *parched.*"

I dutifully headed toward the restaurant's small bar. But I was feeling crankier than ever. Sometimes I wished Shana could be a little more . . . well, a little more like Jane. Down-to-earth. And it would be pleasant if she were more appreciative of the world around her. Unlike Jane, Shana tended to search for the negative in any situation and then point it out for everybody else to notice.

"Tell them not to put too much ice in my soda!" Shana called after me.

I cringed. *It wouldn't hurt if my girlfriend were a little nicer too,* I reflected. As I approached the bar, I realized how weird the whirl of thoughts in my brain was.

The whole point of the deal Jane and I had made was to turn Jane into a girl like *Shana* so that a guy like me would go for her. *But a guy like me would go for Jane just as she is!*

119

And then it hit me. What Jane had needed wasn't a so-called transformation. Not at all. What Jane *did* need was access. Up until now she had never had the chance to spend any significant amount of time with guys like Charlie and me. But once a guy got to know her and realized how great she was, of course he would be interested!

Well, tonight Jane was getting exactly the opportunity she had needed all along. She would be sitting at a table with Charlie, and she would have his full attention. This was it! Jane was about to fulfill her dream. . . . *So why do I feel so lousy?*

By the time we sat down twenty minutes later, I had progressed from merely hungry to totally starving. *That's probably why I'm in such a bad mood,* I thought. Hunger.

I was seated next to Shana and across from Jane. Good. This way if Jane got nervous, I could cast her encouraging glances across the table. I was going to be supportive, no matter *how* cranky these hunger pangs were making me.

"Hi, my name is Olga," our waitress greeted us. "I'll be your server tonight."

"Olga?" Charlie asked. "That doesn't sound Italian. . . . Are you sure you're qualified to work here?"

Olga raised an eyebrow. "You don't look old enough to be able to afford an expensive meal. . . . Are you sure you're qualified to *eat* here?" She stuck out her hip and batted her eyelashes.

120

I resisted the urge to roll my eyes. Yeah, I believed in being friendly to waitresses. But I didn't approve of Charlie's overly familiar style of banter. It was . . . sort of embarrassing.

I glanced at Jane, but she seemed totally oblivious. She was carefully studying the menu, expressing delight over several of the dishes.

Luckily Olga started to recite tonight's specials, so Charlie didn't have the chance to pelt her with another insult slash come-on.

"And finally, we have a special pesto pizza that comes with eggplant and sun-dried tomatoes," Olga concluded a full two minutes later.

Charlie leaned forward in his chair. "What, no oysters?" he asked. "We were all hoping for an aphrodisiac to get us in the *mood*."

Olga giggled. "Seems to me like you're *already* in the mood."

Now I really was embarrassed. I hated it when Charlie pulled out this immature mating ritual—especially on a date! He should have been giving all of his attention to Jane, not the well-endowed waitress.

But nobody else seemed bothered. Shana was giggling behind her napkin, and Jane still seemed to be absorbed in her menu. *Take it easy, Max,* I told myself. *Just have a good time—like you're supposed to.*

After we did our round of ordering, I grabbed a piece of hot, fresh garlic bread from the basket in the middle of the table. I was positive that as soon as I had something in my stomach, I would be able to lighten up.

Once Olga was gone, Charlie shifted his focus squarely onto Jane. He turned around in his chair so that they were looking at each other straight in the eyes. Now—this was more like it!

"How come you haven't been around more, Jane?" Charlie asked. "I can't believe I've never noticed you before."

"Oh, uh, we actually have a class together," Jane told Charlie. "English with Mr. Atkison."

He snapped his fingers. "*Right.* Jane Smith, literary genius." He squinted in her direction. "Is it true that you're the smartest girl in the whole school?"

Jane's face turned a soft, pretty red. "I don't know. I mean, no, of course not—"

"Do brains like to have fun?" Charlie interrupted. "Like, how far have you gone with a guy?"

"Uh . . . what?" Jane's face was now bordering on crimson, and I felt like punching Charlie in the middle of his ruggedly handsome face.

He snorted with laughter. "Just kidding!" He pounded the table. "But I had you going, huh?"

I felt like slipping out of my seat and spending the rest of the evening hiding under the table. Shana could feed me rolls, and I could have Olga set down my chicken marsala on the floor.

But I couldn't abandon Jane now. She was glancing at each of us in turn, and I got the feeling that she was racking her brain for something now. So far, she hadn't contributed much to the conversation—except for Charlie, nobody had had the chance to get a word in edgewise.

Jane cleared her throat, and we all looked at her expectantly. "So, um, Charlie, have you read that book by Jon Krakauer, *Into Thin Air*?"

"Nope. Never heard of it." Charlie took a bite of garlic bread and chewed contentedly.

"Oh," Jane said, sounding disappointed. "I thought you might have because it's sort of a 'guys' book. It's about a group of people who climbed Mount Everest—"

"Sounds boring," Shana interrupted. "I'd rather read about romance and intrigue than a bunch of nature buffs."

"I read the book," I told Jane. "It was awesome. I felt like I was on the mountain with all of those people while they fought for their lives."

Jane's eyes lit up. "Have you seen the IMAX movie of Everest?" she asked me.

"Yes!" I exclaimed. "I went back twice." Of course, I tried to get Shana to go to the movie with me, but she refused to see any film that didn't star either Julia Roberts or Cameron Diaz.

"The giant IMAX screen is so amazing," Jane continued. "I loved the one about the deep sea. . . . It was the closest I've ever been to scuba diving."

I wished I could talk to Shana about this kind of stuff. I loved exchanging views about movies and books, but somehow those subjects never came up when Shana and I were on a date.

What do we talk about? I wondered, turning to look at my beautiful, popular girlfriend.

Shana caught my gaze. She gave me a megawatt

smile and leaned forward. A moment later she snaked her arms around my waist and gave me a kiss on the lips.

"Now, that's better than any stupid movie," Shana declared.

I nodded. But . . . did I really agree?

"So . . . what do you think of Jane?" I asked Charlie when the girls took off for what Shana called the "powder room" in between dinner and dessert.

Charlie pursed his lips, scanning the dessert menu. "Huh." He mulled over the question. "She's cute. I think I'm going to have the tiramisu."

"I *know* she's cute," I answered, feeling a wave of frustration. "But do you *like* her? You know, really *like* her."

Charlie shrugged. "She's kind of boring—not really my type."

"Boring?" I echoed. In my experience Jane was a lot of things—boring wasn't one of them.

"Yeah . . . like, she didn't laugh at any of my jokes." Charlie was warming up to his subject now. "And I was doing some really good stuff!"

In my opinion, Charlie's jokes hadn't been all that funny. In fact, if I had to apply the word *boring* to any of us, it would have been him. Or maybe *boorish* was the better word. But I wasn't about to share my thoughts with Charlie—after all, he was one of my best friends. Most of the time.

"That's too bad," I replied instead. "But you know, maybe it'll just take a little more time for you

124

two to get comfortable with each other. Jane really is an awesome chick."

"Maybe." Charlie didn't seem too concerned with the outcome of his date. He was probably wondering what the baseball score was.

I wasn't sure how to feel about Charlie's luke-warm reaction to Jane. Part of me was relieved. Deep down, I didn't believe that Charlie was good enough for Jane—friend of mine or not.

But another part of me was disappointed. This date meant so much to Jane. I was sorry that Charlie hadn't immediately fallen head over heels in love with her, as I was sure she wanted him to.

I sighed deeply, suddenly not feeling so hungry for dessert. This "bargain" with Jane had turned into something a lot more complicated than I ever could have imagined.

Fourteen

Jane

FRESHLY LIP GLOSSED and powdered, I followed Shana toward our table. *I should have said more to Shana while we were redoing our makeup,* I realized, my gaze on the straight line of the other girl's back. Girl talk was an essential element of a double date, right?

But I had been too busy making sure I didn't smudge my mascara to do much chitchatting. Besides, what would I have said? My emotions and thoughts were so scattered that even *I* wasn't sure what I was thinking.

We got to the table . . . and my eyes immediately went to Max. I almost gasped when I saw that he was staring right back at me. I had never seen him look so *intense.* I could barely breathe as we looked into each other's eyes. Three. Two. One. I forced my gaze to move from Max to Charlie—where it should have been all along.

What was wrong with me anyway? Tonight was my big chance with Charlie—the culmination of everything I had been dreaming about for four years. But so far I had spent most of the night making mental notes about how good Max's dark green shirt looked on him. The color made his hazel eyes appear a deep, aqua green.

And I couldn't stop thinking about how much Max and I had in common, how much we had to talk about. Books, movies, music . . . I felt like I could talk to Max forever and never run out of things to say.

Yes, the only reason I was even at this restaurant, on this date, was because I had been in love with Charlie since forever. But . . . but . . . every time Shana leaned over to kiss Max, I felt as if someone were driving a knife through my heart.

I am seriously deranged, I decided. *This is categorically nuts!* I simply had to ignore these confusing feelings and focus on my goal. From this moment forward, I was going to put into practice every single thing Max had taught me. I would use my newfound womanly wiles to drive Charlie mad with desire!

"Hi, guys, did you miss us?" I asked, batting my eyelashes in Charlie's direction.

"Uh . . . yeah." He sat up a little straighter and reached over to pull out my chair.

I slipped into my chair, crossed my legs at the ankles (in true ladylike fashion), and fixed my attention on Charlie.

"Have you two decided on dessert?" Shana asked, placing her hand in Max's and leaning her body against his.

"Personally, I'm stuffed," I informed the table. "Charlie, is it okay if I just have a bite of whatever you order?"

"Yeah. Yes, of course." He flashed me the same smile that had made me fall for him all those years ago.

"So, Charlie, have you seen any good bands lately?" I asked.

"Yeah! I went to see Radio Active at Wally's the other night. They totally rocked!"

"I've been dying to see them!" I declared, my voice practically bursting with enthusiasm. "I wish I'd known Radio Active was playing—I definitely would have checked them out."

Lies. Lies. Lies. I had never heard of the band or, for that matter, of Wally's. But I doubted that Charlie was going to grill me on the subject. And for the first time tonight he actually seemed interested in something I had to say. This was getting kind of fun.

"The Ringmasters are playing next week," Charlie told me. "But I can't go—we've got a big game against JFK High."

"Bummer!" *Note to self: Research the Ringmasters on the Internet.*

"Tell me about it," Charlie answered, sounding crestfallen. "But hey, them's the breaks. If we want to have a shot at the major leagues, we've got to be dedicated."

Huh? Did Charlie really think he was going to

128

be a professional baseball player? I couldn't imagine wanting to spend that much time around guys whose main hobby was spitting on AstroTurf.

The conversation continued. Charlie threw out the names of bands, cafés, and Web sites, and I responded accordingly. Luckily I had gotten enough coaching from Max that I actually had something to say about the majority of the bands Charlie mentioned.

But my heart wasn't really in it. Sure, I enjoyed the fact that Charlie Simpson appeared to be flirting with me. And mindless banter wasn't all bad—I laughed several times. Yet . . . I knew this kind of interaction would never be enough for me. Not for hours on end.

I liked *real* conversation. I liked to debate, and argue, and have my ideas challenged to the point that I had to question my own beliefs. Somehow I didn't think Charlie would be thrilled at the prospect of an in-depth discussion of a presidential election.

"You should go to Langly's Coffee Shop sometime," Charlie was saying. "They serve free chocolate-chip cookies every Tuesday night. . . ."

As I nodded along to Charlie's steady stream of conversation, I allowed myself to steal a quick glance at Max, who was talking quietly with Shana on the other side of the table.

I expected him to shoot me an encouraging smile or a discreet victory sign. But he didn't. In fact, he didn't even look in my direction. He was staring at some point over Shana's shoulder . . . and he looked, well . . . glum.

I moved my gaze from Max to Shana. She was frowning at her water glass, and I noticed that she was biting her lip. Weird.

I looked back at Charlie, who was still mid-story. But my mind wasn't on his words. Instead I was worrying about the progress of the night. Charlie seemed oblivious to everything but his own jokes, but Max and Shana clearly weren't enjoying themselves.

Was it my fault? Had I done something wrong? And if so . . . what?

I didn't say much during the short drive from the C & O Trattoria to my house. I sat in the dark backseat with Charlie, half listening to the detailed discussion he and Max were having about the various baseball recruiters who had been showing up at practice. Shana hadn't said more than three words since we'd left the restaurant.

"Here we are, Jane," Max announced, pulling up in front of my house. "We have delivered you safely to your abode."

"Thanks, everybody," I said. "I had a great time."

As I opened the door of the car, I half expected Max to get out and walk me to the door. After all, he was the person in the car who I had the closest connection to. But Charlie dutifully hauled himself out of the Ziffs' sedan and walked me up the brick path that led to my family's front door.

"This was fun," Charlie said as I slid my key into the lock. "Hey, I'll see you around school."

"Right . . . see you." I gave Charlie a smile, and he bent forward to give me a kiss on the cheek.

I slipped into the house and closed the door behind me. This night had been nothing like what I had expected. A week ago, if someone had told me that Charlie Simpson would be giving me a kiss on the cheek, I would have said that it was more likely that I would win a Lotto jackpot.

Now it had happened. And I felt let down. I didn't even care that Charlie hadn't asked me for another date. I was just glad to be inside my house, minutes away from scrubbing off my makeup and changing into a pair of soft cotton pajamas.

I walked into the den, where my parents were watching an A&E mystery classic. "I'm home," I announced.

My mom smiled. "Did you have fun, honey?"

I shrugged. "It was . . . interesting."

"We want to hear all about it in the morning," Dad added. "But we won't make you give us a full debriefing until you've had a chance to sort out your thoughts."

I laughed. My parents had never debriefed me in my life. Then again, I had never gone out on a double date on a Saturday night (or any night, for that matter) before. This day was definitely one for the record books. Plain Jane Smith had gone out with one of the most popular guys at Union High—and lived to tell the tale. There was only one problem. There wasn't much of a tale. No sordid details. No giggled confessions or wistful glances. It was just . . . a date.

Upstairs, I took off my new dress and carefully hung it up in my closet. I was getting more depressed by the minute now that I was alone with my thoughts. But why? I had accomplished one of my major goals tonight. I had gone out with Charlie, and I hadn't made a complete fool of myself. I even had the feeling that if I had tried just a little bit harder, I could have obtained that ever elusive second date.

"What's eating at you, Janie?" I asked myself, pulling on my favorite pair of pajamas. "Why are you so down in the dumps?"

But I knew why I felt so low. The answer had been staring me right in the face, almost since the moment that I opened the door and found myself face-to-face with the guy of my dreams. For the first time I had realized, somewhere deep inside, that my crush on Charlie had been totally superficial. It had been stupid, and childish, and based on nothing but a pair of bright blue eyes and a winning smile.

It's all been meaningless, I realized, pacing back and forth across my room. I had spent four years fantasizing about Charlie, but there hadn't been any *real* basis for my infatuation. Sure, he had been nice to me one time at a skating rink. But so what?

The truth was undeniable. My quest to transform myself into the kind of girl that Charlie would go for had been superficial—based on hair and makeup rather than any personality deficiency I might have had. And my crush had been equally superficial. I had fallen for Charlie because he had a great smile and broad shoulders.

But I had never really known him. I had never had a single real conversation with him—at least, not before tonight. I'd liked him because he was cute, and popular, and dazzling. Not because we had anything in common or found the same things funny or believed in the same causes.

Basically I've had a crush on a celebrity, I thought. I might as well have spent my time dreaming about Brad Pitt. Charlie was a face and a name to me—not a real, living, breathing person. How meaningless!

I charged into my bathroom, anxious to scrub away the seven layers of makeup on my face. The lather of the soap felt good in my hands and even better on my face. I massaged the soap into my skin, making it tingle.

How could I have been so stupid? It had taken me all this time to realize that what I felt for Charlie had no more substance than cotton candy. I had moped and mooned and pined for all this time . . . for absolutely no reason. I, Jane Smith, thought by some to be the smartest girl in school, had attached enormous importance to something (or, in this case, someone) that turned out to be totally unimportant.

I turned on the cold water tap and doused my cheeks, forehead, chin—sort of a metaphorical slap in the face. Now maybe I could see my life clearly and not through the gauze of my desperate attempt to "fit in."

At least one truth was already emerging from the fog. There was a real reason why I couldn't stop thinking about Max . . . couldn't stop dreaming about him. I *knew* Max. He was a real person, with whom I'd shared real conversations and real laughter. We had gotten to know each other in a way that I had never known another guy before.

As I was patting my face dry with a fresh towel, the phone on my nightstand rang. *It's got to be Nicole,* I guessed. Christy never called after ten o'clock.

"Hello," I answered, preparing myself for the half-hour grill session that would inevitably ensue.

"Hey, I hope you're not asleep yet." The voice didn't belong to Nicole. It was Max.

I placed my hand over my heart, willing it to stop beating so wildly within my chest. My blood pressure felt like it had risen astronomically during the last two seconds.

"Hi, Max. No . . . uh, I'm not asleep yet." *And now that you've called, it will probably be another three hours before I wind down enough to close my eyes,* I added silently.

"I just couldn't wait until Monday to hear what you thought about the date," Max told me. "Was it everything you had hoped it would be?"

I thought about lying and saying, yes, the date was beyond my wildest dreams. But what was the point? Charlie and I, as a couple, were never going to happen.

"I had a great time . . . but to tell you the truth, I don't think the date part between Charlie and me went that well."

"I know Charlie was being totally obnoxious, but hey, maybe he was nervous. He's probably never been out with a girl as cool and smart as you are."

I smiled. Leave it to Max to say something totally nice at exactly the right moment. He always came through.

"There's nothing wrong with Charlie," I assured him. "But—well, I don't think we really clicked the way I had hoped we would."

"You didn't?" Max didn't sound as disappointed as I thought he would. Probably because Charlie had already told him on the drive home that he never wanted to see me again.

"I think it would be best if we forget the whole thing," I suggested to Max. "Charlie, the transformation, all of it. I mean, your term papers will be finished, right on schedule . . . but . . . let's just leave it at that."

"No!" Max burst out. "We have to give it another shot!"

"Max—," I started, intending to tell him that I was happy with the progress I had made but that I thought I would be okay on my own from here on out.

"Things were just a little off tonight," he interrupted. "There was a weird vibe in the air. I think . . . I think there was just too much pressure on all of us—especially you." He paused. "But I'll think of something to fix it. I swear!"

I closed my eyes and sank into my pillows. More than anything, I wished I could tell Max that Charlie wasn't the one I wanted to go out with. I wished I could open up my heart and tell Max that I had fallen for *him*—and for all of the right reasons.

The transformation was superficial and fake and has nothing to do with why someone should go for me, I wanted to shout into the telephone.

But I couldn't. A relationship between Max and me was an impossibility. He was in love with Shana, and that wasn't going to change. That much was obvious from the way they kept kissing each other during dinner.

"Come on, Janie," Max urged. "Tell me you'll give Charlie another try. Please."

I bit my lip. I couldn't say no. Not to Max. He had done so much for me, and he was so determined to help me that I didn't have the heart to disappoint him. I would have felt terrible if he thought I was giving up on him in any way.

"One more shot," I agreed finally. "But if things don't work out with Charlie and me, I'll live. Really."

On the other end of the phone Max breathed a huge sigh of relief. "You won't be sorry, Jane. I know what I'm doing."

I almost felt like laughing. Max might know what *he* was doing. But I had no idea what *I* was doing. . . .

Fifteen

Jane

I GLANCED IN the girls' bathroom mirror on Monday morning, debating whether or not to apply another coat of lipstick. Last Friday, I would have seized any opportunity to ensure that my makeup was picture-perfect. Today . . . I didn't care all that much. Besides, I didn't really like the lipstick I had bought—it tasted bad.

"Hey, Jane," Shana greeted me, breezing into the bathroom, brush and makeup bag already in hand. "I need to do a quick repair job." She gave me a pointed look. "And so do you."

"Hi, Shana." Dutifully I pulled the tube of lipstick out of my backpack. I couldn't very well tell Shana that after all of her hard work, I had decided that I was okay with looking more or less the way I had for the last four years.

"So . . . was Saturday night the best evening of your life—or what?" Shana inquired, dabbing concealer onto the nonexistent zits on her face.

"Uh . . ." How to answer that question? In some ways Saturday night *had* been great.

I had finally seen the truth, liberating myself from the pathetic crush that had dominated my waking hours for as long as I could remember. And I had also realized, at long last, that a person was more than a hairstyle, gleaming white teeth, and the right attitude.

But the date had also been horrible—and not just because my Charlie bubble had been burst. Now that I had realized what I *really* wanted—Max—the fact that I couldn't have him was more painful than anything I had experienced regarding Charlie. Of course, that particular piece of information was the *last* thing I would ever share with Shana.

"Charlie is, like, the funniest person I have ever met," Shana continued. She had moved on to powder, carefully dusting her face, then blotting with some kind of cotton pad. "He *totally* cracks me up."

"Yeah . . . he's really funny." Actually, I didn't have much of an opinion on whether or not Charlie was witty. I had spent the majority of the evening sneaking glances at Max—not appreciating Charlie's particular brand of humor.

"I don't know *what* was wrong with Max that night," Shana went on. "He was so uptight. I've never seen him act so . . . lame."

"Lame?" I asked, my voice a tiny squeak. "I didn't think Max was being lame."

Shana rolled her eyes—not an easy feat in the midst of applying a fresh coat of black mascara. "Sometimes Max is just so not fun. He's lucky that he's so cute—otherwise I wouldn't stick around for the bad times as well as the good ones."

I couldn't believe Shana felt this way. She had to appreciate Max for more than his dark hair and entrancing hazel-with-gold-flecks eyes. Didn't she feel like the luckiest girl in the world to be dating a guy who was so intelligent and sensitive and interesting and funny and . . . I had to stop myself. I couldn't think about Max like that. It was wrong, wrong, wrong.

Sure, any girl in her right mind would love the way Max *looked.* But that wasn't the most important thing about him—far from it. Appearance was . . . well, just that. *Appearance.* It didn't have anything to do with what was inside.

I had learned that much for myself—Saturday night. Which was why, unlike Shana, I would be spending prom night home alone, with a bag of Ruffles and an expensive aromatherapy kit.

Of course, it had taken me four years to learn the lesson. I couldn't blame Shana for not having the exact same epiphany I'd had.

"Hey, maybe you'll get lucky with Charlie," Shana said, her tone a combination of condescending and encouraging. "There's always a chance he'll ask you out again."

I didn't bother to tell Shana that I didn't think I *cared* whether or not Charlie asked me for another date. She wouldn't understand. Just like she didn't understand a lot of things—like Max's amazing personality. . . .

The last thing on my mind as I walked into Mr. Atkison's class was English literature. I was about to see Charlie—and Max. Since late Saturday night I had been wondering how I would feel when I saw Charlie again. Maybe when we were in class— where my crush had developed into a four-year-long obsession—I would rediscover the magic. Maybe.

I walked into the classroom, scanning the desks. Almost immediately my eyes fell on Charlie. He was unwrapping a package of frosted Pop-Tarts to go with the small carton of chocolate milk on the top of his desk.

He glanced up and caught my eye. "Hey," he greeted me. Then he turned back to the foil wrapper.

"Hey." I continued past his desk and took a seat in the back of the classroom.

Max was still nowhere in sight, so I decided to use the last few moments before the bell rang to dissect my reaction to Charlie. I closed my eyes, tuning out the sounds of scraping chairs, laughter, and rustling notebook pages.

I had seen Charlie. He had nodded and said hi. I had nodded and said hi. And that was it. There had been no lingering anxiety. My palms hadn't been sweaty, and my heart hadn't raced. I had felt neither happy that he said hello nor *unhappy* that *all* he said was hello.

The truth was clear. I felt nothing for Charlie Simpson. Nada. Zip. Nil. Absolutely, positively, definitely *nothing*. My crush was over. The spark was officially, unequivocally dead.

It was as if a huge weight had been lifted from my shoulders. I was free! From now on I could roam the corridors of Union High without feeling compelled to be vigilant about searching for a Charlie sighting. I would no longer have a sick knot in the pit of my stomach when I heard a rumor that Charlie had been spotted making out with one of the cheerleaders under the football-stadium bleachers.

Unfortunately I still felt like a fool for harboring such a meaningless crush for so long. Who knew what interesting and dynamic thoughts I might have had during the time I had spent fantasizing about Charlie? Maybe I could even have met someone—someone like Max—if I hadn't been longing for a guy I didn't even know.

I opened my eyes just as Max was entering the classroom. Zing. Zing. Every nerve in my body felt charged with electricity as my eyes followed Max's easy gait.

Don't think about Max like that, I ordered myself. I had to put him out of my mind completely— at least as anything more than a good friend. I tore my gaze away and stared at my notebook. A moment later I felt Max looking at me, but I didn't glance up. If it's true that a person's eyes are the windows to her soul, I didn't want Max to look into mine and see how I really felt.

I waited for everyone else to file out of the classroom before I finally picked up my backpack and headed for my next class. I didn't want to talk to Max now—I wasn't ready.

"Hey, slowpoke, what took you so long?" I felt Max's hand on my arm before I registered his voice.

I stopped short, just outside the classroom door. "Oh, hi, Max. I was just, uh, making sure I had my calculator for calculus."

Max pulled me out of the throng of students crowding the hallway. "I've got a plan."

"A plan?" I repeated back to him, trying in vain to ignore the way his hand on my arm had sent little shivers up and down my spine.

Max nodded. "Jason Frango is having a party on Friday night. Charlie is going to be there—and so are you."

I frowned. A month ago, even a week ago, I would have been jumping up and down at having received an actual invitation to an actual party where there would be actual cool people. But now . . . Well, the prospect of watching Max and Shana slow dancing and making out wasn't the first thing on my list of fun weekend activities.

"I barely even know Jason. I don't think he'd want me at his party." It wasn't the real reason I didn't want to go, but it was true.

Max gave me the head shake. "No way, Janie.

You're not getting out of this." His gaze was piercing, and I could barely breathe. "You promised to give you and Charlie one more shot, and Friday night is the perfect opportunity. I'm sure this time you two will totally click."

"Charlie barely bothered to say hi to me in English class," I pointed out. "I really don't think he's interested."

"How can he *not* fall for you?" Max wondered aloud. "You're the coolest chick I know. . . . I mean, uh, aside from Shana, of course."

Of course. I wasn't likely to forget that fact! "Max, I really appreciate all you've done." I was going to say a firm no to the party. I really was. But looking into Max's eyes, I simply couldn't let him down. "And I'd like to go to the party. It's a great idea."

He nodded. "Good. Now, there's one more thing we need to talk about."

His tone had changed—it was all business. My heart sort of shriveled as I remembered the real reason Max had been hanging out with me at all. He valued me, all right—but only because I was the one who was writing his term papers.

"I've told you five times that your papers will be done, typed, and spell checked right on time," I informed him, sounding a little testy.

"Listen, Jane, I've been doing a lot of thinking." He paused, shuffling his feet and staring at the floor. "Um, I don't want you to write the papers. It's just not right. I'm going to do them myself."

I had to put my hand over my mouth to keep

143

my jaw from dropping to the ground. Was Max saying what I thought he was saying? After all he had gone through, he wasn't even going to bear the fruits (in the form of twenty pages of carefully written exposition) of his labors?

"Max, I don't know what to say. I mean, we had a deal. . . ."

He grinned. "Let's call our deal to a close—officially. I think we both got a lot out of it, but it's time to call it quits."

Call it quits. No more Max and Jane, working together to make our lives better. We wouldn't be spending any more afternoons together in the library, quietly researching Max's history term paper. Our business was finished.

"If that's what you want, Max, then I'll give you the note cards I've made. You can go from here."

"Thanks, Jane. For everything." His tone had a good-bye in it.

"If the deal is off, it's off," I told him. "We can just forget about Friday night and the party and Charlie—"

"No way!" Max interrupted. "Friday night is on the house. You *are* going to be there!"

I watched Max take off down the hall, feeling more confused than ever. Max had agreed to help me—and he wasn't going to get anything out of it. That meant . . . Well, it meant that we were friends. Max *really* wanted Charlie to fall for me—and not just because he felt obligated.

Even as our partnership was drawing to a close, I felt closer to Max than ever. Closer—and more in love.

Sixteen

Jane

"DO EITHER OF you want to join me for a John Travolta movie marathon this week-end?" Christy asked Nicole and me at lunch on Thursday. "We can start with the seventies and *Saturday Night Fever* and keep right on going through the nineties."

"Count me in," Nicole answered. "As long as you promise to leave *Phenomenon* out of the lineup. Once was enough."

"Deal," Christy said. She turned to me. "So, Jane, any special Travolta requests? *Broken Arrow*? *Get Shorty*? The seminal classic, *Perfect*?"

"I don't know if I can join you guys for the fest," I said, opening a can of Dr Pepper. "I, uh, might have plans."

I had been hoping to avoid this conversation. So

far, I hadn't mentioned Jason's party to either Nicole or Christy because I still wasn't totally committed to going. And I knew that discussing the matter would only stir all of the confusing emotions I had been experiencing all week.

"What gives?" Nicole demanded. "You've been acting weird all week."

"It's Max," I told them. "Actually, it's Charlie. No, it's Max *and* Charlie." Jeez. I was confusing *myself.*

"You had better start from the beginning," Christy told me. "This sounds complicated."

In the simplest possible terms I explained to my friends that my feelings for Charlie had changed. I had simply lost interest in the guy who had been my obsession for all of high school.

"But Max is insisting that I go to a party at Jason Frango's on Friday night. He's positive that Charlie and I will hit it off this time around."

"Maybe you will," Christy said hopefully. "I mean, crazier things have happened."

I shook my head sadly. "Even if Charlie was interested, there's no way I'd rekindle my crush." I paused. "I'm . . . in love with somebody else."

Phew. It was the first time I'd allowed myself to *think* those words, much less say them aloud. I felt exhilarated and sick all at the same time.

"I think we have a tiny inkling who," Nicole said with a smile, and Christy nodded.

I glanced up at both of them in surprise. My best friends had known it even before I did. I was the only person I was keeping it a secret from.

146

"That's so great!" Christy said, then paused. "Uh, is it great?"

"It's terrible." I had been thinking about nothing but Max, Charlie, and the party all week. And any way I examined the situation, I came out a big, fat loser. "First of all, Max already has a girlfriend he's totally in love with. Second, Shana has become a friend of mine. Third, even if Shana wasn't in the picture, I doubt that Max would ever view me as more than a buddy."

Nicole frowned. "Max seems like a really nice guy, but I don't know how you can consider Shana Stevens to be a friend. Her favorite pastime is ragging on people like us."

"She's really not like that," I assured my friends. "She's been so nice to me. Shana even offered to help me get ready for the party Friday night so I would have a better chance with Charlie."

"If you don't want to go to the party, why did you tell Max you would?" Christy asked.

I sighed. "He was just so sweet about wanting me to have another shot with Charlie. . . . I couldn't say no."

Nicole snapped her fingers. "Hey, there is a bright side to this!" she announced.

"What?" I had been searching for a bright side all week, and I hadn't found one.

"If you go to the party," Nicole began in a cheery voice, "and Charlie ends up asking you to the prom . . . Well, there are worse things in the world than going to the dance with a gorgeous guy

147

you've fancied yourself in love with for your entire high-school career. Even if you don't still have a crush on him, it would be fun."

"And," Christy added, "if there's zero chemistry with you and Charlie and he *doesn't* ask you to the prom, then at least you'll get to spend a little more time around Max."

They were right. Going to the prom had been one of my lifelong dreams. And if I couldn't go with the guy of my real dreams, that didn't mean I couldn't go with someone else. If that person turned out to be Charlie Simpson, so much the better. Hey, at least I'd have a great photo of me in a prom dress with one of the hottest guys at Union High.

And if Charlie doesn't ask me . . . no harm done. I had managed to hang out around Max and Shana while they were making out before. Once more wouldn't kill me.

"I'll go!" I told my friends. "And I'll give Charlie everything I've got—for old times' sake."

It wasn't as if anything *bad* would come of me going to Jason Frango's party. At the very least I would get to see how the other half lived. *Who knows?* I thought. *Maybe I'll even have a good time.*

"Tonight is going to be a total blast," Shana chirped, twirling around her bedroom in a new skirt. "Jason's parents are out of town for, like, a week, so it's going to be a total rager."

"Cool." I pictured drunk jocks swinging from chandeliers while their dates did striptease acts on the dining-room table. Was I getting in over my head? Would cops show up?

This whole night was shaping up to be totally surreal. I, not-so-plain Jane Smith, was hanging out with Shana Stevens in her bedroom—which was awe inspiring in and of itself. Pink wall-to-wall carpet. Pink curtains. Pink walls. A four-poster bed with a white comforter and pink pillows. I felt like I was visiting a Barbie Dream House.

"So what are you wearing tonight?" Shana asked. She slipped on a pair of high-heeled sandals and looked at herself in the mirror that took up an entire wall of her bedroom.

I looked down at myself. "Uh . . . this." Flowered, knee-length miniskirt, white T-shirt, white sandals. Shana had *liked* the outfit when she picked it out for me at the mall last weekend.

"Oh. Well, you look nice." She studied me from head to toe, and I didn't need to be a rocket scientist to realize that she wasn't blown away by what she saw.

"But?" I was starting to panic. I hadn't brought anything else to wear, but I would feel totally self-conscious walking into her crowd's party in an ensemble that Shana, queen of fashion, didn't approve.

"What you're wearing would be perfect for school—or an afternoon baseball game. But it's not really right for Jason's party . . . especially if you want to get Charlie's attention."

"Oh." I looked at myself in Shana's mirror. I thought I looked pretty good, but what did I know? Shana was the expert.

"You probably don't know this, Jane, but Charlie has a major thing for leather." Shana's voice was low and conspiratorial, as if she were revealing the identity of Gossip Girl.

"Leather?" I squeaked. I had an image of myself dressed up in a red leather bustier, carrying a whip and a chain.

Shana nodded. She opened the door of her huge walk-in closet and pulled out the smallest skirt I had ever seen—at least, I *thought* it was a skirt. It could have been a halter top. It was black leather, and it looked like something Cher would have worn in the 1980s.

"This baby will drive Charlie wild," Shana declared. "*Trust* me."

I gulped. Could I really walk into a crowded room wearing that . . . garment? I had gained a certain measure of self-confidence, but donning a leather micromini was testing the limit.

Nonetheless, I obediently put on the skirt, along with a tight, bright red tank top that Shana pulled out of the bottom drawer of her dresser. At Shana's urging, I added a pair of black stilettos.

"I don't know, Shana. . . . It's not really me." I pivoted in front of the mirror. This outfit was appropriate for an MTV music video, but I felt downright foolish.

"Charlie will love it," Shana assured me. "He'll go totally wild when he sees this side of you."

I bit my lip. So far, Shana hadn't steered me wrong. Maybe this outfit wasn't Max's ideal, but he wasn't the one I was trying to impress. A prom date was what I was after—which meant Charlie. And if I was going to do this flirting thing, I might as well do it right.

"I'll wear it," I announced. "Thanks, Shana."

She grinned. "My pleasure—believe me."

I walked back and forth across the carpet, trying to get the hang of those superhigh heels. Now I knew how those Olympic gymnasts felt when they were performing on the balance beam in front of a stadium full of people.

Shana sifted through her jewelry box, looking for the perfect accessories to go with her new outfit. "So, Jane, what's your plan tonight?"

I teetered, then caught myself on one of the bedposts. "Plan?"

"With Charlie," she said, inserting a small diamond stud into her ear. "How are you going to get him to fall head over heels for you?"

"I, uh, don't know. . . ." Up until now, I had intended to be myself, plus a little mindless chitchat, and hope for the best.

"Can I give you a little friendly advice, Jane?" Shana asked, her voice suddenly serious.

"Of course." I wasn't about to turn down pearls of wisdom from the girl who had managed to snare the heart of the guy of my dreams. Clearly she knew something—lots of things—that I didn't.

"You were too nice to Charlie last Saturday night," Shana informed me. "You know . . . too eager to please."

"I was?" I had thought the opposite was true. As soon as I had abandoned conversation that had centered around *my* interests and focused instead on those subjects that Charlie liked, he seemed to perk up.

"Yep." Shana took her blush brush and added another layer of color to my cheeks. "See, Jane, Charlie loves nothing more than to be insulted by a girl. You've got to bait him."

Huh. This was a form of flirting that was entirely new to me. Then again, Charlie *had* seemed to enjoy his vaguely insulting banter with our big-busted waitress. Maybe Shana was making sense.

"Are you sure, Shana?" I asked. "I don't have a lot of experience with insulting popular, gorgeous jocks."

Shana gave me a warm, encouraging smile. "Jane, you're the smartest girl in school. I *know* you can do this."

I nodded. *What do I have to lose?* I asked myself. It wasn't as if I'd had a lot of luck with Charlie going about things *my* way. And Shana knew Charlie a hundred times better than I did. If she said this was the way to go, well, then, this *was* the way to go.

I didn't have a lot of confidence in my ability to trade funny insults with a hot guy, but I might as well go for it. Even if that meant acting totally outside the normal realm of my personality.

I'll do my best, I resolved. At the very least, I would try to make Shana—and Max—proud. And maybe, just maybe, I would end the night with an invitation to the prom. Like Nicole had said, worse things had happened . . . right?

Seventeen

Max

ON FRIDAY NIGHT I circled what Jason had jokingly referred to as the hors d'oeuvre table. It consisted of a folding-card table laden with unopened bags of potato chips, jars of salsa, and tins of room-temperature nacho cheese.

I opened a bag of Ruffles and stuffed a couple into my mouth. But as I was chewing, I realized that I had absolutely no appetite. The potato chips made my stomach churn. *What's wrong with me?* I wondered.

Usually I was hungry twenty-four hours a day. But all week I had been feeling sort of queasy. And a couple of nights when I had been hanging out with Shana, I had gotten splitting headaches. It was almost as if my body was trying to tell me something . . . but I didn't know what.

"Yo, Max, where's the squeeze?" Jim Grange

called from the other side of the living room. "Did she dump you or what?"

I rolled my eyes. The guys I hung out with had their good points, but tact wasn't among them. "Shana's meeting me here," I informed Jim. "And she's bringing Jane Smith with her."

Jim nodded. "Cute chick. Nice legs." He paused. "A little too brainy, though. She probably spends most nights reading Plato or learning a foreign language."

I didn't respond. Why bother? I knew how cool Jane was. And that was all that mattered. Besides, I had a feeling that after tonight, a lot more people were going to realize how amazing Jane really was.

I left Jason standing next to the chips table and headed for the kitchen. I needed ginger ale. Or maybe some seltzer water. Anything to calm my stomach.

"Hey, Ziff, you ready to get wild?" Charlie asked as I entered the kitchen. He was mixing a batch of infamous party punch.

"Uh . . . yeah. Sure." I grabbed a 7UP from the fridge and walked out.

The sight of Charlie had made me feel worse than ever. Why? We were friends. Good friends. But I found myself, inexplicably, hating his guts.

Suddenly I wished I hadn't encouraged Shana when she suggested that she help Jane get ready for tonight. Shana had said she wanted Jane to get her "special treatment." At the time the extra "tutor" session had seemed like an awesome idea.

I remembered Shana's promise. *Max, you have*

my word that tonight there's no way Charlie will fail to notice Jane. I'll make sure of that.

I had told Shana that I was hoping tonight would be *the* night for Jane and Charlie. But my gut was telling me something different. The truth was that I dreaded the idea of Charlie and Jane hooking up tonight. I hated to think of them making out in some dark room of Jason's house.

I took a sip of the 7UP and tried to push the image of Charlie holding Jane close out of my mind. But it was quickly replaced by another. Prom night. What if Charlie really *did* ask Jane to the prom?

I knew for a fact that he still hadn't decided who he was going to invite. Charlie had told me at practice just the other day that he was tired of all the girls we hung out with. He had said he wanted some "fresh blood."

Ugh. I pictured Jane in some slinky, shiny, strapless dress. She was slow dancing with Charlie, and he was pulling her closer and closer as they swayed to some cheesy eighties tune. Jane gazed up at her dream guy, batting her eyelashes and giggling. *Yuck!*

I paced up and down the Frangos' front hallway, holding the cold can of soda to my damp forehead. What really got to me was Jane's part in all of this. How was it possible that she had fallen for a guy like Charlie? I was disappointed in her. Profoundly disappointed that her taste would be so, well, predictable.

Didn't she realize that Charlie was just like all of the other so-so guys at Union High? I expected more from Jane. Worst of all, I felt like I didn't know her as well as I thought I did. Was she really the person I thought she was?

Yes, I had set out to change Jane. But in truth, I felt like *she* had changed *me*. Jane had made me realize how superficial my whole world was. I wasn't thrilled to see, at this point, that Jane's transformation had been a success.

I had done exactly what Jane asked—turned her, at least on the surface, into the kind of girl that I would go for. A girl just like Shana. *And that's the problem,* I thought.

Jane had made me realize, unintentionally, that Shana cared more about my letterman's jacket than she did about *me*. As for myself . . . Did I really care about *her*? Or did I just like her because she was gorgeous and popular and made the other guys jealous of me for having her as my girlfriend?

Yes, I liked Shana. But my emotions toward her were totally different from my feelings toward Jane. With Jane, I could be myself. With Jane, I laughed, debated, *talked*. I was always thrilled to see Jane come into a room, and I was always sorry to see her leave.

Oh, man . . . My stomach dropped into my feet as I realized what I must have known in my heart of hearts for a while now. *I'm in love with Jane!* At some point, between teaching her how to act casually around guys and arguing with her over opera, I had fallen head over heels in love with Jane Smith.

As soon as I realized the truth, my heart sank.

Jane had made it totally clear that she wanted Charlie—the guy she was planning to win over this very night, at this very party, in this very living room.

It's hopeless, I thought. *Jane will never be mine . . . especially after tonight.*

Miles Evans and John Gold appeared in the hallway. "Hey, Max!" Miles called. "Want to check out Jason's new Xbox game before all the girls get here?"

"Where is it?" I asked. I'm not really the videogame type—but I was searching for anything to take my mind off Jane and Charlie.

"Upstairs," John informed me. "In Jason's room."

"Count me in." I headed up the front stairs two at a time.

Anything was better than watching Jane enter the party and start making her moves on Charlie. If I had to watch them flirting with each other, I might literally lose my mind. My head would explode, and there would be brain matter all over the Frangos' white plush wall-to-wall carpet. That would be bad. Very, very bad.

With any luck at all, I could stay upstairs all night, avoiding Jane, avoiding Charlie, and avoiding Shana. Hey, maybe I could even avoid the pathetic mess my *life* had become. . . .

Eighteen

Jane

BY THE TIME Shana and I pulled up in front of Jason Frango's house in her white Cabrio convertible, the street was lined with cars. I saw Max's dad's car parked in the driveway and breathed a sigh of relief. Seeing Max would be painful, but at least I knew that I would have someone to talk to if I turned out to be a party flop.

"Good. We're fashionably late." Shana jerked on the parking brake. "I *always* make an entrance. And tonight—so will you."

"Can't wait." I got out of the car, mentally preparing myself to walk into a house full of cool kids wearing a skirt so short it might as well have been a belt. This wasn't going to be easy.

I tailed Shana up the front walk with a moderate degree of success (one trip, one twisted ankle).

Shana didn't bother to ring the doorbell. With a measure of confidence I could only dream of, she threw open the front door and strode in. I followed, wishing in a major way that I at least had a sweater to drape over my bare shoulders.

"Hi, Shana!" Madison sang out as soon as we entered.

Shana sent her friend a smile, then turned to me. "Good luck, Jane. I'll be watching from the sidelines."

Uh-oh. We weren't ten seconds into the party, and already I had been abandoned. At least for now. *Be strong,* I ordered myself. I was armed with all of my new knowledge. There was no reason I couldn't take this party by storm . . . or at least blend into the crowd.

I edged around the perimeter of the living room, scanning for Max. Unfortunately he was nowhere in sight. *Maybe that's for the best,* I decided. As long as Max was around, I was going to have a tough time staying focused on my target—Charlie.

By the time I reached the far end of the living room, I realized that I wasn't quite as inconspicuous as I had thought I was. Several people were not only *glancing* at me—they were *staring.*

I backed up against the wall, wanting to hide. Why had I let Shana talk me into wearing this outfit? It was . . . outrageous. I had no business baring this much of my skin to a viewing public. It was practically indecent!

"Hey, Jane!" Jason called from the kitchen. "There's punch in here if you want some."

"Uh . . . thanks." Huh. Maybe I was imagining

the stares. Jason hadn't looked at me as if I were a stripper—he had merely been friendly.

They're probably just not used to my new look, I decided. The fact that everyone was doing a double take when they saw me didn't mean I looked *bad.* It meant just the opposite. Shana herself had assured me that I looked amazing. And she was the most fashion-conscious—and fashion-critical— person I had ever met.

And this is what Charlie likes, I reminded myself. *That's what matters.* I sighed. *For tonight anyway.*

Despite the fact that I kept telling myself I was here to put the moves on Charlie, I hadn't stopped searching the crowded room for Max's face. Every time my eyes fell on a guy with dark, curly hair, my heart skipped a beat. But so far, nothing. Didn't he even care enough to say hello?

Man. This whole night was shaping up to be a disaster. Max didn't like me. And I was too shy to go up to Charlie and start a conversation. Besides, if this was the outfit I had to wear to get Charlie's attention at a party, what would he expect me to wear to the prom as his date? I had a flash of myself in a short, metallic, mesh dress. Yikes! Not a pretty picture.

I'll just tell Shana that if this *is what Charlie likes, then, well, this isn't who I am.* Why go through the motions of attracting a guy under false pretenses? Was it even fair? Besides, if I bowed out of this whole charade, then I could go home—and be off the hook. I could get into bed and read a book, or do a crossword puzzle, or catch up on the piles of homework that I had been neglecting.

Suddenly Shana loomed at my side. And she didn't look happy. "Jane, why are you standing over here in the corner?" she demanded. "You're supposed to be mingling—with Charlie."

"Shana, I . . ." My voice trailed off as Nicole's and Christy's words echoed in my brain.

You've got nothing to lose. Hey, maybe you'll fulfill your lifelong dream and get to go to the prom. You've got nothing to lose. Nicole and Christy were right. I was here—I might as well go for it. Worst-case scenario, Charlie ignored me. Then I could slip quietly out of the party, knowing that I had done my best.

"I've just been trying to figure out what to say," I told Shana. "But I'll go over there. Right now."

Steeling myself, I threw back my shoulders, stuck out my breasts, and sauntered (or staggered) toward Charlie. He was standing with a group of football players, and they were all laughing hysterically as one of them crushed an empty can of root beer against his forehead. *Not an easy group to infiltrate,* I thought warily.

I stopped right next to Charlie. "Hi!" I exclaimed, heralding my presence in the only way I knew how.

Charlie turned. "Hey, Jane." He raised his eyebrows. "You're looking . . . good."

"Thanks." I wanted to say something else, but I was at a loss. So I just stood there with a stupid smile on my face.

Charlie turned back to his friends. Oops. I had

let my first opportunity pass right by. I needed to make a splash, and I needed to do it fast. Otherwise I was going to lose my nerve, not to mention my interest, altogether. I tuned back into the conversation and realized that Charlie was in the middle of telling a story.

Shana's advice ran through my brain like a ticker tape. She had told me to be aggressive. She had said Charlie liked to be baited and taunted by a girl. If I wanted to get his attention, I really had to be *out* there.

". . . So I told the guy to *bite me,* and then I walked off!" Charlie finished.

As the rest of the guys laughed, I planted myself directly in front of Charlie's line of vision. *Ready, set, go.*

"Is being a dumb jock as painful as it looks?" I asked sweetly, batting my eyelashes à la Olga the Waitress.

Charlie's mouth dropped open. "Gee, Jane, I've never really thought about it," he answered. "Let me get back to you on that one."

"Sure thing," I said. "I'll be waiting with bated breath for your insightful, compelling answer."

"Okay . . ." Charlie gave me a strange look, then turned back to his friends again.

This little performance wasn't going all that well. If anything, Charlie seemed annoyed. I glanced over at Shana, who was standing several feet away with Rose and Madison. She flashed me a thumbs-up and an encouraging smile.

For a few moments I was silent, smiling and nodding along with the general flow of conversation.

When there was a lull, I decided to jump in again.

"Charlie, did you know that the number of muscles a guy has are in indirect proportion to the size of his brain . . . among other things?"

Charlie stared at me with a confused look on his face. Clearly I had stumped him. "Do you need me to explain what 'indirect proportion' means?" I asked, lowering my voice in what I hoped was a sultry, seductive manner.

Charlie ran a hand through his hair, gazing at me through hooded eyes. His expression was blank. "Jane—"

"Careful," I admonished. "You might mess up the pound of gel in your hair." I was really on a roll now. The insults were sliding off my tongue with no effort at all.

I felt like I was having an out-of-body experience. This wasn't Jane Smith talking. It was some foreign being who had no sense of tact, decency, or restraint. In a weird way, I felt liberated. But I also felt . . . fake.

"And another thing—" I stopped midsentence, crashing back to reality.

The music had stopped. And everyone in the room was looking at me. Not just looking. *Staring.* And not in a nice way. They seemed . . . horrified.

Charlie glared at me. "Hey, Shana!" he called. "Can you do something about your friend? She's totally pathetic." He laughed. "And she's too mean—even for me!"

*   *   *

She's pathetic. All of the blood drained from my face as Charlie's words registered. I felt like I was going to faint, or throw up, or both. *She's pathetic.* With every passing second my sense of horror increased exponentially.

This isn't happening, I told myself. *I'm having a nightmare.* Or maybe it was all a big misunderstanding. Maybe everybody staring at me with disgusted expressions on their faces was some kind of cool-kids' party ritual that Max and Shana had forgotten to warn me about.

I looked over at Shana, willing her to come to the rescue. But she didn't give me another thumbs-up. And she didn't rush to my side to explain to everyone that they had the wrong impression—that I was actually a totally cool person who everyone should make an effort to get to know.

Shana is laughing, I realized. She was laughing with her friends, and they were all pointing at me as if I were some piece of garbage on one of their pristine bedroom floors.

I was frozen to my spot, unable to move, to speak, to breathe. This was the worst moment of my life. And I was utterly powerless to do anything about it.

After what seemed like three lifetimes, but was probably only a few seconds, Shana broke away from Rose and Madison. She strolled to my side and led me away from Charlie and his friends.

"Jane, did you *really* think I was going to help make you popular?" she asked. Her beautiful smile had turned into an ugly sneer, and her eyes were shooting poisonous darts in my direction.

"I . . ." No words would come.

Shana laughed again. "I only agreed to help Max with his little 'lab experiment' to keep him happy," Shana informed me. "But as long as I had to do my good-girlfriend duties, I figured . . . hey, why not have some fun of my own?"

"You're . . ." I wanted to tell her that she was the lowest form of life. I wanted to tell Shana that she and her friends didn't deserve to be on the same planet as me, much less use me as a tool for their perverse kicks. But I couldn't speak.

"You see, Jane, my friend Rose has had her sights set on Charlie for a while now. There was no way I could help *you* snag the guy that my *real* friend wanted for herself." She smiled. "You understand that, don't you?"

Out of the corner of my eye I saw Max heading down the front stairs with a couple of guys trailing behind him. *Max.* Had he been in on this sick joke? Had he and Shana been laughing behind my back all along?

"Hey, Jane, no hard feelings," Shana chirped. "I didn't mean any harm."

Get out! From the deep recesses of my soul an inner voice spoke to me. *Get out now!*

I jerked away from Shana, pushing my way through the living room full of people. I kept my eyes fixed on the front door, determined not to cry right here, right now, where all of these horrible people could watch.

"Jane!" Max called out. "Janie, wait!"

I ignored Max. Like a girl possessed, I stumbled to the door. Still holding back my tears, I yanked open the door and sprinted into the dark night. I raced down the street, struggling to put as much distance between myself and that party as I could, as fast as I could.

"Jane . . ." Max's voice was fainter now. I was halfway down the block, and I kept on running.

I wouldn't stop until I was home, upstairs and safe in my own room. This had been the worst night of my life. In the space of half an hour my entire world had collapsed into a heap of ashes.

I had been humiliated, degraded, metaphorically spat upon. And it was all my fault. I had trusted the enemy. And now I was paying for it.

Nineteen

Jane

BY THE TIME I reached the front door of my house, I was sweating and my feet were covered with blisters from Shana's shoes. The walk had numbed me, blocking out the image of Shana's laughing face, of Charlie's angry glare.

But as soon as I entered our front hallway, I was flooded with emotion. At last the tears flowed freely down my face. I tore off the offending high heels and threw them into the corner of our front-hall closet. After I slammed the closet door shut, I was aware of a deafening, overpowering silence.

At least I have one thing to be grateful for, I thought. Mom and Dad had gone to a dinner party, and they wouldn't be home for hours. By that time I would be buried under my blankets, totally hidden from their well-meaning concern.

I used the last of my strength to sprint upstairs and into my room. I closed the door and leaned against it. I had thought I would feel better once I was back in my own room, with my own things. But I didn't. If anything, I felt worse.

Now that I wasn't running away from the scene of the crime, every grisly detail was playing over and over in my head. How could I have been such a fool? I had even *defended* Shana to Nicole and Christy, telling them that once I had gotten to know her, I had liked her. Stupid!

I had to get out of this ridiculous outfit. Now! I peeled off the leather miniskirt and stripped off the tank top. Then I rolled them both in a ball and stuffed them in the bottom of my trash can. If I'd had more guts, I would have burned them.

Wearing just my bra and underwear, I lurched into the bathroom. I turned the hot water on full blast, then scrubbed off every bit of the garish makeup Shana had painted my face with. Stupid! I had *known* I didn't look attractive with all that blue stuff around my eyes—unless one thought looking like a Las Vegas showgirl was a good thing. But I had let her dress me up like some kind of anti–Barbie doll anyway.

Why? I asked myself, staring into the mirror, as I had so many times in the past week. *Because you didn't think you were good enough,* I told my reflection. I had been willing to put all of *me* away in some imaginary closet just so that a group of shallow, self-involved people would think I was *somebody*.

I had brought tonight on myself. I had trusted Shana. I had trusted . . . Max. Fresh tears streamed down my face as I thought about Max. Had he known Shana was planning to humiliate me?

I pulled my hair back into a loose ponytail, thinking of Max. I couldn't believe that was true. I *knew* Max. He was my friend. Or was he? My entire world had turned upside down, and I felt like the truth was a lie and lies were the truth. Everything in my life had lost its meaning.

I walked to my dresser, taking deep breaths, willing myself to stop crying. Those people didn't deserve my tears. They weren't worth it. I opened the bottom drawer of my bureau and pulled out my favorite pair of faded blue jeans. I hadn't worn them since I had begun my transformation, and I experienced a wave of comfort as I slid the soft material over my body.

"That's more like it," I announced to an imaginary audience. "And to complete the ensemble, I will be donning a ratty old T-shirt." I grabbed my favorite one, a relic from my grandparents' pilgrimage to the Grand Canyon, and pulled it over my head.

I was me again. Plain Jane Smith, doer of homework, acer of tests, baby-sitter extraordinaire. From this moment forward I vowed to be one hundred percent myself, one hundred percent of the time. I had learned that anything else led to utter disaster.

I flopped onto my bed and put a pillow over my head. *You still have to go to school on Monday*, I reminded myself. Ugh. I could already hear the giggles,

169

the snide comments. There would probably be a sign posted in the cafeteria: Plain Jane Smith—Loser of the Year.

All I had wanted was a date to my senior prom. Was that evil? Did wanting to be a part of things make me a pathetic, terrible person? Clearly the answer was yes. I had set out to upset the scales of popularity, breaking all rules of high-school social strata.

And my reward for making this one mistake was that I had been humiliated by the very crowd that I had been trying to be a part of. Even worse, I had been betrayed. Not to mention that I was heartbroken. I had found my own version of hell, and it consisted of Shana Stevens, Charlie Simpson, and Jason Frango's living room. And Max.

Max. Max. Max. We would never go bowling together again. There would be no more discussions about opera or movies or books. I would never make Max laugh again. Or see his eyes twinkling at me with that special light that made me feel excited, and faint, and warm all at the same time.

But Max wasn't the person I'd thought he was. There was no way a guy who loved Shana could be the right guy for me. It was obvious that his bright exterior hid something. Otherwise he never would have let this happen to me.

But none of that matters, I told myself. Who Max was or wasn't didn't concern me anymore. I never wanted to speak to him again.

I threw the pillow across my room and heaved

myself off the bed. I needed to listen to some music—at full volume—to drown out the images, the thoughts, the words that were torturing me. I headed toward my stereo, wiping away what I hoped were the last of my tears.

Staring at my CD collection, which included the new ones Max had suggested, nothing seemed right. Joss Stone—too soulful. Jewel—too romantic. Rob Thomas—too *male*. And opera was out. I wished I had some heavy metal that I could blast for all of the neighbors to hear.

Ping. "What . . . ?" I stood up straight and turned toward my bedroom windows.

I had heard something. Or had I? It was probably my imagination. I was overwrought, and now I was hallucinating the presence of some nefarious prowler. *Reality, Jane. We're dealing with reality* only *now.*

Ping. There it was again. The same noise. I walked slowly toward my window, unsure about what to expect. *Ping. Ping.* I had locked the front door. The police were only a 911 call away. I was safe—more or less.

My window was open. A small pebble missed the glass and fell onto the hardwood floor of my bedroom. I leaned out of the window and looked down into our front yard.

And I saw Max. He was holding a fistful of tiny rocks, and he was about to let another one fly.

"Jane!" he called. "Janie, we have to talk!"

Talk about nerve! Who did he think he was? I

couldn't believe he dared to speak to me, much less show up at my house. "Go away, Max!" I shouted. "I never want to talk to you again!"

He didn't move. "Jane, you *have* to let me come inside. Please."

I snorted. "You and your friends didn't have enough fun the first time around?" I asked. "You want to come inside and enjoy part two of the *Plain Jane Show*?"

"It's not like that, Janie. Please, let me explain."

"I've been *humiliated, Max.*" I fought back a new batch of tears as I stared at his beautiful face. "I don't want to face you—or anyone else—ever again."

Max was shaking his head in a way that had become painfully familiar. "I'm begging you," he called. "Just give me five minutes, and then I swear I'll leave you alone."

I knew I should shut the window, turn up the music, and climb into bed. But I couldn't say no to Max. *Isn't that how I've gotten myself in all this trouble?* I thought ruefully. *I'll give him three minutes, and then it's good-bye forever,* I resolved.

"I'll come down," I told him. "But only because you begged."

The trip from my bedroom to the front door seemed to take forever. As much as I told myself that I hated Max, there was still a part of me that couldn't wait to see him face-to-face. *I really am pathetic,* I thought.

★   ★   ★

"So . . . talk, Max." We were standing in the foyer. I wasn't about to invite him to sit down and make himself comfortable

"Jane, I'm so sorry," Max began, wringing his hands. "I had no idea what Shana was up to. I swear."

I shrugged. "I'll get over it. You and your friends had your laughs, but I'm a stronger, better person than they'll ever be."

"Yes. You are." Max took a step forward. For a second I thought he was going to reach out and touch my arm . . . but he seemed to think better of it.

"Is that it?" I asked. "Are we done now?"

"No, we're not *done*," Max responded. "I want to tell you something. And when I'm done, if you tell me you hate me, I promise I'll never bother you again."

I sighed. I wanted to be able to turn off my feelings for Max like a water faucet. But it was impossible. Even now I knew that I was in love with him. And I couldn't shut him down . . . at least, not until he had said what he came to say.

"I'm listening," I said, this time with a little less frost in my tone. "Go on."

"I had no idea what was going on when I came downstairs at Jason's tonight. I knew you were upset, but I didn't really understand what had happened." He took a deep breath, seeming to search for the right words. "After you left, I found out what Shana had done."

"And?" I believed Max that he hadn't known what Shana was planning. Deep down, I didn't think he was capable of that kind of cruelty. But that didn't change the fact that Shana was the girl he loved and admired. In some way that made him implicitly guilty by association.

"I dumped Shana on the spot—in front of everybody," Max announced. "I had been planning to break up with her anyway . . . just not in front of a roomful of people."

Huh. That I hadn't expected.

Max was quiet for a moment. "Jane, you asked me to metamorphose you into the kind of girl a guy like me would go for, but that girl was there all along. *I'm* the one who needed to change, to become the kind of guy that a girl like *you* would go for."

"I . . . I . . ." No words would come. Was he really saying these things, or was I having one of my usual fantasies?

He smiled. "I guess we've both learned a lesson through all of this, huh? I'm in love with you, Jane," Max said simply, taking a couple of steps toward me. "And there's a tiny little part of me that's still holding out a flicker of hope that maybe, just maybe, you're in love with me too."

I felt a hot tear slide down my cheek. But for the first time I understood what people meant when they said they had cried tears of joy. I had never been so incredibly happy in my life.

And this wasn't a joke. And it wasn't part of our

deal, or our bargain, or whatever Max and I had called our strange relationship. This was *us,* two people who understood each other better than anyone else in the world. I knew that with every iota of my being.

"I love you too, Max," I whispered.

The next second he was pulling me into his arms. I smelled the rugged scent of his soap, felt the soft cotton of his shirt against my cheek. This was the best moment of my life. But I was so shocked that all I could do was hold Max tight.

He pulled away, placing his hands on either side of my face. "Jane Smith, will you make me the happiest guy in the world by agreeing to go to the prom with me?"

I couldn't speak. I just nodded, gazing into those hazel eyes. I knew I was grinning like a lunatic, but I didn't care. I knew Max understood. Just like he understood everything else about me.

"I'll take that as a yes," Max murmured. And then he slid his arms to my waist and pulled me against him.

Max's lips captured mine, and it was as if my dream had literally come true. His kiss was warm, and then hot, and then it melted my very bones. We kissed on and on, unable to get enough of each other. I felt his touch to my toes, and I never wanted to let go.

The worst night of my life had just turned into the best night of my life. And all of it had happened while I was *me.* The same plain old Jane Smith—in

175

the same jeans and T-shirt and ponytail—I had been forever. Best of all, I was the girl I *wanted* to be, and I was in love with a guy who wanted that girl too!

"This is what it's all about," Max whispered into my ear when we finally broke apart. "*You're* what it's all about."

"Thank you, Max," I whispered back. "Thank you for helping me realize that I never needed to change at all."

Then his lips found mine again. And we didn't say anything else for a long, long time. . . .

Justin & Nicole

One

Nicole

I WASN'T THE kind of girl who rushed home to read her horoscope in the back of *CosmoGirl* every month. I didn't care whether or not all astrological signs indicated that I would fall in love sometime during the thirty-one days of May. And I never daydreamed about guys on horses sweeping me off my feet or stared at engagement rings in jewelry-store windows.

I, Nicole Gilmore, have never been accused of being a romantic. During my seventeen years on the planet, I have never carved a boy's initials in a tree or doodled his name on my notebook.

But there was something about the floor-length, lavender silk dress that hung in the window of Claire's Boutique that took my breath away. I had been working after school and on weekends at

Claire's for several months now, and during every shift I expected someone to come in and purchase that dress for the upcoming senior prom. So far, the dress was still on the mannequin, and the prom was less than a week away.

Not that the senior prom was relevant in *my* life. I didn't have a date, and I didn't want one. None of the guys at Union High had fallen prey to my particular brand of charm. Consequently I would be staying home on prom night, watching reruns of *Desperate Housewives* and eating cookie dough.

I had told my two best friends, Jane Smith and Christy Redmond, over and over again that I didn't care about the stupid dance. But in those rare moments when I peered deep into my soul, I had to admit, at least to myself, that the prom fantasy held some pretty powerful images.

Even I could appreciate the attraction of a gorgeous date, a beautiful corsage, and a romantic slow dance with the guy of my dreams. But it was just that—a dream. Because there was no gorgeous date. There was no date, period. So why make myself feel bad?

I pushed all thoughts of the prom out of my mind and turned to the inventory list that my boss, Claire, had asked me to compile. *Boring,* I thought, but I tried to concentrate. Anything to keep me from stealing stares at the dress. *My* dress.

The bell over the door of the shop chimed, and I glanced up to see Christy and Jane entering.

"Hey, guys!" I called. "I thought you'd never get

here." I had been looking forward to seeing my friends all afternoon.

"Are you kidding?" Jane asked. "I have been *dying* to try on my new and improved prom dress."

"Me too," Christy agreed. "I want to make sure that Claire cut off enough from the bottom so that I won't be tripping over my own feet the whole night."

I walked over to a rack behind the cash register and pulled off two plastic-covered dresses. "Don't worry. They're perfect," I assured the girls. "Since you two are my best friends, Claire promised she was going to do her absolute best on these dresses—she says her tailoring is like performance art."

Jane took her dress from my outstretched hand. "When Max sees me in this, he's going to forget that any other girl exists."

I politely resisted the urge to roll my eyes. Ever since Jane and Max had realized a week ago that they were madly in love, Jane had talked about little else. Who could blame her? Max was a best friend, a gorgeous guy, and a prom date—all rolled into one. Jane deserved to be happy—even if happiness meant that she was now limited to one topic of conversation: Max Ziff.

"I wish I were as excited about the prom as you are, Jane," Christy commented.

I felt a wave of sympathy for Christy. Her mom had been sick for a long time, and the main reason Christy wanted to go to the prom was to fulfill her mother's longtime wish to see Christy in a long taffeta dress with a corsage pinned to her waist.

"I'm in la-la land again, aren't I?" Jane asked, wincing.

Christy and I laughed, nodding in an exaggerated way.

"Okay, okay," Jane said, her blue eyes sparkling. "But you know, Nicole, I still think you should ask Leon Strickler to the prom. The dance isn't going to be the same if you're not there with us."

"No way," I answered quickly. "I'm not going to a dance with a guy who would rather dissect a frog than kiss a girl good night." I paused. "If I can't do the prom right, I don't want to do it at all."

Almost involuntarily my eyes wandered back to the lavender dress. I had meant what I said—I wasn't about to beg my biology-lab partner to accompany me to the prom just so I could show my face in the gaudily decorated gym on a Saturday night. I had way too much pride for such a desperate measure. But there was no doubt that I wished I could wear that dress.

"Nicole, you've been mooning over that dress in the window every single time I've been in here," Christy said. "Why don't you try it on?"

I shook my head. "No way."

Jane raised one eyebrow. "Come on. Isn't there a tiny little part of you that wants to put on a beautiful dress and join the rest of teenage America in this grand rite of passage?"

I snorted. "No offense, but you're both attaching *way* too much importance to the prom. I mean,

4

what's the big deal? People come, they drink punch, they dance badly, and then they go home."

"There's a *bit* more to it than that," Christy insisted.

"Oh, right. I forgot the part about how all the couples get a cheesy picture taken of themselves standing under some trellis covered with fake roses. Then they tack the photo to the bulletin board hanging over their desk for the next twenty-five years." I was really getting into my speech. "Face it—the whole ritual is idiotic. Especially considering the paltry selection of guys at Union High!"

Jane had been watching me with a patient expression on her face during my entire diatribe. Now she smiled in a Mona Lisa kind of way. "If you *really* don't care about going to the prom, then why is trying on one little dress such a production?" she asked. "Why don't you just humor Christy and me?"

I sighed. Once those girls had an idea in their heads, there was no way to convince them to let it go. I glanced at my watch. My shift was officially over in one minute . . . and I really *did* want to try on the dress. Just for fun. It wasn't as if seeing that beautiful piece of material on my body would do any *harm*.

"Fine! I'll do it." I walked over to the store window and unzipped the dress. Then I slipped it over the mannequin's head.

"I hope she doesn't get arrested for indecent exposure!" Jane commented, pointing at the now naked mannequin.

5

I laughed and covered the mannequin with a beautiful pink dress. "Can you guys keep an eye on the register? Claire should be back any second."

"No problem," Christy answered. Twice during visits to the shop, Christy had been asked by Claire to watch the register while we dashed in the back to fix an irate customer's dress. "Maybe if I make a sale, Claire will give me a discount on my dress."

"Don't count on it!" I called as I stepped into one of the boutique's three dressing rooms.

I pulled the curtain shut, then kicked off my penny loafers and slipped out of my black pants and white button-down blouse. Inexplicably, my heart was beating wildly in my chest as I pulled the prom dress over my head.

Reaching back, I pulled up the long zipper of the dress and clasped the tiny hook at the neck. I took a deep breath and turned to view myself in the three-way mirror.

"Wow!" I exclaimed. I looked, in a word, amazing.

The pale lavender silk contrasted beautifully with my dark, mahogany skin. The sleeveless cut of the dress set off my long, slender arms and pronounced collarbone. I looked like a prom queen in this getup!

Who am I kidding? I asked myself, sighing. I hadn't had a decent date since the middle of my freshman year, and there were zero prospects on the horizon. I needed this dress about as much as I needed an extra arm attached to my body. There was simply no way that I was going to score a date to the senior prom. And that was that.

It's not like some totally gorgeous guy is going to walk up to me out of the blue and ask me to the prom, I reminded myself. As if! All right, all right. I *did* care that I wasn't going to the dance. And because I cared, I had no desire to dwell on the hopeless situation.

I couldn't wait to get this stupid dress off my body. I was ready to transform back into my usual nonromantic self, who didn't care about stuff like corsages and slow dancing.

"Get out here, Nicole!" Christy ordered from outside the dressing room. "We want to see you in that awesome dress!"

"Too late! I've already changed back into my clothes!" I called—an outright lie. Why have Christy and Jane ooh and ah over how great I looked for absolutely no reason?

"We don't believe you," Jane practically shouted. "And if you don't come out, then we're coming in."

"Yeah," Christy agreed. "We didn't badger you into trying on the dress just so you could hide in the dressing room."

Again I sighed. I never should have caved about trying the dress on in the first place. But since I *had,* I knew that those two wouldn't shut up until they had seen me with their own four eyes.

"Okay, okay. You guys win." I opened the curtain and walked out into the boutique.

"Hello!" Christy yelled. "Can you say 'cover girl'?"

7

Jane was beaming, the way people in love are constantly beaming and casting loving glances at anyone in a five-mile radius. "Nicole, you look absolutely amazing. Beautiful!"

Christy and Jane's praise made me feel suddenly shy. "Yeah, well, I guess I clean up okay," I murmured. "I mean, who wouldn't look decent in a dress this pretty?"

"Me, for one," Christy commented. "And a lot of other people too."

I strutted back and forth in front of the mirror, admiring myself. I pivoted, then found myself staring into the biggest pair of chocolate brown eyes I had ever seen. Suddenly I teetered in my high heels.

The guy standing in front of me was one of the hottest male specimens I had ever laid eyes on. He was over six feet tall, with dark, smooth skin, and close-cut hair. The rest of the face and body definitely did justice to that amazing pair of eyes.

"Excuse me . . . ," he murmured tentatively.

My heart pounded. Could this be the mysterious stranger I had been fantasizing about just a moment ago? *Will you allow me the honor of accompanying you to your senior prom?* I mentally finished for him.

"Yes?" I responded, flashing him my most dazzling smile.

"Does, uh, anyone know if this place has a juniors' section?" he finished.

I blinked. And then I saw that my Mr. Wonderful was standing in front of a little girl. Well, not so little. Maybe eleven or twelve. Since he was about my age, she must be his sister.

My face suddenly felt like it was on fire. "Uh, not—not really," I stammered. "Try a store called Girl Kraze. It's on the first floor of the mall."

"Thanks." He turned to the girl and nodded toward the door of the store. Unfortunately she waylaid him at the basket of rhinestone barrettes. Great! There was no doubt I was going to feel stupid for my involuntary daydream until Beautiful Boy exited Claire's Boutique.

"I've got to get out of this thing," I informed Jane and Christy. "Claire's not back yet. And we could have customers anytime."

"Speaking of customers, look who's heading this way," Jane said, her eyebrows raised.

I rolled my eyes as Madison Embry and Rose McNeal flounced into the shop. They were two of the most popular—and meanest—girls at Union High. A couple of weeks ago their best friend, the Queen Mean, Shana Stevens, had conspired with Madison and Rose to humiliate Jane in front of half of the senior class. Luckily Jane had come out of the situation with no visible scars (plus one cute boyfriend).

Since then I had made it my personal mission to let the girls know exactly how I felt about them. They hadn't seemed too thrilled when I announced in the crowded cafeteria one day that a pet rock had a better personality than their entire clique put together.

Now Rose stopped right in front of me. Slowly she studied me from head to toe, then gave me a look somewhere between a sneer and a frown.

"Can we get some *help?*" Rose asked, her voice dripping with snotty attitude. "Some of us actually *have* prom dates—and *need* a dress."

I felt like I had been punched in the stomach. This afternoon wasn't going well. And I had a sense that it was about to get worse.

Two

Nicole

WHITE-HOT ANGER FLOWED through my veins as I stared at Rose and Madison. Maybe I wasn't an airheaded cheerleader, but I wasn't exactly wallflower material either. And the Snob Patrol had no right to speak to me as if I were some scared, dorky freshman. Who did they think they were?

I gave them an acid smile. "For your information, I *am* going to the prom. And I'm wearing *this* dress."

Out of the corner of my eye I saw Christy and Jane glance at each other. But they kept their mouths shut—luckily.

Rose snorted. "Who's your date? Your cousin? Or maybe an older brother?"

Madison snickered, and I bit my lip, trying in

11

vain to ignore the painful knot forming in my stomach. I had opened my enormous mouth, and now I was about to pay for it. I looked wildly around the large shop, searching my brain for the name of a guy—any guy.

And then my gaze landed on *him*. Mr. Made-to-be-Naomi-Campbell's-dream-guy. Actually, I was staring at his back. He and his sister were headed out the door. But even from behind, he was beautiful.

"If you must know, my date is right over there," I said, pointing toward the mystery man. "He stopped by to check out my dress."

Rose's eyebrows shot up into her bangs, and Madison seemed on the verge of drooling.

"Bye!" I shouted across the store. "See you later!"

Why did I just do that? I asked myself. As if I hadn't dug myself into a deep enough hole by announcing this guy was my prom date . . . now I was giving him the chance to unwittingly cause the most humiliating moment of my life.

The guy turned around. He looked confused—understandably. *Please don't expose me,* I silently begged.

"Uh—bye." He gave me a half wave and sauntered out of the store.

I breathed a huge sigh of relief. I wasn't going to be humiliated—at least, not yet. I turned back to Rose and Madison. "Is there anything else?" I asked, my voice dripping sugar.

I was afraid that Madison was going to chase down my so-called prom date and ask if I were telling the truth. Instead she simply shook her head and returned my fake smile.

"There's nothing here I like. So I guess we'll see you two on prom night," she said. "If he's really your date, that is."

I was doomed. "I can't wait."

With a quick sneer in Jane and Christy's direction, Madison and Rose flounced out of Claire's Boutique. As soon as they were gone, I flopped into a chair next to the dressing rooms.

"What have I done?" I groaned, staring dolefully into the sympathetic eyes of Jane and Christy. "Just put a gun to my head and shoot me now."

"It's not that bad," Christy said encouragingly. "They probably won't even remember this conversation by prom night."

"Right!" As if Rose and Madison *wouldn't* be counting the minutes until they had the chance to rub my face in my lie.

"We'll think of something," Jane promised. "Don't worry, Nicole."

I closed my eyes and sighed. If only I hadn't tried on this stupid prom dress. In the space of ten minutes my once peaceful life had been turned upside down.

13

Nicole's Journal

Where do I begin? I mean, I like guys. I don't think they're evil or worthless or generally inferior to the female half of the species. Hey, my dad is a man, and he's a great guy. Most of the time anyway. But at least when they're young, guys have a tendency to act like complete fools. And here's how . . .

First of all, there are *way* too many guys in this world who think that being good at sports means they rule the planet. They believe that their letterman's jacket is, like, an aphrodisiac. I'm sorry, but watching a bunch of boys run around on a football field, hitting one another as hard as they can, doesn't get me in the mood for a romantic walk in the park.

Then there's the other category of teenage male. These are the ones (the science dudes, the valedictorians, the school-newspaper reporters) who nurture their brains plenty—but don't worry about developing an actual personality. They spend all of middle school playing elaborate cyber–video games in their bedrooms, then think they're going to charm girls by expounding on Doom or demonstrating their ability to solve a difficult physics problem.

Here's what I want to know. Where are the guys who like to *talk?* I'm looking to have actual conversations, about actual things. And I'd like to be able to joke around with my dates, the way I do with my friends.

I want a guy to look into my eyes and see *me* for *me*. I want him to care more about that than my chest and cheekbones. And I want to care about him for who *he* is.

Is that too much to ask?

Three

Justin

"CAN I GET shoes to go with my new dress, Justin?" my sister, Star, asked for the tenth time since we had arrived at the mall.

I was staring at a huge, plastic-encased map of the shopping center, searching for the location of Girl Kraze. "We'll see," I said, also for the tenth time. "It depends."

"And I need something for my hair," Star added. "Like a headband. Or some barrettes."

I nodded absently. "This way." I took off in the direction of the store, praying that this would be our last stop.

I had never realized how much effort it took to get a sixth-grade girl ready to go to her first dance. We had been all over two malls, and Star still hadn't found the "right" dress. I was beginning to think that she'd have to wear jeans and a T-shirt to the big event. It was either that or find an outfit that had Star Banks written across the front of it.

But Star's dire need for the perfect outfit wasn't the only thing on my mind. I couldn't stop thinking about that group of girls I had seen in Claire's Boutique. There had been something about them . . . well, *one* of them. But what?

"I think that girl in the fancy dress shop liked you!" Star exclaimed, breaking into my thoughts. "She was, like, totally staring at you."

I rolled my eyes. The moment Star had hit sixth grade, she had begun to talk nonstop about boys—and girls and boys. My little sister saw her eleven-year-old version of romance behind every corner—or dress rack, in this case.

If only Mom were still here, I thought, as I did a thousand times a day. She would have known how to talk to Star about this kind of stuff. I was clueless.

"Nobody was staring at me," I informed my sister. "And you should be more worried about the spelling test you have tomorrow than who *is* or *isn't* looking at who."

"Well, exuuussssee me!" Star retorted. She flipped her long hair over one shoulder and glared at me.

I laughed. Star had a habit of getting on my nerves, but the girl was funny. And I *had* been thinking about those girls from Claire's Boutique. *There was something about one of them . . . ,* I thought yet again.

18

Not that I was interested in anything remotely romantic with *anyone*. I had learned that lesson the hard way. *Don't go there,* I told myself. What had happened last year was old news. The important thing was that I knew what I wanted—and what I didn't want.

I had sworn off the opposite sex until I was at least thirty. Right now I had my hands full taking care of my little sister. And that was all the headache I needed!

"Spell *extracurricular,*" Dad told Star, glancing at the list of words for her spelling test.

"*E-x-t-r-a . . .*" Star's voice trailed off, and she bit her lip in concentration.

Dad, Star, and I had finished dinner half an hour ago. Now we were all lounging in various areas of the living room, and Dad was quizzing Star for her test tomorrow. This was our tiny family's nightly ritual—our way of keeping things at least seminormal now that we didn't have Mom around to make our house a home.

I turned back to *The Grapes of Wrath,* by John Steinbeck, the novel I was reading for my senior English class. I was totally into the book, but my eyelids kept drooping sleepily. All of my years playing various sports hadn't prepared me for the amount of energy it took to spend an afternoon shopping with a preadolescent girl.

"*. . . c-u-r-r-i-c-u-l-a-r!*" Star finished triumphantly.

My dad beamed at her. "Excellent, sweetheart," he exclaimed. "Now all you have to do is spell *archeology,* and you're done for the night."

I put down my book and waited expectantly for Star to spell the word correctly. Before last year I hadn't been the type of older brother who worried about his little sister's quizzes or knew the names of all of her friends. But now . . . well, everything had changed.

" . . . *o-g-y.*" Star's voice interrupted my thoughts. *"Archeology!"*

"Exactly right," Dad announced. "You get an A."

Star grinned. "Can I go call Alison now?"

"Yes, you may." Dad put down the spelling list as Star sprinted from the living room. He turned to me. "Who is Alison?"

"Star's new best friend of the week," I explained. "They bonded during a field trip to the museum."

Dad sighed in this sort of wistful way that always made me feel sad. "Star really is growing up fast, isn't she?"

I nodded. "Sometimes when I overhear her talking to her friends, she sounds like she's older than *I* am."

Dad took off his reading glasses and slipped them into his shirt pocket. "I guess there's nothing we can do about it—you can't stop nature."

"Nope." I wished there was something I could say to my father to make him feel better. But I knew that it was at times like this that he missed Mom most. We all did.

"She would have loved to take Star shopping for

that dress," Dad commented, as if reading my mind. I knew that the "she" he was referring to was my mother. "And she would have loved to see you play in the basketball championship last winter."

"We're doing okay, Dad," I said softly.

And we were. All things considered. It had been over a year since Mom lost her battle with breast cancer. At first Star, Dad, and I had walked around the house like zombies. We had eaten nothing but takeout Chinese food and frozen pizza. The dishes had piled up in the sink, and nobody had bothered to clean the shower. It was dismal.

Then Grandma Banks had come to visit. She reminded us that we couldn't stop living—that was the last thing that Mom would have wanted. And so . . . we had gotten our acts together. For the most part.

My father nodded, and I saw his eyes drift toward a family picture that stood at the center of the mantelpiece. "Before Elaine died, I promised her that I would try to be a mother as well as a father to both of you." He sighed. "But seeing Star changing at the speed of light . . . I don't know if I'm doing such a great job in the mom department."

"Don't worry, Dad," I assured him. "Star is happy. And she's a good kid. She'll be fine."

"And how are you?" he asked me, giving me a penetrating stare. "Are you hanging in there?"

"Sure." I gulped. Talking about my emotions wasn't exactly my forte. I preferred to be the strong-and-silent type.

Dad's gaze was so intense that I felt like he was looking straight into my brain. It was a talent that made him the excellent father he was. It was also unnerving.

"You should go out more, Justin. Have some fun." He grinned at me. "I'm sure you would enjoy taking a nice girl to a movie or out to dinner."

"Dad, I'm *fine*," I repeated. "You're doing a great job of taking care of us. Really."

He reached over and gave me a paternal pat on the shoulder. "How about some ice cream?" he offered.

"Sounds good." I turned back to the photograph as Dad retreated into the kitchen.

Looking at the picture now, I still found it difficult to believe that Mom was actually gone. I would never forget the last months of her life. It was as if we were all living through a nightmare. Poor Star. She had been so young, so confused.

I closed my eyes, and images of that terrible time flooded through my memory. I remembered sitting in the waiting room of the hospital with Star, waiting for Dad to come out of Mom's room to tell us how she was doing.

I had known then that Mom's death would be the hardest of all on Star. Her face had been so sad. . . . It had broken my heart into a million pieces.

The waiting room. My eyes popped open, and I snapped my fingers. Now I remembered. I had seen the girl from Claire's Boutique in the waiting room of the hospital. I'd overheard the doctor talking about *her* mother's condition. And it wasn't good.

22

Her mom had cancer too, I recalled. The disease hadn't progressed as far as my own mom's, but the doctors were pursuing a heavy-duty course of chemotherapy. I could still see the girl's tearstained face as she absorbed the news.

I wondered how she was doing—and how her mother was. I hope she didn't have to go through what I experienced last year. *But I'll probably never know,* I thought. Most likely I would never see the girl again.

Justin's Journal

I don't *have* any trouble with girls. None. *Nada.* I know better than to *let* girls cause me any trouble. Not that I have anything against them. They're enjoyable to look at, they can be great lab partners, and I've been known to enjoy conversation with a few of them over a disgusting lunch in the Jefferson cafeteria.

But I realized a long time ago that it's dangerous to allow a girl to matter too much to me—unless she's related by blood. I mean, who needs the hassle? I don't want to walk around with my head in the clouds and my heart in the palm of some female's tight grip. I prefer to keep my senses about me at all times.

I guess I need to amend my first statement. I don't have any trouble with girls *now.* I have had trouble in the past—major, major trouble. I fell in love one time, and it's not something I'm looking to repeat. It was one of the worst experiences of my life.

So what was the trouble with *that?* Basically, I trusted a girl with all of my heart. And she took that trust and threw it in my face. Oh, sure, she said she was sorry and gave me the standard it's-not-you-it's-me line. But her eyes were so cold—icy, really—that her mere glance now sends chills down my spine.

I learned the hard way that girls are, in fact, nothing *but* trouble. Unless you keep them at a nice, safe distance where they have no power to inflict any pain whatsoever. Which is why I've decided to devote myself to anything and everything *not* related to females.

Having said all that, I have to admit that I miss hugging and kissing and holding hands. I miss that feeling that I used to get right before my girlfriend answered her front door. Maybe . . . well, maybe that *is* the trouble with girls. I miss them.

Four

Nicole

"**D**O YOU HAVE this in orange?" The mother of a girl in one of the dressing rooms held out a long, black skirt for my inspection.

"Uh . . . no." *Thank goodness,* I added silently. I assumed the daughter wanted to look like a prom queen—not a pumpkin.

I turned back to the stack of receipts next to the cash register. I had made over a dozen sales that afternoon, and each one had required me to make at least a dozen laps around the store, searching for sizes, colors, and matching shoes. I was beat.

And I still had another hour to go. This was already my fourth shift this week at Claire's Boutique, and I was getting behind on my homework. But if I wanted to pay Claire back for that gorgeous lavender prom dress, which she had let

27

me buy on credit, I had no choice but to work double time.

"Do you know where I could *find* this skirt in orange?" the woman called. "Maybe at another store?"

I shook my head. "No, ma'am," I answered sweetly, sounding more like a friendly salesgirl than I felt. "But I think the pink one would look amazing on your daughter."

"Pink?" She brightened. "You know . . . you might be right."

I knew I should walk over to the dress rack and pull out the appropriate garment, but I couldn't seem to make myself abandon my post on the stool in front of the register. *If she can't find the pink skirt herself, I'll offer to help,* I promised myself.

This situation was ridiculous. I was working like crazy to pay for a dress that I was never going to have the chance to wear. As of now, I was no closer to having a prom date than I had been when I announced to Rose and Madison that Mr. Gorgeous was my official date. *Idiot!* I told myself. What had I been *thinking?*

I looked up from the receipts when I heard tinkling from the small silver bell over the door of the boutique. Jane and Christy breezed into the shop and headed toward the cash register. Finally!

"Did you find him?" I demanded, practically pouncing on my two best friends. "Please, tell me you found him." I had sent them deep into the mall with one mission: Find Mr. Beautiful. Once I had him right in front of me, I'd simply ask him to go to my prom with me. If I didn't lose my nerve.

I had been searching for him myself—with zero luck. During every one of my breaks, I roamed the food court, keeping my eyes peeled for a gorgeous guy splitting a basket of french fries with his little sister. I had spotted plenty of cute guys—and a plethora of little sisters—but my mystery man simply hadn't been on the scene since the day I'd first laid eyes on him.

Sending Jane and Christy out to look for him had been my latest attempt to dig myself out of the potentially humiliating situation I faced on prom night. I was hoping that two pairs of fresh eyes would bring me good luck.

Christy shook her head. "Sorry, Nic."

"We searched the place from top to bottom," Jane informed me. "We even went aisle to aisle in the, like, fifteen sporting-goods stores. He's not there."

"To tell you the truth, I don't even really know what the guy *looks* like," Christy told me. "I only saw part of the side of his face and the back of his head when we were all in here the other day."

"Well, *I* saw him!" Jane announced. "And I can unequivocally say that I haven't seen him since that day."

I sighed. Things were looking pretty grim. If I didn't show up in my lavender dress at the prom with *that guy,* Rose and Madison were going to have proof that I lied. And I had no doubt that the girls would divulge that fact to anyone and everyone within a mile range.

29

I have to find him, I thought for the thousandth time. *It's the only answer.*

By ten o'clock that night I was more convinced than ever that the final weeks of my high-school career were about to go up in flames. I had trekked around the mall two more times with no more luck than I'd had before.

Apparently my mystery guy didn't have a habit of cruising malls. I had to accept the possibility—no, the *probability*—that I would never see him again. Much less convince him to take me, a total stranger, to the senior prom.

I stared at the history book sitting in my lap. I had read the same paragraph about the Great Depression three times. And I still had no idea what it said. *Great Depression,* I thought. *Something I should be able to relate to.*

There was a soft knock on my bedroom door, and I gladly looked up from the textbook. "Yes?"

The door opened. My twenty-year-old sister, Gwen, stuck her head through the doorway. "How are you doing, Nic?" she asked. "You barely said a word during dinner."

Gwen's a sophomore at a college a hundred miles away, but she periodically comes home to eat what she calls "real" food and do about a dozen loads of laundry. Usually I loved having my sister back home, but tonight I had been too distracted to grill her about college life.

"I'm having a crisis," I blurted out. "My life is over."

Gwen laughed. "Wow! In that case, it's a good thing I'm here." She walked into my bedroom and shut the door behind her.

I wasn't crazy about the idea of revealing the stupid move I had made with Rose and Madison. Nonetheless, I had a feeling that trying to hide the truth from Gwen was going to be impossible. She had a way of making me tell her everything—even when I didn't want to.

Gwen climbed onto my bed and stuffed a couple of pillows between her back and the wall. She stretched her legs out in front of her and raised her eyebrows at me. "So? What's the story?"

"I don't even know where to begin. . . ." Should I tell her about my showdown with Shana, Rose, and Madison in the lunchroom a few weeks ago? Or should I explain that I hadn't had a date since freshman year because guys had heard I was so picky that there was no way anyone would ask me out?

As Gwen waited for me to spit out whatever it was that I was planning to say, I noticed her eyes drifting toward the open door of my walk-in closet. Her gaze fastened on the floor-length lavender dress that was hanging from a hook on the closet door.

"Hey, is that what I think it is?" she asked.

I nodded. "Yep. A prom dress." My voice was flat.

Gwen grinned. "Who's the lucky guy?"

I could see visions of corsages and boutonnieres dancing in her eyes as she studied the graceful cut of the dress. Gwen, unlike me, had spent every free

31

minute during high school going on dates.

"There *isn't* a lucky guy." I moaned, grabbing a pillow and burying my head in it.

Gwen frowned. "Uh-oh . . . does the dress have something to do with whatever it is that's bothering you?"

I took the pillow away and tossed it across my bedroom. "I'm a complete and total idiot!" I announced to my sister.

She laughed. "I've known you since you were born, Nicole. You might be a little annoying at times, but you're definitely not an idiot."

"You'll change your mind once you hear what I did," I said, sighing deeply.

Gwen leaned forward, preparing to listen intently to my saga. "Well . . . don't keep me in suspense!" she begged. "Tell me what's going on!"

"I told two of the nastiest girls at school that I had a date to the prom," I explained miserably. "But it was a lie."

"Hmmm . . ." Gwen was silent for a moment, gazing at the lavender dress. "So—ask somebody. Anybody."

"I can't ask just *anybody*," I responded, realizing for the millionth time that I had been suffering from temporary insanity when I had told Rose and Madison that Mr. Wonderful was my date.

"Okay . . . I'm missing something." Gwen leaned back against her stack of pillows and looked at me expectantly.

Yeah. You're missing the fact that your sister has the IQ of

32

a termite, I thought. *No, lower than a termite. An amoeba.*

"I told Rose and Madison that I was going to the prom with a certain gorgeous guy. I have to show up with *him,* or I'll be humiliated in front of the entire senior class." I cringed just thinking about the imminent ugly scene with the so-called popular girls.

"You're a beautiful girl," Gwen said in her reassuring-big-sister voice. "I'm sure if you explain the situation to the guy, he would be happy to take you to the prom—as long as he doesn't already have a date."

Of course Gwen thought I was beautiful—she's my sister! But my mystery man was another story. "Well, there's a huge catch—I don't even know the guy's name. He happened to be in Claire's Boutique when Rose and Madison started in on me about not going to the prom . . . and, well, I accidentally pointed to him and announced that he was my date."

"How do you *accidentally* announce that someone is your prom date?" Gwen asked.

I shrugged. "I wasn't thinking. . . . It just sort of popped out of my mouth before I could understand the implications of what I was doing."

"And now you have no idea how to find this mystery dude," Gwen finished, getting the picture.

"Do you think Mom and Dad will let me stay home from school for the rest of the semester?" I asked hopefully. "I could help around the house, or do some work for Dad at his office, or—"

"Not a chance," Gwen interrupted. "I suggested the same thing when I had a series of the grossest zits you've ever seen during the first semester of my junior year in high school."

"Maybe I could alter my appearance, like one of those people in the witness-protection program," I suggested. "You know, wear a wig and sunglasses and a big gauzy scarf around my face."

Gwen reached out and squeezed my hand—a sure sign she was about to give me a well-intended but ultimately useless big-sister lecture. I braced myself for the ineffectual pep talk.

"I know this seems like a really big deal right now, Nic," she began, warming up to her role as the older, wiser one. "But trust me, not having the right date to the prom isn't something that will scar you for life."

"I'm not worried about being scarred for life!" I retorted. "I'm worried about giving Rose and Madison a reason to think they're better than I am!"

Part of me knew that I was being ridiculous. I should have been confident enough not to care what a bunch of jerky girls said about me at school. After high school I would never have to deal with that crowd again.

But still . . . I *did* care. I didn't want to get a copy of my senior yearbook and find myself described as Union High's biggest loser. Sure, I was being shallow. But I had been responsible, and deep, and studious for the last four years. Just once I wanted to be a totally frivolous teenager. I wanted to wear a beautiful dress to the prom—and have an equally beautiful guy on my arm.

And I want to prove to Rose and Madison that I'm not some geek. I'm as attractive and likable—if not more—than any of the girls they hang with. Somehow the prom had become important to me. I simply *had* to go.

"Nic, I really don't believe that your little white lie is going to turn into a life-altering tragedy." Gwen grinned. "*But* if this is really that important to you, then let's go about it the right way."

"The right way?" I squeaked. What was the "right way"? I had already searched for Mr. Adorable numerous times.

Gwen nodded. "You need a plan. A good plan."

I wasn't about to argue with that point. "Go on."

"Here's what you've got to do . . . ," Gwen started.

I grabbed a notebook and pen off my desk, prepared to take notes. I was going to absorb every word Gwen uttered, and then I was going to follow her advice.

Thank goodness for big sisters, I thought. Gwen might be full of lectures. But she was always there when I needed her. *And I definitely need her now!*

Five

Nicole

"WHAT ARE YOU *eating?*" Jane asked, warily eyeing the bag of grains I had brought from home for lunch on Monday.

"Power food," I explained. "Gwen says this stuff helps her get her brain in gear when she's got to put in a long night of studying."

Christy wrinkled her nose. "It looks like something I used to feed the horses when I went through my riding-lessons phase."

"This stuff doesn't taste that great," I admitted, biting into another mouthful of the dry, bland mixture. "But if I'm going to find my mystery guy this week, I need all the help I can get."

Jane and Christy exchanged a glance that I mentally characterized as "worried." But neither of them said a word.

"What?" I asked. "Did you find Mr. Beautiful? Does he have a girlfriend? Did he say he would never, ever consider taking a stranger to the prom, no matter how desperate and pathetic she was?"

Jane set down her taco. "Unfortunately, we *didn't* find him." She shot another glance at Christy. "And to be honest, we don't think we're going to."

"Nicole, we think you might want to forget about this whole thing," Christy added. "I mean, it doesn't look like your dream man is going to show his face again."

"And the prom is *this* Saturday!" Jane chimed in.

"Maybe if you don't say anything else about it, Rose and Madison will lay off." Christy's voice was mild, but her message was clear: *You're doomed.*

I heard what they were saying. I really did. But after my sister-to-sister talk with Gwen last night, I was more committed than ever to finding Mr. X. Still, there was no way I could search on my own. I needed to have my two best friends as resources.

But how could either of them understand what it felt like not to have a date for the prom? Jane was going with Max—of course. And Christy was going with Jake Saunders, who she claimed wasn't her favorite person but was incredibly cute nonetheless.

Just as I was opening my mouth to launch into the details of the plan Gwen had helped me come up with, I noticed two extremely unwelcome individuals heading our way.

"Uh-oh," I muttered. *I think I might be about to say something I'll regret.*

38

"Hi, Nicole," Rose greeted me. As always, she didn't try to hide the disdain in her voice.

"Hey," I responded casually. "What brings you two to this side of the cafeteria?"

As in all lunchrooms across America, there was an unwritten law at Union High that the cafeteria was divided and subdivided. Students rarely ventured out of the area where they sat every day.

"We were curious . . . ," Madison said. "Has your date come up with an excuse to get out of going to the prom with you yet?"

Yep. Now I was *positive* I was about to say something I would later regret. But there was no way to avoid it. Not unless I was ready to give up the fight.

I fluttered my eyelashes and forced my face into an expression of total serenity. "As a matter of fact, he's completely psyched about the dance," I assured them. "And he decided that the two of us should go to La Serenara before we make our entrance at the prom."

"How interesting," Rose responded, her eyebrows raised. "That happens to be where *we're* going to dinner."

"Then I guess I'll see you there." I couldn't believe how confident I sounded. It was almost as if I actually believed every word that was coming out of my mouth.

As Rose and Madison sashayed toward their side of the cafeteria, Jane scowled. "Those girls get friendlier by the day," she commented wryly. "They bring sunshine to everyone they encounter."

"Uh, Nicole . . . you do realize that you just

dug yourself deeper into this mess, right?" Christy asked, looking concerned.

"Before you two go through the blow by blow about why I should abandon my search for the mystery date, let me tell you about my new plan." I set aside the bag of brain food and leaned forward to deliver the verbal blueprints of my new strategy.

"We're listening," Jane assured me. "But we reserve the right to declare you totally nuts and unable to make your own decisions."

Make this good, Nic, I ordered myself. Without Jane and Christy's help I didn't know if I would have the nerve to conduct an all-out search, my sister's brilliant idea.

"We know he isn't a student at Union High," I said. "And we know he doesn't hang out at the mall all that often."

"I'm with you so far," Christy chimed in. "But you're not telling us anything we don't already know about him."

"*However,* he must go to a high school that's close by," I reasoned. "Otherwise he never would have been at the mall in the first place." Now was the part where I begged them to help me. I took a deep breath. "All *we* have to do is check out the other schools during lunchtime and right after school, and eventually we'll find him—hopefully."

"Nic, there are, like, ten high schools in our vicinity," Jane pointed out. "Do you know how hard it's going to be to find him?"

"And remember . . . I didn't even get a good look

at the guy," Christy reminded me. "I'll be virtually useless when it comes to picking him out of a crowd."

What my friends said made a certain amount of sense. But not enough sense to convince me to abandon my project.

"What if Max was the guy we were trying to find?" I asked Jane. "Would you still believe that looking wasn't at least worth a try?"

"But I *love* Max," Jane answered, her face turning slightly red from embarrassment. "The only reason you want to find this guy is to prove a point. . . . At least, that's what you said."

The truth was that my desire to find Mr. Hottie now went beyond the need to save face in front of Rose and Madison. I *wanted* to go to the prom. And I wanted to go with *him*. There had been something about that guy. . . . I had seen him in my dreams several times over the past few days. I almost felt like I knew him.

"I just know that I won't be able to graduate from high school with a clear conscience unless I at least *try*," I responded, my voice soft and pleading. "Will you guys help?"

Christy grinned. "Of course we will, Nic," she assured me. "We would both do anything for you—you know that."

I breathed a huge sigh of relief. I had the two best friends in the world. And as soon as the three of us found Man with Soulful Eyes, I was going to give them each a huge hug and a big kiss. No, *first* I was going to beg the Guy to take me to the prom.

41

Then I would give them a hug and a kiss.

I just hoped that moment would come to pass. Finding *him* had come to mean everything to me.

"Ms. Gilmore, would you care to respond to the question?" Mr. Schneider's voice interrupted the intense concentration I was directing toward the piece of paper in front of me.

Oops. "Uh, sorry . . . what was the question?" I asked meekly. Usually I was the one raising my hand—not the one doodling in the back row. But it was now Friday afternoon, and how was I supposed to concentrate on anything except for how many hours and minutes I had left to find my so-called prom date?

"Never mind, Nicole. Just try to stay with us for at least the last ten minutes of class." Mr. Schneider gave me a smile, then pointed at Brian Landry, a none-too-bright jock type who was snoozing in the corner of the room. "Mr. Landry, maybe *you* could enlighten us."

I tuned back out as Brian began to stutter unintelligibly. There was simply no chance that I was going to pay even an iota of attention during this U.S. history class. My mind was occupied with far more pressing matters than the Wall Street stock-market crash of 1929.

Like locating my knight in shining blue jeans. Jane, Christy, and I had cruised the parking lots of every high school within a fifteen-minute radius. We had checked out McDonald's, Burger King,

Pizza Hut, and a 7-Eleven. And nothing. Not even a glimmer of the guy I had sworn to take to the prom.

Twenty-four hours from now almost every girl in my class would be primping and preening, preparing for their big night. And I would be home alone, counting the minutes until Rose and Madison used the cafeteria as a stage on which to make me eat dirt!

I turned back to the single sheet of paper on my desk. On it I had written a list of every place where I could realistically expect to find my mystery man. Now that all of the original places hadn't panned out, I was trying to come up with more options. *Car wash,* I wrote. But I knew I'd be struck by lightning, sitting at this desk, before I'd find *him* at the exact moment on the exact day at the exact car wash he decided to use.

Desperate, I wrote next, in big, bold capitals. It wasn't a place, but the word definitely suited my frame of mind.

"Nicole?" Mr. Schneider's voice once again broke into my thoughts.

I snapped my head upward and smiled apologetically. "Uh, sorry, what was the question?"

He laughed. "There's no question, Ms. Gilmore. I just wanted to inform you that class is over."

I glanced around the classroom. It was empty, except for a couple of girls who were redoing their lipstick before venturing into the hallway. Man! I had been so into my own head that I hadn't even noticed the loud shrill of the last bell. I was losing it!

"Thanks, Mr. Schneider," I responded sheep-ishly. "I'll, um, see you on Monday."

I grabbed my backpack from underneath my chair and sprinted toward the door of the classroom. If I stayed in there one more second, I was positive that Mr. Schneider would start grilling me about why I hadn't been paying attention. And a well-meant lecture was the last thing I was in the mood for.

I headed toward my locker, racking my brain for a good spot to search for my mystery man. Unfortunately, my mind was a big, fat blank.

"Maybe I should check out North High again," I said to myself, spinning the combination on my locker.

"Nicole!" Jane appeared at my side and threw an arm around my shoulders. Her face was flushed, and she was grinning as if she had just discovered that chocolate didn't, in fact, have any calories.

"What's up?" I asked. "Did Max tell you he loved you for the hundredth time—or are you just happy to see me?"

"*This* is up!" She pointed to a large, stuffed canvas bag at her feet. "You're not going to believe what I got!"

"What?" I asked. I hadn't seen her this excited since she announced that she and Max were now an official couple.

"I have in the bag last year's yearbooks for every high school in our area!" she practically shouted. "I

44

had a brainstorm during my study hall, paid a visit to the Union High yearbook editor . . . and voilà!"

"I don't get it." I knew Jane was going somewhere with this, but I couldn't quite connect the dots (or the yearbooks, in this case).

"All you have to do is flip through these until you find Mr. Wonderful," she explained. "Once you see his picture, we'll know his name, his school, and all kinds of other vital information."

In a flash it clicked. If I weren't so excited, I probably would have fainted with gratitude. "Jane Smith, you are brilliant!" I yelled.

"We're just lucky that the yearbook editor keeps copies of all of the other schools' books for ideas," she responded.

"Have I told you lately that you're the smartest, best friend a girl could ever hope to have?" I gave her a huge hug, then grabbed the first yearbook out of the canvas bag.

"Don't thank me yet," Jane warned. "First we've got to find your guy."

Jane and I knelt down on the semigrungy floor of the corridor. We each opened a yearbook and began to flip through the photos as fast as we could. Page after page of nameless faces passed by me. I began to worry that maybe I *wouldn't* recognize him.

Sure, I had seen him in my dreams (a fact that I alone was aware of), but there was a possibility that I had changed his face in my imagination. Could a mortal man actually be as goodlooking as the guy in my dreams had been?

"Look through this one," Jane advised, handing me the yearbook from Jefferson High. "It feels lucky to me."

I opened the book to the section that pictured last year's class of roughly three hundred juniors. *Adams. Ali. Allen. Alton.* I skimmed through the A's, then started in on the B's. *Babbit. Babson. Bacon. Bailey. Banks—*

"Banks!" I shouted. "Banks!"

"You found him?" Jane slammed the Washington High yearbook shut and leaned over to look at the book in my lap. "Where?"

"Justin Banks," I announced. "Right here." I pointed to the small photograph. Even in a two-by-two picture, the guy was gorgeous. And he looked *exactly* like I had remembered him.

Jane whistled. "He's cute, all right. And that's definitely him." She studied the photo for another few seconds, then frowned. "Nicole, is it really possible that a guy who looks like *that* doesn't have a girlfriend?"

I shrugged. "If he does, I'll just have to buy her off. Because now that I've found Mr. Justin Banks, there's no *way* I'm going to let him turn me down."

"In that case, let's go find Christy," Jane suggested. "If we hurry, we can get over to Jefferson before all of the kids leave—and you're going to need all the moral support you can get."

My heart was pounding as I followed Jane down the hallway toward Christy's locker. Now that I knew Mr. X's name and school, I had only one problem. What was I going to say when I found him?

Six

Justin

"JUSTIN, I'M TELLING you, this girl is really pretty," Sam insisted. "You've *got* to go out with her tonight."

I rolled my eyes. My best friend, Sam Patton, had been trying to set me up on dates for the past three months. No matter how many times I said no, he just kept coming at me.

At the moment we were hanging out on the grassy lawn in front of Jefferson High, decompressing after a major chemistry test. Sam was trying to persuade me to double-date with his girlfriend and her cousin, who was visiting for the weekend. On Monday, the first time he'd asked me, I had told him I wasn't interested. He was *still* asking me now that it was Friday afternoon.

"First of all, you have no idea whether or not

47

Maya's cousin is pretty. You've never even met her." With Sam it was sometimes necessary to point out the obvious.

He grinned. "How could a girl related to Maya *not* be pretty? It's simple genetics, my friend."

"You know I have a rule against dating," I reminded him. "Why would tonight be different from any other night?"

"Justin, I love you like a brother, but this whole I-don't-need-anyone-because-I'm-an-island-unto-myself attitude has got to go." He paused. "Besides, I already promised Maya that we would help her entertain her cousin."

I appreciated the fact that Sam cared about my social life (or lack thereof), but it was also a quality that I found totally irritating. After all, this was *my* life. If I wanted to stay home on Friday night and read a book, well, that was *my* business. And I refused to be guilted into having a so-called good time.

"For the last time the answer is *no*," I announced firmly.

There was no way that Sam was going to change my mind. I wasn't about to open myself up again to the kind of hurt I had experienced last year. That lesson had been learned—and I had no interest in learning it all over again the hard way.

"Justin, you've really got to—" He stopped midplea, and his eyes drifted off to some point over my shoulder.

"What?" I asked, turning around to look.

"Check out those girls!" Sam told me. "They are *hot*—and they're not from Jefferson."

I scanned the parking lot automatically, searching for unfamiliar (but pretty) faces. And then I saw them. Three girls were piling out of a red Honda, and Sam was right. They weren't Jefferson High students.

I frowned. There was something about the girls, though. . . . I felt like I'd seen them before. *If not at school, where?* I wondered, searching my memory.

"Maybe my reputation as the best boyfriend in the world has spread to other high schools, and I'm being pursued by the masses," Sam speculated.

"Yeah, you're a regular Leonardo DiCaprio," I retorted, resisting the urge to snort. Sam was a lot of things—modest wasn't one of them.

"Hey, one of them is heading straight toward us!" Sam said, jabbing me in the side. "Have you been hiding a girlfriend from me?"

I shook my head, studying the girl who was walking toward us. She was tall, with smooth black skin and silky hair. Wearing faded jeans and a white tank top, her well-sculpted arms swung at her sides. *Where have I seen her?* I asked myself again.

I closed my eyes. In my imagination the girl wasn't wearing blue jeans . . . she was in a long, lavender dress. I snapped my fingers. "The mall," I exclaimed.

Yep. That's where I had seen this girl before. Immediately my eyes traveled to one of the other two girls. There she was again. The girl I had recognized from the hospital that day in the dress shop.

Today the girl was smiling, and there were no signs of the tears I had seen streaking down her face in that horrible waiting room. But even from this distance I could see that her grin didn't quite reach her eyes. She had the same sort of distracted air about her that I had had during my own mother's illness.

Her mom's condition hasn't improved, I guessed. As the thought formulated in my brain, my heart went out to her. Unfortunately, I knew exactly how she felt. Just seeing her face, I felt a rush of the grief that had become so familiar during the last year. It was never far from the forefront of my mind.

I was still looking at the girl from the hospital when I realized that the first girl was standing, like, *right* in front of me. I blinked and found myself staring into a pair of huge brown eyes.

"You're Justin Banks," she announced, her hands on her hips.

I glanced at Sam, wondering if he had somehow orchestrated this whole event. But he looked as baffled as I felt. "Uh, yes, I am," I replied. "Do I know you?"

Man. This girl was totally beautiful, and for some strange reason, she seemed to know me. At another time in my life (like, a year ago), I would have thought I was experiencing my own male, teenage version of heaven on earth. But I had trained myself not to care about the way a girl looked—or about anything else that in any way, directly or indirectly, related to the subject of dating.

"You don't know me," she said. "But I have to talk to you."

My mind raced. Had I unknowingly *done* something to this girl? Rear-ended her car in a parking lot? Accidentally knocked over a rack of expensive, breakable merchandise in Claire's Boutique? *There's nothing,* I thought. *I have done nothing wrong.*

"Okay . . . I'm listening." I felt like I was in an episode of *The X-Files* or maybe on *Candid Camera*. A complete stranger (who happened also to be an extremely attractive girl) had appeared out of thin air and demanded to talk to me. Why?

She glanced over at Sam. "Uh . . . *alone?*"

This scenario was getting weirder by the second. I looked over at Sam and shrugged. He backed away, grinning.

Great. Now I was going to have to spend the next few weeks convincing Sam that I hadn't been cruising malls or secretly logging on to the Internet to meet strange girls. He would never buy that a random girl just happened to want to talk to me for no apparent reason—even if she did announce to anyone within earshot that I didn't know her.

"Say no more. I'm out of here." Sam flashed me a thumbs-up and sauntered toward the other end of the lawn.

And then it was just us. The mystery girl and me. I crossed my arms in front of my chest and waited nervously for her to say something. I focused on her eyes, willing the butterflies that had for some reason formed in my stomach to go away.

"So . . . ," she said.

And with that one word I had the feeling that my life was about to change. I just didn't know what form that change would take. . . .

Seven

Nicole

"So . . ." I MANAGED to get out exactly one word before my mouth transformed itself into a giant cotton ball.

My hands were shaking, my palms were sweating, and my knees had become ill-formed lumps of jelly. *Get it together,* I ordered myself. *You're never going to convince him if he thinks you're a total psycho.*

But I couldn't help being overwhelmed with a kind of heady terror. This was the bravest (not to mention craziest) moment of my life. And Justin Banks was just so . . . cute. *Beyond cute,* I amended. He was even hotter than I remembered—which was saying a lot.

You're not asking Justin for a real date, I reminded myself. This would be a business/begging-for-mercy transaction only. Unless . . . well, unless he actually liked me.

"*So . . .*" Justin's voice interrupted my daydream. "What do you want?"

I felt several pints of blood rushing to my face. I had to spit out my request *now*. If I didn't speak in the next second and a half, I knew I would simply turn and run.

"I want to take you to my prom tomorrow night," I blurted out. "The Union High senior prom."

He didn't even hesitate. Without taking one *moment* to consider my request, Justin started to shake his head. "Um . . . thanks. But no thanks."

My heart sank, and I felt like all of the air had left my lungs. That was it. A flat-out no. *This isn't happening,* I told myself. *You're so paranoid that you imagined his refusal before he even had a chance to properly respond.*

"Sorry," Justin added. And I knew that it *hadn't* been my imagination. He had turned me down outright.

"Oh. You have a girlfriend." That had to be the explanation, right? Otherwise he wouldn't have answered so quickly.

Besides, I was nuts to have thought for even a minute that a guy this gorgeous didn't have a girlfriend. Or two. Or three. He could probably date anyone he wanted to.

But again Justin shook his head. "Nope. No girlfriend."

No girlfriend? *What is up with this guy?* I wondered. In the next moment I realized the obvious truth. He hated me! Justin Banks had taken one look at my face and decided that I was the least prom-worthy girl on earth.

I wanted to turn around, sprint to the car, and peel out of the parking lot, never to be seen or heard from again. Justin Banks wasn't my dream guy—he was a jerk.

Then again, who could blame him for turning me down? He probably thought I was some insane stalker who had been secretly plotting to get him to take me to the prom for weeks. Of course, that description wasn't *entirely* inaccurate.

I couldn't walk away. Not with schoolwide humiliation staring me in the face on Monday morning. I opened my mouth and willed something brilliant, articulate, and witty to come out.

"Justin, you have to go to the prom with me," I exclaimed, sounding like an idiot. "I mean, you don't *have* to, obviously, but I really, really need you to be my date."

"Ah . . ." Justin's eyes were narrowed suspiciously, but he was listening. That was all that mattered.

"You see, there are these girls in my class who are really mean and nasty and stuck on themselves. And they came into the shop where I worked and started to make snide remarks about the fact that I didn't have a date for the prom. Of course, I *could* have a date, but, well, I'm picky." I took a deep breath. "But that's a whole other story."

"Uh-huh . . ." Justin was so beautiful—his picture in the yearbook definitely didn't do him justice.

You're babbling, I told myself. But I couldn't stop. Not now. "Anyway, you happened to be in the shop at the time, and I told them you were my prom date, and then you left, and I've been trying to find you ever since. Which wasn't easy . . ."

My mind seemed to separate from my body as I continued to tell Justin the story in one long, rambling run-on sentence. I could *see* myself standing there, talking like an idiot, but I was powerless to shut my mouth.

Finally Justin held up his hand, indicating that I should stop speaking. Abruptly I clamped my mouth shut. *Say yes,* I begged silently. *Please, say yes!*

"I hear what you're saying . . . but, uh, I don't know. . . ." He looked friendlier than he had a few minutes ago, but I could read on Justin's face that I hadn't won him over.

I glanced over at the parking lot, where Jane and Christy were hanging out next to the car. They nodded and smiled at me, sending silent messages of encouragement. I took a deep breath, preparing to take the final plunge.

"I'll give you fifty dollars to do me the favor of taking me to the prom," I announced. "And, of course, I'll pay for the entire evening."

Hey, what were a few more shifts at Claire's Boutique at this point? I was already going to have to work there until I was thirty to dig myself out of debt!

"I'll agree to take you to the prom," Justin said

after several *long* moments of utter silence. "But fifty dollars isn't what I want."

I raised an eyebrow, trying to keep focused on the matter at hand. But I was having a tough time thinking about anything besides how incredibly good Justin looked in the pair of worn khakis he was wearing. *Hello!*

"What *do* you want?" I asked. If he asked for a hundred, I was going to have to sell myself for medical experiments.

"I, uh, want to meet your friend." Justin's gaze traveled toward the parking lot, and he pointed at Christy.

So much for study dates, walking in the park, falling in love, and marital bliss. Only ten minutes into our relationship, Justin had already fallen for another girl. One of my best friends, to be exact. I willed away the sinking feeling in the pit of my stomach and forced myself to concentrate on the positive aspect of this conversation.

I'm going to get what I need, I thought. *That's all that matters.* Besides, I didn't even know this Justin Banks guy. Sure, he was gorgeous. But for all I knew, he had the personality of a goldfish. Anyway, the only reason I even wanted to go to the prom in the first place was to teach Rose, Madison, and the rest of their friends a lesson.

"No problem," I answered, managing to sound at least semicool and semicollected. "I'll get you a date with Christy."

Gulp. *Sorry, Christy,* I added silently. I wasn't in

57

the habit of promising virtual strangers that one of my friends would go on a date with them. But maybe I was doing Christy a favor. She'd said that her prom date, Jake, was the last guy she would want as a boyfriend. Why she was even going with Jake the Jerk (that was her name for him) was beyond Jane and me, but Christy wasn't forthcoming when we pressed her.

Anyway, what warm-blooded girl *wouldn't* want to go out with Justin?

I stuck out my hand. "So . . . it's a deal."

"Deal." Justin shook my hand, then looked into my eyes for slightly longer than was strictly necessary. "By the way—do you always use this kind of, uh, unorthodox method to get your dates?"

"It's not a real date," I reminded him. "And no, I don't."

Usually I don't use any methods at all, I added to myself. I literally couldn't remember the last time I had laid eyes on a guy I would want to walk in the moonlight with.

I pulled a small scrap of paper and a pen out of the back pocket of my blue jeans. "I'll pay—but you have to drive," I told Justin.

"Fair enough," he answered.

I wrote down my address on the slip of paper and placed it into Justin's outstretched hand. When my fingers brushed his skin, I felt an electric spark shoot all the way up my arm.

It's just nerves, I assured myself. *One little spark doesn't mean I'll be totally crushed if Justin and Christy*

fall in love and I have to spend the rest of my days watching
them go gaga over each other the way Max and Jane do.
Right.

"Pick me up at seven o'clock," I added. "We're going to dinner at La Serenara before the dance."

Justin whistled. "La Serenara? That's the nicest restaurant in town."

Tell me something I don't know, I thought. "It's a long story," I pronounced. "And I doubt you want to hear me babble on about it for another fifteen minutes."

Justin laughed, and it was one of the most amazing sounds I had ever heard. Deep and rich and infectious. If only . . . well, if only.

I tore my gaze away from Justin's face, pivoted, and strode toward the parking lot. "See you tomorrow night!" I called over my shoulder.

"Wait!" Justin shouted. "I don't even know your name!"

I stopped in my tracks and turned around to look Justin in the eye. "Nicole Gilmore," I informed him.

Then I marched toward the car, resisting the urge to jump up and down or do a victory dance. *I did it!* Just now the enormity of my feat was sinking in. Mr. X was going to be my date to the Union High senior prom.

Even if Justin didn't like me, the prom was going to be a night I would never forget. And I was going to look absolutely fabulous in my strapless lavender gown—if I did say so myself!

59

Justin's Saturday To-Do List

A List of Annoying Tasks I Must Complete Before I Go to the Union High Senior Prom with a Virtual Stranger

1. Rent a tuxedo (otherwise known as a strait-jacket). Hope that I'm not stuck with something resembling a 1970s leisure suit.

2. Wash my car. The least I can do is shepherd this girl to her prom in a car that is not covered with dust and bird droppings.

3. Practice dance moves in the privacy of my own bedroom.

4. Shine my good shoes.

5. Shower. Use my superstrong deodorant soap to stave off any impending malodors.

6. Shave. Be particularly careful to avoid nicks and cuts since I don't want to go to the prom with bits of toilet paper stuck to my face (even if it's not a real date).

7. Contemplate splashing on a little aftershave. Reject the idea on the grounds that nobody but James Bond (007) can wear aftershave and not seem a bit cheesy.

8. Don tuxedo. Make sure that Star is on hand to help me with the bow tie and cummerbund.

9. Allow Star to take exactly one (1) picture of me in my tuxedo.

10. Pick up Nicole. Be sure to wipe my potentially sweaty palms on my pants leg before I go to her front door.

Eight

Justin

A S I WALKED through the mall on Saturday morning, I was regretting the moment of weakness I had shown when I agreed to go to the prom with Nicole Gilmore. I didn't even know the girl. *Then again, who cares if I don't know her?* I thought. It's not like we were going on a real date. I was doing a favor for a stranger. Period.

"This is the place," Sam announced. "Joe's Tuxedos."

Sam, Star, and I stopped in front of the small shop. "With my luck all they'll have left is a powder blue tuxedo with a ruffle-front shirt," I commented.

"Well, *I* think you should rent a red cummerbund to go with your tux," Star informed me. "That'll make you totally stand out."

"I don't *want* to stand out," I retorted.

Bringing Star along on this little shopping excursion wouldn't have been my first choice. As soon as she had heard I was going to the Union High prom, my little sister had gone headfirst into hearts-and-flowers mode. She seemed to believe that going to a dance was up there with being crowned the king of England and winning the state lottery.

But I'd *had* to include Star in the outing. Dad worked every Saturday, and I had promised Star that I would take her to the mall to get a new pair of sneakers. Since I'd done so well in the patience department until she'd found her perfect dress and shoes and headband for her own dance, I was now her designated shopping partner. Besides, she had been so excited at the prospect of tagging along with Sam and me that I probably wouldn't have had the heart to say no even if I could have.

"Let's go behind door number one," Sam exclaimed. "If we don't get in there and get you a tux, you're going to have to go to the prom in jeans and a T-shirt."

"Fine with me," I muttered.

But I couldn't help feeling just a little excited as we walked into the shop. I hadn't been out of the house on a Saturday night in months. And there were only so many games of backgammon a guy could play with his dad before he went a little nuts.

"Welcome to Joe's Tuxedos," a small man with

wiry gray hair greeted us. "I'm Joe." He beamed at us and gave Star a wink. "How may I help you lovely people this afternoon?"

"I need a, uh, tux," I said. "I'm going to the prom tonight."

"Tonight!" Joe exclaimed. "Oh, my, we've got much work to do. Let's get started right away."

Star giggled as Joe took me by the arm and led me toward a small platform in front of a three-way mirror. I stood as still as a mannequin while Joe took my measurements.

"And who is the lucky girl?" Joe asked, tsking over the length of my arms.

"She's the most beautiful girl I've seen in ages," Sam informed him when I didn't say anything. "Aside from *my* girlfriend, of course."

"Do I get to meet her?" Star asked. "I really, really want to."

"No," I said firmly. The last thing I needed was to make this prom date into a family affair.

"I'll be right back," Joe said. "Don't go anywhere." He disappeared behind a red velvet curtain, still talking to himself.

"Your ugly brother got lucky with this one," Sam told Star. "For some crazy reason, she thinks he's hot stuff."

"Please, stop with the compliments." I stepped off the platform and paced nervously around the small shop. What if Joe didn't have a tux in my size? What would I do?

"I wonder who I'll go to *my* senior prom with,"

Star speculated. "Maybe Aaron Trent will take me. He's cute."

I rolled my eyes. "Easy there, little sister. You've got a few years before you've got to start shopping for a prom dress."

The velvet curtain opened with a flourish, and Joe emerged holding a perfectly pressed black tuxedo. "Ta da!" he exclaimed. "I have exactly what you need, young man."

"Phew." I had spent the last five minutes imagining myself driving from store to store, trying on ill-fitting tuxedos.

Joe placed the suit in my hands, then more or less shoved me into a tiny, brightly lit dressing room. I pulled off my clothes, praying that the pants of the tuxedo wouldn't come up to my knees.

"I'm so psyched you're going to the prom!" Star yelled from the other side of the door. "I'm sick of you skulking around the house every weekend!"

"Tell the whole world how you feel, Star," I called back. The girl certainly wasn't shy. I viewed the pants in the mirror. A perfect fit. *Joe will be proud,* I noted.

Still, it was great to see her so enthused. It was almost as if seeing me reenter the world at large was lifting a heavy burden from Star's shoulders. If I was getting on with my life, so could she.

Which is exactly why I'm not going to tell her the real reason I agreed to take Nicole to the prom, I thought, pulling on the trendy black tuxedo shirt. I didn't want to tell my sister about Christy, reminding her

66

of the hospital and the waiting room and the doctors and the machines. She was too young to be dragged down with those kinds of images. I wanted her to forget them as quickly as possible.

I hadn't told Sam the real reason I was going to the Union High prom either. He had been a great friend—the best—throughout my mother's illness. But I didn't want to open up with him about all of this mushy stuff. It was too hard.

I just hope I can help Christy, I thought, buttoning the shirt. Or maybe . . . well, maybe I was hoping to help *myself.* As soon as I had seen Christy in Claire's Boutique, I had felt an urge to talk to her.

Speaking with someone who was going through what I had been through would allow me to let go of some of the pain, I theorized. It would be a catharsis. *And I have to let the pain go,* I realized. Wallowing in grief wasn't only harming me—it was probably hurting Dad and Star as well.

I finished buttoning the shirt, pulled on the jacket, and surveyed myself in the mirror. Wow. I looked halfway decent in this thing. I flashed a game-show-host grin in the mirror and did a miniature waltz around the dressing room. Not bad.

If I was totally honest with myself, I would have to admit that wanting to reach out to Christy wasn't the *only* reason I had acquiesced to Nicole's request. After all, I could have walked over to Nicole's car and introduced myself to Christy on the spot.

The truth was that I had admired how gutsy Ms. Nicole Gilmore had been. I could see how nervous she was when she walked up to me. Despite her casual bravado, her hands had been shaking, and she had seemed a little wobbly. But she had managed to walk up to a perfect stranger and ask him to the prom. And *then* she hadn't taken no for an answer. A person had to have confidence in the core of her being to pull off a move like that.

"Are you ever coming out of there?" Sam called. "If you stay in the dressing room much longer, Star is going to talk me into wearing a paisley bow tie with *my* tux at the Jefferson High prom next weekend."

I laughed. Somehow I didn't think Maya would appreciate that kind of apparel on Sam—even if she did love him for his quirky sense of humor. "I'm coming!"

I opened the door of the dressing room and stepped back into the shop. "Wow!" Star whispered. "You look like a movie star."

"Well, I don't know about that. . . ."

"She's right," Joe proclaimed. "I am a genius. I couldn't have done better with that tuxedo if I'd had a month to fit you."

"Thanks, Joe." I couldn't help grinning. *You'd think he was going to the prom,* I thought.

Sam got up from the small sofa he and Star had been lounging on while they waited for me to come out of the dressing room. He bowed deeply in front of Star and held out his hand.

"Madam, may I have this dance?" he asked, using a fake English accent.

Star giggled. "I would be delighted, kind sir," she responded, rising from the sofa.

Immediately Sam and Star began to do a variation of the fox-trot around the shop. "One, two, three, one, two, three," Sam chanted, spinning Star in small circles.

"Hey, you're not bad," I commented. *A lot better than I am,* I added to myself.

Sam grinned. "What I'm about to tell you can't go beyond these walls." He paused dramatically. "Maya has been making me take dance lessons."

I threw back my head, laughing. I couldn't remember the last time I had felt so free . . . so young. *It feels good,* I realized. I needed this.

I'm glad Nicole Gilmore appeared out of nowhere, I thought. A little dancing and some disgustingly sweet fruit punch were just what I needed. As long as I remembered to keep my hands off my gorgeous date.

I might be ready to go out and have a little fun. But nothing more. After tonight I would never see Nicole again.

Nicole's Preprom Checklist

Things I Must Accomplish before Justin Banks Arrives at My Door

1. Pluck eyebrows. (Note to self: Be sure to *carefully* follow plucking instructions from *Cosmo,* as I don't want to rip off half of my face in the process of trying to beautify my brows.)
2. Give myself a manicure and a pedicure. Be sure to allow ample drying time to avoid the kind of nail-polish fiasco that occurred when Jane, Christy, and I designated one Friday last winter as Home Spa Night.
3. Allot at least two hours for hair styling. Don't panic if the first three attempts at the upsweep fail. Practice makes perfect.
4. Allot one hour for makeup. Use Cindy Crawford's *Basic Face* to get that natural-but-beautiful look Cindy talked about on *Oprah*.
5. Have Mom help me steam press my perfect (and pricey) prom dress.
6. Assemble the whole package (dress, hair, and makeup). Add jewelry and Gwen's high heels.
7. Stare at myself in the mirror, searching for tiny flaws that will seem like major disfigurements.

8. Convince myself I look fine despite the major zit I can feel forming on my forehead. Who's going to let a minor skin irritation keep her from the prom?

9. Think of no less than three witty, cutting remarks to make to Rose and Madison, should the need arise.

10. When the doorbell rings, descend the stairs with the attitude and composure of the late Princess Diana.

Nine

Justin

WHY IS MY heart beating so fast? I asked myself as I stood outside the Gilmores' redbrick house. I was having a minor panic attack as I prepared to ring the doorbell.

Okay, so I was feeling a little nervous. But not because of *Nicole*. I just hadn't been on a date in a long time. Not since . . . well, not for a long time. I was out of practice. *How firmly do I shake her father's hand? Do I open her car door for her? Am I supposed to tell her she looks nice—even though this isn't a real date?*

I wasn't going to figure out the answers to these pressing questions by standing here. *Might as well go for it.* I pressed the bell, then took a step back from the door and waited.

A moment later the door opened. I found myself face-to-face with one of the tallest men I had ever seen. Just my luck. My first date in months, and her father was one of those totally intimidating types who liked to crush the fingers of his daughter's dates in his steel handshake.

"Uh, hi. I'm—I'm Justin Banks," I stuttered.

Mr. Banks smiled, and all of my tension began to dissipate. His warm smile reminded me of a teddy bear's. "Great to meet you, Justin," he said, firmly shaking my hand. "Come on inside."

I walked into the house. "Hi, Justin," Mrs. Gilmore called, walking down the stairs. "Nicole will just be a minute."

"Nice to meet you, Mrs. Gilmore." I absorbed the motherly details of her presence, feeling instantly bathed in a warm glow.

We all stood there, looking at each other. Funny. Even though this wasn't a real date, I felt like a *real* guy, meeting a *real* girl's *real* parents. I sent a silent thanks to Joe for hooking me up with such a dignified-looking tuxedo. I would have been sweating like a pig if I'd had to stand here wearing some kind of magenta leisure suit. Instead I felt perfectly presentable.

"Nicole never told us how you two met," Mrs. Gilmore said in a soothing voice that reminded me of my own mom's. "Maybe you could fill us in while we wait for her."

"Oh. Um." What should I say? *Your daughter tracked me down in front of my high school* didn't seem appropriate. "It's really kind of a funny story—"

"Whoops. I guess we'll have to hear about it

later," Mr. Gilmore interrupted. "The girl of the hour is making her entrance."

I turned toward the staircase—and my breath caught in my throat. *Whoa!* Nicole looked . . . well, absolutely, in a word, *incredible.* She was wearing the same lavender dress she'd had on that day at the boutique. Only now she was wearing high heels and a sparkly necklace, and she had her hair piled atop her head back in some kind of girl-hairdo thing, complete with pink roses. And how was it possible that I hadn't noticed those perfect cheekbones the first time I had laid eyes on her?

"Hey, Justin," Nicole greeted me as she glided down the stairs as if she were walking on air rather than four-inch heels.

"Uh, hi." I blanked. *Name. Name. Name.* "Nicole!" I blurted out finally. Phew. Forgetting their daughter's name wasn't the impression I wanted to make with the Gilmores. *Not that it matters,* I amended.

"You look great," I told Nicole as she reached the bottom of the stairs. Hey, it would have been rude just to stand there mute.

"Honey, you're absolutely gorgeous," Mrs. Gilmore gushed. "Dad and I want to get a picture of you and Justin before you go off and have a great time."

"Mom, no pictures!" Nicole responded. She raised her eyebrows in my direction and flashed me an apologetic smile.

Mrs. Gilmore frowned. "But we need a photograph!"

"Of course we do," I added, stepping forward. "I mean, it's not a prom without a picture, right?"

Could I have sounded any stupider? This was exactly the kind of awkward moment that made guys' palms sweat. And it was about to get worse—because it was almost time for the Pinning of the Corsage.

I held out the small box that contained the single white rose that Star had convinced me to buy for Nicole this afternoon. My sister had simply refused to leave the mall until I had purchased a corsage for my prom date.

Nicole took the rose out of the box, then handed it to me. "Do you, uh, want to put it on for me?" she asked.

I nodded, and my palms started to sweat, right on cue. The corsage felt tiny in my big hands, and I was half afraid that I was going to gouge Nicole with the pins the florist had given me.

"Got it," I announced finally, breathing a sigh of relief.

"Good job," Nicole complimented me. She touched the flower lightly, her fingers moving like a butterfly's wings.

"Thanks." I brushed my palms against the legs of my pants and followed Nicole and her parents into their spacious living room. Mrs. Gilmore herded Nicole and me toward the fireplace.

Mrs. Gilmore put a small digital camera up to her eye. "Stand a little closer together," she instructed, peering through the lens.

I inched closer to Nicole and placed my arm around her slender waist. The fabric of her dress was cool against my hand, but I couldn't help notice the slight tingle that traveled up my arm. *It's been a long time since I touched a girl,* I realized.

"Smile!" Mr. Gilmore ordered.

Dutifully Nicole and I grinned for the camera. A moment later the flash went off.

"Perfect!" Mrs. Gilmore exclaimed. "Now we just need one more—for Justin's family."

Nicole and I smiled again, and Mrs. Gilmore took the photograph. "Let's get out of here," Nicole whispered. Parent time was now over, and the night was officially about to begin.

"I'm ready when you are," I answered. I followed Nicole out of the living room toward the front door.

"Bye, Mom. Bye, Dad." She kissed each of her parents on the cheek.

"It was nice to meet you," I told Mr. and Mrs. Gilmore, reaching out to shake Nicole's dad's hand again.

"Have fun, kids," Mrs. Gilmore called.

"Don't stay out too late," Mr. Gilmore added. "And no drinking and driving. Period."

"We *know,* Dad." Nicole rolled her eyes at me as I pulled open the front door.

Seconds later we were outside, surrounded by the warm spring air. I inhaled deeply, appreciating the scent of the honeysuckle bushes that lined one side of the Gilmores' yard. I had a good feeling about tonight. It was going to be fun.

"Hey, thanks for the corsage," Nicole said as soon as the door shut behind us. "Even though this isn't a real date, I appreciate the niceties."

"Oh . . . right, no problem." Oops. For a moment I had almost forgotten that this *wasn't* a real date.

The dress, the flowers, the picture, the parents—the evening had all of the ingredients of an actual, real-life date. *But I'm glad it's not,* I reminded myself. *I never would have agreed to a real date.*

But Nicole was a beautiful, intelligent girl. I was going to have to be careful tonight . . . very, very careful.

Ten

Nicole

BY THE TIME Justin and I strolled into La Serenara for our dinner reservation, I felt at least halfway confident about walking in the super-high heels I had borrowed from Gwen. With any luck, I wouldn't trip on the way to our table.

"It smells awesome in here," Justin commented, inhaling deeply. "I feel like a young millionaire, out on the town."

"I know what you mean," I answered, clutching his arm for support as I walked up the small set of steps that led to the main dining room.

Sure, after tonight I would be a pauper, toiling for weeks on end to dig myself out of debt. But for this one night I felt like a princess. I had it all—the gown, the guy, the corsage. This might be a grand illusion, but it *felt* real.

"Two for dinner," I said to the maitre d'. "The name is Gilmore."

He scanned the list of names in front of him, then gave us a warm smile. "Ah, yes. Prom night, yes?"

"Actually, we're going to a monster-truck rally," I joked, squeezing Justin's arm.

The maitre d' fluttered his eyelashes. "Young love," he said with a sigh. "So tender, so sweet, so light at heart."

"And so hungry," Justin added.

"But of course." The man pivoted toward the main dining room. "Follow me."

As we wended our way through the elegant, dimly lit restaurant, I scanned the tables for Madison and Rose. Of course, if they were there, I probably wouldn't have had to *look* for them—I would have heard the girls' grating, shrill giggles from halfway down the block.

There was no sign of Rose and Madison or their dates. But I had no doubt that they would turn up eventually. I would simply bide my time until it was time to show off the fact that I had the hottest date around.

We stopped in front of a small table next to a huge window, and Justin pulled out my chair. "Thank you," I said, wishing more than ever that the class jerks were there to see Nicole Gilmore being treated like a prom queen.

"My pleasure, Nicole." His deep, slightly husky voice sent a small, almost imperceptible shiver up my spine.

Justin slid into his seat and immediately picked up the pale blue linen napkin that was resting on top of the table. He put the napkin in his lap, then straightened the array of silverware placed in front of him. Wow. The guy was gorgeous *and* well mannered. A rare combination in any high-school boy.

Thank goodness Justin's not some total louse, I thought. *I really lucked out.* The truth was that I had picked Justin Banks as a prom date completely at random. I had been in the throes of desperation, and he had been the cutest guy in a three-shop radius. But I had had zero knowledge that he wasn't a complete jerk. *Phew!* A date who was a complete embarrassment was worse than no date at all. Any girl with a modicum of self-respect knew that much.

"Have you ever been here before?" Justin asked, opening his menu.

I shook my head. "Nope. But I've heard the food is amazing."

I stared at the menu, but I wasn't reading any of the words. Instead I was racking my brain for something else to say. *Nice weather we're having* was one totally dull option. Or I could go the twenty-questions route. *What's your favorite color? Do you have a middle name? Have you figured out what you're going to major in at college?*

But I didn't want to bore Justin to sleep with typical first-date conversation (not that I'd had many first dates). I wanted to be charming and witty and intelligent. Basically I wanted to prove to the guy that I wasn't a complete psycho who could

81

only get a date by hunting someone down through their yearbook photo—even if that was sort of the truth.

"Have you decided what to order?" Justin asked, breaking the silence.

"Not yet." *Actually, I haven't even read the first item on the menu,* I added silently. "Everything looks so good, I don't know what I want."

Justin coughed. "Um . . . yeah. The entrées sound . . . interesting."

I forced myself to focus on the menu, quickly reading the description of each dish. My eyebrows shot up as I absorbed the contents of various entrées. These weren't just fancy pasta dishes or T-bone steaks.

"The goat brain looks especially tasty," I commented dryly.

Justin nodded solemnly. "Yes, I'm always tempted to order brains. But tonight I may be adventurous and go for the tongue."

"Are you sure?" I asked, struggling not to laugh. "Because I've always found that the walnut glaze the tongue is served with can be a bit heavy—not conducive to dancing."

"You've got a good point, Nic," Justin responded with a grin. "On second thought, I think I'll order the chicken."

Nic. He called me Nic. "What an amazing coincidence!" I exclaimed. "I've been craving chicken all day."

Justin closed his menu. "I guess we're not cut out for haute cuisine."

82

"I beg to differ," I countered. "After all, we're going to get the escargot for an appetizer."

"We are?" Justin asked, his face a study in snail phobia.

"Did I say 'escargot'?" I asked, wide-eyed. "I *meant* to say 'fried zucchini sticks.'"

Justin laughed, and I couldn't help but notice that his smile was one of the warmest I had ever seen. And his eyes were like laser beams as he gazed at me from the other side of the tiny table.

"If you're with me . . . I've got a radical idea," Justin announced. "But feel free to wimp out if you're not up for the challenge."

"I'm *always* up for a challenge," I assured him. "What is it?"

"Let's order the escargot. I'll eat snail meat if you will."

"I'm with you," I responded. "After all, we don't want to disappoint our waiter."

As if on cue, a waiter wearing a white tuxedo appeared beside our table. "Have mademoiselle and monsieur decided?" he asked with a French accent.

Justin started to give the waiter our order, and I found myself on the verge of a hysterical giggling fit. I picked up my napkin from my lap and held it over my mouth, feeling like a seven-year-old trying not to laugh during a church service.

When the waiter finally walked away, Justin gave me a mock glare. "You were *no* help," he accused me. "I can't take you anywhere."

83

I couldn't help myself. I started to giggle. Within seconds Justin was laughing even louder than I was.

"We have to be *serious,*" I proclaimed. "This is a *serious* establishment." But just looking across the table at Justin was making me giggle.

"You're right," Justin answered. "This is no time for joking around. We're surrounded by sophisticated people eating sophisticated meals . . . consisting of cow intestines."

As I grinned at Justin, I caught sight of a flash of pale pink taffeta in my peripheral vision. I blinked, then turned my head. Madison and Rose were cruising through La Serenara in their pairs of five-inch heels as if they walked the runways in Milan every day.

Whoa. *I forgot they were coming,* I realized. During the last twenty minutes it hadn't occurred to me even once to check the door for the Witch Brigade's grand entrance. I had been having such a good time that I had lost sight of the evening's true mission—to prove to those snobs that I could get the best-looking date ever.

I reached across the table and tapped Justin's forearm. "There are the girls I was telling you about," I whispered. "The ones who inspired me to track you down and beg you to be here tonight."

Justin twisted around in his chair. "Where?"

"Don't look!" I hissed. "Just act like you're in love with me." I paused, realizing that more or less barking at a guy in order to get him to cozy up wasn't the best idea in the world. "Please."

"Gotcha." Justin scooted his chair around the table so that it was next to mine.

The next thing I knew, he had slipped his arm around my shoulders, and he was holding me close. He tilted his head so that his lips were just millimeters from my ear.

"How's this?" he whispered. "Should I actually pull you into my lap—or do you think they're getting the picture?"

Justin's words washed over me like liquid fire. I felt blood rushing to my face at a rate of approximately ten liters per second, and I felt like I wasn't going to be able to breathe for the rest of the night. *It's just nerves,* I assured myself. *You're feeling hypersensitive because this is your big moment with Rose and Madison.*

"This is perfect," I whispered back. "Keep it up."

I shifted my body so that I was resting against Justin's torso, virtually nestled in his arms. Then I gazed across the room until Rose and Madison caught my glance. *Eat your hearts out,* I told them silently, hoping the mental telepathy found its way into their heads.

I watched as each girl studied Justin. *That's right—he's gorgeous.* After several long seconds the girls nudged each other. Madison raised her eyebrows and mimed that she was tipping her hat to me. Rose flashed a discreet thumbs-up sign.

I wanted to glare at the horrible twosome. But I couldn't control the grin that was spreading across my face. I had accomplished my goal. Rose and Madison were admitting defeat, and I had come out on top.

"So, what's the verdict?" Justin asked quietly. "Am I up to par?"

I shifted in my seat again so that I could look him in his eyes. "You're *more* than acceptable," I assured him. "With your help I have successfully avoided having prom night be the worst night of my life."

I wished I had the words to express what that meant to me. For all of high school I had resisted the urge to do whatever stupid things were necessary to "fit in" with the right crowd. I had turned down dates offered by mindless jocks, refused to be drawn into debates about Nike versus Reebok sneakers, and hadn't even been tempted to try out for the cheerleading squad.

But tonight I had shown, in some small way, that I *could* have done any of those things. I had maintained my integrity for four years, and dumb of me not to care, now girls like Rose and Madison were forced to realize that I wasn't a loser. I was just . . . me. Well, I was me *plus* one great date.

"Thank you," I told Justin. "This night means a lot to me—for a lot of different reasons that I won't bore you with."

"You're welcome," he answered. "For a lot of different reasons that I won't bore *you* with."

Huh. *Interesting response,* I noted. I was dying to

ask Justin to expand on his cryptic statement, but I sensed that he didn't want me to pry. And then it came to me. *Duh.* He was referring to Christy.

He's psyched that I'm going to give him an introduction to her—and he probably knows that it won't hurt her opinion of him that he's dressed to the nth degree in that tuxedo.

"Do you want me to go back to my side of the table now?" Justin asked, breaking into my thoughts. "Or should we continue the show for a few more minutes?"

"Um . . . let's let them observe our state of romantic bliss for a little while longer," I suggested. "You know, to make sure they get the point."

"No problem." Justin adjusted his position so that one hand rested on my waist while the other rested lightly against mine on top of the table.

There was simply no getting around it. Every time Justin's skin came into contact with mine, I felt a tingle travel the length of my entire body. This wasn't a case of nerves—it was pure, animal attraction.

Suddenly I didn't care about Madison or Rose or any of their friends. They had stopped being an issue. Now I had a bigger problem than the (now defunct) possibility of being humiliated at the senior prom. A much bigger problem.

I'm falling for Justin, I admitted to myself. And there was zero chance that he would ever return my feelings. The only reason Justin had agreed to go on this nondate was that he wanted the opportunity to meet Christy. He had made it perfectly clear that he never would have been my date just because he *wanted* to be.

The waiter appeared with our escargot, and Justin moved back to his side of the table. My waist and hand felt bare now that his fingers were no longer brushing against my skin.

"It's our moment of truth," Justin commented. "To snail or not to snail, that is the question."

I stifled a huge, dramatic sigh. After years of avoiding dates with total jerks, I had stumbled on a diamond in the proverbial rough. And I couldn't have him.

I glanced at the gray lumps sitting on the tiny plate in front of me. *I know how you guys feel,* I thought. Unwanted, icky, slimy . . . the list went on.

Yes, I had completed the mission I had set for myself. But it wasn't enough anymore. It wasn't *nearly* enough.

Eleven

Nicole

THE PARKING LOT at Union High was almost full by the time Justin and I arrived for the prom. Clearly the entire senior class had decided to show up for this age-old rite of passage.

"I should warn you right now that I'm not the greatest dancer," Justin said as we walked across the parking lot toward the gym. "In fact, my little sister spent half the afternoon trying to give me a crash course."

"That's too bad," I joked. "I'm the Union High lambada champion."

At the door of the gymnasium I handed our prom tickets to Mrs. Learner, the home-economics teacher. "Have a wonderful time," she sang out. "It's a magical night."

I rolled my eyes at her cheesy enthusiasm, but as

we walked into the prom, I had to admit to myself that there *was* something magical about the transformation that the prom committee had executed in the high-school gym.

We were staring at a winter wonderland in the middle of May, complete with twinkling lights, fake snow, and dozens and dozens of red poinsettia plants. The bleachers were gone. In their place were tiny wrought-iron tables with matching chairs. A disco ball hanging from the ceiling bathed the huge room in otherworldly light.

"Nice!" Justin exclaimed. "You guys really know how to throw a party."

"Yeah . . . I guess we do." Not that I could take any of the credit. I would have laughed in the face of anyone who had tried to convince me to help with the prom decorations. But the joke would have been on me. Because this place was amazing.

I led Justin into the crowd, still not quite able to absorb that I was actually here. *I can't believe I almost missed this,* I thought. Now that I could hear the music and the laughter and see the hundreds of beautiful dresses and elegant tuxedos, I realized that the prom really *was* an essential part of the high-school experience. It was sort of a symbol of our impending transition from teenagedom to adulthood.

In a weird way Rose and Madison had done me a huge favor when they had shoved their snobby attitude at me. If those girls hadn't given me the challenge of a lifetime, I never would have taken it upon myself to find a date to the dance. I would have scorned the whole event, then made snide comments when Christy and Jane filled me in on the details on Monday.

But this night beat baby-sitting the Fiedler twins by a mile. True, my feet were already starting to ache, and I was fairly sure that mascara was covering at least half of my face. But it was better than burning my finger on the Fiedlers' toaster oven in a misguided attempt to make the twins s'mores. In fact, it was pretty amazing.

"It feels good to be out!" Justin shouted over the music. "Thank you!"

It feels good to be out? What did that mean, exactly? A guy like Justin was probably out every Friday and Saturday night. I wouldn't have been surprised to learn that ten different girls from ten different schools had asked him to the prom. He was, after all, the African American version of Cinderella's Prince Charming.

But every girl couldn't provide what I could. Justin wanted to meet Christy, and that was why he was here. It was a fact that I was going to have to repeat to myself over and over again for the rest of the night.

And I had every intention of keeping my end of the bargain. Justin had shown up, and he had more than fulfilled his end of our deal. It wasn't as if a corsage and a cuddling session at the restaurant had been part of our contract.

Now it's my job to introduce him to Christy, I realized.

After that, Justin and I would be even. We could go our separate ways, not owing each other a thing. The thought filled me with sadness, but I shoved aside the wistful longing that was washing over me.

I was going to enjoy my evening—even if it wasn't going to end with the hearts and music (and good-night kiss) that would have completed a perfect picture. Being at the prom with Mr. Gorgeous was what I had wanted. And that's what I had gotten. To have expected more would be . . . greedy.

"Nicole!" I heard Jane call my name before I actually caught sight of her. But as she emerged from the crowd, I whistled.

In a sleeveless pale blue silk dress, Jane looked absolutely beautiful. Her blond hair was swept into a French twist, and she wore a choker made of crystals around her long, slender neck.

"You look like a supermodel." I gave her a big hug and grinned at Max, who was standing a few feet away in a black tuxedo.

I still hadn't spotted Christy and her date, Jake, but I had no doubt that they were around here somewhere. And Jane was the ideal source for that particular bit of information.

"So do you," Jane assured me. "And your date ain't half bad either," she added, lowering her voice.

I felt a pang. If only Justin were a real date. Then I would be as radiant as Jane was. Instead I felt like something of a fraud. I was parading Justin around as if he were the love of my life when he was really nothing more than a hired helper.

Behind Jane's shoulder I saw that Justin and Max were introducing themselves to each other. They looked like they were getting along, but I didn't know how much longer Justin would be willing to wait before he expected the big introduction.

"Nicole, how come you never told anyone you had a boyfriend?" Max asked. "Jane and I could have been going on double dates with you guys if you hadn't kept Justin a secret."

"Uh . . . l-long story," I stuttered.

"Why don't we go get the prom queens some sickeningly sweet punch?" Justin suggested to Max. "I still have the taste of snail in my mouth."

"Good idea!" Jane piped up. "Nic and I need to talk. I mean, we need to freshen up our makeup."

"Don't spend all night in the girls' room," Max said, pulling Jane close. "I want to get out on the dance floor and hold you in my arms."

I was practically drooling as I watched Max and Jane exchange a long kiss. *You'd think they were saying good-bye for a month—not ten minutes,* I thought, hating the fact that I was feeling the tiniest bit jealous of their fairy-tale romance.

"I'll, um, see you in a few," Justin said in a way that let me know he was feeling as awkward as I was about viewing this oh-so-public display of affection.

After what seemed like an hour, Jane and Max finally broke apart from each other. Max gave Jane one last, yearning glance, then disappeared into a throng of prom goers with Justin following close behind.

Jane grabbed my arm and pulled me in the direction of the bathroom. "I want to hear everything," she informed me. "And don't leave out one single second of the action."

I sighed. Unfortunately, there wasn't "everything" to tell. In reality, there wasn't *anything* to tell. On the outside, my night was a total triumph. But inside, I was feeling turmoil.

And if I knew Jane as well as I thought I did, then there was almost no doubt that by the end of our imminent girl-to-girl rap session, my emotions were going to be laid out on the bathroom floor in a big, messy heap of confusion. I could hardly wait.

"Max has kissed me so many times tonight that I've already redone my lipstick three times," Jane said giddily as we walked into the packed women's locker room at the far end of the gymnasium. "Uh-oh," she added, turning to me. "I'm being totally sickening again, aren't I?"

I laughed and nodded. "You two are a great couple," I told her. "It's like you were made for each other."

For a brief moment I fantasized that it was Jane who was telling *me* that Justin and I were made for each other. I imagined my coy smile and fluttering eyelashes as I shyly agreed with her assessment. *It must be amazing to find a person who can make you feel like that,* I thought wistfully.

"Tell me all about dinner," Jane ordered, pulling a lipstick out of the tiny pale blue handbag she had

94

bought to go with her dress. "How are things going with you and Mr. Wonderful?"

I uncapped a tube of mascara and leaned close to the mirror. There were globs of black gunk all over my lashes. Whoops. Apparently my makeup job had been far from expert.

"Nicole, I'm dying for details!" Jane insisted. "Tell me about La Serenara—and Justin."

I shrugged, staring at myself in the mirror. "There's nothing to tell. He's a guy, he showed up, Rose and Madison saw us. Mission accomplished."

Jane caught my gaze in the mirror. "That's *it*? Mission accomplished?"

"Yeah. I mean, I guess Justin is nice enough, but he's really not my type." I concentrated on applying a new coat of mascara in order to keep a telltale quiver out of my voice. "To tell you the truth, he's sort of a bore."

Jane finished her fresh lipstick job and stepped away from the mirror. "He's *boring?*" she asked, sounding suspicious. "Justin seems like a lot of things—gorgeous, sweet, funny, charming. But I wouldn't put 'boring' on the list."

"I just spent two hours with the guy, Jane," I replied huffily. "If I say he's boring, he's boring."

"Then how come I could see your toothpaste smile from all the way across the dance floor the second you walked into the prom?" she asked.

I shrugged again. "I don't know. . . . Maybe I was thinking about something funny I saw on TV last night."

My excuses sounded lame even to me. But as soon as I admitted out loud just how much I really did like Justin, my feelings would become real. And that was the last thing I wanted.

Jane gave me one of those looks that said I-don't-believe-a-word-you're-saying-so-don't-even-try-to-lie-to-me. "Well, according to my extrasensory perception, you *do* like Justin," she informed me. "And judging from the way he was looking at you, I think he likes you too. A lot."

I slipped the mascara back into my purse, giving up the idea of achieving the perfect cover-girl lashes. "Can we drop this?" I pleaded. "Justin and I are at the prom together. That's it—end of story."

Jane shook her head. "I don't get it, Nic. You should be totally psyched . . . but you seem upset." She paused. "You're not telling me something—what is it?"

I bit my lip. I wasn't proud of the fact that I had used the promise of meeting Christy to entice Justin to go to the prom with me. So far, I had kept the deal a secret. But it was going to come out eventually. And now seemed like as good a time as any to reveal the bargain I had made with Justin. Besides, telling Jane the truth would definitely put an end to her inquisition.

"Justin didn't agree to go to the prom with me because he actually wanted to be my date," I admitted. "The first time I asked him, he told me no, flat out."

"So?" Jane asked. "That doesn't mean he didn't

change his mind. I mean, he's here, isn't he?"

"He's only here because I promised him something in return for the favor of helping me avert total social ruin."

Jane looked concerned. "What did you promise?"

"I promised that I would introduce him to Christy," I informed her. "Because that's what he wanted. We were standing in front of his high school, and Justin said he would accompany me to the dance on only one condition—that I introduce him to my friend. Then he pointed to Christy."

"Huh." Jane was quiet for a few moments, contemplating this new piece of information. "Well . . . maybe there's an explanation. You could have misinterpreted what Justin meant by that."

I shook my head. "I know what I heard, Jane. He likes Christy—not me."

I tried to ignore the way my guts were twisting into a big, tight knot. This wasn't the time to fall apart because some guy I barely knew didn't think I was the girl of his dreams. I was determined to have a good time tonight—no matter what the circumstances.

"Where is Christy anyway?" I asked Jane, hoping my tone sounded as upbeat as I wanted it to. "I haven't seen her since we got here."

"I don't know," Jane responded. "I haven't seen her since we first arrived."

"Weird. I thought she'd spend all of prom in the bathroom, avoiding Jake. I know she was dreading having to spend the whole evening with the guy."

Christy had made it clear that Jake wasn't boyfriend material. She found him rude, obnoxious, and self-centered. But for some reason that Jane and I hadn't totally figured out, our friend had agreed to go to the prom with the guy anyway.

Jane snapped her fingers. "Hey, I just had a brilliant idea."

"What?" I asked. Maybe she had some new insight into the dubious art of mascara application.

"Why don't you avoid introducing Justin to Christy for as long as possible?" she suggested. "Maybe Justin will fall for you in the meantime."

It was a tempting notion. After all, it wasn't as if Justin and I weren't getting along. He had seemed to enjoy our dinner . . . and he *had* said I looked pretty in my dress.

But no. It wouldn't be right to try to manipulate Justin like that. He had held up his end of the bargain, and it wasn't fair for me to renege on *my* promise. Besides, if Justin had decided he liked me, he could have told me to forget about the introduction to Christy. And he had said no such thing.

Finally I shook my head. "Nope. A deal is a deal."

Jane sighed. "I'm really sorry, Nic. I wish tonight had turned out differently for you."

I smiled. "Hey, it's no big deal," I lied. "Let's get back out there—you've got an appointment to slow dance with your adorable boyfriend."

I followed Jane out of the bathroom, willing myself back into the great mood I had been in at La

98

Serenara. The last thing I wanted was for Justin to sense that his desire to go out with one of my best friends was bringing me down. The whole point of tonight had been to *avoid* embarrassment—not to invite it.

As soon as were outside the locker room, Jane made a beeline for Max. I didn't blame her. This was probably the most romantic night of her life. I, on the other hand, had work to do.

I stood on my tiptoes and scanned the dance floor. After several seconds I finally spotted Christy. She was in the middle of the crowd, dancing with Jake. *Good, I can get this stupid introduction out of the way . . . and at least* try *to enjoy the rest of the night.*

Luckily at the exact moment that I saw Jake and Christy, I noticed that Justin was heading in my direction.

"There you are!" Justin exclaimed, handing me a cup of now lukewarm punch. "I thought you'd decided to ditch me by climbing out of the bathroom window."

I set the punch down on a nearby table and grabbed Justin's hand. "Actually, I've been hard at work," I told him.

He raised his eyebrows. "I don't get it."

"Let's go," I said, pulling Justin toward the dance floor. "I'm about to hold up my end of this bargain." *And it's going to break my heart . . .*

Twelve

Justin

I'M GOING TO *hold up my end of this bargain.* Nicole's words echoed through my brain as she pulled me toward the dance floor. I knew what she was planning to do. Nicole was going to introduce me to Christy, just as I had asked her to do.

But now wasn't the right time. I had noticed Christy dancing with her date as I had been wandering around the prom with Nicole's glass of punch. As soon as I had seen her, I had stood at the edge of the crowd and watched Christy.

She had looked happy and carefree, her hair flying around her head as she danced to a retro seventies tune. And as I found her again with my gaze, I saw that she still looked like she was having a great time. The haunted look in her eyes that I had recognized that day in front of Jefferson

101

High was gone, and she was laughing.

My whole plan has been sort of off, I realized, watching Christy's date dip her almost to the floor. She obviously hadn't recognized me from the hospital. She hadn't even blinked the last two times I had seen her.

And the night of the girl's senior prom wasn't exactly the best time to walk up to her and say, "Hey, I recognize you from the cancer ward. Want to get together and form a support group?"

Nope. Now was not the appropriate time to make Christy's acquaintance. She seemed happy, and I didn't want to remind her of the illness that was undoubtedly the most painful thing in her life. Not now.

I pulled Nicole to a stop, trying not to notice how great her soft hand felt inside mine. *Putting off the introduction to Christy isn't entirely for Christy's sake,* I realized.

"Where are we going?" Nicole asked as I led her back to the edge of the crowd. "Christy is *that* way," she added, pointing toward her friend.

"I just want to talk to you for a second," I explained. "Hold up."

For the first time in a long time I felt like a regular guy. The kind who laughed and danced and gave my date little paper cups filled with nasty fruit punch. It was a foreign sensation. But . . . well, it was *fun.* And I didn't want it to end. Not yet.

"What's wrong?" Nicole asked. "This is your big moment."

102

"I, uh . . ." What was I going to say, exactly? It wasn't as if I had filled Nicole in on *why* I wanted to meet her friend. She was completely in the dark.

"You, uh, *what?*" she asked, sounding more than a little annoyed.

"I noticed that Christy looks pretty involved in what she's doing," I said, gesturing toward the middle of the dance floor, where Christy's date was twirling her around in some kind of swing move. "Maybe now isn't the best time to interrupt her."

Nicole dropped my hand. "Whatever you say, Justin. It's your call."

Why did she sound mad? It was almost as if Nicole couldn't *wait* to get rid of me. *She wants to dump me off on her friend now that I've done my duty,* I thought, feeling strangely let down.

But I wasn't ready to let Nicole off the hook. She had asked me to be her date to the prom, and that's exactly what I was being. Even if the so-called date was more than a little unconventional. I wasn't going to be gotten rid of—not yet anyway.

"Why don't we get out on the dance floor ourselves?" I suggested. "Those girls you were trying to impress would probably think it was pretty weird if you didn't even dance with your date."

Nicole's eyes lit up. "Good point," she proclaimed. "Besides, there's no reason we can't have some fun together. 'No dancing' wasn't written into the bylaws of our agreement."

"So what's it going to be?" I asked. "The foxtrot or the cha-cha-cha?"

Nicole grinned. "I don't think either of those dances is quite right for this tune. Why don't we get out there and let our spirits move us?" she suggested. "But no *Saturday Night Fever* moves. We've got a reputation as the coolest couple at the prom to uphold."

I clasped Nicole's hand in mine again, surprised at how easy it was to talk to her. A lot of girls needed to hear a constant stream of compliments in order to have a good time, but Nicole was all about witty banter and intelligent conversation. It was a nice change from . . . what I had been used to in the past.

We stopped in the middle of the dance floor, directly under the disco ball. "Do you think we're front and center enough?" I asked, semishouting over the band's rendition of "Brick House." "We wouldn't want your 'friends' to miss the show."

"This is a great spot," Nicole assured me. "As long as I don't fall on my butt in front of the entire senior class."

"If either of us hits the floor, we'll make it look like a never-before-seen dance move," I told her.

Just as Nicole and I started to dance, "Brick House" came to an abrupt stop. A moment later the band launched into a version of some slow song that I had heard on the radio but never bothered to pay attention to. *Uh-oh, it looks like we're in for a full-contact dance number,* I thought. Was I ready for this?

Nicole seemed to sense my hesitancy. "Why don't we sit this one out?" she suggested. "This is a song for people on *real* dates."

104

I was torn between wanting nothing more than to slide my hands around Nicole's waist and feeling terrified of what dancing with her *that* way might do to me. But in the next second the decision was made for me. I saw one of the girls from the restaurant staring at us from several yards away.

I didn't even bother to respond to what Nicole had said. I simply stepped forward and took her in my arms. For a split second Nicole looked confused. Then she melted into my embrace, and we began to sway to the soft, sultry music.

"This is nice," Nicole murmured quietly. "I feel like this is the kind of moment the prom was invented for." She paused. "I mean, you know, if I were into that kind of thing."

I nodded, too distracted by the softness of Nicole's skin to reply. I inhaled deeply, absorbing the scent of her perfume, the silky texture of her hair, the delicate fabric of her long, sexy dress. All of my senses had shifted into high gear as I became more and more tantalized by the essence of the girl I held in my arms.

Gently I pulled Nicole even closer, and she rested her head against the lapel of my tuxedo jacket. When was the last time I had felt like this? It had been so long that it was difficult to remember that I had ever been the kind of guy who delighted in the soft touch of a beautiful girl.

The homecoming dance sophomore year with Laurie, I remembered. That was the last time I had allowed myself to be swept away by the presence of another human being. Suddenly images of Laurie washed through my consciousness. I saw her at the school fair, eating cotton candy. And sitting beside me in the car, singing along to the radio.

And then I saw her face—cold, distant, unknowable. In an instant I felt gripped in a familiar sense of pain and longing. *No!* I shouted to myself. *No!*

I took ahold of Nicole's arms and pushed her away. I had to get out of here. I didn't want to be surrounded by smiling faces and shrill laughter. I needed to be alone, away from Nicole.

"I, uh, need to get some air," I told her, already several feet away from her still outstretched arms. "I'll catch up with you later."

I ignored the hurt look on her face and turned away. I pushed my way through the dancing couples, desperate to find that huge steel door that led to freedom—and peace. Striding through the made-over gymnasium, I kept my gaze fixed on the far side of the door. It was imperative that I *not* catch sight of Nicole again.

After what felt like forever but was probably less than forty-five seconds, I found myself in front of the entrance to the prom. I walked straight past the grinning face of the dance chaperon and pushed on the door.

A moment later I was bathed in fresh spring air. The prom seemed a million miles away as I jogged across the parking lot, searching for a quiet place where I could be alone.

I can't believe I did that, I thought, chastising my

106

weakness. For a few minutes—maybe even for a few hours—I had forgotten my promise to myself. I had allowed Nicole to get under my skin, into my brain.

I let myself start to fall for her, I realized, mentally cursing the fact that I had ever agreed to this non-date to the prom. I should have realized the moment I saw Nicole that it would be next to impossible to maintain the cordial-yet-distant air of friendly acquaintances.

I should have recognized the temptation that Nicole Gilmore represented and stayed as far away from her as humanly possible. *But it's not too late to save myself.* I would forget the smell of her hair, the feel of her skin, the bright light of her smile. I would shut those qualities out of my mind, where they would stay buried forever.

I simply couldn't afford to let myself fall for another girl. No matter how much I wanted to.

Thirteen

Nicole

I STOOD IN the middle of the dance floor, staring at the space that Justin had filled just moments ago. What had happened? I felt like I had entered a bizarre alternate universe. One second I had been slow dancing with my date, then the next second he had vanished into thin air.

He hates me, I thought. *I repulse him.* I blinked back tears as I pushed my way through the crowded dance floor. This was the worst. Tonight had been a roller coaster—up and down, up and down, up and down. But I felt like the ride had come to a screeching halt, and my heart had been left on one of the loopity loops.

I had been upset earlier, after I realized that Justin was a great guy who was interested in my friend rather than me. But I had been handling that emotion with a certain amount of dignity. I had told myself that the end of my senior year was a lousy time to fall in love anyway. I had five exams to study for, two papers to write, graduation to prepare for. Who had time for dates?

Had all of my excuses equaled one massive rationalization to keep myself from feeling like a crushed grape? Yes. But those lame excuses had also allowed me to enjoy the evening for what it was—or had been, before Justin bolted.

But I had really started to believe there was something between us, I admitted to myself now. I went over the evidence in my mind. First, Justin had decided that he wanted to wait to meet Christy. Then he had asked me to dance. *Then* he had pulled me close for a slow dance. *And closer, and closer, and closer . . .*

I could still feel the delicious tingle of his arms encircling my body. And when I rested my head against his chest, I had felt like I was dancing on top of a cloud. The image was cheesy, but it was *true*. Justin had brought out sensations in me that I had never before experienced.

And then he had left me standing all alone like a complete idiot. No explanation, no chitchat, no funny one-liner. He had simply fled. In his wake I felt like I had been punched in the gut by a heavyweight-boxing champion.

Well, he wasn't the only one who could be rude. I wasn't going to say another unnecessary word to Justin for the rest of the night. Then again, for all I knew, the night was already officially over. Maybe Justin had jumped into his car and peeled out of the parking lot in an effort to get away from me.

But he wouldn't leave before he gets to meet Christy, I reminded myself. I had accomplished my stated goal, and I had no doubt that Justin wanted to accomplish his. In fact, he was probably outside, figuring out exactly how he was going to charm Christy into falling for him. Maybe that was why he decided to wait a little longer before taking advantage of the big introduction—he had needed time to mentally prepare himself to wow her.

I was almost at the edge of the dance floor when I felt a strong hand take hold of my arm. *Justin! He's back!* My heart leaped, and an unbidden smile (which was more like a huge grin) formed on my face.

I spun around—and found myself face-to-face with a guy who was definitely *not* Justin. My heart sank, and I felt fresh tears threatening to spill over onto my cheeks.

Luckily the guy seemed oblivious to my distress. "Hey, you're Nicole, right?" he asked.

"Yes." Great. Justin had probably given this guy a message for me. *Something polite about how he enjoyed the evening but was suddenly called home to watch a rerun of* Saturday Night Live. "Who are you?"

He smiled. "I'm Doug McGraff," he introduced himself. "We had biology together sophomore year."

"Oh . . . right." I didn't want to be a jerk, but I

wasn't in the mood to reminisce about frog dissection.

"So, do you want to dance?" he asked.

It was the last thing I had expected to come out of his mouth. For a moment I didn't know what to say. Then I took in Doug McGraff's appearance. Over six feet tall, with curly blond hair and bright blue eyes, the guy definitely fell into the hottie category.

I shrugged. "Why not?" Just because Justin didn't realize what a catch I was didn't mean that nobody else had good taste.

Another slow-dance number—something by Celine Dion—was playing. Doug put his arms around me and guided me toward the center of the dance floor. Who knew? Maybe this guy had an alias. Doug McGraff: aka Prince Charming.

"Where's your date?" I asked Doug. If we were going to be dancing cheek to cheek, we might as well get some kind of rapport going.

"I came alone," he explained. "I haven't been dating anyone in particular, so I decided to take my chances that other people's dates wouldn't go as well as they had expected." He gave me a warm smile. "And right about now, I'm thinking I made the right call. I can't think of anyone I'd rather be dancing with than you."

"Thank you," I said, feeling genuinely flattered for the first time in a long time. Doug was turning out to be just the right prescription for my heartache.

As we continued to dance, I forced all thoughts

of Justin out of my brain. *Carpe diem,* I ordered my-self. Seize the day. Doug was the guy that was here, and he was the one who deserved my full attention. Unfortunately, I couldn't think of anything else to say to him.

Suddenly I felt Doug's hot breath in my ear. "You know what would look good on you?" he whispered.

Well, it wasn't a traditional icebreaker, but what the hey. "What?" I asked, tilting back my head to look into his sky blue eyes.

"Me," he answered.

Eeew. It took a moment for me to realize just how disgusting and inappropriate a come-on line that was. *Now I know the* real *reason the guy doesn't have a date,* I thought.

"You know what would look good on *you?*" I retorted.

He grinned, obviously not getting the fact that I wasn't digging his brand of wit. "Tell me," he said smugly. "What would look good on me?"

I stepped away from Doug and dropped my arms. "A glass of punch," I informed him. "Unfortunately, I don't have one at the moment—which is why I'm going to leave you standing here while I head for the refreshment table."

I strode away, wishing that Justin had been around to hear my snappy comeback. He would have gotten a kick out of it. *Not that it matters,* I reminded myself.

So much for Prince Charming. Doug had

turned out to be a lower form of life than those frogs we had dissected in biology class. The guy had turned out to be as big a jerk as the rest of the ones I had encountered during my four years of high school. Big surprise!

This evening has gone from great to bad to worse in the space of fifteen minutes, I thought. It was time to put myself out of my misery. Who wanted to spend another two hours circulating the gym, looking for moron after moron to dance with?

I wanted to cut my losses and get home as quickly as possible. If Rose and Madison noticed that I had been ditched by my so-called date, they would have fresh ammunition with which to torture me. *Now* that *would be the perfect end to a perfect evening,* I thought dismally.

I scanned the dance floor, searching for a sign of Christy. I wanted to introduce Justin to my friend and get this whole thing over with. As far as I was concerned, the clock had struck midnight, and I had turned back into a pumpkin.

"Christy, where *are* you?" I wondered aloud. I hadn't talked to her once since I had arrived at the prom—she was like a phantom tonight.

I continued across the winter wonderland of a gym, keeping my eyes peeled for either of my two best friends. Christy, apparently, was hiding in some dark corner. But I spotted Jane and Max next to the stage the band had set up. They weren't even making a show of dancing. They were simply standing in one place and making out, seemingly

114

unaware that they were surrounded by hundreds of people.

"Sorry to interrupt, Janie," I murmured under my breath. "But I'm getting desperate."

I walked up to Jane and Max, then tapped Jane lightly on the shoulder. When she went right on smooching Max, I tapped again—harder this time.

Finally Jane turned around. "Hey, Nic!" She peered over my shoulder. "Where's Justin?"

"He's either in the parking lot, the bathroom, or halfway home," I informed her. "But assuming he's still somewhere in the vicinity, I need to find Christy. It's an emergency."

"Sorry, I saw Christy leave a few minutes ago," Jane responded, her eyes filled with empathy.

I groaned. Wonderful! Now what was I supposed to do?

Fourteen

Justin

SITTING ON THE empty bleachers beside the Union High football field, I looked out into the dark night and tried to clear my head of all negative thoughts. I focused on the sound of crickets chirping, the distant hum of laughter, the bright stars in the inky black sky.

But I have to think about bad stuff, I told myself. It was imperative that I remember all of the totally sane reasons why I didn't want to get involved with another girl. Otherwise . . . I didn't want to think about otherwise.

Besides, I didn't even know how Nicole felt about me. True, I had felt some definite chemistry when we had been dancing. And I had made her laugh approximately thirteen times over the course of the evening (not that I was counting). Then

117

there was that misty, soulful look in her eyes when I had caught her gaze over chocolate mousse at La Serenara. . . .

"Stop it!" I ordered myself aloud. "Stop thinking about Nicole like that."

Instead I pictured Laurie Swanson, the first— and only—girl I had ever fallen in love with. She was petite, with short, short hair and chocolate brown skin. And when she had looked at me with her almond-shaped eyes, I had felt like I was melting into a huge puddle of butter. I blinked at the image. Thinking of my ex-girlfriend was painful, but necessary.

I had met Laurie the first day of our freshman year at Jefferson High. I had come to Jefferson from JFK Junior High, and Laurie had come from North Junior High. We had accidentally been assigned the same locker, and the moment our hands had met at the dial of the combination lock, I had fallen deeply, irrevocably in love.

Or so I had thought. I had learned the hard way that love didn't last forever. If Laurie had *ever* loved me. She had certainly *acted* like she had. But maybe that's all it had been—an Oscar-worthy performance. And I had been the straight man, believing every word she uttered, like the fool that I was.

But the two years Laurie and I were together had been wonderful. We were inseparable, the kind of couple people referred to as JustinandLaurie, as if we were one person. There had been movies, study dates, walks in the park. We had eaten lunch together every day in the cafeteria, and we had even arranged our school schedules so that we could have as many classes together as possible.

Back then, I had been a different person. The Justin Banks people knew *before* had been outgoing, social, funny. I had been the first guy to suggest throwing a huge Halloween party and the last one to view the world through a lens of cynicism or pessimism.

Everything in my life had started to fall apart the day I was told that my mom was sick—*really* sick. She had been diagnosed with breast cancer, and doctors immediately ordered a mastectomy and a powerful course of chemotherapy. The news had been more devastating than anything I ever could have imagined, and I turned immediately to Laurie for the love and support I needed to get through every day of watching my mother suffer.

At first Laurie had been there for me. She had held my hand, hugged me, even allowed me to cry bitter tears on her shoulder. She had been the one person in the world with whom I had shared the extent of my pain. With everyone else I kept up a brave front. Mom was dealing with enough, and I had wanted to stay strong for Dad and Star.

And then, so slowly at first that I hadn't even noticed, Laurie started to pull away. She avoided coming over to our house, and our time together dwindled to the point that I would go a whole weekend without hearing from her.

On the morning that we checked my mom into

the hospital, I had shown up unannounced at Laurie's door, hoping to escape from the sadness that had become my life for just a few hours. But Laurie hadn't been happy to see me.

The moment I had looked into her eyes, I had felt cold all over. Laurie had asked me to come inside, then invited me to sit down on the sofa in her family's formal living room rather than in the den where we usually hung out for hours on end. She had perched at the edge of a Victorian-style ottoman, and she had looked like she was sitting in the dentist's office, waiting to go in for a root canal.

In her sweet, melodious voice Laurie had told me that she thought it would be better if we were just friends. She said she needed time and space to "find herself." But I had known the *real* reason for the breakup. Cancer. She didn't want to deal with the pressures of having a boyfriend with a sick mother. And worse, she didn't want to have to cope with the inevitable end of that illness.

As the memories washed over me, I stood up and made my way down the bleachers. If I was going to think about this stuff, I needed to be on the move. Otherwise I might just hang my head and sob. I headed back toward the parking lot, focusing on putting one foot in front of the other as I remembered those dark months.

I had left Laurie's house that day for the last time, feeling like my entire world had been turned upside down. Until that moment I think I had held out hope that somehow, some way Mom would pull through. But everything came crashing down around me as I realized that life wasn't the rosy prospect I had always believed it to be. Girlfriends broke hearts . . . and mothers . . . died.

From that day on, life had become a downward spiral. Mom's health had deteriorated day by day until the last flicker of hope that she would recover was extinguished. Aside from the bright moments I spent laughing with my mother at her bedside, I was engulfed in sadness.

Sam had tried to help, but I hadn't been able to let him get close. I wasn't used to talking to other guys about something so emotionally devastating. Talking about basketball and watching *The Shield* reruns was a lot different from confessing one's deepest fears about the future. Letting go in front of Sam simply hadn't been in my nature—at least, not back then.

When my mom died at the end of a long stay in the hospital, I felt completely and utterly alone. I had felt like I was a robot going through the motions of life without connecting to anyone or anything. Laurie had shown up at my mom's funeral, but the words we had exchanged had been awkward and distant. If anything, seeing Laurie that day made me feel even worse than I already had.

In the weeks that followed my mother's death, I had resolved to myself that I would never trust and depend on another girl the way I had Laurie. Never let another girl get under my skin. I reserved my love for my dad and Star, the two people in the world who needed me the most.

And for over a year I had avoided any romantic situation with a ten-foot pole. And so far, my plan had worked. But tonight I couldn't help wondering . . . was it possible that Nicole was different?

Nicole was so *real,* so open, so honest. I couldn't imagine her acting the way Laurie had, no matter what tough situation she was confronted with. Then again, a vow was a vow. . . .

My thoughts stopped midstream as I noticed a girl rushing out of the door of the gymnasium. I was still halfway across the parking lot, but I recognized Christy immediately. Something instinctive made me quicken my pace. I jogged toward prom central, keeping my eyes glued on Christy's advancing figure.

As I got closer, I saw that tears were running down Christy's cheeks, and her skin was so pale that she looked almost like a ghost. *Now,* I thought. *Now is the time to talk to her.*

I rushed forward. "Christy?" I called out.

She stopped. "Hey . . . Justin, right?" She was drying her eyes as she spoke and clearly attempting a weak smile.

"Right." I paused, not knowing exactly how to proceed. "Do you, uh, want to tell me what's wrong?" I asked hesitantly.

"Nothing's wrong," she responded, her voice overly bright. "Everything is just fine."

I knew she was lying. And I was fairly sure that she knew I knew she was lying. What she didn't know—or at least remember at the moment—was that I understood what she was going through.

Despite the long, black, strapless dress and strappy high heels, Christy looked like a lost child. My heart went out to her, just as it had the day I had spotted her in Claire's Boutique.

"Christy, you and I have actually met once before," I explained. "Well, not officially, but your face has stuck with me ever since."

I had to talk to her. With every passing moment I was more sure that Christy's tears were related to her mother's illness. And it was imperative that I reach out . . . that I try to lend my support in any way I could.

She looked confused. "We met? Where? At the mall?"

I shook my head. "No, at the hospital. We were both in the waiting room of the cancer ward. My mom was sick too."

"Oh," she responded softly, recognition slowly dawning in her eyes. "Right."

"Are you crying because of your mom?" I asked gently. "You can tell me. Really."

"Yes," Christy whispered. The tears began to flow again, and she pulled a rumpled Kleenex from her tiny silk purse.

"Is it bad?" I asked. "Has she gotten worse?"

Christy nodded, dabbing her eyes with the Kleenex. "I appreciate your concern, Justin. I really do."

"But . . . ?" I asked.

"But please don't tell anyone that you saw me—especially that you saw me crying. I know my friends care about me, but I'm not ready to share my feelings." She took a deep, steadying breath. "I don't want anyone's pity. I just can't handle that right now."

"I won't tell the others," I promised without hesitation. "You can trust me."

I knew from personal experience that each person handled something like a parent's illness in his or her own way. It wasn't my place to tell Christy what she did or didn't need. All I could do was let her know that she wasn't alone.

"Thanks, Justin," she responded. "I just . . ."

"You don't have to explain," I assured her. "Remember, I've been there."

"Your mom . . . didn't make it?" she asked. But I could see in her eyes that she already knew the answer to that question.

"No, she died last year," I told Christy, feeling the same deep ache I felt every time I said that sentence out loud.

"I'm so sorry, Justin—"

"I'm okay," I interrupted, not wanting to put Christy in the position of having to comfort *me* at a time like this. "It gets easier to deal with every day."

She nodded mutely. "Well, I had better go . . . but thanks for talking to me. It helped."

I took the stub of my prom ticket out of the inside pocket of my tuxedo and handed it to Christy. I had written my phone number on the back of it earlier in the evening before I had realized that pushing myself on her when she was having a good time wasn't such a bright idea.

"Promise that you'll call me if you ever want to talk," I said to Christy. "I really do know what you're going through."

Christy smiled. A real smile this time. "I just might take you up on that, Justin."

I watched as she turned and headed across the parking lot. Well, I had done it. I had met Christy and offered her my support. There was nothing more I could do, at least not right now.

I walked toward the door of the gymnasium. Now that I had faced some of my demons, it was time to go back inside and find Nicole. She was either having a great time dancing with some other guy—or she was mad that I had stranded her on the dance floor. Or both.

Just as I was about to enter the prom, none other than Nicole herself walked out of the gym. "Hey," I greeted her. "I was just about to come inside and find you."

She raised her eyebrows. "I wasn't sure you were still on the premises," she said icily.

Oops. She *was* mad. "Listen, I didn't mean to rush off like that," I apologized. "I just needed to get some air."

She held up one hand to silence me. "Don't worry about it, Justin."

"Okay—"

"Here's the thing," she interrupted. "It's over. The night is a failure."

125

Fifteen

Nicole

I STARED AT Justin, my hands on my hips, and waited for him to respond to my statement that the night was a categorical flop. But he didn't say anything. Justin was just looking at me like I was crazy.

"Why is the night a failure?" he asked finally. "What happened?"

Justin was so mellow, so sweet, looking at me with real concern. It was hard to ignore the feelings that had been stirring inside me all evening. *Remember that you're mad at him,* I ordered myself.

"Christy left the prom already," I explained. "I went to find her, and Jane said she left a few minutes ago." Justin didn't look particularly disappointed. Maybe he didn't get what I was saying. "So I can't introduce you to her tonight," I said, spelling out the problem. "I can't hold up my end of the bargain."

"Oh, well," Justin responded mildly. *"C'est la vie."*

Jeez. Justin was one surprise after another. The guy who had flat out refused to go to the prom with me—until I had promised him a chance with my friend—now seemed totally unperturbed by the fact that he had wasted his time.

Don't read anything into this, I told myself. *He's just being nice.* Justin wasn't the type to throw a tantrum or do anything that resembled rudeness (aside, of course, from leaving me in the middle of the dance floor for no apparent reason).

"We can go now," I announced. "You've done more than your part tonight."

Justin was silent for a moment, then he grinned. "Why don't we hang out for a while longer?" he suggested. "The band is playing good music. We could take another stab at dancing."

"I don't know. . . ." Justin was an enigma—one I doubted I would ever fully understand. *Not that I'll have the chance.* Cold, hot, warm, cool, hot, cold. I never knew exactly where he was coming from.

"Come on, Nicole," he urged. "It would be a shame to waste our finery when there's still so much of the night left."

Time seemed suspended as I considered what Justin had said. There was a big part of me that wanted to leave the prom this very minute. The less time I spent with Justin, the better. I knew, deep inside, that the more hours I passed in his company,

128

the more I would fall for him. And I didn't want to step knowingly into a minefield of disappointment. Not when I was this close to finishing my senior year without the complication of having fallen for the wrong guy.

But there was another voice inside me. The one that had made me track down Justin and beg him to go to the prom with me. Sure, I had pledged to avoid social ruin by bringing the hottest guy I had ever seen to the dance. But it wasn't as if I were the kind of person who would lose sleep over a couple of members of the Witch Brigade making fun of me. There had been some essential part of my being that had *needed* to go to the prom.

There was also some essential part of my being that found the prospect of spending another few hours with Justin totally and completely irresistible. The guy of my dreams was standing right in front of me, and I wanted to be with him more than anything else in the world. *Hey, we'll always have the prom,* I thought, already resigning myself to the heartache that would inevitably follow this evening.

"Okay," I agreed at last. "Let's stay."

Justin smiled and held out his arm for me to take. "Madam, your chariot awaits."

I took his arm, unable to resist the urge to laugh. I was Cinderella again, back at the ball. Now all I needed was a real-life fairy godmother to sprinkle me with magic dust and tell me that I was going to get everything I wanted.

★　　★　　★

Two hours later my feet were in considerably worse condition, but my mood had improved by about a hundred times. Justin and I had danced together to a dozen pounding rock tunes, laughing, twirling, and shaking like all of the other couples at the prom. At one point we had even formed an impromptu (and ridiculous-looking) conga line with Max and Jane.

A few weeks ago I wouldn't have believed that I could have so much fun engaging in such stereotypically teenage activities. Now I couldn't imagine having stayed home or having passed the night building up my meager savings with a baby-sitting job. Whatever I had spent (and I shuddered when I thought of the total dollar amount) was more than worth it. Tonight a whole new side of Nicole Gilmore had decided to stand up and be counted.

"If I drink one more glass of this punch, my blood-sugar level is going to be too high for me to drive legally," Justin commented.

"Maybe we can find a cup of coffee and try to bring you down," I suggested.

We were standing near the refreshment table (which was now strewn with crushed paper cups and cookie crumbs), taking a break from dancing. The crowd had thinned out, and the floor was littered with bedraggled decorations.

Justin ladled himself another glass of the neon pink punch. "Then again, I like to live dangerously."

I smiled, trying in vain to ignore all of the subtle (and not so subtle) signs that the prom was almost over. I wished it would go on forever so that I wouldn't have to say good night—and good-bye—to Justin.

"Ladies and gentlemen, you've been a great audience," the band leader announced from the stage. "We've got one more tune for you. Pair up and cuddle up—it's gonna be a slow one."

Pair. Cuddle. Slow. Those key words echoed through my brain, and my heart started to pound. Justin and I hadn't danced to any ballads since he had come back inside. And I wasn't about to put my dignity on the line by asking him to dance to this one. If he said no, I wouldn't be able to handle it.

My heart actually skipped a beat as I watched him set down his full cup of punch on the table. My mouth was so dry that I wasn't sure I would be able to speak when Justin turned to me.

"May I have the last dance?" he asked, his gaze so intense that I felt like he was looking straight into my soul.

"Uh, yeah. I mean, yes, of course. Prom wouldn't be prom without the infamous last dance."

Justin took my hand and led me into the middle of what was left of the crowd. Once again we were face-to-face under the disco ball. Hopefully Justin wouldn't bolt in the middle of the song this time.

He placed a hand on each side of my waist and pulled me close. "I'm glad it's a slow one," he said softly. "I was, um, getting pretty tired."

"Same here," I responded. But the fact that I

131

was happy about the tune being a ballad had nothing to do with being tired.

As we started to move to the music, small shivers traveled up and down my spine. I never knew that a guy's hands could feel so good. Justin's fingers brushed against the soft, tender skin on the underside of my wrist, and I felt a tingle that was more like the spark of a firecracker.

I can't breathe, I thought. *Yes, I can. No, I can't.* I struggled to focus on the music and the other couples on the dance floor. Anything to distract me from the tantalizing feel of Justin's arms around me.

"I guess there's a reason why people get so excited about the prom," Justin said. "Until tonight I couldn't understand why anyone would want to subject themselves to this kind of thing."

"I know what you mean," I answered. Did that mean Justin was glad he came along, despite the fact that he hadn't actually gotten to meet Christy? "I'm glad Rose and Madison acted the way they did. Otherwise I would have stayed home tonight."

I couldn't believe I had just admitted that. I wasn't one of those girls that babbled every thought that came into her head. And I'd had no intention of telling Justin that the night had come to mean more than a dare to me. But . . . well, looking into his eyes, it was hard not to be totally honest.

A companionable silence fell between us. For some amount of time that was either less than a minute or forever, we simply swayed to the soft sounds of the music. I sighed contentedly, wishing I could fall asleep right here in Justin's warm, safe arms.

Justin cleared his throat. "Nicole, I really want to thank you," he said. "I haven't had an evening like this in a long time."

Okay, *now* I couldn't breathe. For real. Or speak. I wasn't even sure if my ears were working right. I must have imagined the husky tone in Justin's voice.

"I, uh, you're welcome." I could have shut my mouth and let it go at that. But I was compelled to press on. "What do you mean?"

He didn't answer right away, and I thought that perhaps I had just thought those last words rather than speaking them out loud. "It's just . . . well, I forgot how much fun it is to dance and laugh and . . . just hang out with somebody besides my friend Sam."

I closed my eyes. I hadn't been imagining the husky tone in his voice. I had heard it again, and this time I was positive. *Please, let him be talking to me the way a guy talks to a girl he's really into,* I pleaded with the universe.

But I couldn't let down my defenses. I wasn't going to fall into that trap. Especially since I had spent the last several hours convincing myself that I could say good-bye to Justin without regrets. If I started to believe that there was the tiniest possibility that he had feelings for me . . . it would all be over.

"I'm sorry you didn't get more face time with

Christy," I said tentatively. "I know that's the only reason you agreed to come tonight."

I held my breath, praying with every fiber of my being that Justin would lean forward and whisper in my ear that he didn't care if he *ever* met Christy. I wanted him to take my face in his hands and kiss me, right here under the disco ball. *I don't even care if Rose and Madison are watching,* I thought. *This kiss would be for me and me alone.*

Justin shrugged (as well as he could with my arms wrapped around his neck). "Don't worry about it," he said easily. "I'll catch up with Christy another time. I'm sure of it."

I exhaled, and as the breath left my lungs, so did all of the good feelings I had been storing inside myself for the last few hours. That was that. I didn't need to hear anything else to know that nothing had changed between the time I had approached Justin yesterday afternoon and now.

Okay, one thing had changed. I was no longer just the bizarre stranger who had accosted Justin outside his high school. Now I was something of a buddy, a pal, a *compadre*. Maybe Justin would want to hang out and watch a baseball game together or share a basket of cheese fries at the food court in the mall. Or, even worse, maybe Justin would want to double date. He and Christy, and me and some nameless, faceless jerk.

But he hasn't forgotten about Christy. Not for a second. My heart was in the soles of my feet as the band finished the song. As soon as the last strum of the guitar faded into silence, the blaring lights of the gymnasium came up.

The winter wonderland was gone. In its place was a colossal mess. Even the disco ball now seemed totally out of whack with the rest of the gym. Couples were streaming out of the prom as chaperons walked around and picked up empty cups and discarded paper plates.

The fairy tale was officially over. I felt my face getting hot, and there was a tremendous squeezing sensation in my chest. Oh no! I knew what was coming. Any moment now tears would start to run down my cheeks.

"I'll meet you outside," I told Justin, my voice barely more than a squeak. I couldn't just stand there like my heart hadn't been flattened into a crepe. I had to get away from Justin.

Before Justin had a chance to say anything, I turned and raced across the floor of the gymnasium. I was too proud to run, so I executed a sort of race walk that I'd seen middle-aged women in my neighborhood doing every morning.

Don't cry, I ordered myself. *Not now.* But as I continued to speed across the floor, one tear and then another slid down my face. I couldn't help it. This level of misery couldn't be contained within a pair of dry eyes.

I broke out of the fast walk and began to run. But as I neared the door of the gym, I tripped on the hem of my long, stupid dress. "Ouch!" I yelped, falling to my knees.

I stood up quickly, hoping no one had seen me. But as I started to move again, I realized that something was wrong. My legs weren't working quite right. I lifted the hem of my dress and looked down. Perfect! The heel of one of my shoes had broken off.

Gwen is going to kill me, I thought. This was her favorite pair of shoes. But I didn't stop to look for the missing heel. I couldn't. I had to get out to the parking lot as quickly as possible—and as far ahead of Justin as possible.

I needed at least a minute alone to pull myself together before Justin drove me home. I was upset enough as it was. I didn't need the added humiliation of having Justin see me so emotional.

At last I reached the parking lot. The air had cooled, but it was still a beautiful night. I slipped off both of my shoes and walked slowly toward the car, catching my breath as I swung the ruined heels at my side.

I inhaled deeply, willing myself to find that calm, distant room in my head. The one that was safe and closed and protected from the outside world. *You're all right, Nicole,* I told myself. *You don't need anyone.*

I took one last deep breath. I had gone from deep depression to a sort of numbness. At least for now. But all I needed was to get through the next twenty minutes. Once I got home, I would be free to sob into my pillow until I turned thirty.

It was strange. I had thought tonight was all about the Witch Brigade and their evil attitude. But it had turned out that the night had been about me . . . and the fact that I was fundamentally unlovable.

136

Sixteen

Justin

I FOUND NICOLE in the parking lot, waiting by the side of my car. She didn't exactly light up when she saw me coming.

"Hey," I greeted her. "Why did you rush off?"

She shrugged. "I was ready to get out of there. Once the lights came up, the place looked like a winter *wasteland*. It was depressing."

Okay. Apparently Nicole didn't like bright lights. Or maybe she wasn't being totally honest. There was always the possibility that Nicole had been afraid that one of the chaperons was going to recruit her to help clean up the totally trashed gymnasium. More than one of them had suggested to me on my way out that I could stay for the "cleanup party."

"Well, Max and Jane asked us to wait a few

minutes before we take off," I informed her. "Jane wanted to say good-bye to you."

Nicole opened the passenger-side door of the car. "Jane can call me tomorrow. I'm tired."

All righty, then, I thought, unnerved by Nicole's 180-degree change of attitude. Had I done something wrong? Or did Nicole magically turn into a shrew when the clock struck midnight?

I slid into the driver's seat and started the car. I had been planning to ask Nicole if she would let me take her out for a late-night cup of coffee, but clearly that was a bad plan. She wasn't hiding the fact that she wanted to rid herself of my company ASAP.

"Thanks again for tonight," I said pleasantly, hoping her bad mood was a passing phenomenon. "I had fun." I pulled out of the parking lot and started toward the Gilmores' house.

Nicole sighed deeply, settling into her seat. "I broke one of my heels," she announced. "But it's not *my* heel. It's my sister, Gwen's, heel."

"That's too bad." I switched on the radio and turned the dial, searching for a station playing some kind of soothing, classical music. "Maybe you can get it fixed."

She shook her head. "I *can't* get it fixed because I lost the stupid heel. Okay?"

"Okay." Man. This girl had some serious personality issues. One would have thought that *I* had broken her shoe.

Nicole sighed again—this time it was sort of a

resigned, tired, I-know-I-was-just-really-rude-but-I-don't-want-to-say-I'm-sorry kind of a sigh. "Listen, Justin, I appreciate your concern. But there's nothing you can do, so why don't we just drop it?"

"Good idea." I didn't have much to say on the subject of women's shoes anyway. Nor was I much good at coaxing girls out of a weird state of mind.

Nicole closed her eyes, and the conversation was officially over. Just like the prom. I stared straight ahead at the road, trying to figure out what was going on. Nicole just didn't seem like the sort of person whose life fell apart over a broken heel. And from what she had said about her sister during dinner, I doubted that Gwen was really going to give her that hard a time about it.

So what is it? I asked myself. I was in a state of utter confusion, and I had no idea how I was supposed to wade through that confusion to figure out what was going on. I glanced over at Nicole. Her eyes were still closed, and she looked a million miles away.

I shouldn't even be wasting my time thinking about this, I realized. It wasn't as if I wanted to go out with Nicole. Her bad mood simply wasn't my problem to cope with. She could be a grouch for the rest of her life—it meant nothing to me.

After what seemed like the longest ride since man first flew to the moon, I finally turned onto Nicole's street. "Wake up, sleepyhead," I said. "We're almost there."

She opened her eyes but didn't bother to respond.

I pulled up in front of the Gilmores' house and turned off the car so that I could walk Nicole to the door. But before I even had the chance to undo my seat belt, Nicole had opened her car door and jumped out.

"Wait!" I called. But Nicole was already heading toward the front path that led to her front door. "I guess you don't want me to walk you to the door," I said softly.

What if her parents are watching from the window? I thought. *They'll think I'm the rudest date in history.*

I didn't want to care. But I did. Nicole's attitude hurt. I had thought we were becoming friends, but she obviously didn't agree. I got out of the car anyway, determined to say a proper good night. Maybe Nicole was comfortable ignoring the niceties—but I wasn't.

By the time I started up the front path, she was already sliding her key into the lock of the front door. "Thanks again, Justin," she called.

"You're welcome," I called back. "But I'm the one who should be thanking you."

The door opened, and Nicole slipped into the house. So much for attempting the niceties. I stopped in my tracks. As I was about to turn back to the car, Nicole stuck her head out of the doorway.

"And I really am sorry I didn't get you your big 'date' with Christy!" she added.

A date? I had never wanted a *date* with Christy. I just wanted to offer her an ear. Obviously Nicole had misunderstood my intentions.

"Nicole, I—"

"Good night," she interrupted. A moment later the door slammed shut.

Well, that's that. Good-bye, prom. Good-bye, Nicole. This morning I had wanted nothing more than for this evening to come to a merciful end. Now I felt totally deflated.

And sad. Nicole Gilmore had disappeared from my life as quickly as she had entered it. Absurdly, I felt like a part of me had vanished too.

"Juuuustinnn!" Star's voice penetrated my unconscious, and I pried open my eyes. Light was streaming in through the window, and the clock beside my bed read 9:12 A.M. "Justtttiiiiin!"

I had been having a dream. Something about circus elephants and house cats wearing prom dresses and broken high-heeled shoes. *I'm getting weirder as I get older,* I noted.

And then it all came back to me. The prom. Nicole. Meeting Christy. Nicole basically refusing to speak to me in the car on the way home. The whole night ran through my mind on ultra-fast-forward in vivid Technicolor.

"I'll be down in a minute!" I shouted to Star. Since Mom died, we had made a habit of fixing a big Sunday morning breakfast together every week.

Now I know why I'm so tired and groggy, I thought. I had lain awake most of the night, going over every detail of the night in my head. I had tried everything to fall asleep—counting sheep, pacing the floor, even drinking a little warm milk (which was disgusting). But every time I closed my eyes, another image from the evening would pop into my head.

I pulled on a pair of sweatpants and one of my softest, oldest T-shirts. I was going to eat breakfast, read the paper, maybe go for a jog. Once I got back into my routine, I would forget all about the whirlwind of emotions I had experienced last night. My strange, early morning dreams had been my way of putting a period at the end of the whole event. I had been expunging all extraneous memories from my subconscious.

Walking out of my room, I inhaled deeply, absorbing the aroma of pancakes emanating from the kitchen. Great! A stack of pancakes topped with Star's special peanut-butter-and-banana spread was exactly what I needed to dissipate that nagging feeling of disappointment that was refusing to go away.

"It's about time," Star said the moment I walked into the kitchen. "Did you stay out all night or something?"

"Nooo," I responded. "I just wanted to sleep in for a while. Sue me."

Star raised her eyebrows with the kind of avidly curious expression that only a sixth-grade girl can muster. "I thought you would be in a better mood after your big date!"

"Who said I'm in a bad mood?" I asked, taking over at the griddle. "It's a beautiful morning. Hey, where's Dad, anyway?"

And if you want to know about bad moods, talk to Nicole, I added silently. I flipped a couple of pancakes, then slid them onto a plate. Star took the plate and went to work with the peanut butter and bananas.

"He went to get a newspaper," she explained. So?" she added, spreading the peanut butter an inch thick. "How was the prom? Are you in love?"

I laughed. "In love? Of course not!"

Star added some bananas to her creation. "Well, do you at least *like* her?" she asked.

I thought for a moment. Of course, I *liked* Nicole. Aside from the fact that she had decided she hated me at the end of the night, she was the perfect girl.

"Yes, I like her," I said finally. "She's a great person."

I only had to look into Star's eyes for a split second to know that she was far from done with the game of twenty questions. She had probably spent most of last night composing a list of everything she wanted to know about my experience at the Union High senior prom.

Might as well give her the breakdown of the entire evening, I thought. I would never get out of this kitchen otherwise.

"We had an awesome time," I declared. "Nicole took me to this really fancy restaurant. We ate snails and made fun of the waiters, and Nicole pretended for a while that she didn't speak English."

I laughed at the memory. The girl was nuts! I

143

could still see the confused look on the busboy's face when Nicole tried to ask him for another glass of water in a made-up language. Star started to laugh too.

"She sounds funny," Star proclaimed. "I think I'd like her."

I nodded. "You would. Man, *she* could help you shop for a dress. You should have seen what she was wearing. . . . She looked beautiful."

Then again, Nicole would look beautiful in denim shorts and a ripped sweatshirt, I thought. She had the cheekbones of an Egyptian goddess.

"What about the prom itself?" Star asked. "Were the decorations nice? Did you dance? Did you meet any cool people?"

"Yeah, the Union High gym looked pretty amazing," I told her, remembering the thousands of tiny lights, the huge disco ball, and the pretty little tables. "Nicole suggested we try to start a pickup game of basketball to see if anyone would abandon the dance floor for the hoops."

"Did you slow dance?" Star pressed. "Was it romantic?"

Yes, it was romantic, I thought. But I wasn't about to tell Star what it felt like to hold Nicole in my arms. There were some things a guy needed to keep to himself. And that was definitely one of them.

"We danced," I said casually. "After all, it was the *prom.*"

"You know, for a guy who isn't in love, you're talking an awful lot about Nicole," Star commented.

144

"Are you guys going to go on another date?" she asked as I handed her another plate of pancakes.

I groaned. "Star, you ask way too many questions," I told her. "And for your information, no, we're *not* going out again."

But she was right. I was sort of going on and on about Nicole. But that was just because it had been so long since I'd been out with a girl. Just because I had sworn off girls didn't mean I wasn't a normal guy with normal desires. That didn't mean I had to *act* on those desires. I knew better.

"Besides, Nicole totally turned on me at the end of the night," I continued. "She would barely talk to me in the car on the way home. One second we were dancing . . . and the next thing I knew, she, like, hated me." I paused. "But who cares? It wasn't a real date."

"I don't get it." Star frowned at the jar of peanut butter. "How could going to the prom with somebody not be a *date?* That's, like, the *definition* of a date."

I shook my head. "Not in our case." I poured another ladle full of batter onto the griddle and watched tiny bubbles appear on the pancake. "You're too young to understand. Why don't you just forget it?"

Her eyes flashed, and she put her hands on her hips. I wanted to laugh. In her ice-cream-cone-patterned pajamas, my little sister was hardly threatening. But I knew that if even one giggle escaped, I would have a very angry sixth-grader on my hands.

"Why don't *you* just explain why it wasn't a real date?" she demanded. "I'm not a little kid, you know. I have *insights*."

This time I couldn't help myself. I laughed out loud. "Okay, Miss Know-it-all, I'll explain why it wasn't a *real* date," I relented.

She finished the second plate of pancakes and set them on the table. "Do you remember a girl with long brown hair from the hospital?" I asked, sitting down across from Star. "She was in the waiting room of the cancer ward a couple of times."

Star furrowed her brow. "I think so . . . but I'm not sure. It's hard to remember anything about that time except for how sick Mom was."

I nodded, and we were both quiet for a moment . . . remembering. "Well, her name is Christy, and she's a friend of Nicole's," I explained. "I recognized her at the mall that day you were on the endless hunt for the perfect dress."

"I remember," Star told me through a mouthful of pancakes.

"When Nicole asked me to the prom, I said no at first," I admitted. "But then I saw that Christy was with her, waiting by the car."

Star gulped half her glass of orange juice, then looked at me with confusion in her eyes. "So . . . you really wanted a date with Christy?"

"No! I didn't want a date with *anybody*." I couldn't believe I was discussing this stuff with my little sister. Sam would have been laughing his head off if he had been around for this conversation. "I wanted to meet Christy and offer her some help," I explained. "I mean, I know what it's like to have a sick mom—and there was something in her face. . . . I could tell that her mom wasn't doing well."

"The Look," Star said quietly. She was young, but she knew a lot about pain. Too much.

"So I told Nicole that I would go to the prom with her on one condition. She had to introduce me to Christy."

Star took another bite of her pancakes, studying my face as she chewed. Finally she swallowed. "Justin, it's obvious you have a crush on Nicole."

"I—"

"Let me talk!" she interrupted, waving her fork in my face. "As I was saying, it's *obvious* you like Nicole. A lot. And I think she likes you too."

"Star, I told you—by the end of the night Nicole was a totally different person. She was cold and distant and . . . she didn't even let me walk her to the front door of her house."

The image made me feel sad all over again. The sound of Nicole slamming the door still echoed through my head. I was never going to see her again. . . .

"Duh!" Star exclaimed, tapping me on the forehead with her sticky fork. "Nicole is obviously *so* into you. But she turned cold at the end of the night because *she* thinks *you* like *Christy*."

"Huh." I was momentarily speechless.

Was it possible that Star was right? A tiny flicker of hope ignited within my heart. What she'd said *did* make a certain amount of sense. I went over the evening again in my head. And there had been one other point at which Nicole was less than her usual charming self. It was when I had left her alone on the dance floor. She had even said that she had thought I'd gone home without her.

"Justin, she *likes* you," Star repeated. "I'm a girl. I know about this kind of thing."

Maybe Star was right. But that didn't change the fact that I had no desire for a girlfriend. Even one as awesome as Nicole.

"Nonetheless, I don't want to get involved with anyone," I told Star, repeating myself for probably the hundredth time. "So it doesn't matter."

Star pushed away her now empty plate. "Justin, you're living in the past," she announced. "I know what happened with Laurie. I'm young—but I'm not stupid."

"What does Laurie have to do with anything?" I protested. "I haven't even *mentioned* Laurie."

"I know," she responded. "But you're using your past with Laurie to keep yourself from moving into the future. A future that *doesn't* include Mom."

"Mom doesn't have anything to do with this either!" I practically shouted. "I don't want to date for my own, very sane, reasons."

Star shook her head. "This *does* have something to do with Mom," she insisted. "Her life is over, but ours *isn't*."

"I know that," I said quietly. "I'm here; you're here. Life goes on."

"But you're *not* letting life go on," Star continued. "By not letting yourself risk getting hurt again, you're living in denial of reality." She paused. "There's always going to be the chance you could get hurt, Justin. That doesn't mean we shouldn't take chances."

I looked down at my plate. My pancakes were mostly eaten, but I couldn't even remember bringing the fork to my mouth. Star's words had gotten to me. And she was absolutely right.

If Mom's death has taught us anything, it's that life is the most precious thing there is, I thought. My mother wouldn't have wanted me to cloister myself away and stop taking chances. She would have wanted me and Star and my dad to go on without her. She would have wanted us to live the best, happiest lives we could—even without her.

And there was no doubt that I couldn't be totally alive without opening myself up to the possibility of hurt. It just wasn't possible to go through every day without feeling moments of pain, loneliness, even desperation. But it also wasn't possible to go through life without those moments of joy. And lately . . . I hadn't been feeling *anything*.

Until last night. Last night I had been on top of the world. Not just because it was fun to be at a dance or eat at a nice restaurant. I had been on cloud nine because of Nicole. She had made me feel like a real human being again.

"You're right," I said to Star. "You may be only in sixth grade, but you've got a lot of insights."

149

Star grinned. "At last! He sees the light!"

"You're pretty smart," I told my little sister. "You know that?"

"Yes, I know that!" she declared. "But we're not talking about my brain right now. We're talking about how you're going to convince Nicole to go on another date with you—a *real* date this time."

But I was one step ahead of her. I had already started to formulate a plan . . . one that would show Nicole that she was more than simply a "business transaction" to me. *And if it works . . . I'll be the happiest guy in the world.*

Seventeen

Nicole

BY LATE SUNDAY morning my eyeballs felt like they had been pried out and put back into their sockets with Krazy Glue. I hadn't been this tired since I had stayed up all night to watch a Nick At Nite *Wonder Years* marathon. By my best estimation, I had managed to get about two and a half hours of sleep.

I promised myself I wasn't going to lose sleep over Justin, and that's exactly what I did, I thought. I had sat up in bed, hour after hour, going over every detail of my nondate with Justin in my head.

I just didn't get it. Justin didn't even *know* Christy. How could he be so stuck on her . . . especially after the two of us had had such an awesome time together? Yes, Christy was pretty—she was beautiful. But it wasn't as if I belonged in the dog pound. Plenty of guys had let me know in crude but no uncertain terms that I was an attractive girl.

"Maybe he *didn't* have a good time," I speculated aloud. Maybe he really was just being a gentleman when he laughed at my jokes and gazed into my eyes and cut to the front of the punch line when I said I was about to faint from thirst.

I pulled on my favorite pair of faded denim overalls and a graying white tank top. I probably wouldn't put on another dress until the day of my high-school graduation. And after that . . . maybe never again.

The single white rose Justin had given me was sitting on top of my desk next to the stub of my ticket to the dance. I picked it up and breathed deeply. The smell was already fading—I hoped my memories would drift into the ether as quickly. *But I want to save the corsage,* I decided. A girl went to her senior prom only one time, and it was an event that deserved to be memorialized for posterity.

I had learned how to press flowers at Girl Scout camp in the fourth grade. My knowledge of the process was vague at best, but it would have to do. I pulled volume *A* through *O* of my *Oxford English Dictionary* off my bookshelf and set it on the desk.

I opened the enormous book and leafed through it until I reached the approximate middle. *Forwrought. Foryellow. Foryeme. Foryield. Forzando.* Too bad *failure* wasn't on this page. It would be slightly more appropriate.

"Good-bye, rose," I said, feeling like a total dork. I

152

rested the corsage gently between the pages, laid the ticket stub next to it, then carefully shut the huge book. Next I took the other volume of the *OED* from the bookshelf and placed it on top of the first one.

"There," I announced. "In two weeks I'll have one ticket stub and a beautiful, dead, dry flower as proof that I actually went to the prom."

In the meantime I had no desire to spend the rest of the day staring at the lavender dress hanging from my closet door. In fact, I never wanted to see it again. I crossed the room toward the closet, remembering the soft touch of the lavender silk against my legs as I had danced.

"You served me well," I told the dress, re-covering it in the pink plastic garment bag from Claire's Boutique. "But it's time for retirement."

I walked all the way into the roomy closet and hung the dress at the very back of the rack. Knowing the way things disappeared in there (Gwen called it the Bermuda Triangle of closets), I doubted the item would resurface until sometime in the year 2020. Which was fine with me.

I firmly shut the closet door, then collapsed onto my bed. That was it. I didn't have anything else to do until it was time for my 3:00 P.M. shift at the store. Neither Christy nor Jane had answered their phones earlier, and Gwen had gone camping for the weekend. I had all day to sit here and pine over what could never be.

Oh, joy! I thought sarcastically. I almost wished I hadn't finished that math assignment Friday night.

For some reason, I always found working with concrete numbers soothing. At least I didn't have to worry about seeing Rose and Madison on Monday. They would be giving me nothing but props for my totally hot date.

I sighed deeply, thinking about the prom photo that my mom had snapped the night before. When she and Dad had taken off for a day of errands this morning, she had asked if I wanted her to take the film by One Hour photo. I had said no, but now I wished I had taken her up on the offer. I was longing to see Justin's face—even if that face was two-dimensional.

Of course, looking at the picture would be mental torture. It would remind me of everything I had lost when the clock had struck midnight. For one night I had been Cinderella. *Too bad Justin isn't going to appear at my doorstep with a glass slipper—or in my case, a glass heel.*

I was still trying to figure out how to break the news to Gwen about her favorite pair of shoes. I would have offered to buy her a new pair, but I was already up to the bib of my overalls in debt. Then again, after I told Gwen the whole sob story about Justin, she'd probably be in a pretty forgiving mood. . . .

The doorbell rang. It was probably a magazine salesman. Or an ax murderer. *Either way, it'll be someone to talk to.* Who knew? Maybe the person at the door was Ed McMahon with my ten-million-dollar check from the Publishers Clearing House sweepstakes.

I took the stairs two at a time. At the front door I peered through the window to make sure my visitor didn't have horns or big, spiky teeth. My jaw dropped open when I saw who was standing on the front steps.

It wasn't a monster. It was Justin Banks.

My first thought was that I must have left something in his car. My second thought was that he had shown up to demand that I take him over to Christy's house for an introduction. My third thought was that I must be hallucinating.

I opened the door. This wasn't a mirage—Justin stood before me, looking as gorgeous as ever in jeans and an old T-shirt. "Justin!" I said as soon as I found my voice. "This is, uh, a surprise." *One that's making my heart beat like there was a hummingbird in my chest,* I added silently. "Did you forget something? I mean, did I forget something?"

He smiled and held out his left hand, which had been hiding behind his back. "I found this," he announced. "And I believe it belongs to you."

I stared at Justin's palm, trying to decipher what the object in his hand was. It was silver and about four inches long and looked like it would be a perfect eye-gouging tool. Finally it clicked.

"My heel!" I exclaimed. "I mean, Gwen's heel!" I grinned as I took it from Justin's outstretched hand. "Where did you *find* it?"

Justin looked down for a moment, then gave me a sort of tentative smile. "Uh . . . in a trash can outside Alta Vista," he explained.

155

I looked at the heel, and then I looked at Justin. Wow. He found it in a garbage can. Which meant that he had gotten up this morning and driven back to school and dug through trash for who knew how long.

"It must have taken forever to find this," I said, not knowing quite what to make of his actions. "Thanks a lot."

I was truly touched that Justin had gone to such lengths to find my missing heel. I was also relieved. I could get the shoe fixed before Gwen ever knew that it had been broken.

He shrugged. "I, um, knew it was important to you. I mean, I didn't want your sister to renounce you or anything."

Immediately I felt guilty. I had gone on so much about the broken heel in the car that I'd actually made Justin feel bad. And the truth was that losing the heel hadn't been a tragedy. I had just been worried in the car that if I didn't focus on something specific, I would start to cry.

"Well . . . thanks again," I said, wishing I were holding Justin's hand instead of the broken heel. "And I promise that I'll get Christy to call you."

I expected Justin to smile, wave, and disappear into the sunset. But he didn't. He just kept standing there, giving me a weird look.

"Do I have something on my face?" I asked, rubbing my nose.

He laughed. "No, your face is fine, Nic." Justin was staring into my eyes now, and I felt my knees threatening to give way. "It's more than fine. It's beautiful."

I was starting to think I was on a TV prank show. Had Justin Banks just told me that I was beautiful? "I—I, uh . . ." Nothing came out.

"I actually talked to Christy last night," Justin informed me, seeming not to notice that I was stammering and stuttering. "But not for the reason you think."

Okay. I had entered some parallel universe in which nothing I had previously known made any sense. "Why, then?" I asked.

"It's a long story," Justin said. "And one I'll tell you about someday . . . but not right now."

Someday. He had said someday. As if we were going to see each other again. *Don't get started, Nicole,* I ordered myself. I had gone down the path of hope before, and it had led to a total dead end.

"All right. I *won't* have Christy call you," I announced. "So . . . I'll see you around."

"Since I met Christy on my own, I'd like you to fulfill your part of our bargain in another way," Justin informed me.

"You want the fifty dollars?" I asked.

Justin laughed. "No! Of course not!"

"What, then?" I was searching my brain for something I had that Justin could possibly want. But unless he had a thing for girls' clothing or old dolls, he was going to be out of luck.

"I'd like you to go to *my* prom with me next weekend," he said matter-of-factly.

157

"Why?" I asked, dumbfounded.

He shrugged. "Let's just say I'm trying to impress someone very special."

And then it hit me. The answer was totally obvious. Justin didn't have a crush on Christy anymore—he had said as much just now. He had feelings for someone else. Somebody he wanted to see at the Jefferson prom. And he thought (probably rightly) that he would be more attractive to this girl if he had a date on his arm. In my experience, guys did stuff like that all the time.

"If I do this for you, it means we're even, right?" I asked. "No more favors, no more conditions?"

"Right," Justin said. "But—"

"I'll do it," I interrupted. "Pick me up next Saturday at eight."

With that, I shut the door in Justin's face. I didn't want to stand there and listen to him talk about this mystery girl. And I didn't want to chat about the weather. All I wanted to do was go upstairs, climb into bed, and forget that next Saturday night I was going to have to endure a whole other evening being tortured by the fact that I was with a guy who loved someone else instead of me.

Eighteen

Nicole

"NIC? ARE YOU in there?" Gwen called, knocking softly on my bedroom door.

"Come on in!" I called back.

I was halfway inside my closet, digging for my prom dress. Now that it looked like I was going to wear it again, I didn't want the thing to turn into a wrinkled mess.

I heard the door open and close behind me. "What are you *doing?*" Gwen asked with a laugh. "I've never known you to do any voluntary spring cleaning."

"I was looking for my prom dress," I explained, backing out of the closet with the plastic-covered dress clutched in my right hand. "I put it way back on the rack so that I wouldn't have to see it again until I was sixty years old."

Gwen looked confused. "Correct me if I'm wrong, but I detect there's a story here." She glanced at the dress. "And it definitely has something to do with your big night at the prom—which, by the way, I want to hear all about."

"I don't want to talk about it," I informed her.

She snorted. "Come on, Nic. Why do you think I came home today? I've only got one tiny load of laundry with me."

I hung the dress back up on the closet door, then sort of catapulted myself onto my bed. "Dinner was awesome. Rose and Madison had to eat their words." I delivered the prom rundown in a toneless voice, as if I were a robot. "The prom was awesome. Justin and I danced for hours and had a great time. The end."

"All that sounds great," Gwen announced. "What's the problem?"

I picked up the heel Justin had brought me and held it up for Gwen's inspection. "This, for one. I broke your shoe."

Gwen took the heel. "Okay . . . that news doesn't thrill me. But it's hardly a reason to dismiss your prom as a failure. There *are* shoe repairmen in this town, Nicole."

I moaned. It seemed that Gwen wasn't going to let me off the hook gracefully. She wanted to know every ugly detail.

"Justin doesn't love me," I told her. "He barely even *likes* me."

I had already figured out why he had gone to all

160

the trouble to find the missing heel. He was afraid I wouldn't agree to go to his prom, so he wanted a little extra guilt ammunition.

"How do you know?" Gwen asked. "I mean, did he come right out and tell you that he doesn't want to see you again?"

"Not exactly," I admitted. "We're actually going to *his* prom together next weekend."

Gwen reached over and rapped my forehead. "*Hello?* This is a *good* thing."

"For a normal guy and a normal girl, yes, this would be a good thing," I agreed. "But Justin and I don't operate the regular way. The only reason he even wants me to go to the prom with him is so that he can scope out some girl that he apparently wants to ask out on a real date."

"Did he actually express that fact in words?" Gwen asked. "Or are you using ESP to deduce this information?"

I shrugged. "A little bit of both," I admitted.

Gwen was quiet for a moment. "You know what I think?" she said finally. "I think you should go to the prom with Justin as if this was a typical date between a typical guy and a typical girl. I think you should drink punch and dance and forget all about this other, theoretical girl."

"But that's not going to help anything," I insisted. "I'll just fall for Justin even harder—and be hurt that much more."

"Maybe. But maybe not." She reached out and gave me a sisterly pat on the shoulder. "I don't

161

think you're giving yourself *or* Justin enough credit. If he has any brains at all, the guy will fall madly and deeply in love with you."

"Thanks, Gwen." I appreciated that my older sister thought I was girlfriend worthy, despite all the evidence I had seen to the contrary. If only Justin saw all of the qualities in me that Gwen did . . .

"But there is one hitch," Gwen informed me.

"What's that?" I was almost afraid to hear.

"You're going to have to get yourself a new pair of shoes," Gwen proclaimed. "I'm not loaning you mine again until you're in college."

I laughed. I wished I could be as lighthearted and carefree as my sister. But how was that really possible? The man of my dreams had just asked me to go to his prom for the sole purpose of impressing "someone very special." This wasn't exactly a banner day.

But I would take Gwen's advice. I would have a good time at the prom, simply enjoying what little time I was going to have with Justin. After all, it wasn't as if a few more dances with him were going to make me feel *worse*. My heart was already broken.

"You're in this place almost as much as I am," Claire said to me later that afternoon in the middle of my shift at the boutique. "I'm beginning to think I should retire and let you take over."

I shut the drawer of the register. "No way," I told her. "I like dresses as much as the next person, but I definitely don't have your out-and-out passion for taffeta and silk."

Still, I was actually glad that I had to work this afternoon. Hanging clothes, ringing up sales, and cleaning the supply closet were simple, concrete tasks that had effectively kept my mind off Justin (more or less) for the past three hours.

I had even managed to tell Claire about the prom without getting totally upset over the lack of romantic possibilities between Justin and myself. The rhythmic activities of work had cleared my head and allowed me to attain a state of semiserenity. Justin was just a guy—not a god. There was no logical reason why I should allow myself to fall apart because Justin didn't think I was the girl of his dreams.

"How close are you to being out of debt?" Claire asked.

I groaned. "Don't even ask."

She grinned, her green eyes twinkling. "Well, I have a surprise for you." Claire reached under the counter and pulled out a small white envelope. "It's a graduation present, but I figure I'll give it to you now."

"Thanks, Claire," I said, taking the envelope. "But you didn't have to get me anything."

"I wanted to, Nic," she assured me. "Having you around has been good for business. Not just because of your skill as a salesperson, but because practically everyone you know bought their prom dress here."

I opened the envelope. Inside there was a graduation card. There was some kind of Hallmark poem printed on it, but I didn't stop to read it. My gaze fixed on the thin, prettily decorated slip of paper that Claire had slipped into the card. This Certificate Entitles *Nicole Gilmore* to One Lavender Silk Prom Dress, Courtesy of Claire's Boutique.

Tears sprang to my eyes as I absorbed the meaning of this single piece of paper. "Claire, I can't accept this," I announced. "It's way too big a gift."

She tossed her long, curly red hair over one shoulder and arched her eyebrows. "You can and you *will* accept it," she informed me. She opened up a notebook and scanned some figures. "Now— since the dress is a gift and you've worked so many extra shifts during the last few weeks, my calculations tell me that I owe you *more* than enough to cover your prom tickets and that expensive dinner at La Serenara that you put on your credit card."

"Thank you, Claire." I felt a huge wave of relief wash over me. Financial freedom! Yeah! I put my arms around my boss and gave her a huge hug. "I can't tell you how much this means to me."

My day had gone from bad to okay to great. Now I could even buy a new pair of high heels to wear to Justin's prom—not that it really mattered what I wore.

I was still smiling when the bell over the door of the shop chimed, and Jane walked in. I noticed immediately that her eyes were red and her face looked pale.

"What's wrong?" I asked. "Did you and Max have a fight after Justin and I left last night?"

Jane shook her head. "I just found out that Christy's mom went into the hospital last night. She's not doing very well—at all."

"What?" I suddenly felt numb. I knew that Mrs. Redmond had been sick, but I had no idea that she needed to be hospitalized. Christy never wanted to talk about it.

"That's why Christy left the prom so suddenly last night," Jane explained. "She found out her mom had gone into the hospital, and she left to be with her."

"She didn't tell us . . . ," I whispered. "Why didn't she tell us?"

Jane shook her head. "I don't know, Nic. But we know now."

"Don't worry about your shift," Claire told me. "Go be with your friend."

"Thanks, Claire. Again."

I grabbed my backpack and followed Jane out of the store. Suddenly the prom and Justin and the Witch Brigade seemed like the most unimportant things on earth. Our friend was in trouble, and she needed us. *And we'll be there for her,* I thought. *No matter what happens.*

Nineteen

Justin

SITTING ACROSS THE table from Nicole at Pete's Lobster House on Saturday night, I could hardly believe this was the same girl I had accompanied to her senior prom just a week ago. Nicole was being nice enough, but she hadn't made one joke about wagging lobster tails or filling squirt guns with the butter sauce.

Nicole looks beautiful, but she seems tired, I thought. *Tired and sad.* For the first time in a long time, I realized that I felt . . . well, like someone's boyfriend. Not that Nicole had done anything to make me feel like I deserved that title. When I had called her during the week, she hadn't been any more effusive than she had been last Sunday when I was standing on her stoop.

I was beginning to accept the fact that Star had

been wrong. Nicole didn't like me at all. She hadn't wanted to go on a real date with me, and she *hadn't* cared that in her mind I had only agreed to go to her prom because I had a crush on Christy. Still . . . now that I had opened my heart, it was hard to close it. I had to try to get through to her.

"Nicole, do you want to talk about what's bothering you?" I asked. "I mean, you can't be frowning like that just because I'm taking up your Saturday night—unless you were dying to watch the *Mad About You* marathon on Nick at Nite."

She shook her head and gave me a small smile. "Nah . . . I don't want to bring you down right before the prom. You need to be at your best to impress that special someone."

Special someone? Suddenly the words I had spoken to Nicole last Sunday echoed through my mind. She had thought I was talking about someone *else*. So maybe there was still hope. Maybe I still had a chance!

But there was something I needed to do. I needed to tell Nicole the whole truth. I had to tell her about my mom, and Laurie, and the real reason I had wanted to meet Christy. Otherwise she was never going to understand why I had been so hot and cold . . . why even though I had wanted to more than anything else in the world, I hadn't let my defenses down enough to kiss her on the dance floor when I'd had the chance.

"Nicole, there's something I need to tell you," I said softly.

She looked up from her lobster. "What is it?" she asked. "Something about how I'm supposed to act when we see the special someone?"

"No," I said firmly, shaking my head. "I need to explain the real reason that I asked you to introduce me to Christy—the reason that that was my condition when you invited me to your prom."

As soon as I finished speaking, I saw that tears had started to well in Nicole's eyes. One escaped and slid down her cheek, and she raised her hand to brush it away. The truth began to dawn on me, but I was almost afraid to ask.

"It's Christy's mom, isn't it?" I asked, before Nicole had a chance to say anything. "She's getting even sicker than she was last week."

Nicole nodded miserably. "Mrs. Redmond has been in the hospital since last Saturday night. At first Christy insisted that it was only temporary . . . but now . . . I'm not so sure."

I felt a tight knot in my chest, and for a moment I wasn't sure I was going to be able to breathe. I felt transplanted in time, back to when my own mother was lying in a hospital bed.

"I'm sorry, Nicole," I said, because there was really nothing else to say.

She rubbed her eyes, then gave me a baffled glance. "I don't understand—how did you know that Mrs. Redmond is sick? I never told you that."

"That's what I was going to tell you about," I told her. "The reason I wanted to meet Christy was that I recognized her from the hospital cancer ward.

169

I saw her in the waiting room there last year . . . when my own mom was dying from breast cancer."

Understanding began to dawn in Nicole's eyes. For a long time she didn't say anything. She simply sat there, looking sad and vulnerable and adorable in the lobster bib that now seemed absurdly out of place.

"Justin, I didn't know. I mean, you never mentioned your mom. . . . I figured you two didn't get along or something. I, uh, didn't want to pry."

"Sometimes talking about her is just too painful," I admitted. "She died last year, but often it feels more like last week."

"You wanted to talk to Christy about her mother?" Nicole asked. "That's why you wanted to meet her?"

I nodded. "At first I thought I wanted to talk to Christy just because I thought I might be able to offer her an empathetic ear." I paused, realizing that this was the most open, honest conversation I'd had with a girl since Laurie and I broke up. "But I finally realized that I need Christy's help too. I wanted to talk with someone about what it felt like to have a sick mother so that I could get some of my own feelings off my chest."

"I wish Christy would talk more to Jane and me," Nicole said, her voice contemplative. "It's like she believes that as long as she doesn't talk about her mom's illness, it won't be real."

"But you've been there for her," I stated. The fact wasn't even a question in my mind—I knew

170

there was no way Nicole Gilmore would abandon a friend in need. "That's the important thing."

She nodded. "Jane and I have been at the hospital during every free moment. But Christy barely talks to us. . . . That's probably why she didn't tell me about your mom. She's sort of lost in her own world right now."

I knew how that felt, and my heart ached for Christy. But another part of my heart felt lighter than it had since my mother died. And that was because of Nicole.

"Do you want to go home?" I asked. "I'll understand if you're not in the mood to go to a dance."

"No way," Nicole proclaimed. "Christy found out that we were going to your prom tonight, and she practically made me sign a written contract saying I wouldn't back out on her account." She paused. "Now I understand at least part of why she felt so strongly. . . . Christy probably realizes that it's important for you to live your own life, now that there's nothing you can do for your mom."

And Christy was right. Just as Star had been. I glanced at my watch, shocked to see how much time had passed while Nicole and I had been talking.

"Nic, we've got a lot more to talk about tonight. But I think we better continue this conversation at the prom. It started half an hour ago."

As she stood to leave, I admired her all over again. Now that we had started this dialogue, I

171

hoped I would succeed in convincing Nicole that she was the only "someone special" I wanted in my life. And if I was lucky . . . maybe tonight would end with a kiss rather than the supreme brush-off I received at our *last* prom. Anything was possible.

Twenty

Nicole

THE JEFFERSON HIGH prom committee had clearly outdone themselves. While the Union High prom had been a winter wonderland, this one was a Caribbean paradise. There were huge fake palm trees, thatched huts, tiny umbrellas in the punch, and sandboxes everywhere. Naturally everyone received a lei at the door.

"This is really something," I said to Justin. "You guys know how to throw a party."

Justin smiled and pointed toward the ceiling. "You'll notice that we too have the requisite disco ball."

"I'm impressed."

I felt my spirits lift as I watched dozens of couples approximating hula dances as the band played something that sounded vaguely Hawaiian. So what if Justin was just using me to get to some girl? He had become a good friend, and that was going to have to be enough.

Out of nowhere I felt a large hand clamp down on my shoulder. "So this is Nicole!" a deep voice announced. "We've never officially met, but Justin's been talking about you so much for the past week that I feel like we're already friends."

I turned around to find a guy with dark brown curly hair and warm hazel eyes grinning at me. A petite blond girl was standing beside him. "Uh . . ."

Justin stepped closer to me. "Nicole, this is my overly enthusiastic best friend, Sam. And this is his girlfriend, Maya."

"Hi. Nice to meet you," I greeted them. I was still reeling from the fact that Justin had been talking about me all week.

"Are you guys going to dance or *what?*" Sam asked. "Maya and I have already been out on the floor for almost an hour. I'm totally sweaty."

"Charming, isn't he?" Maya asked, her eyes sparkling. "But Sam is mine, and I love him."

I grinned at both Maya and Sam. They were exactly the kind of people I would have been friends with if I had gone to Jefferson High. If Justin and I were going out, I could imagine double dating with Sam and Maya every weekend. *Don't think like that,* I admonished myself. *It's not going to happen.*

So much had happened tonight that I was having a tough time remembering that tonight was just payback for last weekend. Justin and I had such a rapport. . . . It was as if we had known each other years, not days.

"If you guys don't mind, I think I'll follow Sam's advice and ask my date for a dance," Justin announced to his friends. He turned to me. "Nicole, will you do me the honor?"

I curtsied. "*Mai oui,* monsieur."

Justin took my hand and started to lead me toward the dance floor. It felt like déjà vu. But this time we weren't putting on a show for Rose and Madison. We were going to dance for the benefit of some nameless, faceless girl—who despite myself, I hated.

When we were a few steps away from Sam and Maya, Sam suddenly lunged forward and clasped my arm. "You're the best thing that's ever happened to Justin," he whispered. "I feel like I've finally got my best friend back."

I didn't know what to make of Sam's words as Justin and I continued toward the dance floor. Tonight was all about mixed signals . . . and I was more confused than ever.

"So where is she?" I asked as soon as we were on the dance floor. "Where is that special someone?"

I figured that if I said that phrase enough times, I would be able to accept the horrible fact that lay behind it. So far, it wasn't working.

The band struck up a slow tune, and Justin put his arms around me. His embrace was becoming tantalizingly familiar, and it was hard not to melt into him.

"Before I tell you about the 'special someone'

you keep mentioning, I want to finish the conversation we started at dinner," he told me softly.

"I'm not sure now is the time to talk about Christy's mom," I replied. I wasn't going to be able to keep it together if Justin and I allowed ourselves to think about Christy, at her mother's bedside at the hospital.

He shook his head. "This isn't about Mrs. Redmond—at least not directly," he told me. "It's sort of about my mom . . . but most of all, it's about me."

I nodded. Gazing into Justin's warm brown eyes, I probably would have agreed to talk about *anything*. And I was touched that he trusted me enough to discuss something that was obviously so painful. I wanted to be there for him—even if it was only as a friend.

"I used to have a girlfriend," Justin began. "Her name was—still is—Laurie, and I thought I was going to be in love with her for the rest of my life."

"Uh-huh . . ." Hearing a monologue about Justin's ex-girlfriend wasn't exactly what I had been expecting.

"When my mom got sick, Laurie bailed," Justin continued. "She couldn't deal with it. . . . She didn't *want* to deal with it."

"That's awful!" I exclaimed. I couldn't imagine leaving a friend—or a boyfriend—at a time like that.

He nodded. "It *was* awful. And my breakup with Laurie made my mother's death even harder than it already was. I felt totally isolated."

"You must have been so lonely. . . ." Thinking about Justin's grief made my eyes fill with tears. More than anything, I wished I had known him

176

then. I wished I could have been there for him during that horrible time.

"Somehow my mom's death and my breakup with Laurie got all mixed up in my head." His voice was quiet, but I could hear his words clearly, despite the band music. It was as if I was tuned in to Justin's thoughts as he spoke.

"I don't know what to say," I responded. "I can't imagine what that must have been like."

He smiled. "Don't be sad, Nic. I'm getting to the happy part of the tale." He paused. "Anyway, I convinced myself that if I swore off girls forever, I would never experience that pain again. I thought I could stay safe, living life like I was surrounded by an unbreakable bubble."

"But there's always pain," I said softly. "It's part of life."

"Exactly," Justin agreed. "But that's something I didn't realize—until this past week. I was shutting out pain—or so I thought—by not allowing myself to get close to another girl." He paused. "But I was also shutting out happiness."

"And now?" I asked.

He grinned. "And *now* I realize that I have to move on with my life. I'll always miss my mom, but that doesn't mean I should cut myself off from all that life has to offer."

"Is this where the 'special someone' comes in?" I asked. I hated to bring up the subject, but I couldn't help myself.

He nodded. "*You're* the special someone, Nicole.

You're the girl I was hoping to impress tonight."

"I . . . I . . ." I was speechless. And euphoric. And utterly turned upside down.

"Can I put one more condition on tonight?" he asked. "Just to make things even between us?"

"What is it . . . ?" I couldn't breathe.

"I want this to be a real date," he said softly, folding me even closer into his embrace.

I felt my entire body sort of light up. I would have thought I had misheard Justin, but there was no mistaking the heat in his gaze.

"I don't understand . . . ," I whispered. "Last week you didn't . . . I mean, Justin, you were so . . ." I couldn't find any words to express what I was trying to say.

"I wasn't interested in finding romance, Nicole," he said simply. "Like I said, I had sworn off girls for good." As he paused, I resisted the urge to fall deeper into his arms like a limp noodle. "Then I met you . . . and I can't ignore my feelings." He reached out and took my hand. "You're the girl of my dreams—only I didn't even know I was dreaming."

If the floor had opened up and swallowed me whole at that moment, I would have left the earth a happy girl. But the floor didn't open up. This was real. *It's just like a fairy tale after all. . . .*

For all of high school I had refused to compromise. I hadn't gone out with jerks on the football team just because they were considered the gods of Alta Vista. And I hadn't dated the nicer guys who made me yawn halfway through a conversation just so I would have something to do on Saturday night.

I had spent my time bonding with Jane and Christy, the two best friends a girl could have. And I had read books and listened to music, discovering who I was and who I wanted to be. There had been times when I was lonely, tempted to enter the mainstream of high-school life just so I could blend in with the crowd.

But I hadn't. And my patience had been worthwhile. The cocoon had slipped away, and I had emerged a butterfly, worthy of being the prom date of the greatest guy I had ever met.

"Nicole?" Justin's voice reached me through the haze of my whirling thoughts.

"What?" I asked, pinching myself on the arm— just to make sure.

"Is your answer yes? Will you agree that this is a *real* date . . . and will you agree to go on another one with me?"

"Yes!" I answered. "Yes!"

"There's one more thing I wanted to ask you," Justin said. We weren't even dancing now. We were just standing under the disco ball, staring into each other's eyes.

"What?" I asked again.

"This . . ." Justin held me in his arms, and I felt like I was defying gravity, floating on air.

For a long moment we looked at each other. Then he lowered his head . . . and kissed me. My heart melted as I felt his soft, firm lips against mine. I slid my arms around his neck, and the kiss deepened. The firecrackers I had experienced the times

179

Justin's fingers had grazed my bare skin were nothing compared to the sparks zipping through my veins now.

Until this moment I hadn't allowed myself to process just how intense my feelings for Justin had become. I had been too afraid of getting hurt to admit to myself just how much I wanted him to be a part of my life. Now . . . I felt more alive than I had during the past four years of high school.

At last Justin pulled away from me. "Thank you for finding me, Nicole," he said quietly. "You've changed my life."

Like I said before, I had never been the kind of girl who chased boys or dreamed about knights on white horses or wanted to wear a guy's picture in a locket around my neck. But all of that had changed the day that Justin Banks walked into Claire's Boutique with his little sister. Now I was a believer in long walks on the beach, candlelit dinners, and late-night study dates. I was a new woman—and I liked it.

"You've changed my life too," I whispered back.

And they lived happily ever after . . . , I thought, finishing the fairy tale that my life had become during the past few weeks.

Then I kissed Justin again . . . and realized that the *real* story was just beginning.

Jake & Christy

Prologue

The Summer Before Eighth Grade

CHRISTY REDMOND RUBBED her hands against the fabric of her favorite white skirt and hoped that Jake Saunders wouldn't notice how sweaty her palms were. This was the most significant night of her thirteen years on the planet, and she wanted every detail of the evening to be perfect.

So far, so good, Christy thought. Mr. Saunders had dropped them off in the parking lot of the Star Diner, and he hadn't said anything embarrassing about how cute they looked all dressed up or commented in that *parent* voice that they were really "all grown up now." That would have been totally humiliating!

"Ready to go inside?" Jake asked, pulling open the door of the diner.

"Uh, yeah." Duh. Christy wished she had said something clever, but tonight she felt completely tongue-tied.

Usually she felt so comfortable around Jake that he had a hard time shutting her up. But tonight was different. Tonight they were on a *date*. Jake had asked, and Christy had accepted. So even though they'd been buddies forever, even though they'd practically grown up together because their moms were best friends, Christy knew that something had changed between them.

And that something was the fact that friends didn't kiss. But people on dates did.

And for a couple of weeks now, all Christy could think about was what it would be like to kiss Jake Saunders. Her best friend. He must have been feeling the same way since he was the one who asked her out—on a real date.

Her first real date. And so far, it was everything she'd imagined. Everything really was different tonight. Jake even *looked* different. He was wearing khaki pants that she had never seen before and a white, button-down shirt that he had actually bothered to tuck in.

"We'd like a table by the window," Jake informed a waiter as he and Christy walked into the restaurant. "Preferably a booth."

The waiter rolled his eyes. "Do I look like a maitre d', kid? Sit wherever you want. Preferably *not* a booth since it's just the two of you."

Christy cringed. A shot of red crept up Jake's cheeks.

"Does he want a tip?" Jake asked, loudly enough for the waiter to hear him. "Sue me for wanting a nice table."

2

"Forget him," Christy whispered in Jake's ear. "He probably hates teenagers. Let's just sit down. I see a table over there."

Jake smiled. "Okay."

They sat down at a table for two by the window. A large, green hanging plant was right over Christy's head. *Please don't fall on me,* she prayed as another waiter dropped two menus on the table. *That would be just what I need. A head full of dirt on my first date!*

The waiter returned, snapping open his order pad and removing a short pencil from behind his ear. "What'll it be?"

Christy's mouth was watering. She knew exactly what she wanted: a bacon double cheeseburger, medium rare, well-done fries, some coleslaw, an extra pickle, and a large Coke with a lemon wedge. "I'll have a tossed salad, dressing on the side, and an iced tea, please."

Jake raised an eyebrow. "What else?"

Christy shut her menu. "That's it." She smiled at the waiter, handing her menu to him.

Jake stared at her as if there was something wrong with her, then shrugged and turned his attention to the waiter. He ordered everything Christy had been dreaming of except he got a milk shake instead of a Coke. When the waiter left, Jake said, "You knew we were going to have dinner, so why'd you eat something before?"

Huh? she thought. What was he talking about? "I didn't. I haven't eaten anything since breakfast. Why would you think I did?"

3

"Why else would you order just a salad, then? And since when do you drink iced tea?"

Christy felt herself redden. "I'm just trying to eat lighter these days, that's all." Okay, that was a total lie. But she couldn't eat like a pig in front of Jake. Not tonight anyway. Did he have to make such a big deal about what she ordered?

"So I'm really psyched for the movie we're going to see," she told him, dying to change the subject. Jake's eyes lit up at the mention of the film. They talked excitedly and easily about their expectations of it, and Christy felt herself relax. This was more like it. *This* was a date.

"Yum," Christy said as she saw the waiter headed toward them with their orders. "There's nothing like a crisp, green salad."

Again Jake looked at her like she had two heads. "Usually you eat like there was no tomorrow."

She felt her cheeks flame again and then realized she was more angry than embarrassed. That comment wasn't very nice. Who was he to say anything about how much or how little she ate? *Calm down, Christy,* she told herself. *Guys aren't known for their sensitivity*. Christy decided to let it pass—in the name of love. Besides, she *did* have a tendency to eat a lot.

"Here you go, kiddies," the waiter announced. "One salad, one cheeseburger with the works."

Jake glared at the waiter. "We're not—"

"Going to need anything else, thanks!" Christy cut in brightly. The waiter left, and Christy

4

breathed a sigh of relief. The last thing she needed was for Jake and the guy to get into a fistfight. "Just forget it, okay?" she whispered urgently to Jake. "Don't say anything rude if he comes back with more water or something."

"Why should I let him talk to us that way?" Jake demanded. "Who does he think he is? And he's not that much older than we are. He's like seventeen or something."

"Your fries are getting cold," she told him with a smile. "Let's dig in, okay?"

Jake nodded, grabbing the squirt bottle of ketchup. He turned it upside down over his fries and squeezed, but nothing came out. He shook the bottle, then tried again.

"Do you need help with that?" she asked, reaching for the bottle.

"Nope." Jake shook the bottle vigorously. "I can handle it."

Then he squeezed the bottle, using what looked like all of his upper-body strength. The ketchup shot out of the bottle as if it were coming from an old-fashioned cannon. And it landed all over the pale yellow cotton sweater she had so carefully chosen from her closet less than an hour ago.

"Oh no!" Christy shrieked. "It's all over me."

"Sorry!" Jake turned bright red as he grabbed a fistful of napkins from the dispenser. "Here, let me help you."

But as he leaned across the table with the napkins, his sleeve caught on the straw that was sticking out of

5

his milk shake. In a split second the entire contents of the glass landed on her skirt.

"Jake!" she cried. "I can't believe you! You're such a—"

He froze, napkins in hand. "Such a *what?*"

"Look at me!" she shrieked. "My outfit's completely ruined!"

"I'm *sorry,*" he yelled. "Jeez! It was an accident."

Christy grabbed the napkins out of his hand and wiped futilely at her skirt and sweater. This whole date was turning into a disaster. She didn't want to leave the table, much less go to a movie theater looking like this.

She put the wet pile of napkins on the table and glared at Jake. A little while ago she had thought he was the greatest guy in the world. But now . . . he didn't even look cute. Okay, he *did* look cute. But still . . . this date wasn't anything like she'd thought it would be.

Jake stared in horror at the mess he had created. He felt bad about what had happened, but truthfully, it *was* an accident. He hadn't meant to squirt her with ketchup. And as for the milk shake spilling onto her skirt . . . he had just been trying to help!

What was he supposed to do? She was completely freaking out. It wasn't as if she had broken her arm—she just had a little food on her clothes. No biggie.

"Calm down," Jake told her. "Everybody is staring at us."

In particular, Jake had spotted three guys from the eighth grade, sitting at a table on the other side of the diner. They were pointing at Jake and Christy's booth and laughing hysterically.

"Hey, Saunders!" one of them called. "You want one of us to pinch-hit on your date? It doesn't look like you're doing such a great job of it yourself."

Humiliation. Total and utter humiliation. He slid down in the booth, hoping to avoid any further comments from the boys.

"Shut up!" Christy yelled at the guys. "Nobody asked for your opinion!"

They howled. "Oh, she's a blast!" another called.

Could he die now, or would that be too much to ask for? It wasn't like he could challenge them to a fight over Christy's honor. They would kill him! Each one was practically twice his size.

"Why don't we get the check?" Jake asked Christy. "I've suddenly lost my appetite."

She looked up from the fresh bunch of napkins she was using to dab at her sweater. "Good idea," she agreed. "If I don't soak these clothes soon, they'll be ruined forever."

But the waiter was one step ahead of them. Before Jake could even catch his eye, he placed the check in front of him on the table. "I'll take that whenever you're ready, *sir*."

"I'm ready now," Jake responded. He reached into the back pocket of his khakis to get his wallet.

But nothing was there. Quickly he reached into the other pocket. Nothing. No wallet. No money.

7

Just a lint ball from the dryer. Suddenly his face felt like it was on fire. Jake knew exactly where his wallet was. On the top of his dresser, where he had put it just before he slipped into his pants.

"What's wrong?" Christy asked.

Jake took a deep breath. "I forgot my wallet," he whispered, not wanting the waiter to know.

"You forgot it?" she repeated loudly. "Jake!"

"I—I'm sorry," he stammered, for what felt like the hundredth time since their date had begun such a short time ago. "I just—"

"I'll pay," Christy interrupted. "Luckily I brought my baby-sitting money." She opened up her small purse and took out several bills.

"Thanks." He gulped, wishing the floor would open up and swallow him whole—along with that stupid ketchup bottle.

But there was still hope. Maybe Christy could go home and change, and they could start the whole date over again. Well, minus the part that included eating.

He didn't want to give up yet. Jake had spent the last few months building up the courage to ask Christy out on a real date, and he wanted it to be perfect. But even if it couldn't be *perfect,* he still wanted it to *be.*

"Do you still want to go to the movie?" he asked. "We can catch a later show."

She looked into his eyes, then smiled. "Okay. Yes, I'd like that."

They both slid out of the booth and headed for the door. Trying to regain his gentleman status,

8

Jake took Christy's arm to help her down the steps that led to the parking lot.

"I think I can get out most of the—" Christy's voice suddenly broke off as she missed one of the steps.

One second she had been right next to him, her arm in his hand. The next second she was sprawled on the parking lot, holding her ankle and moaning.

"Are you okay?" he asked, kneeling beside her.

"It's these shoes," she explained, wincing. "I'm not used to heels."

He looked at the shoe she was now holding in her hand. It had one of those skinny heels that his mom wore when she and his dad went out to dinner.

"Why are you wearing those?" he asked. "You should have worn your sneakers, like you always do."

Christy's eyes filled with tears. "Excuse me!" she shouted. "I was trying to be grown-up for a change."

Uh-oh. He had made another blunder. "I didn't mean anything by it," he said quickly. "I just, uh, don't understand why you're trying to act like you're twenty years old or something."

There. That was a compliment. He had told her that he liked her just the way she was. She didn't need to do anything fancy to impress him.

Christy stood up, hopping on her good ankle. "I guess you would have preferred it if I acted like a five-year-old and spilled ketchup all over you!" she blurted out, her face a bright, angry red.

"I *said* I was sorry about that," he yelled back. "How many times do you want me to apologize?"

She sighed, looking defeated. "I didn't mean it that way," she exclaimed. "It's just that this date isn't at all like I thought it would be. . . . I thought you were going to make an effort."

Make an effort? He had shaved for the first time in his life this afternoon just to make an effort. If she didn't appreciate that, then it was her problem.

"Maybe we should skip the movie," he suggested, still hoping against hope that she would disagree with him.

She scowled. "If that's your attitude, then maybe we should."

"Fine!" he exclaimed.

"Fine!" she yelled.

He kicked an empty Coke can across the parking lot. "I'm going to walk home *that* way," he shouted, pointing in the opposite direction of the way they had come.

"Good. I'm going to walk home the *other* way." With that, she turned and limped across the parking lot.

Jake stood, watching her go. After almost a minute he had a strange sensation that he wasn't alone. He glanced toward the diner and saw the guys who had been making fun of him staring at him from the other side of the window.

Great! Not only had he ruined things with Christy, but his reputation would be damaged forever. And it was all her fault. If he never saw Christy Redmond again, it would be too soon.

One

Christy

I POURED A tablespoon of olive oil onto the center of the large frying pan, then tilted the pan from side to side until the oil was spread evenly across the Teflon surface. Next I cracked an egg on the edge of the counter and carefully spilled the contents onto the now sizzling oil. I turned up the heat and stood back to wait until the over-easy egg was ready to slide onto one of the plates I had warming in the oven.

A year ago nobody would have said that I, Christy Redmond, could boil a pot of water, much less believe that I would wake up at dawn to perfect another breakfast item I was adding to my slowly building repertoire of dishes. Then again, a year ago nobody would have said a *lot* of things about me that were now true.

For instance, nobody, and I mean nobody,

would have predicted that I would be going to my senior prom at Union High with Jake Saunders. I still couldn't believe I was stuck going to the dance with that annoying collection of irksome personality traits. *But there's a method to this madness,* I reminded myself. Or if not a method, at least a *reason.*

It was the reason that lay behind most, if not all, of the innumerable changes in my life. I held back tears as I stared at the frying egg. My mom used to be the one who got up early every morning to cook breakfast. But she hadn't been able to do that for a long time. Not since she had been diagnosed with breast cancer and undergone a double mastectomy eighteen months ago.

I eyed the egg, assessing how close it was to being done—firm white, runny yellow. *Another ninety seconds,* I guessed.

Mom had suffered through a major operation and a radical course of chemotherapy. She had won a few battles against the cancer, but I knew, deep down in the darkest part of my soul, that she probably wasn't going to win the war.

I slipped on an oven mitt, opened the oven door, and pulled out one of the plates. After I put the egg on the plate, I would add two slices of toast and half a grapefruit. This was my dad's favorite breakfast, although I had cut him down to two eggs per week after we studied the effects of cholesterol in AP biology last month.

Making breakfast every day wasn't much, but at least I felt I was doing *something* to help out my parents.

Early in the morning, with sunlight streaming in through the kitchen windows, I could almost believe that everything was okay. It wasn't until later, when I went upstairs to spend time with Mom, that I would come crashing back down to reality.

As I slid two pieces of bread into the toaster, I remembered the time in third grade when Jake and I had tried to make grilled-cheese sandwiches in the toaster. What a fiasco! It was a miracle we hadn't set the entire kitchen on fire. Of course, that was back when Jake and I had been friends—it seemed like a lifetime ago.

I had practically grown up with Jake. His mom and my mom were best friends, and their family lived down the block. We had spent our summers together—lemonade stands, kick the can, running through every sprinkler on the block. Jake had been my first confidant, and for a while I had thought I was in love with him. Then again, I had also thought I was in love with Barney the dinosaur.

A date with Barney probably would have gone better than the one Jake and I went on, I thought as I watched the toast pop up. It had been the summer after seventh grade. Jake and I had been flirting for months, which mostly involved us daring each other to eat gross foods and having splashing fights at the neighborhood pool. And then "it" had happened.

He was wearing a green-and-blue-striped shirt with short white tennis shorts (hey, guys don't develop their fashion sense until at least the tenth grade). Jake showed up at the screen door at the

13

back of our house, stammered for approximately thirty seconds, and then asked if I would like to accompany him to the diner for dinner and then to a movie at the mall. By the time I had finished saying yes, he was already halfway down the block.

I had stood motionless at the screen door for what felt like an hour, going over and over the invitation in my mind. That afternoon I had been the happiest girl in the world.

Too bad I didn't have the wisdom to stay home and practice putting on eye shadow the night of our so-called date, I thought now, slicing through a grapefruit in one swift motion. That evening had been a total fiasco.

Jake and I never recovered after that night. We'd been forced together the very next day for a family function—*big mistake*. Our delicate thirteen-year-old egos had been too recently stomped on, by each other, no less. We'd glared at each other. Made obnoxious comments under our breath. And with each passing day, we grew further and further apart. And suddenly weeks, months, and then years had gone by.

Dad's breakfast was ready, so all there was left to do was whip up some French toast for my mom and me. Her appetite had been terrible lately, and I was hoping that one of her favorite foods would entice her into eating something substantial.

I was still thinking about Jake as I cracked three eggs, one after another, on the side of a large glass bowl. It was almost unbelievable that Jake and I were still locked in our version of a Cold War, especially because we were still thrown together all the time—an unfortunate by-product of our parents' longtime friendship. We'd always hid our animosity from our parents, but not from each other.

I stuck a fork into the bowl of eggs and began to whip them into a frothy batter. Both Jake and I had become experts at the verbal one-two punch. Lately every time Jake and I got into it, I had taken to using a three-word attack from a list of Shakespearean insults I had downloaded off the Internet. Lumpish, idle-headed measle. Churlish, bat-fowling minnow. Reeky, spur-galled ratsbane.

Too bad my mom was so set on the idea of me going to the prom with none other than the vain, toad-spotted pig-nut himself. My mother, Rose Redmond, was a completely normal person in almost every way. She was intelligent, had a great sense of humor, and doled out the kind of advice that I hoped to give to my daughter someday. But the woman had a *thing* about the senior prom.

Probably because the first real date my mom and dad ever had was the night of their own senior prom. Since then Mom had been convinced that it was a night made for magic. And somehow, someway, she thought that Jake Saunders plus Christy Redmond equaled abracadabra.

I doubted that it was Jake's idea to pop the big question. I was ninety percent sure that Mrs. Saunders had talked him into it. Nonetheless, Jake didn't *have* to agree to ask me to be his date. As much as I hated to, I had to give him credit for his part in making Mom's dream come true. I had no illusion that Jake actually *wanted* to be my date, which meant that the guy was basically sacrificing his prom.

Unfortunately, going to the prom with Jake meant that even if Matt Fowler—the Boy of Sparkling Blue Eyes and Perfect Teeth—asked me to go to the prom with *him,* I would have to say no.

I plopped a piece of wheat bread into the egg batter, my heart beating just a little faster at the thought of Matt. He had transferred to Union High last year, but he hadn't reached his full hot-guy potential until *this* year. More important, Matt hadn't started to flirt with me until exactly two weeks ago. It had been in AP bio, and he had offered me a Pez. Nothing shouts romantic interest like a small piece of rectangular-shaped, tart candy that comes out of the mouth of a miniature, plastic Batman.

As the French toast sizzled in the pan, I imagined myself slow dancing with Matt. I would stare into his blue eyes, and all of the worries and anxieties that kept me awake at night would melt away as if they had never existed. . . .

Not! I reminded myself. Instead of swaying to a ballad with Matt, I would probably be exchanging snappy one-liners with Jake next to the refreshment table. I would spend most of the evening watching Jake ogle every girl in a low-cut dress within a hundred-foot radius of whatever corner we planted ourselves in.

Maybe I'll try to get out of the date with Jake, I

decided, thinking again of Matt's spectacular gaze. *I would be doing* both *of us a favor!*

Dad walked into the kitchen just as I was turning off the heat under the French toast. He was whistling, but he looked tired.

"How is she?" I asked.

He paused next to me and dropped a kiss on the top of my head. "She's okay, honey. Not great—but okay."

"I made French toast," I said brightly. "Mom *loves* my French toast."

Dad slid into a chair at the kitchen table, and I set his breakfast down in front of him. For a moment he just stared at the plate, almost as if he didn't recognize what it was. I knew what he was thinking about. Mom.

Finally he picked up his fork. "Rose has always loved French toast," he murmured. "Maybe it will tempt her."

I picked up Mom's plate and set my face in grin position. I made sure that the first time my mother saw me every morning, I was smiling. I wanted her to believe I was happy . . . no matter what I was feeling inside.

TWO

Christy

I KNOCKED SOFTLY on the door of my parents' bedroom. There was no response, so I nudged the door open with my hip and stuck my head into the room. My mother lay in the middle of her bed, propped up against a wall of pillows. Her eyes were closed, and I could tell from the expression on her face that she was sleeping lightly.

"Mom . . . ," I whispered. "Time for breakfast."

Her eyes fluttered open. For a split second I watched the muscles of my mother's face contort with pain. Then her gaze landed on me, and she smiled. I grinned back at her, holding up the breakfast tray for her inspection.

"Good morning, sweetie," she greeted me, as she did every day. "How nice of my wonderful daughter to make me such a delicious breakfast."

19

I felt a warm glow from the praise. Now that Mom was sick, I treasured these little things I could do to make her happy. "Do you feel up to eating?" I asked, my voice hopeful.

She moved to the side of the bed and took the tray from me. "For you, I would eat liver, or snails, or cow's tongue," she assured me. "At least . . . I would try."

I laughed. "As long as you manage a few bites of the French toast, I'll be satisfied."

I perched on the overstuffed chair beside my parents' bed and waited anxiously to see how much my mom would eat. She had been steadily losing weight since her surgery, and it seemed that every pound she shed was a bad omen.

"This is delicious, Christy," Mom told me, swallowing a bite. "Maybe you should take some gourmet-cooking lessons—you've got talent."

I rolled my eyes. "Mom, it's two slices of bread fried in egg batter. I don't think I'm quite ready for the Cordon Bleu in Paris."

She didn't answer. Mom was now staring at the food as if it were her worst enemy. I bit my lip, holding back the tears that suddenly threatened to slide down my cheeks. I knew what the look on her face meant. She had lost her appetite, and one more bite would probably make her want to throw up.

I took the tray. "I'll leave it over on the dresser," I told her. "You can have some more later."

She nodded. "Thanks, honey. I guess I wasn't as

hungry as I thought I was." She leaned back against the pillows, her eyes heavy with fatigue.

That was my cue. It was time to leave my mother to rest so I could finish getting ready for school. I took a deep breath, pushing away the sense of doom that I felt as I studied her face. I couldn't succumb to any dark thoughts about the future. Mom needed my optimism.

"I'll see you after school," I told her. "Just tell Mrs. Saunders that I put a lasagna in the fridge to heat up for lunch."

Mom nodded sleepily. "Molly and I will have a feast," she whispered.

I started to tiptoe from the room, believing that Mom had fallen into another light sleep.

"Christy," she called as I reached the door. "Can you do me a favor before you leave?"

I turned around. "Sure, Mom. Anything." *Maybe she wants to try the french toast again,* I hoped.

"I'd love it if you would open the window," she asked. "I want to smell the fresh spring air."

I smiled. Spring had always been my mother's favorite season. She was way into gardening, and she used to spend hours on her hands and knees in the backyard as soon as the final snow melted. Now her red gardening clogs and big straw hat were at the back of her closet. . . .

I walked over to the window and opened it wide. The air was cool and clean, and I could hear birds singing in the trees outside the house. I inhaled deeply, relishing the fact that my mother

21

wasn't too sick to enjoy a beautiful day.

"That's wonderful," Mom murmured. "Mornings like this always make me think of romance."

Me too, I thought. I had practically been foaming at the mouth, thinking about Matt while I cooked breakfast.

"Which reminds me . . . as soon as you pick up your prom dress from Claire's Boutique, you'll have to do a fashion show for me."

"I will," I promised. "The dress is gorgeous—you'll love it."

All signs of fatigue gone, my mother's eyes shone at the thought of seeing me in my floor-length gown. As I said, she had a thing about the prom.

"You and Jake are going to have a wonderful time," she mused. "I wish I could be a fly on the wall at the dance. It means the world to me that you two are going together."

"Uh . . . yeah. It'll be a blast," I agreed.

How could I even have *considered* getting out of the date with Jake? It meant so much to my mom to see the two of us together. . . . There was no way I could let her down. No matter how distasteful I found the wagtail.

Her eyes closed again. "I think I'll just lie here and listen to the birds awhile," Mom said softly.

I walked back to the door. "Hey, Mom?" I called quietly.

"Yes, pumpkin?" she asked, her eyes still closed.

"I can't wait to show you my dress." The image of her smile in my mind, I slipped out of the room.

I'm going to the prom with Jake, I reaffirmed to myself. And I was going to pretend to love every minute of it—for my mother.

In my room I pulled off the sweatshirt I had worn to cook breakfast. It was splattered with oil and syrup. My cooking skills might be improving, but I still managed to make a mess every time I went near the stove.

As I slipped into a white cotton shirt, I caught sight of myself in the full-length mirror that stood in one corner of my bedroom. I stopped and stared at my face. My skin was almost as pale as the white cotton, especially in contrast to my dark brown, shoulder-length hair.

I walked closer to the mirror, feeling like I was looking at a reflection of a ghost. There was so much on my mind that I hadn't really *looked* at myself lately. And I couldn't help but notice that I wasn't exactly a pretty sight. I looked like Morticia—on a bad day.

There were faint dark circles around my hazel eyes, and there were little lines around my mouth, as if my lips were superglued into a permanent frown. Ugh! I hadn't been sleeping well lately, but I hadn't realized that my insomnia showed so much. Under normal circumstances, I was sure that my mom and dad would have been taking my temperature if I came downstairs looking this bad. But like me, they had something else to worry about.

"This is no good, Christy," I told myself. I

didn't want to walk around Union High looking like a total stress case.

I finished buttoning my shirt and walked into my bathroom, which was something of a wreck. I was mastering the art of cooking . . . but my cleaning habits left a lot to be desired. At the bottom of an old shoe box I kept next to my sink, I found a bright pink shade of blush.

A few strokes with the blush brush added much needed pink to my pale cheeks. Next I coated my eyelashes in mascara that I'd purchased circa 1997. *Note to self,* I thought. *Update your makeup supply.* Finally I coated my lips with a subtle shade of dusty rose.

I looked a lot better. But there was still something missing from my face. A smile. Lately I had only been bothering to pull out smiles for Mom and Dad. But that was going to change.

I didn't want anyone to notice the mounting fear that was keeping me up nights. It was vital that I stay strong for my parents, and part of staying strong meant that I carried on my life as if nothing were wrong. As much as I appreciated the concern my best friends, Jane and Nicole, had for me, I didn't want their pity. I didn't want *anyone's* pity. It wouldn't help Mom—and it would just make me feel worse.

I practiced several different smiles in the mirror above the sink, testing which one looked the most natural. Finally I settled on a casual grin that *almost* reached my eyes.

"Good enough," I declared. "Christy Redmond, I think you're ready for your public."

Hi, Matt. How's it going? I rehearsed in my mind, checking the status of the grin. I nodded to myself in the mirror.

My friends—and Matt—weren't going to know how scared I was. As far as the world was concerned, I was a normal, happy, healthy teenager without a care in the world.

Ha.

Three

Jake

"COME ON, RAMONA," I begged. "I know you can do it, baby." I turned the key in the ignition of my Volkswagen GTI for the third time, praying for some kind of life from the engine.

But there was no sound from the car's internal organs, and I knew getting the engine going within the next three minutes was impossible. It wasn't the first time the fifth-hand used car I had bought with the lawn-mowing money I had saved last summer had refused to cooperate with me. And I was sure it wouldn't be the last. Ramona, my car, had an extremely temperamental personality.

This was the last thing I needed. I was running way late, and Mrs. Clark had informed me last week that I was going to have to stay after school if I was tardy one more time. At the age of seventeen, staying after school was a downright humiliating experience.

I gazed down the block, trying to figure out my next course of action. My dad had already left for work, and my mom was in the shower. But if I walked to school, I was going to be at least twenty minutes late.

And then I saw none other than Christy Redmond racing out of her house. Her arms were loaded down with books, as always. I sighed. Christy was the last person I wanted to ask for a ride to school. But she was also the only person on this street about to head to Union High.

Pride or detention. Pride. Detention. Okay, I would sacrifice my pride in the name of avoiding detention. It was the only sane thing to do. I jumped out of the car and slammed the door behind me.

Swinging my backpack over one shoulder, I jogged down the block, waving my arms. When I was about fifty feet from the Redmonds' house, Christy looked up from the door she was unlocking.

"You can stop waving, Jake," she informed me. "I see you."

"Can I have a ride to school?" I asked. "Ramona is in one of her moods."

She shrugged. "Get in."

Huh. That was easy. This wasn't the first time I'd had to swallow my pride and ask Christy for a lift to school. But usually she tortured me for a couple of minutes before she grudgingly agreed to let me grace the inside of her precious car. I tossed my backpack into the backseat of her Honda and slid into the passenger seat.

Christy barely seemed to notice me as she started the car and put it into gear. Her eyes were focused on the road, and she seemed to be in some sort of meditative trance.

"You're losing your touch," I commented, glancing sideways at her dark hair and ivory skin.

She raised an eyebrow. "What's that supposed to mean?"

"I haven't received one insult since I got into this car," I pointed out. "We've been together for almost three full minutes, and you've neither commented on my poor taste in girls *nor* called me a ruttish, reeling-ripe puttock."

"Maybe I've matured," she responded. "Maybe I've realized that it's a waste of time to expend even an iota of mental energy on sparring with you."

Right. And I'm the proud owner of a brand-new Porsche, I thought. "I've got another theory," I informed her. "I think you're harboring a hidden, burning passion for me. It's written all over your face."

Now *that* got her attention. Christy took her eyes off the road just long enough to glare at me. "I might have a burning *disdain* for you," Christy retorted. "But as for giving you a ride, I'm only doing what's right. My parents always taught me to take pity on stray animals."

Ouch. I never should have opened my mouth. But now that I had . . . there was no way I was going to let Christy get the last word.

"Speaking of animals, I saw your ex-boyfriend making out with some freshman in the cafeteria the other day. He was kissing her in between showing off his ability to snort milk out of his nose to his buddies."

"He must have been making out with Leanne Nelson," Christy came back at me. "Isn't she the girl who turned you down for a date last month?"

Ouch again. Christy was an expert at getting under my skin. Why did I find it necessary to provoke her the minute I got into the car? *Because you're an idiot,* I told myself. But it was too late to take it back. So far, this day was getting off to a stellar start.

For the tenth time I regretted the fact that I had let my mom talk me into asking Christy to the prom. Not that I had resisted the idea. I knew that Rose Redmond had always had a not-so-secret hope that Christy and I would fall in love. Making her happy by taking Christy to the prom was, like, the least I could do for the woman who had been basically like a second mom to me since I was five.

It was ironic, really. I could have named at least six guys who would have killed to take Christy Redmond to the senior prom. And I, her archenemy, had asked her to the dance as a favor to her mother. *At what point is life going to start making sense?* I wondered as Christy slammed on the brakes to avoid going through a yellow light.

"So have you thought up a good excuse to get out of going to the prom with me yet?" Christy asked, almost as if she had been reading my mind with an X-ray machine.

"Why?" I asked. "Have you found some no-brained jock you'd rather go with?"

I had never understood Christy's taste in guys. She flitted from one amiable, good-looking bone-head to another. Apparently she enjoyed the company of guys who resembled friendly puppies. Naturally, none of these relationships (and I use that term loosely) lasted for more than three or four weeks. Sometimes I thought she chose her dates based solely on who would provide the best material for my stinging barbs.

"For your information, David Foster was a National Merit semifinalist," she retorted, referring to her last sort-of boyfriend. "Not everyone finds it necessary to flaunt their smarts in order to get attention."

I decided not to respond to that particular comment. I knew Christy thought I tended to be obnoxious—it wasn't new information. Luckily there were others who *appreciated* my strong personality. Wendy Schultz, for instance. She was an adorable junior who had been giving me The Eye in the cafeteria lately.

Now, there's an ideal prom date, I thought. Wendy was pretty, smart, and, most important, *pleasant.* I would have loved to put my arms around her for a few rounds of slow, slow dancing.

"Well, don't worry," I assured Christy. "Once we get to the dance, you can flirt with any National Merit semifinalist you want to."

31

"I *know,* Jake," Christy declared. "We'll do the limo, we'll do the corsage, we'll do the pictures. After we make nice for the parents, we're both free to do whatever we want once we arrive at the prom."

She had repeated back to me exactly what I had said to her when I asked her to be my "date." I guessed that bringing up the same subject again had hurt her girlish sensibility.

"Unless you *want* to be real dates," I said quickly. "I mean, it's not like I'm going to refuse to dance with you or anything."

She snorted. "I'll have plenty of people to do the lambada with," she assured me. "Don't you worry your tickle-brained little head."

"Say no more," I answered. "I'll be *more* than happy to leave you to your own devices."

"Good." It had the ring of a definitive, final statement. She was done with the conversation. Had we not been confined to the front seat of a small car, Christy probably would have waved her hand to dismiss me from the room.

That's fine with me, I thought. Who cared if Christy didn't want to talk to me? I didn't want to talk to her either. I would sit here in silence until we pulled into the school parking lot.

Still, Christy's attitude was just a tad irritating. Even beyond her usual brand of irritating. She didn't have to be quite so bummed about going to the prom with me. It wasn't as if I were a total loser. For that matter, I wasn't any kind of loser. Not that

32

I would ever let Christy know that she had even slightly gotten to me. I might not be too proud to cop a ride, but I had my limits.

Besides, lots of girls would have jumped at the chance to go to the prom with me, if I did say so myself. Wendy Schultz, for instance. I would have been willing to bet anyone fifty dollars—no, a hundred—that she would have done somersaults if I'd invited her to be my date.

I was getting the sinking feeling that prom night was going to be a replay of the Date from Hell after seventh grade. *At least it can't be any worse,* I thought.

Sometimes it was hard for me to believe that at one time in our lives, Christy and I had been almost inseparable. She was the first girl I really got to know. In truth, she was the first girl I ever loved.

During long summer days in grade school, I had learned that girls could be playing with a doll one minute, climbing a tree the next. I had learned that girls were a lot more sympathetic when it came to scraped knees than boys were. I had learned that . . . well, just because girls had longer hair and softer skin didn't mean they couldn't be a blast to hang out with.

I sighed quietly, glancing at Christy out of the corner of my eye. Now that we weren't engaged in verbal combat, I could really study her face. She looked as beautiful as she always did . . . but something was off.

She's got circles under her eyes, I realized. *She's tired.* Sure, she was wearing blush and lipstick and whatever else it was that girls wore to make themselves look totally put together. But beyond the makeup, I could see that Christy was exhausted.

Suddenly all of the fire seeped out of my bones. Next to me sat the girl I had grown up with. And she was going through the worst time of her entire life. I felt a deep pang of sympathy—but I knew better than to say anything aloud to Christy.

She wasn't the type of person who wanted to acknowledge any kind of weakness. If I let her know that I sensed her pain, it would only make her feel worse. There was, however, something I *could* do.

I could offer Christy what I always offered her. A person with whom she could argue and vent and relieve some of the tension that must be building up inside her. Hey, it wasn't much . . . but it was all I had to give.

Four

Christy

"DO YOU THINK Max would still like me if I cut off all of my hair?" Jane wondered aloud.

It was Tuesday, and Jane, Nicole, and I were having lunch at our usual table in the Union High lunchroom. Since the cafeteria was serving an orange glop they had the audacity to label "macaroni 'n' cheese," I was glad that I'd had the wisdom to bring a smoked-turkey sandwich on seven-grain bread from home.

"You mean, like, cut it *all* off, in the military style?" Nicole asked. "Or do you mean cut it off Sienna Miller style?"

"Duh," Jane responded. "I'm not going to go *bald*."

"I'm not going to the prom," Nicole said, changing the subject completely. "I'm simply not going to go. No biggie."

"Part of me thinks Max would find the new haircut sexy," Jane said, ignoring Nicole's comment. "Aren't guys supposed to be intrigued by unexpected change?"

I almost laughed. Jane Smith and Nicole Gilmore had been my two best friends for as long as I could remember—well, since ninth grade anyway. The three of us had developed our own form of communication during the last four years. Often our conversations consisted of three simultaneous monologues. But somehow everybody managed to hear what everyone else was saying.

"Let's face it," Nicole declared. "The guys in this school are *lame*." She glanced at Jane. "I mean, except for Max."

Jane and Max Ziff had starting going out a couple of days ago, and the relationship had made Jane deliriously happy. It also seemed to be making her overly preoccupied with her hairstyle.

"Maybe I'll just get a new sweater," Jane decided. "If I get my hair cut, then Max won't be able to run his fingers through it. And he loves doing that . . ."

As Jane went on in her dreamy tone and Nicole cut in every now and then to zap Jane back down to earth, I resisted the urge just to close my eyes, put my head down on the table, and let their conversation swirl around me like a gentle stream. I had never thought the sound of my friends' voices could be so . . . soothing.

Sure, their problems were minor compared to

what I was dealing with. But that's exactly what I liked about having them around. Nicole and Jane had made a tacit agreement not to push me to talk about my mom's illness. They knew I wasn't the type to pour out my problems, and they respected my wish to maintain my privacy. At the same time, I knew they were there for me if I ever wanted to talk.

"What do you think, Christy?" Jane asked, interrupting my thoughts. "Should I get my hair cut—or buy a new sweater with one of those plunging necklines?"

This time I *did* laugh. Jane sounded so serious—as if she were discussing a Middle East peace agreement rather than what kind of fashion statement she wanted to make on her date Friday night.

I pushed away the image of my mother's face, etched in pain. There was nothing I could do for her right now—except preserve my sanity by throwing myself into the Life of a Normal Teenager.

"Go with the sweater," I advised her. "Max likes your hair just the way it is."

"I agree," Nicole added. "Max loves you for your sparkling personality—but he also loves you for your cute ponytail."

Jane's eyes lit up. "Do you really think he *loves* me?" she asked. "Or is it a strong case of *like?*"

I settled more comfortably in my chair, ready to launch into a long and detailed discussion about the exact state of Max and Jane's relationship. Friends. What would I do without them?

*   *   *

37

I stood several feet away from one of the industrial-sized garbage cans at the back of the cafeteria. I took aim and tossed my diet Coke can toward the huge receptacle.

"She shoots . . . she scores," I announced as the can landed in the trash can.

"You should think about going pro," I heard a voice behind me comment as I held up my arms in victory.

I didn't need to turn around to know who had spoken to me. I had kept one eye out for Matt Fowler all through lunch period, but the cafeteria had been so crowded that I hadn't been able to catch sight of him.

"Hi, Matt," I said, pivoting in what I hoped was a somewhat alluring manner.

He grinned. "Christy, you're just the person I was looking for."

Okay, time to go into full-flirt mode, I told myself. This was exactly the kind of intro I had been waiting for during the last two weeks.

"Is there something I can do for you?" I asked, executing a subtle eyelash flutter as I attempted to dazzle him with a hundred-watt smile.

"I come to you as the bearer of excellent news," Matt informed me. "AP biology is canceled this afternoon."

Okay. It wasn't the pickup line I had been hoping for . . . but it *was* good news. Biology was my last class of the day. If it was canceled, that meant I could leave school early and spend a little extra time

38

with my mom. She was usually in pretty good shape during the afternoon.

"What happened?" I asked. "Was there a bomb scare in the lab?"

Matt laughed. "Nothing quite so dramatic. Word has it that Mr. Burgess has a nasty case of the flu. The kind that makes you throw up every five minutes."

I knew altogether too much about throwing up. I had held Mom's hair back for her at least a dozen times as she had thrown up after chemotherapy treatments. And later . . . she hadn't had any hair to hold back. The powerful chemicals in the chemotherapy had caused almost all of it to fall out.

"Thanks for letting me know," I told Matt. "That was sweet of you."

I expected him to turn around and walk off, but he didn't. Instead Max fixed his startling blue eyes on mine and stayed rooted to his spot.

"Is there something else?" I asked. *Maybe my makeup is wearing off,* I thought. *Maybe he's wondering why I look so darn tired.*

"I thought you and I could take advantage of the free time," he said, giving me a delicious smile. "I, uh, was wondering if you'd like to join me for a little afternoon air hockey at Jon's Pizza."

"Oh!" This was the invitation I had been waiting for. But now that it had been issued, I wasn't sure how to respond.

I was torn between the prospect of a date with my crush and a little extra quality time with my mother. Ninety percent of me wanted to go home and see how Mom was doing. But the other ten percent of me found myself staring into Matt's twinkling, mesmerizing blue eyes.

"Air hockey sounds great," I heard myself saying. Maybe a little recreation with a cute boy was exactly what I needed to decompress.

As Matt walked away, I gave myself a mental pat on the back. Sure, Jake Saunders thought I was about as attractive as the bride of Frankenstein. But what did he know? Matt Fowler had just asked me to accompany him on something that definitely resembled a date. I still had it.

"Keep your eye on the puck," Matt instructed. "Don't get distracted."

We were at the back of Jon's Pizza, where there were a couple of air-hockey games, three pinball machines, and a somewhat rickety Foosball table. The minute Matt had dropped two quarters into the slot and the table had come to life, I knew I was in trouble.

Matt had scored five goals off me in less than ten minutes—I had only managed to block the puck one time. Luckily he wasn't one of those guys who found it necessary to lord his hand-eye coordination over others. He had stopped the game and given me some key pointers. I was still losing, but at least I wasn't totally humiliating myself.

"Here it comes!" Matt warned. "Remember, *keep your eye on the puck.*"

I zeroed in on the small, round, plastic disk and leaned over the table. I felt the faint breeze of the air coming off the game as I kept my eyes glued to the puck that was whizzing toward me. *Three, two, one.* I moved my "stick" a fraction of an inch and made contact with the puck. *Zoom!*

The plastic disk shot across the table—and into Matt's goal. "Score!" I shouted, throwing up my arms. "I did it!"

Matt grinned. "Move over, Mark Messier—here comes Christy."

"Did you let me score on purpose?" I asked suspiciously.

"No way," Matt insisted. "I'm too competitive to let someone get a goal off me—even someone as pretty as you are."

My heart skipped a beat. Matt had said I was pretty. This was exactly what I had been waiting for, and it felt good. It had been a long time since I had enjoyed such a typical, seventeen-year-old moment.

"Let's celebrate your triumph with a couple of slices," Matt suggested. "I don't want you to get air-hockey elbow."

I slid into a corner booth and watched Matt as he went to the counter for our slices of pizza. I felt more relaxed than I had in days. With Matt I could almost—but not quite—forget about what was going on at home. At least for this hour I was just a normal girl with normal, everyday problems.

Matt is so easy to be with, I thought. He was the exact opposite of Jake, whose idea of a good time was needling me to the point of extreme exasperation. Matt just liked to have a good time—he wasn't obsessed with outsmarting me every second of our conversation. *This is what I needed,* I decided, glad I had taken Matt up on his offer.

When Matt appeared at the booth with a slice of pepperoni pizza for me, I flashed him my best smile. "Thanks for inviting me out today," I told him as I sprinkled my pizza with Parmesan cheese.

He finished chewing the huge bite he had taken from his slice of Italian sausage. He swallowed, then dabbed at his lips with a paper napkin. *Hmmm . . . a gentleman,* I noted. *A bonus point for good table manners.*

"You don't need to thank me," he responded finally. "I've been wanting to ask you out for weeks."

I felt a tingle of pleasure that is particular to a guy letting a girl know he's interested. It was excitement mixed with satisfaction. And hope for the future.

"I'm glad you did," I told him. "This has been the best afternoon I've had in a long time."

He smiled. "Good. Me too."

There was a moment of awkward silence. We had both established that we were happy to be here. Now what?

"Well, air hockey was the perfect antidote to all the pressure I've been under," I offered. "My mom is really sick . . . and sometimes I need to let off some serious steam."

"Yeah, I—I, uh, heard about that," Matt stammered. "I'm, uh, sorry."

"Thanks." I took another bite of pizza and prepared to let the subject drop.

I could tell that Matt was uncomfortable with the idea of my mother having cancer. But that was normal. A lot people had trouble confronting the *c* word.

Matt pushed away the paper plate that had held his pizza. "Hey, how about another game?" he asked. "I don't have to be at baseball practice for almost an hour."

To be honest, I'd had my fair share of air hockey for the day. I would have preferred a pinball challenge. But I didn't want to hurt Matt's feelings. Especially since he had been so nice about giving me pointers.

"That sounds great," I responded. "I can't wait to try out my new moves now that I've been reenergized."

As we headed back to the table, I noticed that Matt looked almost as good from behind as he did from the front. *This is a guy who can take my mind off my troubles,* I confirmed to myself.

Sort of.

No. Definitely.

Because that was what I needed. To escape a little. Stop worrying. Not talk about the big "it."

Right?

Five

Christy

"THERE'S NOTHING BETTER than a teacher with the flu," Matt commented as he drove me back to school. "I feel like we had a snow day."

"Don't tell me you were actually *glad* to miss out on the opportunity to do an advanced dissection of an earthworm," I joked. "I've been looking forward to it all month."

"Maybe we'll get lucky, and he'll be out all week," he said. "We could start a tournament of champions at Jon's Pizza."

Amazingly, I had actually managed to win one of our air-hockey games. Matt had looked so surprised that I'd half expected him to faint from shock.

"Ha!" I laughed. "I don't think beating you one game out of, like, six calls for an entire tournament." I paused. "But I might take you on in pinball."

"It's a date." As Matt spoke, I noticed a few droplets of water spattering against the windshield.

Moments later, rain began to fall steadily. Rivulets of water streamed down the glass, and Matt turned on the windshield wipers. I had always loved the soothing, rhythmic sound of wipers.

"I love rain," I told Matt, cracking the window of the passenger-side door. "Especially warm spring rain."

Matt shook his head. "I can't stand it. This means we're going to do sprints in the gym during baseball practice."

"Ugh." I didn't blame Matt for being bummed out about the rain, but I couldn't get enough of the fresh, damp air.

I inhaled deeply, then rolled the window down farther so that I could stick my head out of the car. I held out my tongue and caught several drops on my tongue. Delicious!

Matt laughed. "You're crazy, you know that?" he asked as we pulled into the school parking lot. "Most girls would pay money just to keep from getting their hair wet."

I grinned at him. "Last time I checked, I wasn't 'most girls.'"

Matt drove through the parking lot and stopped next to my Honda. "You're going to get soaked just getting into your car," he noted.

"Don't worry about it." I put my hand on the door latch and turned to him. "Thanks for a great afternoon, Matt."

"It was my pleasure." He hesitated, and it seemed like he wanted to say something else.

"What?" I asked. "Do I have pizza sauce on my face or something?"

"No . . . I, uh, wanted to tell you something." He seemed nervous, so I took my hand off the latch and gave him my most comforting smile.

"What is it?" I asked. *Is he going to invite me to the prom?* I wondered. *And if he does . . . well, if he does, I'll have to say no. Period.*

"I, uh, already have a date to the prom," he blurted out finally. "But if I didn't, I would ask you to go with me."

I tried not to feel the sting of rejection. After all, he wasn't the only one who already had a date. I was shackled to Jake, whether I liked it or not.

"Oh." I couldn't help it. I was hurt.

"You see, Sandra Donell asked me if I would take her to the prom, like, last month," he explained. "I couldn't say no. I mean, I knew she had a crush on me . . . and it probably took a lot of guts for her to get up the nerve to ask. . . ."

"I understand," I said quickly. "I already have a date too." But I wasn't about to go into the details of my bizarre agreement with Jake. "It's a similar circumstance."

He nodded. "Well, then."

"So . . . I guess we're not going to the prom together," I said, stating the obvious.

He nodded again. "True. But that doesn't mean we can't hang out together. I mean, if you want to."

"Yes!" I realized I sounded slightly desperate, so I decided I needed to take it down a notch. "That might be nice."

"There's no law against two people having a good time together," Matt continued. "A date to the prom isn't a binding contract or anything."

"Right," I responded. Of course, in *my* case the date with Jake *felt* like a contract.

"Promise to save me a slow dance at the prom?" Matt asked softly, resting his hand on my arm.

"Definitely," I answered. "I'll save one for you, and you can save one for me." I leaned forward and gave Matt a quick peck on the cheek.

Then I slid out of the car and into the rain. As I felt the water coming down on my head, soaking me from head to foot, I imagined the rain was washing away all of my fear and anxiety. *I'm cleansed,* I thought, holding out my hands to catch more of the rain.

As I covered the several yards to get to my car, I realized something astonishing. I felt almost human again. . . . Now, *that* was an accomplishment.

The moment I put my car into reverse in order to pull out of my parking space and head home, the feeling of well-being I had enjoyed during the last hour and a half started to evaporate. Jon's Pizza, the rain, Matt's blue eyes . . . all of that seemed like a surreal daydream. Now I just wanted to get home and see how Mom was feeling.

I shook my head, willing away the fear I always

felt when it was time to go home. *Will she be worse? Will she be in pain? Is she having a good day? A bad day?* The same questions ran through my mind again and again every day.

I backed out of my parking space and drove slowly through the nearly empty lot. The rain had turned the sky dark, and it felt more like seven o'clock than four. *I need a nap,* I decided. Maybe when I got home, I would crawl into bed with Mom and doze for an hour or so before Dad got home. Even now, there was no place I felt safer than at my mother's side.

She always had the power to soothe whatever chaos was going on inside my head—even when it was her own illness that was the source of that chaos. *A mother's instinct,* I thought. She always knew just what to say.

As I started down the street that led to my block, I caught sight of a lone, dark figure on the side of the street. *I know that walk,* I thought. Because of the rain I couldn't see his face. But there was no doubt in my mind that it was Jake.

I should let him slosh through puddles all the way to Sunset Drive, I thought. After the way he was going after me this morning, the guy deserved to catch pneumonia on his way home.

That was what I *believed,* but I already knew that I was going to pull over and take the boy out of his misery. I couldn't help myself. Jake just looked so . . . pathetic. I stopped next to the curb and blared the horn.

Through the rain I saw Jake's head swivel toward my car. A second later he was jogging in my direction, the ever present backpack banging against his hip. He looked all of about eight years old.

I rolled down my window and thrust my head into the rain. "All aboard for Noah's ark," I called.

He sprinted around the car, yanked open the passenger-side door, and dove into the seat. "Thanks, Christy!" He slammed the door shut and heaved what sounded like a huge sigh of relief. "I was seriously worried that the five pages of notes I have to study for my history test were going to get so wet that the erasable ink was going to run all over the place."

"No problem," I answered. "I mean, it's not like I have to go out of my way to take you home."

And if I were perfectly honest with myself, I would have to admit that I preferred even the company of Jake to the onslaught of concerns that had been ricocheting around my brain. Of course, admitting that to *myself* didn't mean I was going to confess it to *him*.

Jake shook out his shaggy head of dark hair, sending about a million droplets of water in my general direction. I opened my mouth to tell him that it was supposed to be raining *outside*. Then I stopped myself, snapping my jaw shut. He'd sounded so genuinely grateful for the ride home that I decided to allow just this one obnoxious gesture to slide. There were, after all, those moments when I almost liked Jake. They were few and far between, but they did exist.

"You know who you look like right now?" Jake asked, settling into his seat.

"Who?" I steered the Honda back into my lane and headed down the street.

"Ms. Whiskers."

I raised an eyebrow. "And who is Ms. Whiskers?" I asked, knowing that I was going to regret the question.

He grinned. "She was one of my favorite stuffed animals. Ms. Whiskers was a big, pink rat . . . until I left her out in the rain one afternoon. Then she was a big, pink, *drowned* rat."

"Gee . . . thanks." I had stopped to give Jake a ride out of the goodness of my heart, and his reaction had been to compare me to a drowned rat. Touching. So much for that fleeting moment of near tolerance.

"It's not too late for me to stop this car and make you walk," I pointed out. "We rats aren't known for our generous spirits."

"Hey, watch what you say about Ms. Whiskers," Jake countered. "She was a loyal friend—until that fateful day."

"Are you this annoying all the time?" I asked. "Or do you save the 'special' parts of your personality for me and me alone?"

Jake scoffed. "You think *I'm* annoying?" he demanded. "Correct me if I'm wrong, but I could

51

have sworn I saw you driving into the parking lot with Matt Fowler."

Okay. Now he was asking for it. "What's wrong with Matt?" I demanded.

"Nothing . . . he's a nice enough guy if you like the type."

I am not going to respond, I told myself. *This is a trap.* I stared straight ahead, focusing on the movement of the windshield wipers.

Jake cleared his throat. "So, is that the guy you're so psyched to hang out with at the prom?" he asked. "Pretty-boy Matt Fowler?"

I rolled my eyes. "I don't see how that's any of your business," I retorted. "Last time I checked, I didn't need to clear my dance partners with *you*." I paused. "Having said that, yes, Matt and I will probably keep company with each other at the prom."

Jake snorted. "Matt's a really deep guy," he remarked, his voice laced with sarcasm. "But I guess his supposed good looks make up for his lack of personality."

"Ha!" I spat out. "It's not like Wendy Schultz is known for her sparkling conversation."

Jake frowned. "How do you know about Wendy?"

"Please!" I snorted. "You're not exactly a master of subtlety, Saunders. I happened to see you practicing your lame brand of flirting with the girl in the cafeteria the other day."

"So?" he asked.

"*So*, it doesn't take a NASA engineer to figure out that you've got the hots for her." I paused. "Although *why* you'd want to go out with my-name-is-Wendy-and-I-end-every-statement-with-a-giggle is a complete mystery to me."

"Wendy is a very nice person," Matt stated, as if he were giving her a good reference for a potential future employer. "And she's *exceedingly* easy to be around."

"Suit yourself," I told him. "You can date Wendy or Bambi or Candy for all I care."

"Thanks for the stamp of approval," Jake retorted. "Now I'll be able to sleep at night."

The rain had let up considerably in the last few minutes, leaving only a gray drizzle that seemed considerably less romantic than the torrents that had been coming down when Matt and I had been sitting in his car. I found myself wishing for something more dramatic—thunder, lightning, hail. The drizzle was just plain . . . dreary.

I hit the blinker and took a right onto Sunset Drive. Finally. Two car rides with Jake in one day were two too many. The two of us simply weren't meant to be in a confined space together for any amount of time.

I stopped the car in front of my house. "Do you have the strength to make it from here?" I asked.

Jake glanced up the block toward his house. "I think I'll manage," he assured me. Then his eyes moved toward the driveway beside our house. "But I guess my mom can't even walk a block. Her car is here."

I followed Jake's gaze. He was right. Molly Saunders's supermom minivan was parked in our driveway. She had probably driven over a fresh load of frozen casseroles. Ever since Mom had gotten sick, Mrs. Saunders had made it her personal mission to ensure that we never went hungry. I knew Molly used cooking for my mother as a way to deal with the cancer, so I refrained from mentioning that we had enough frozen dinners to carry us through to the *next* millennium.

"Your mom is the greatest," I told Jake. "I don't know what we would do without her."

Jake nodded. "She . . . well, she wants to do whatever she can to help. You know how much your mom means to her."

I did. They had been friends since high school and had gone through every significant event of their lives together. I couldn't imagine how I would feel twenty years from now if Nicole or Jane were diagnosed with breast cancer. It would be devastating . . . almost as devastating as the diagnosis of my own mother.

"How is she?" Jake asked. "I mean, my mom talks about her . . . but she doesn't like to focus on her illness."

Now, *that* was the sixty-four-thousand-dollar question. How was Mom doing? I wanted to say she was doing fine. I wanted to say she was getting stronger every day. I wanted to give him a million different positive responses.

But none of them would have been true. Mom

54

was getting weaker every day, and there was absolutely nothing that I, or anyone else, could do about it.

I didn't even realize that tears had started to roll down my face. It wasn't until I felt Jake's hand on my shoulder that I realized my cheeks were wet. I wanted to stop the tears, but the unexpected gentleness of Jake's touch triggered something inside me.

Maybe it was the knowledge that if someone like *Jake* felt sorry for me, then the situation had to be truly awful. Maybe it was the fact that I had been bottling up my fears for days, weeks, months, and I couldn't hold back for one more second. Or maybe it was simply that it had been a while since someone had come right out and asked me that simple question. *How is she?*

I couldn't help myself. I began to sob. This wasn't quiet weeping. My shoulders were heaving, my eyes were starting to swell, and I was hiccuping. But as I cried, I felt the tension slowly starting to dissolve.

"Christy, I'm so sorry," Jake said softly. "I didn't mean to—"

"It's not your fault," I interrupted. "I'm just . . . I don't know."

Talk about humiliating! Of all times to crack, I had to do it with none other than Jake Saunders sitting next to me. I breathed deeply, willing the tears to stop.

"I don't usually cry," I said finally. "I don't want anyone's pity. It's just that sometimes . . ."

"Hey, don't think twice about it," Jake said, his hand still on my shoulder. "Crying is the most natural thing in the world."

I rolled my eyes. "Yeah, right. I'm sure you bawl all the time." Jake's kindness was threatening to bring on a whole fresh round of tears.

Be strong, I told myself. *Don't let him see how much you're hurting.* Well, it was a little late for that. Jake had already witnessed my total breakdown.

"I do cry," Jake insisted. "Just last week I had this terrible hangnail. Oh, man, I was crying like a baby."

"Uh-huh . . ." I almost smiled. The image of Jake tearing up over a tiny hangnail was beyond absurd.

"And the other day I was watching one of those cheesy long-distance commercials," he continued. "Before I knew what hit me, tears were rolling down my face and I was picking up the phone to call my grandma in Arizona."

I giggled. "Let me guess—you carry around a hankie just in case you happen to stub your toe."

"As a matter of fact, I make it a policy never to leave home without a travel pack of Kleenex." Jake unzipped his backpack as he spoke. A moment later he pulled out, yes, a brand-new packet of Kleenex. "Ta-da!" He handed me a few tissues.

"Thanks." I dabbed at my eyes, then blew my nose loudly and unceremoniously into the Kleenex.

"Those really come in handy when the bullies at school try to steal my lunch money," Jake told me, his voice gravely serious. "One time I wept all through my mystery-turkey casserole."

I giggled again. And then I started to laugh. *Really* laugh. "I hope you never get into carpentry," I sputtered. "I would hate to see what would happen if you accidentally hit your thumb with a hammer!"

"Forget about it!" Jake responded. "We're talking a major flood—a national disaster."

I kept laughing. It wasn't that Jake was so funny—although even I had to admit that the guy had a sense of humor. It just felt *so* good to really and truly laugh that I never wanted to stop.

After what felt like an hour, but was probably about two minutes, the laughter slowly started to subside. Which immediately caused another round of the hiccups.

"I'm a mess." I moaned. "First I'm sobbing, then I'm laughing hysterically." I paused. "I really didn't want anyone to see me like this."

Jake shrugged. "Hey, as far as I'm concerned, this never happened."

I nodded. "Do you mind just leaving me alone?" I asked. "I don't want to go inside until I'm one hundred percent calm."

"Say no more." Jake gave me a last glance, then slipped out of the car. "Thanks for the ride, Christy," he said, sticking his head back inside. Then he shut the door gently behind him and began to jog toward his house.

I closed my eyes and leaned my head against the back of the seat. I still couldn't believe I had totally lost it in front of Jake. I had sworn to myself I would never do that kind of thing. Then again . . . I had to admit that Jake had been incredibly cool.

For a few minutes I had felt like we were back in sixth grade, laughing and talking like we could with no one else in the world. *I* needed *that,* I realized suddenly. Because . . . wonder of wonders . . . the dull, throbbing headache that had become an intrinsic part of my life had magically disappeared.

Thanks, Jake, I thought. *This one time you really helped me out.* I unbuckled my seat belt and opened the door of the car. I couldn't wait to get inside—I wanted to see my mom. Who knew? Maybe I would even share a few laughs with the woman I loved more than anything in the whole world.

Six

Jake

"I NEED CHOCOLATE-CHIP cookies," I murmured to myself, heading up the stairs from my basement-turned-bedroom two at a time. "Or maybe a ham sandwich."

I had been trying to study for my history test for hours. So far, I had learned two dates and the names of five vice presidents. In other words, my study session was a complete bust—useless. And I knew why. Every time I bent my head over my history notes, I saw Christy's tearstained face staring back at me. Now it was almost midnight, and I was getting desperate. *When the going gets tough, the tough go to the fridge,* I told myself.

"Jake, is that you?" I heard my mother call softly.

I stopped in the arched doorway at the edge of

the living room. "What are you doing up, Mom?" I asked. "You're usually asleep before the ten o'clock news."

She was sitting on the sofa, a huge pile of photographs covering her lap. "I was looking at some old pictures."

I walked into the room and flopped beside her on the couch. "Cooing over my old baby photos?" I asked.

She smiled, but I noticed that her eyes were slightly damp. Jeez. Everywhere I went today, I was making women cry. "Most of these are of Rose and me," she explained. "We must have taken a thousand pictures together over the years."

"You two are really close, huh?" I asked. It was sort of weird to think of my mom in the context of being someone's friend. To me, she was one hundred percent Mom.

She nodded, staring at a photo of herself and Rose dressed up as Laverne and Shirley one Halloween night. "Rose is my best friend. . . . I don't know what I'm going to do without her."

"Without her?" I squeaked. "You mean . . . ?"

I had known that Rose was *really* sick. I had even known there was a chance that . . . well, she wouldn't make it. But until this moment I had never heard my mother speak as if she didn't expect Mrs. Redmond to make a full recovery. Mom had maintained a determined, positive attitude since the day her friend was diagnosed with breast cancer.

A lone tear slid down my mother's cheek as she

continued to gaze at the old photograph. "I'm praying for a miracle, sweetie. And you never know . . ."

"I didn't realize that things had gotten so bad," I
said, thinking again of Christy's tears. "Christy is so
strong. . . . She never talks about it."

Mom sighed. Then she shuffled through the
pile and pulled out a picture of Rose holding
Christy when she was a newborn baby. "Christy
has always been that way. Even when she was a
baby, she rarely cried. It was almost as if she didn't
want to cause anyone a bit of trouble."

"Well, she hasn't changed." I thought of the
firm set of Christy's jaw and her horror when she
realized that I was a witness to her tears.

"If only the same were true of Rose," Mom
murmured, glancing down at another picture.
"She's changing every day . . . growing weaker and
weaker."

"I'm so sorry, Mom," I whispered. "I wish there
were something I could do to help."

My mother reached out and put her arm around
my shoulders. "You *are* doing something, honey.
You're taking Christy to the prom, which as you
know thrills Rose. She's so happy about that."

"Mrs. Redmond might be thrilled, but Christy
isn't," I commented. "She hates me."

Mom pulled me close and gave me one of her
patented maternal squeezes. "Oh, honey, that's not
true. You're one of Christy's oldest friends."

I shook my head. "You don't understand. She
can't stand the sight of me." I paused. "Today I

made her cry. . . . I mean, not on purpose, but still . . ."

My mother set aside the photographs and shifted in her seat so she could look me in the eyes. "Christy is going through a lot, Jake. I think crying is probably a really good thing for her. It's not healthy for her to hold all of her feelings in."

"Maybe . . ." Christy *had* started to laugh after the tears had stopped flowing. And she hadn't seemed angry about me asking her about her mom. She'd just been—sad.

"Christy needs all the friends she can get right now," Mom declared, her tone allowing no room for argument. "Trust me on this one, Jake—even if I am just your mom."

I nodded. I would do whatever I could for Christy. But I doubted I could do much good. As far as Christy Redmond was concerned, I was persona non grata. She had made that clear time and time again. And I didn't think my best foe's opinion on the score was going to change anytime soon. At least, not if today were any indication . . .

The Olympic-sized swimming pool was lit only by the blue glow of an underwater light. But the moon was so bright that I could see clearly the back of the girl who was treading water in the deep end. Her red bikini highlighted her ivory skin, and her dark hair was wet and glistening under the moonbeams.

I walked toward the pool, unsure why I was here or what I was meant to do. I didn't even know why I was wearing my swimming trunks. But the pool—or more accurately, the girl in the pool—was drawing me forward. The air was warm and sultry, and a light breeze blew through my hair as I continued to put one foot in front of the other.

Turn around, *I thought, staring at the back of the girl's head. But she didn't. She simply continued to tread water, seemingly unaware of my presence.*

I was acutely aware of my surroundings as I finally reached the edge of the pool. The scent of honeysuckle and jasmine filled my nostrils, and the grass under my bare feet was crisp and cool. Every nerve in my body felt hypersensitive, as if my entire life had led up to this one moonlit moment.

Standing on my tiptoes, I held my arms over my head. Then I dove into the water, swimming for several seconds until I burst through to the surface. I found myself just feet from the girl.

"Who are you?" I asked.

When she turned around, it was like the sun coming up. "Who am I?" she echoed. "Jake, you know me."

And I did. It was Christy. Beautiful, sexy Christy— my very own mermaid. "I've missed you."

She smiled. "How could you miss me?" she asked. "I've been here all the time."

"Yes, but . . . not like this." I couldn't take my eyes off her.

Was this the same girl I had climbed trees and played kick the can with? She was all grown up now.

Christy tossed her head backward, showering me with drops of cool water. Her light, sparkling laughter filled the night as she swam toward me. "You're different too, Jake. . . . I like it."

It was as if her eyes were laser beams and she was staring straight into my heart and mind. Almost of their own volition, my arms reached out, and I clasped Christy around the waist. I pulled her toward me, her body weightless in the pool's deep, blue water.

"What took you so long?" she asked, settling her slender arms around my neck. "I've only been waiting for, like, a lifetime."

I didn't respond. . . . I couldn't speak. I could only gaze into her tranquil hazel eyes and thank whatever force of nature had brought me to this spot. Then I closed my eyes and tilted my head toward her.

A moment later we were kissing. Really kissing. Her lips were soft and warm and full and just . . . incredible. The kiss went on and on until I wasn't sure where her mouth left off and mine began. I only knew that I wanted this feeling to last forever—

I woke up suddenly, gasping for breath. Bright, glaring sunlight streamed in through the small window of my basement room, and the clock beside my bed read 6:30 A.M.

"What the . . . ?" My sheets were tangled into knots, and my forehead was covered with sweat.

I kicked away the sheets and sat up, bunching my pillow behind me for support. My mind was filled with a dozen confusing images. A pool. The moon. A girl. Kissing. They were all jumbled together like a mental jigsaw puzzle.

"Wait. Not just a girl . . . ," I whispered to my-self. *"Christy."*

I had been dreaming about Christy. We had been in a pool together, and we had been making out like crazy. I shook my head, pushing away the intense memory of the dream.

This was nuts. Why would I dream about Christy, of all people? Especially . . . like *that.* I didn't even like her, much less want to kiss her. But there was no doubt about it. My heart was still pounding, and I could almost taste her lips on mine, the sensation had been so powerful.

I jumped out of bed and began to pace back and forth across my spacious bedroom. There had to be an explanation . . . and there was. In fact, the dream made perfect sense now that I really started to put the pieces together.

The dream didn't mean anything. When I had finally fallen asleep a little after 1 A.M., Christy had been alive and well in my subconscious. And why not? I had spent almost half an hour talking about her with my mother. It was only natural that she should show in my dreams.

As for the *other* elements of the dream . . . how could I explain the kissing? I stopped pacing and plopped back onto my bed. Okay, Christy *had* looked really pretty yesterday afternoon. Raindrops had clung to her eyelashes, and her cheeks had been incredibly pink—almost like a doll's.

"So I dreamed that I kissed an attractive girl," I

said to the Michael Jordan poster that hung over my bureau. "Big deal."

Dreams didn't mean a thing. Everybody knew that. Still, I was glad I had managed to get my car going last night. I didn't want to run into Christy today. I didn't want to see her until that dream had had plenty of time to fade. . . .

Seven

Christy

"WHAT ARE YOU doing here?" I asked Matt the next afternoon when I walked into AP bio and found him standing at my lab table, holding a stack of slides. "You're not Aisha."

He grinned. "Let me introduce myself. I'm your new lab partner, Matt Fowler."

I shook his hand, then scanned the room. Yep. There was Aisha, standing beside Matt's now former lab partner, Trent O'Grady. "I'm confused."

"It's simple," he explained. "I got here early and begged Aisha to trade partners with me. She, being a sympathetic romantic, agreed."

"Great!" I loved Aisha, but there was no doubt that biology would be a lot more . . . stimulating . . . with Matt as a lab partner. Plus he was making it very clear that he liked me.

At the front of the large classroom Mr. Burgess—still looking slightly green—cleared his throat. "I'm sure you all missed me yesterday," he announced. "But the good news is that I'm back. And we can all get started on our earthworms."

"So how was the rest of your afternoon yesterday?" Matt asked as we started to diagram the earthworm on sheets of grid paper.

"It was . . . weird." I stared at the piece of paper, thinking of the scene between Jake and me in my car.

"Weird?" Matt glanced up from the diagram. "That sounds interesting. Were you, like, visited by aliens or something?"

"Not quite." I wasn't ready to tell Matt about my crying fit. Somehow I knew he wouldn't understand.

Matt shrugged—a sort of far-be-it-from-me-to-interpret-a-girl's-bizarre-statement shrug. "So, what should we name the little guy?" he asked.

I stared down at the worm. "He looks like a George," I announced.

"Huh. I was thinking he looked more like a Skipper," Matt mused. "But I guess I can live with George."

As we began to slice and dice poor George, I thought of the significance of what we were doing. Sure, it seemed pretty silly right now. It was last period, the sun was shining outside, and we were all thinking ahead to our graduation in a few weeks. Who cared about the insides of an earthworm? But maybe just one of us would really *get* something out

68

of the project. Maybe one of us would even be inspired to go to medical school.

"Wouldn't it be amazing if someone in this class discovered the ultimate cure for cancer one day?" I asked Matt.

He kept his eyes trained on what I assumed was the head of the earthworm. "Um . . . yeah. That would be great."

I was really getting into the idea. "I mean, to us this is just a class we have to pass before we can graduate from high school. But all great scientists have to start somewhere. Who knows what could happen in the future?"

"Um . . . I think I accidentally cut off George's legs—or where his legs would be if he weren't a worm." Matt took a step away from the lab table and handed me the knife we were using. "Maybe you should take over."

I bent over the earthworm, looking at him in a whole new way. He was a portal, a first step, a sign of hope in a universe that sometimes seemed absolutely hopeless. Of course, in my *own* small world it didn't really *matter* if one of us looked at our earthworm and saw the future of cancer research sitting in a small, metal tray. Not for my mom. It was too late.

"I was wondering if you wanted to go out with me on Saturday night," Matt said, breaking into my thoughts. "I thought we could do the dinner-and-a-movie thing."

Truthfully, I was more in the mood to sit

around and brood about the current failings of modern medicine than I was to watch Bruce Willis blow up some building just in time to save the chick from the bad guy.

But it was important that I keep up at least a facsimile of a social life. If nothing else, my breakdown yesterday had made me realize that I needed to find more ways to relieve my anxiety. And Matt was fun—even if he wasn't, as Jake had claimed, "deep."

"Sure," I told him. "I'd like that."

"Cool," he enthused, giving me one of his dazzling smiles. Then he pushed away the tray that held George's somewhat tattered remains. "Now, what do you say we give up on our little guy and go see if Aisha and Trent are doing a better job?"

I shrugged. "Why not?"

It wasn't as if my meager stabs at understanding the inner workings of an earthworm were going to make an iota of difference in my mother's life. I might as well throw in the scalpel and give up.

I lay back in the afternoon sun and propped my ice-cold can of diet Coke on my stomach. The fresh air smelled especially good after the overpowering odor of formaldehyde that had permeated Mr. Burgess's classroom. Nicole, Jane, and I had congregated on the lawn in front of Union High, where we were whiling away the few free minutes Nicole had before she had to leave for work at Claire's Boutique.

"I can't believe Matt asked you out for Saturday

70

night," Jane was saying. "I mean, of course I *believe* it since you're gorgeous and intelligent and funny. But given the fact that he's already going to the prom with one of the most popular girls in the senior class . . . this is a major coup."

"I guess so." I wished I could feel more excited about the upcoming date. But right now nothing seemed terribly exciting.

"I wonder if Sandra knows that you guys are going out this weekend," Jane continued. "If I were her, I'd be crushed."

Nicole waved her hand as if to dismiss the thought. "Come on—all Sandra cares about is the fact that she's got a hot date for her preprom photos. Why else would she have secured Matt *so* far in advance?" She raised her eyebrows. "Besides, I heard the only reason she asked him was to make her ex-boyfriend, Ed Polanski, jealous."

"Great," Jane said. "Then Christy has nothing to worry about. Matt is free and clear of obligation."

Nicole bit into a handful of Chee-tos. "I'll say this. Matt is extremely good-looking. He's not my type, but he's objectively outstanding in the blue-eyes-and-blond-hair department."

"Yeah, he is," I agreed. And he was. So what if he didn't want to talk about the possibilities of cancer research? Most high-school seniors were more interested in deciding where they were going to go to college than in obsessing over their mother's illness.

"And Matt is really easy to talk to," Jane added.

"He's not totally stuck-up like a lot of the other jocks."

"He's easy to be around," I confirmed. "But I don't know. . . . Do you think he's *deep?*"

"Deep?" Nicole crunched more Chee-tos, pondering the question. "Well . . . I wouldn't compare him to the Pacific Ocean. Then again, I don't think you're going to break your neck diving into the shallow end."

"It sounds like he's not afraid to let you know he cares," Jane added. "That's the important thing."

"Yeah . . . he does care," I responded. "As long as caring doesn't involve talking about my mother's illness. That subject totally freaks him out."

"You talked to him about that?" Nicole asked, sounding surprised. "You don't even talk to *us* about it."

"I didn't really *talk* to him about it. I just mentioned it a couple of times. That's all."

Even so, somewhere deep inside, it bothered me that Matt hadn't been more responsive to my casual references to my mom's cancer. Sure, I understood that it was an uncomfortable subject. But if *I* was willing to bring it up . . . then it seemed like a guy who was a potential boyfriend would want to hear what I had to say. Even *Jake* had been attentive to my need to vent. And he had the sensitivity of a droning, fly-bitten jolthead.

"Give him a chance," Nicole suggested. "It takes guys a while to open up." She paused. "At least, that's what I read in *Cosmopolitan.*"

72

I sat up and took several gulps from my can of soda. I thought of Matt's friendly smile and the warmth of his hand on my arm yesterday afternoon. Nicole and Jane were right. Matt was a great guy—any girl would consider herself lucky to have a date with him on Saturday night. I was going to have an awesome time . . . and I *certainly* wasn't going to let anything Jake Saunders had to say stand in the way of that awesome time. I couldn't wait!

The first thing I was aware of when I opened my eyes on Saturday morning was that I felt incredibly well rested. The second thing I was aware of was the sound of my dad whistling coming from somewhere downstairs.

I felt a sudden jolt of adrenaline and sat up ramrod straight in my bed. What was Dad doing up already? I always set my alarm clock so that I would be the first one awake, even on the weekends. Getting up early to make breakfast was a duty I took very seriously—it was my one consistent contribution to our family unit.

I looked over at the digital clock that sat on my nightstand. 10:30 A.M. I had overslept!

"Oh no!" I threw myself out of bed and reached for the robe I had thrown over my chaise lounge the night before. What had gone wrong? Had I accidentally turned off the alarm in my sleep?

I had my arms halfway into the sleeves of my robe when I heard a soft tap on my bedroom door.

"Dad, is that you?" I called. "I'm sorry it's so late—I don't know what happened."

"It's not Dad." The door opened, and I saw my mother smiling at me. "Good morning, sleepyhead," she said, her voice bright. "I told Dad to sneak in here this morning and turn off your alarm. We thought you deserved a few extra hours in bed."

"Oh . . . thanks." For a brief moment life felt almost normal again. Sleeping late. Dad whistling. Mom greeting me with the mug of herbal tea she was holding out to me. It was all so routine. Wonderfully, magically, awesomely routine.

"How do you feel, honey?" She walked into the room and over to the windows, where she opened the blinds to allow the sun in.

This morning Mom was wearing one of the three beautifully made wigs she had bought before she started chemotherapy. She had known her hair was going to fall out, and she had wanted to be prepared. But most days she was too tired to bother with them. She just wore a colorful scarf around her head and called herself Rhoda.

"I feel great," I responded, inhaling the delicious scent of the chamomile tea. "How are *you?*"

Mom sat down on my bed and pulled me next to her. "Christy, I woke up at six o'clock this morning, and I knew in my bones that this was going to be one of those precious, rare, *good* days."

I set the mug on the nightstand and wrapped my arms around my mother's waist. "Really, Mom?"

She nodded. "It's a reprieve. My body's out on furlough, so to speak."

I laughed. "How can you make jokes about this?" I asked, hugging her tight.

She kissed my forehead, then ran her fingers through my hair the way she had done when I was a little girl. "As long as I can laugh, this cancer hasn't gotten the best of me," she explained. "Christy, no matter what happens in the future, I never want you to forget the power of laughter."

"It's the best medicine, right?" I joked.

She squeezed me. "Right." I felt like my heart was going to burst, I was so happy to have my mom sitting on my bed and giving me advice. It was the best kind of Hallmark moment.

Finally my mother stood up. "I've got a brilliant idea," she announced.

"What is it?" I sipped my tea, thinking of all the "brilliant ideas" my mother had come up with before she got sick.

There was the picnic we went on one February afternoon. And our all-cotton-candy dinner when I was seven. Then there was the time that Mom decided at the last minute that she, Dad, and I should take a week off from work and school so that we could hike to the bottom of the Grand Canyon.

"Let's invite the Saunders family over for dinner tonight," she suggested. "We'll all stuff ourselves and then play a round of charades."

"But I—" *I have a date with Matt.*

Mom looked at me with a question in her eyes,

obviously wondering why I had stopped speaking midsentence. "What, sweetie? Do you have plans tonight?"

I shook my head. "No! I was just going to say that I think we should play Pictionary instead of charades."

"Then it's a plan," Mom declared. "We'll even let you and Jake be a team in the Pictionary game."

"Perfect." *Good-bye, date with Matt. Hello, evening with the urchin-snouted boar.*

But there was no date on earth that would make me give up spending a few hours with Mom when she was feeling this good. I hadn't seen her cheeks this bright in months. And if a family dinner with the Saunderses would make her happy, then I was going to put on a smile and be Jake's best friend for the duration of the evening. Anything to see her smile the way she was right now.

"Now all I have to do is call Molly and make sure their schedule is free . . . which I assume it is, since she's taken to bringing me a truckload of movie rentals every Saturday night."

"Can I make a call first?" I asked. "I just, uh, want to remind Nicole that she's got my history book."

"Of course, hon. Just come downstairs when you're off. Dad is making chocolate-chip pancakes."

As soon as she was gone, I picked up the receiver of the Hello Kitty phone I had gotten for my thirteenth birthday. It was a slightly embarass-ing possession for a seventeen-year-old, but hey, it

76

did the job. I dialed Matt's number, which I had memorized the first day he had flirted with me in science class.

He answered the phone on the second ring. As soon as I heard Matt's voice, my heart sped up a little. This was the first time I had called him, which was a major step.

"Hey, it's Christy," I announced, hoping I sounded as cool and casual as I wanted to.

"Hi, Christy. How's my favorite lab partner?" His voice was low and sexy and made me a little bit sorry that we weren't going out tonight.

"I'm good," I responded. "Actually, I'm great."

"Does this mean you're psyched for tonight?" he asked. "I was just sitting here, looking at movie times."

I could picture Matt sitting at the kitchen table, a newspaper spread out in front of him. He was probably drinking a glass of milk and eating a huge bacon-and-eggs brunch. And he probably looked gorgeous, even if he was just wearing old sweatpants and a T-shirt.

I cleared my throat. "Unfortunately, I'm going to have to take a rain check," I told him. "You see, my mom is feeling really decent for the first time in, like, a long time . . . so we're having a kind of family dinner."

I didn't add that Jake was going to be there. I didn't want Matt to get the wrong impression. Guys could be weird that way.

"Oh." He was silent for a moment. "Did you

explain that you've got a date tonight? I mean, maybe you could get out of it."

I twisted the phone cord around my finger, pondering Matt's question. I could sort of understand where he was coming from. Most seniors in high school didn't do a victory dance when they discovered they were going to spend Saturday night with their parents.

But I was different. "I *want* to stay home with my parents," I explained. "The thing is, Matt, I don't get to spend a lot of so-called quality time with my mom. She doesn't feel all that well most of the time."

"Right. Sure, I understand," he said quickly. "Hey, it's no big deal. We'll do it another time."

"I'd like that." Maybe Matt didn't want to get into a major discussion about my mother's "good day," but that didn't mean he wasn't sensitive.

"I'll call you tomorrow," he promised. Once again Matt's alluring voice made me feel a twinge of regret that I wasn't going to get to sit next to him in a darkened movie theater tonight. Instead I would be trading glares with Jake.

As I hung up the phone, I was already scanning the titles of the cookbooks I had started to collect. After the dozen or so pancakes I was going to eat for breakfast, I planned to prepare a veritable feast. I was going to make sure that tonight was an evening none of us would ever forget.

Eight

Jake

"IT SMELLS GREAT in here," I announced on Saturday night as I walked through the swinging door that led to the Redmonds' kitchen. "I feel like I'm walking into the kitchen of a five-star restaurant."

Christy looked up from the pan in which she was sautéing some kind of green vegetable. "Hey, I didn't hear you all come in."

I wasn't surprised. Judging from the number of dirty pots and pans in the sink and the five cookbooks on the kitchen counter, it looked like Christy had been so deep into making dinner that she probably wouldn't have noticed an earthquake.

"We got here about five minutes ago," I informed her. "Your mom looks great."

Christy nodded, beaming. "I know. She's been

like this all day. It's . . . I can't even explain how great it is."

She didn't have to explain. The expression on Christy's face said it all. Her eyes were shining, her cheeks were flushed, and her smile was so big that it seemed to take up her entire face. I couldn't help grinning back. This kind of mood was infectious.

"Thanks for coming tonight, Jake," Christy said quietly. "I'm sure there were a million things you would have rather done with your Saturday night than come here to hang out with me and my family."

"Nah," I said, shrugging. "All I had to look forward to was me, a bag of microwave popcorn, and the World Wrestling Entertainment on TV."

Okay, that wasn't exactly true. I had been planning for the last two weeks to go to a baseball game tonight with two of my best friends, Bill Feldman and John Hernandez. But as soon as my mom had told me that Rose was feeling up to having our family over for dinner, I knew I was going to be bagging my plans for the game.

I wasn't stupid. I knew there was the possibility that this was the last time our families would ever spend an evening together. Maybe hanging out with Christy wasn't first on my list of fun things to do now, but we'd had a lot of awesome times together as kids. And I knew that it meant a lot to my mom to have me there, rounding out the picture of two happy families.

Tonight I wanted to recapture the warmth and

security of childhood, when the only thing I worried about was whether or not I could have another bowl of ice cream and if it would be warm enough Sunday afternoon to play softball. I just hoped that Christy could experience that same sense of well-being. She needed it even more than I did.

"So are you going to stand there and stare at me, or are you going to make yourself useful?" Christy asked.

I grabbed an apron that was hanging on a hook next to the oven. It wasn't until I had already put it on that I realized it read Women Who Cook Know How to Turn Up the Heat.

Christy giggled. "Don't worry. I won't tell any of your friends about this particular fashion choice."

"If you do, I'll deny everything," I joked.

I walked over to Christy and peered over her shoulder. She had four different pots and pans on the stove, each of which contained something I couldn't identify. Of course, my idea of cooking a meal consisted of heating up a can of tomato soup or dialing Pizza Hut.

"So, what are we making?" I asked.

"We're preparing baked Brie with pecans, orange tarragon chicken, almond rice, and for dessert, toffee cookie diamonds." Christy was pointing to the various pans as she spoke.

I whistled. "I had no idea you'd turned into such a gourmand. Last I remember, the only things you could cook were hot dogs and packaged tortellini."

81

She laughed. "I've come a long way, baby." She pointed to the stack of cookbooks. "See those? All mine."

I was impressed. "I wouldn't have pegged you as the stay-in-the-kitchen type," I commented. "It seems so 1950s."

She arched an eyebrow. "Gee! Thanks." She set a bowl of almonds in front of me and handed me a knife. "Here. Chop these."

Good going, Jake, I reprimanded myself. Now that we were finally having a pleasant exchange, I had managed to put not only my foot in my mouth—but the sock and penny loafer I was wearing as well.

"I—I . . . uh . . . that didn't come out right," I stammered. "I'm, like, totally wowed by this new-found cooking ability."

I chopped an almond, hoping my faux pas wasn't going to send us into a full-on verbal battle. I just wasn't in the mood to tear Christy to shreds with witty comebacks. Or be torn to shreds *myself,* for that matter.

"Don't worry about it," she said, pulling a tray of chicken breasts out of the refrigerator. "To tell you the truth, the only reason I've been cooking so much is to feel like I'm doing something to help out." She paused. "And it helps somehow . . . it's sort of therapy, I guess."

"I really admire the way you're dealing with all of this," I said quietly, concentrating on the small pile of diced almonds growing in front of me. "I don't know how I would handle it if my mom got sick."

Christy sighed. "I pray to God you'll never have to know how you'd handle it," she responded. "It's not something I would wish on my worst enemy."

"Is that what I am?" I asked. "Your worst enemy?"

She looked at me for a long moment. "Nah. You're just a pain in the butt."

I popped an almond in my mouth. "Right back at you, kid."

Christy put the chicken in the oven. Then she took out a bag of brown sugar and carefully measured out a cup. She was a veritable dynamo. I stopped chopping my almonds and watched with fascination as Christy sped around the kitchen, mixing, whisking, and beating. She was like Julia Child, only a lot better looking.

"I have a proposal," Christy announced, cracking an egg into a clear glass bowl.

Hastily I turned back to the almonds. "What's that?"

"I propose that we don't mention anything related to illness, especially cancer, for the rest of the night," she announced. "For the next few hours I'm going to try to forget that my mom is sick."

I set down the knife and looked Christy in the eyes. "Can you really do that?" I asked. "Can you forget?"

She gave a smile that was so brave, it made my heart ache. "I can try, Jake."

"Count me in," I told her. "I won't even sneeze. I promise."

She examined my almond pile, then nodded approvingly. "Looks good."

"Thanks." It was the closest Christy had come to giving me a compliment since the sixth grade.

"Think you can move on to boiling a pot of water for rice?" Christy asked. "I've got to get the rice ready."

I squinted. "Let's see. . . . Boiling water . . . How do I do that again?"

She groaned. "I'll walk you through it step by step."

As I filled a giant pot with water, I couldn't help thinking that I was experiencing something that people might describe as "fun." Since our usual icy rapport was thawing out, tonight really did feel like old times. And I liked it. I liked it a lot.

"I'd like to propose a toast," Mr. Redmond announced as we were all finishing our chicken and rice. He lifted his glass. "To family, friends, and love."

As he spoke of love, Mr. Redmond turned to his wife and gazed into her eyes. The way they looked at each other almost brought tears to my eyes. I glanced at Christy out of the corner of my eye and saw that she was also studying her parents.

"I love you, Bobby," Rose said to her husband. "I love all of you . . . so much."

I knew with my gut that Christy was looking

into the future and wondering how she and her dad would go on if the worst happened. I wished I could reach out and hold her hand . . . but I couldn't. It wasn't what she needed right now.

"Hey, enough of the mushy stuff," I said. "How about a toast to the chef? This is the best meal I've had in months!"

My mom laughed. "Is that a hint about my cooking?"

Mrs. Redmond winked at Mom. "I think he's a little biased."

"You're an excellent chef," my dad told Christy as he patted his stomach. "I ate way too much. The meal was truly fabulous, Christy."

I saw Christy blush. "I just hope the toffee cookie diamonds come out all right," she commented. "I think I burned the crust."

"They'll be wonderful, Christy," my dad said quickly. "And I'm sure Jake will eat about a dozen of them to prove it."

Rose leaned back in her seat and looked at Christy and me with a sort of beatific gaze in her eyes. "I can't wait to see the two of you on prom night next weekend," she mused. "I know it's silly that I'm so romantic about a high-school dance, but I can't help myself. When Bobby and I went to *our* prom, it was the night he told me he loved me for the very first time."

Beside me Christy was shifting uncomfortably in her seat. "Mom, come on. . . ."

"I'm sorry, sweetie. But surely you can indulge

your old mom when she wants to bask in the re-flected glow of young love."

Suddenly I realized that Mrs. Redmond was under the impression that Christy and I were more than prom dates. She thought we were on the verge of, like, a major relationship. Under normal cir-cumstances I would have no doubt that Christy would disabuse her mom of such a crazy idea. Under *normal* circumstances she would probably have loved nothing more than to go on for hours to her mom about what a jerk I was.

But right now I figured Christy would do just about anything to make her mom smile. And if that included letting her mom believe that she and I were an item . . . it was my job to keep the illusion going.

I took a deep breath, preparing to take the plunge. And then I did it. I casually slung my arm around Christy's shoulders. *Please don't humiliate me by slapping away my hand,* I thought.

When she didn't immediately elbow me in the ribs, I started to relax a little. "I can't wait for the prom either," I announced. "Christy is going to be the most beautiful girl at the dance."

That much was true. Despite her many person-ality flaws, there was no disputing the fact that Christy would be outstanding in her prom dress. I could envision her creamy skin and red lips and soft, shiny hair. . . . *Whoa. Stop. Rewind.* This was Christy who I was thinking about.

So it was Christy. But I was a guy. I was human.

I wasn't going to pretend to myself that I didn't like the sensation of having my arm around her. It felt pretty great, actually. *It's only taken me five years to get another chance to put my arm around her,* I thought. *That must be a world record.*

"Jake and I will dance the night away," Christy said to the group. "It'll be just like a movie."

Then she leaned in close to me. "Just like a *bad* movie," she whispered.

Absurdly, Christy's stinging remark was like getting a knife in the chest. I quickly removed my arm and put my hands in my lap. So much for Ms. Nice Girl. Christy was just being nice to me to please her mother. I should have known.

Yes, I *should* have known. But for that one second, when I had thought that she actually *meant* we were going to dance the night away, my heart had thumped.

You're insane, Jake, I told myself. *You don't even like this girl.* I had been caught up in the moment. That was all. It could happen to anyone.

"A *really* bad movie," I whispered back to let her know that I was in on the "joke."

Still, the magic of the night was gone. When Christy left the table to get the toffee cookie diamonds, I found that I had lost my appetite.

Nine

Christy

"I HOPE THERE'S more to the plot than blowing up buildings and chase scenes," I said to Matt as we settled into our seats at the movie theater on Sunday afternoon. "Special effects only carry a movie so far."

"I'm sure there will also be a beautiful blond girl with an attitude," Matt assured me. "There's always a love interest." He paused. "Of course, *I* prefer brunettes."

"Thanks, Matt. I appreciate that." I held out the giant tub of buttered popcorn we had bought, and he took a handful. "And thanks for calling this morning. I didn't expect you to be so prompt with my rain check."

"Life is short," Matt commented. "You've got to go for it." Then he looked at me and sort of choked on his popcorn. "Uh, sorry. I didn't mean . . ."

I reached over and squeezed his hand. "That's okay. I know you weren't referring to my mom."

He gulped. "Um, would you like some Milk Duds?" He held out the box.

I took a handful and bit into them. "But you're right," I said when I was finally able to swallow the chewy mass. "My mom's sickness has taught me how important it is to enjoy life. Then again, it's also made it *harder* to enjoy life. I mean, I'm sitting here with you, but part of me is still at home, wondering how my mom is feeling."

Matt nudged me. "Uh, they're dimming the lights. I think the previews are about to start."

"Oh . . . right." I turned away from Matt and settled more comfortably into my seat. But as the theater darkened, I knew I wouldn't really be paying attention to the movie.

When I had woken up this morning, I had been filled with hope that Mom was going to have another great day. I had even started to think about plans for tonight, and next week, and next month. But when I brought in her breakfast, I realized immediately that no miracle had taken place. Mom was already awake and reaching for one of her pain pills when I walked into the room. The respite had ended.

Then again, she had eaten almost all of the strawberry-topped waffles I had made for breakfast. Maybe the pain she had felt this morning was one of those fleeting things that would be gone by the time I got home from the movies.

On the screen there were dizzying images of an exploding planet, a beautiful woman running down a long, dark corridor, and a beefy actor scaling the side of a skyscraper. It looked exactly like the preview for every other movie that had come out in the last five years. Boring.

"I can't wait to see this," Matt whispered to me. "We'll have to make it a date."

"Uh, yeah." I wondered if for every action flick I saw with Matt, he would accompany me to an indie film. Huh. Probably not.

The previews ended, and the movie began. As I watched the titles roll across the screen, I thought about last night. It had been so amazing to see my mother feeling like her old self. . . . It was almost as if she had been reborn.

And Jake. I hadn't been able to get him out of my head all day. I had forgotten what it was like to hang out with him minus the acrimonious comments. Part of me had felt like suggesting, *Hey, why don't we let the past go and pick up our friendship where it ended—that fateful night when we were thirteen?*

In fact, there was even a tiny part of me that had wanted more. When I had felt his arm around me, a tingle had traveled from my shoulders to the tips of my fingers. Why? *Just residual emotions from preadolescence,* I told myself, shifting now so that my shoulder was touching Matt's.

But I *had* been impressed by how relaxed Jake

91

had been around my mom. Even Nicole and Jane felt a little nervous about how to act and what to say in front of a person with cancer.

Of course, Matt would probably never meet my mother. First of all, I hadn't stopped her from believing that there might be something going on between Jake and me. Why confuse that issue with Matt? Second, I knew without having to ask that Matt would *definitely* be uncomfortable about Mom's illness. He just couldn't deal with it. Not like Jake.

Don't do that! I told myself. Why did I keep comparing and contrasting Jake and Matt? One had nothing to do with the other. And the fact that I had felt sparks when Jake touched me, whereas I felt only a warm fuzzy when Matt touched me, meant nothing.

In the darkness of the theater I slipped my hand into Matt's. I was positive that once we knew each other better, there would be sparks aplenty. How could there not be? Unlike Jake, Matt was the perfect guy.

I held my pillow over my head, trying in vain to block out the sounds coming from my parents' bedroom. It was almost two o'clock in the morning, and I couldn't sleep. I had woken up from a deep sleep almost an hour ago to the sound of Mom whimpering in pain in her bedroom.

Her soft, muffled crying made my heart feel like it had been shattered into a million shards of glass. I knew it was equally painful for my father. I could hear his gentle, murmuring voice as he spoke. He was probably rubbing her shoulders and whispering to her that everything was going to be all right.

But it wasn't. I was starting to know in my gut that nothing was ever going to be all right again. The feeling had started the minute I arrived home from my date with Matt. Dad had been sitting on the sofa in the living room, just sort of staring at the wall. He hadn't even noticed that I had come inside.

I had walked over to Dad and tapped him on the shoulder. "Is everything okay?" I asked.

He didn't nod or shake his head or say anything at all. He just blinked, as if I had woken him from a deep sleep. I had never seen him look so defeated.

"Dad?" I asked, louder this time. "Is Mom okay?"

Finally he reached up and took my hand. "She had to increase her pain medication, hon."

I hadn't asked him any more questions. I hadn't wanted to. I was too afraid of what the answers might be. I had simply gone upstairs, kissed my mother as she lay sleeping, and locked myself in my bedroom. Then I had buried myself in homework, resolutely pushing away the image of my father's forlorn face.

But now that it was the middle of the night and the house was dark and quiet—except for the soft sounds coming from my parents' bedroom—I couldn't stop the thoughts that were whirling through my brain.

The dark night of the soul, I thought. My mom was sick. She had cancer. Unless a miracle happened, she was going to die.

"She's going to die." I had never said the words aloud before. I wasn't sure if I had ever even *thought* the words. They were the worst, most devastating, most terrifying words in the universe.

Save her, I thought. *If there's anyone out there, I'm begging you. Please, please save my mother.*

I almost wished Mom hadn't felt so good yesterday. Her brief reprieve from her illness made the reality of it even more painful than it had been before. I wished I had never seen what I had interpreted as a light at the end of the tunnel. Now the tunnel was bleaker, darker, and more depressing than it had been before.

And I was exhausted. I was tired of being strong. I was tired of holding in my emotions so that nobody would know that I felt like I was slipping into a black hole. I felt like I was about to burst.

Suddenly the house was completely still. Thankfully, both of my parents had apparently fallen asleep. It was the only time when they didn't have to think about what was going on around us. I was sure that in her dreams, my mom was as healthy as she had been when she was eighteen, walking into her senior prom with my dad on her arm.

But I was wide awake. I felt like I would never sleep again. "I have to talk to somebody," I realized, speaking aloud.

I couldn't go another minute without *telling*

someone about what I was going through. If I didn't, I was going to lose my mind.

I switched on the light next to my bed and picked up the receiver of the Minnie Mouse phone. I would call Nicole. She had her own telephone line, and I knew she wouldn't mind if I woke her up in the middle of the night.

Then I set the phone down again. I knew that both Nicole and Jane would be more than happy to listen to me vent. But where was I going to start? It had been my decision not to talk to them much about my mom's illness. As a result, they didn't know a lot about it. I wanted to speak to someone who *understood*. Or came as close to understanding as someone who wasn't going through this could.

Jake. I don't know what made me think of him, of all people. Maybe it was the fact that he had known my mother practically since the day he was born. Maybe it was because he had just seen her. Or because his mother was Mom's best friend. Or because he was the only one who had asked me about her condition lately.

Maybe it's because he's been there for you before, I thought. I would never forget the day that we had put our dog, Pepper, to sleep. I had been in the sixth grade, and when I got home from school, Mom had told me that Pepper had been hit by a car. The vet had done everything he could, but if Pepper lived, she would be in pain for the rest of her life.

Mom had taken me onto her lap, and she had

95

talked to me like a grown-up for the first time in my life. Together we had decided that the most humane thing to do was put Pepper out of her misery. We had gone to the veterinarian's office, and I had held Pepper while she died.

Up to that point, it had been the worst day of my life. Afterward I had been inconsolable. I was sure we had made the wrong decision. What if they discovered a cure for whatever was wrong with Pepper? What if she had *wanted* to live despite the pain?

That night I hadn't been able to sleep. Once I had cried all of my tears, I realized that I wanted to talk to someone who had known Pepper as well as I had. And that person was Jake. He had been there when I taught her to fetch and to sit. He had helped me dress her up as Yoda one Halloween night. He loved her just like I did.

I had sneaked out of the house, terrified that my parents would wake up and ground me for a lifetime. Then I had sprinted down to Jake's house and thrown pebbles at the window that used to be his bedroom. He had woken up and let me inside, no questions asked. I had stayed for two hours, and when I left, I knew that I would be able to sleep.

I got out of my bed now, feeling like I was running on autopilot. I picked up the pink scrunchie sitting on my nightstand and put my hair back into a loose ponytail. Then I slipped into the jeans I had left lying next to my bed and pulled a T-shirt out of my drawer. There was only one person in the world

I wanted to talk to right now. And it was the very last person I would have ever expected it to be . . .

Outside, the air was cool. There wasn't a cloud in the sky; instead it was filled with millions of stars. I jogged down the block, living completely in the moment. If I stopped to think about what I was doing, I knew that I would turn around and go back to my house, where I would sit up all night, chewing on my fingernails.

I slowed to a walk as I approached the Saunderses' house. I knew that Jake had moved down to the basement. I had heard my mom and Molly talking about it last year—something about Jake "needing more privacy now that his hormones are raging."

I crept to the side of the house. There it was. The front basement window. *Am I really going to do this?* I asked myself. But I had to. I needed to talk, and Jake was the only person who would be real with me. He wouldn't go overboard with condolences or try to pretend that he knew what I was going through. He would just be . . . him. Like he had been the night that Pepper died.

I rapped on the small basement window three times. Then I waited. And waited. I knocked again. *I'll go back,* I decided. *He's sound asleep.* And this was a totally insane idea anyway. By tomorrow I would be fine. I would build back up my defenses overnight, and I would cope.

I started to turn away from the window.

"Christy? Is that you?" I heard his voice behind me, coming from inside the house.

I turned around. He had opened the window, and he was staring straight at me. "Uh, yeah," I whispered. "I just . . . never mind. Go back to bed."

He shook his head. "No. Go around back. I'll let you in through the basement door."

"Thanks." As I headed toward the back of the house, I hoped I was doing the right thing.

Jake was my archfoe, my sparring partner, my surly, spur-galled foot-licker. But was he my *friend?* I reached the door, my heart pounding. *You're about to find out, Christy.*

Ten

Christy

"COME INSIDE," JAKE said as soon as he opened the basement door that led to his bedroom.

I walked into the house and followed Jake down a small, narrow hallway. At the end of the hallway was the door that opened into Jake's bedroom. Actually, it was more like an apartment, complete with a sitting area, a Ping-Pong table, and a minifridge in the corner.

"Is everything okay?" Jake asked anxiously. He was wearing pajama bottoms and a T-shirt, and his hair looked like it had been through a tornado. "Is it your mom?"

I flopped onto an old, half-stuffed beanbag chair. "She's fine. I mean, no, she's not fine. She hasn't been fine for a long, long time. But for some crazy reason I've been going around telling anyone who asks that she *is*. And now I can't do that anymore. . . ." I sighed deeply, sinking farther into the giant beanbag. "Oh, man, I don't even know why I'm here."

Jake perched on the edge of an old couch. It was the same one that had been in their living room before Mrs. Saunders had gone on a Martha Stewart–style redecorating binge. "Christy—"

"I'm going to leave," I interrupted. "This was a stupid idea."

What had I been *thinking*? I had woken up Jake in the middle of the night so that he could sit there and listen to me, probably his least-favorite person in the world, moan and groan about my problems. It was ridiculous. I pushed my hands against the floor and heaved myself off the beanbag.

Jake stood up and grabbed my arm. "Christy, listen to me for *one* second."

"What?" I couldn't exactly refuse to hear what the guy had to say. Not after I had woken him up (probably from a dream about Jennifer Love Hewitt or Elisha Cuthbert).

"I think you should stay for a while. I mean, you obviously came here for a reason. And now you're up, and I'm up . . . and, well, we might as well talk."

I sort of fell onto the sofa. My legs just kind of gave out from under me. I didn't say anything at first. I gazed around Jake's room, taking in every detail. There were trophies, sports posters, and CDs everywhere. A miniature basketball hoop was attached to

100

one of the walls, and his mom's old StairMaster (which Jake seemed to be using as a clothes-hanging device) was in the corner.

It was all so typically *male* that I realized suddenly that this was the first time since sixth grade that I had been alone with a guy in his room. Of course, since that guy was Jake, it didn't really count. My gaze fell on the peewee swimming trophy he had won in fifth grade. I had been on the other end of the lane, cheering him to victory. After the meet both of our families had gone to Jon's Pizza for a celebration.

"Everything used to be so simple," I said finally. "Swim meets, pizza, minigolf . . ."

Jake sat down beside me. "Yeah. Sometimes I wish I didn't have to grow up. I mean, I want to go to college and become independent—but I miss the time that I could fix any problem with a hot-fudge sundae or a trip to the arcade."

"Remember the time we ran away from home together?" I asked.

Jake laughed. "I don't know how far we thought we were going to get with two ham sandwiches, a package of Oreo cookies, and four dollars."

"Hey, we made it all the way to McDonald's," I pointed out. "I think that was the best Happy Meal I ever had."

"And then your mom showed up with a suitcase," Jake continued. "She said that as long as we were running away, she was going to come with us."

I giggled. "To tell you the truth, I think she got

that technique from an old *Brady Bunch* episode."

"It worked," Jake responded. "You were so worried that your dad was going to be lonely all by himself that you insisted we abandon our plan to move to Disney World."

I sighed. "My mom was really something, wasn't she?"

"She still is." Jake scooped up a Nerf basketball and tossed it in the direction of the hoop. It hit the rim, fell to the floor, then rolled in our direction.

"I don't know what we're going to do without her," I whispered. "I'm so scared, Jake. If I even think about the worst-case scenario, I feel like I'm going to completely fall apart."

Jake picked up the basketball again and squeezed it into a tight, orange ball. "It's okay if you fall apart, Christy. You're entitled."

I took the ball from him and threw it. It swished through the hoop. "Two points," I declared.

"Really, Christy, you don't need to pretend that everything is okay. There are a lot of people around who would love a chance to lend you a shoulder."

I shook my head. "I have to be strong. I don't want my parents to know how terrified I am." I paused, again thinking of the way my dad was sitting in the living room tonight, staring into space. "They need me to have a smile on my face, Jake. It's all they've got right now."

"It's at times like these that it's rough to be an only child," Jake commented. "If you had a sister or a brother, maybe you wouldn't feel so compelled to keep a stiff upper lip, as they say."

I laughed softly. "You know what's weird? You're probably the closest thing I have to a sibling." I paused. "Maybe that's why I'm here."

"We were sort of like a brother and a sister when we were little," Jake agreed. He got up and grabbed the basketball. "We used to squabble like two kids stuck in the backseat of a car during a long road trip."

I nodded. "I loved all that bickering when I was young. It made me feel . . . I don't know . . . safe somehow."

Jake threw the ball, and it went through the hoop. "Two points. We're tied." He reached for the ball again, then handed it to me. "We're still pretty fantastic in the bickering department."

"True." I tossed the basketball. It didn't land anywhere near the hoop this time. "But it feels different now."

Jake sighed, then shifted so that his back was against the plush arm of the sofa. "I guess hormones got in the way. We hit puberty and *bam,* everything changed."

I grinned. "You know, we never should have gone on that stupid date. It was the beginning of the end of a beautiful friendship."

My heart skipped a beat. I couldn't believe I had just mentioned that taboo subject. Neither Jake nor I had directly referred to our date since that awful night. I had been so caught up in our conversation that the comment had slipped out before my internal censor weeded it out.

"Man, that was a disaster," Jake said with a laugh. "I was so nervous that my palms produced about a liter of sweat that night."

"Same here." How could I forget? When Jake had tried to hold my hand, I had yanked it away as if he were on fire.

"Really?" Jake asked. He attempted to spin the basketball on the tip of his finger. "You seemed so calm, cool, and collected. I never would have guessed that you were the least bit nervous."

"Ha!" I exclaimed. "Are you *kidding?* That was, like, the biggest night of my life. It was the first time I ever wore lip gloss."

"I warranted lip gloss?" Jake teased. "Wow. I never knew."

"Well, if you hadn't been so busy antagonizing the waiter, maybe you would have noticed that my lips were incredibly red and sensuous for a thirteen-year-old."

Jake set down the Nerf ball between us. "I noticed," he said quietly. "Trust me, I noticed."

I shifted so that I was facing Jake. And I looked at him. I mean, I really *looked* at him. He appeared to be the same boy I had built forts with in his backyard. But he was also someone totally different. He had broad shoulders, and I could see the muscles in his chest lurking somewhere under his T-shirt. Funny. I had never noticed what a square jaw he had . . . or the way his hair brushed his ears in just the right way.

I became acutely aware of two facts. The first was that I hadn't felt this close to another person in ages—not since my mother had received her initial diagnosis, and I had started to pull away from Jane and Nicole. Just being able to really *talk* to someone made me feel like I could start cracking away at the wall I had built around my heart.

The second fact was even more mind-blowing. Out of nowhere, I had become aware of Jake's presence in an entirely different way. I was conscious of his body, his arms, his strong hands resting lightly on the basketball.

And I couldn't take my eyes off his lips. They were full and red and exactly the kind of lips that girls dreamed of kissing. I felt thirteen all over again . . . only not. Now I was seventeen, and kissing wasn't just something I had read about in books. I had done it. And I could imagine what it would be like with Jake.

"Are you wearing lip gloss right now?" Jake asked, his voice so husky that it sent chills down my spine.

He was staring into my eyes. My body felt like it was turning to liquid as I nodded. "Um, a little. It's left over from this afternoon."

He reached out and brushed my hair away from my face. "It looks nice." A vein in his forehead throbbed as if it had a life of its own.

"Thanks." My voice was so low that it was barely a whisper.

Jake leaned closer to me, and I found myself responding to him like a magnet. I moved closer to him, my eyes falling again to his lips.

Time seemed to stand still, and I realized that at this moment, I wanted to kiss Jake Saunders more than I ever could have dreamed possible.

Eleven

Jake

ALL OF THE blood in my body had rushed to my head, and I felt like I was about to faint. At the same time every one of my five senses was hyperalert as I continued to stare into Christy's eyes.

My mouth was so close to her lips that I could practically taste them. It was as if the dream I'd had the other night was coming to life. But this moment was even more intense than it had been in the dream. Because now I could detect the slight scent of apple from the shampoo Christy used on her shiny, dark hair. It was intoxicating.

I'm about to kiss Christy Redmond. For the first time ever, I was aware that this was something I had wanted to do for a long, long time.

I closed my eyes and leaned even closer, closing

the tiny amount of space that was still between us. But I didn't find her lips with mine. There was just empty space where her mouth had been.

My eyes popped open. Christy was on the other side of the couch, as far away as she could get from me. She had jerked away at the last possible second. And she was still staring at me—but now her eyes were flashing with anger.

"Christy, what's the matter?" I felt like the proverbial rug had been ripped out from under my feet.

She scowled. "I don't need your *pity* kiss, Jake." She stood up and crossed her arms protectively against her chest. "I should never have come here."

"What are you *talking* about?" I yelled—as loudly as I could without running the risk of waking up my parents.

"I'm out of here." Christy didn't give me a chance to say anything else.

She spun around and strode toward the door of my bedroom. "Just wait—"

But it was too late. She had started running. By the time I reached the door, she had already fled down the hallway and out the door that led to the backyard. I had to let her go. I couldn't exactly chase a girl down the block in the middle of the night.

Instead I ran back into my room and stood by the window, where I had a view of the street. I watched as Christy sprinted down the block and slipped safely back into her house.

"What just happened here?" I asked myself, gazing at the sofa.

I was confused, frustrated, and annoyed. Christy had *wanted* me to kiss her. I was sure of it. What was her *deal?* I had never met someone who ran so hot and cold.

I bent over and picked up the basketball. Then I threw it as hard as I could against the wall, wishing I could vent some of my pent-up emotion.

Had Christy intentionally come over to get me all riled up so that she could throw it back in my face? It didn't seem possible. . . . Then again, two hours ago I wouldn't have thought it possible that I'd be woken up in the middle of the night by my sparring partner either.

"Nothing makes sense anymore." I moaned, flopping onto my bed.

I felt terrible that Christy's mother was sick, but I also resented the way Christy was treating me. Just because she was going through a traumatic time didn't mean she could use me as an emotional punching bag. I was a human being with feelings! Not that Christy had the power to *hurt* me. I didn't even like her. I didn't! The nonkiss had been . . . what?

A mistake. A moment of weakness. A severe error in judgment. I was *glad* Christy had pulled away. I would have regretted the kiss the second that it ended, if not sooner. I should consider myself lucky that it never happened.

I reached out and flipped off the switch of the overhead light. Unfortunately, I was going to have to wake up in a few short hours. Tomorrow was going to be a complete wash. But it wasn't going to be anywhere near as miserable as prom night. If the way tonight had gone was any indication, the dance was going to be nothing short of a nightmare.

"Jake! Are you awake down there?" My mother's voice at the top of the stairs, combined with the buzz of the alarm clock, jolted me out of a deep sleep.

I turned over and banged my fist against the alarm clock. "I'm up!" I yelled back.

Groggily I slid out of bed and headed directly for a hot shower. As I passed the couch, last night came flooding back to me. Had I been dreaming, or had Christy really shown up at my door in the middle of the night?

Then I noticed a pink ponytail holder lying on the floor next to the sofa. Yep. She had been here, all right. So it was all real. Her showing up. Our conversation. The kiss. *The kiss that never happened,* I amended to myself.

In the bathroom I turned on the shower full blast and stepped inside. As the hot water poured over my head, I mulled over the events of last night. Christy had been incredibly upset when she had arrived—obviously. She never would have come over if she hadn't been totally desperate for someone—anyone—to talk to.

Maybe I had overreacted when I had been so angry that she bolted without a word of explanation. It wasn't as if I knew how *I* would behave under similar circumstances. If my mom were as sick as Rose was . . . I didn't even want to think about what I might do.

110

I stepped out of the shower and wrapped a towel around my waist. I felt considerably more awake—but I also felt guilty. Christy hadn't been the one in the wrong last night. I had been.

She had been totally vulnerable, and she had trusted me. She had shared her fears with me. I was sure she hadn't told anyone else about her need to be strong on the outside no matter what happened. And I was fairly certain that she hadn't voiced her worst fear of all to anyone else . . . that her mother wasn't going to beat this thing.

I wiped away the steam-covered mirror and gazed at my foggy reflection. "You're a jerk," I told myself.

Rule number one in the code of chivalry was never to take advantage of a girl when she was feeling vulnerable. I hadn't *intended* to take advantage of Christy, but maybe it had been wrong of me to try to kiss her under the circumstances.

True, she had seemed as ready for the kiss as I had been. But at the last second she must have come to her senses and remembered that she didn't even *like* me. *I'll apologize,* I decided.

Everything had been so mixed up last night that at this point I wasn't sure who had been right and who had been wrong. But one thing had become clear. My mom had been right. Christy needed friends right now. And I wanted to be in that category.

I wanted to be there for Christy . . . for old times' sake, if nothing else.

*　　*　　*

I spent most of my lunch period searching for Christy so that I could give her a timely apology. Finally, ten minutes before the bell was going to ring for next period, I found her sitting at a corner table in the library. She was eating an apple and staring at her calculus textbook.

"Hey." I stood in front of the table and waited for her to look up from the math problems.

"Jake, what are you doing here?" she asked, sounding extremely suspicious.

So much for crying on my shoulder. "I, uh, wanted to talk about last night," I explained. "I mean, it was pretty weird."

Cut to the chase, I ordered myself. *Just tell the girl you're sorry.*

She laughed. "Forget about last night."

"What?" I had been ready for just about anything. But *laughter?*

Christy set down her apple and folded her hands together on top of the table. "Listen, Jake, last night I had a bad case of temporary insanity."

"You did." I wasn't sure if I was making a statement or posing a question. Christy always had the effect of throwing me completely off balance.

She nodded. "It was late; I couldn't sleep." She gave me a tight, mean (in my opinion) smile. "Consider it an insomnia-provoked dementia."

Showing up at my house might have been a little out of the ordinary. But I didn't think I would have labeled the act *demented.* "Well, whatever it was, I just wanted to let you know that I—"

"Save it," Christy interrupted. "Whatever you're about to say is totally irrelevant. Because we're just going to pretend that it never happened." She raised her eyebrows and gave me a challenging stare. "End. Of. Story."

So she wasn't looking for an apology. Okay. Fine. I was still going to give the friend thing one more shot. For my mom. For Rose. For Christy.

"End of story. I understand," I echoed. "But I wanted you to know that I'm here for you. That's all."

"Thank you." But Christy's voice conveyed anything *but* gratitude. "I'll keep that in mind." She glanced back at her textbook. "Now, do you mind? I'm trying to get my homework done before class."

Nice, I thought. I turned my back on Christy and strode across the library. Our conversation certainly hadn't been worth giving up my lunch for. In fact, it had been a complete waste of time.

From now on I was going to stay as far away from Christy as I could. That was obviously what she wanted—and that's what she was going to get. End. Of. Story.

Twelve

Christy

"I HAVE TO find him," Nicole said for the thousandth time on Monday afternoon. "That's all there is to it."

Nicole had gotten herself into quite a quandary. She'd told two members of the Jerk Brigade (our name for the nastiest clique at Union High) that a certain hot guy was her prom date—a guy she'd never even met! And now she had to track down the guy and beg him to be her date.

The three of us were sharing a basket of fries at the food court in the mall. Nicole was continuing to obsess about finding her man, and Jane and I were mostly nodding.

"The prom is five days away, and I've got *nothing*." Nicole moaned.

"Christy and I will keep looking, won't we?"

Jane announced, nudging me in the ribs.

"Yeah, of course we will," I answered automatically. Jane and I had been with Nicole when she'd pointed out the total stranger to the Jerk Brigade.

Unfortunately, I knew I wasn't going to be all that much help. I had barely seen the guy. My mind, as usual, had been on my mom—not on the cute guy who'd taken his kid sister shopping for a dress at the shop Nicole works in.

"We should check out all of the kids' stores," Nicole suggested. "After all, the last time we actually *saw* the guy, he was with his little sister. And we should get started on checking out the other local high schools."

I nodded absently. I wanted to concentrate on Nicole's problem. I really did. But while she was focused on public humiliation, I was worried about my own, *private* humiliation.

I couldn't stop thinking about last night. I had managed to act nonchalant when Jake had found me hiding in the library today, but inside I had been a mess. When I woke up this morning, I had hoped that the whole scene at Jake's had been some kind of surreal nightmare.

Then I had noticed that I was still wearing the T-shirt I had put on to go over to his house. I hadn't been dreaming. This was real. I had made a total fool of myself, and there was nothing I could do about it.

What was I thinking? I wondered for around the millionth time today. The more times I went over last night in my head, the more embarrassed I was. Going over to Jake's house in the middle of the night had been worse than desperate. It was pathetic!

I shouldn't have let myself get to a place where I would do something so pitiable. I should have been able to stay strong. Or if I simply *couldn't* hold in my emotions another second, Jake was the last person I should have turned to. I was like a thorn in his side—and I had been for years.

I should have called Jane or Nicole or written in my nonexistent diary or called the Psychic Hotline or talked to myself in the mirror. *Anything* would have been better than the dead-of-night call I had inflicted upon poor, unsuspecting Jake.

I'm never going to blubber on Jake's shoulder again, I vowed to myself. I would have to deal with him at the prom on Saturday night, but after that, I was going to steer clear of him as much as I possibly could.

At least I had managed to do *one* thing right last night. I had come to my senses before we actually kissed. That would have been nothing short of total personal ruin. I knew there was no *way* he really wanted to kiss me. He was probably just hoping that a kiss would get me to stop droning on and on about my messed-up life.

True, his eyes had been sort of smoldering when he had been leaning so close . . . but that had most likely been due to fatigue, not desire. I wasn't Jake's type, and I never would be. *Not that I want to be,* I assured myself. I found him just as unattractive as he found me!

"Christy, hello, are you listening?" Nicole asked, waving her hand in front of my face.

I blinked. Whoops. I not only didn't know what she had just said—I had no idea what either of them had been talking about for the last five minutes. "Uh, yes, I was listening," I protested. "I think we should look for the mystery guy at all the pizza places nearby."

Jane raised her eyebrows. "Christy, we were asking if you wanted more fries. We were thinking of sharing another order."

Whoops again. "Sorry, guys. I guess I'm sort of preoccupied."

"What were you thinking about?" Nicole asked gently, her big brown eyes filled with sympathy. "Was it your mom?"

"No, not my mom." For once I could say that in all honesty. My mom had been the last thing on my mind as I had gone over the near kiss in my head.

"What, then?" Jane asked. "Do you want to talk about it?"

I bit the inside of my cheek, pondering the question. I knew I could trust Jane and Nicole with anything. They wouldn't go blabbing to anyone about the scene with Jake. And they would probably come up with all sorts of reasons about why I shouldn't feel humiliated.

But what was the point of spilling my guts? Last

night was over, and I wanted to put it behind me. Besides, the Kiss That Never Happened meant zilch to me. I had analyzed the moment enough in my head. I didn't need to do it again in a friends-therapy session.

Besides, I didn't want to give Jane and Nicole the wrong idea. If I told them about last night and the way my body had totally melted when I stared at Jake's lips, they might not believe me when I told them that I couldn't stand the guy.

"I know!" Nicole exclaimed. "You were thinking about Matt."

Matt. Right. The guy I had a huge crush on. "Well . . ." I let my voice trail off, allowing my best friends to interpret my response any way they wanted to.

"Were you daydreaming about kissing him?" Jane asked. "Before Max and I started dating, I must have imagined our first kiss a thousand times."

"Are you in love?" Nicole teased. "Does thinking about Matt make your heart go pitter-pat?"

I rolled my eyes. "No comment," I informed them. "I'll just let you two use your fertile imaginations to fill in the blanks."

"I wonder what it would be like to kiss the mystery man," Nicole mused. "Not that I'll ever have the chance to find out . . ."

As Nicole launched back into a discussion about how to find the guy from Claire's Boutique, I breathed a small sigh of relief. I loved my friends, but there were some things better left unsaid. Anyway, as soon as Jake and I got this prom date behind us, I could quit worrying about him. And as far as I was concerned, that couldn't be soon enough.

"Are you sure you're up for this?" I asked my mother on Friday afternoon. "Because if you're tired, we don't have to stay."

Mom put her arm around my shoulders and gave me her patented squeeze. "I'm fine, honey. Really. I took a long nap before you got home from school, and I woke up feeling quite refreshed."

The prom was tomorrow, and Mom had surprised me when I got home from school by telling me that she had made an appointment for me to get my hair cut and highlighted by a woman at Bijin, the best salon in town. And she had insisted on coming with me.

This was the first time in almost two months that we had been out, just the two of us. I was worried about Mom, but I was also walking on air. It felt great to be doing such a typical mother–daughter activity together.

I returned her squeeze, just like I always did. "Okay. If you're sure."

As we walked into the salon, I saw Mom's eyes shine. Before her hair had started to fall out from the chemotherapy, she had prided herself on what she called "creative expression through hair." Mom never dyed her hair blue or purple, but she had been a blonde, a brunette, and a redhead at various points during my childhood. Her theory was that change on the *outside* fostered growth on the *inside*. I had rebelled by maintaining the same hairstyle since third grade.

"Good afternoon, Mary Ann," my mother greeted her hairstylist enthusiastically. "Christy has finally agreed to go under the scissors—for more than the biannual trim she usually consents to."

Mary Ann grinned. "I've been wanting to get at that head of hair for a decade," she proclaimed. "Christy, this is going to be the first day of the rest of your life."

I resisted the urge to roll my eyes. I thought the two of them were making a little much of a simple haircut and highlight, but I wasn't going to argue. Whatever made Mom happy made *me* happy.

"I'm in your hands, Mary Ann," I proclaimed. "You have complete power over my hair." I smiled. "But please, be gentle."

Fifteen minutes and one shampoo, condition, and head massage later, I was sitting in Mary Ann's chair with a giant smock covering most of my body. Mom was several feet away, sitting across from her favorite manicurist, Eula.

"I feel ten years and five chemo treatments younger," Mom declared. "I should have been getting weekly manicures for the last eighteen months."

"I feel nervous," I admitted. I looked up at Mary Ann. "You're not going to give me a Mohawk or anything, are you?"

"I promise that you're going to have the best hair at the prom tomorrow night," Mary Ann assured me. "Trust me."

"So Mom told you about the prom?" I asked.

I wasn't surprised. She had been talking about it all week. The dress, the hair, the makeup, the shoes. I had never realized that going to a dance involved so many accessories.

"Your date sounds like a real hottie," Mary Ann commented as she started to paint sections of my hair with some gooey, bad-smelling concoction.

"Jake is adorable," Mom chimed in. "And he's one of the nicest young men I've ever met."

Usually my mom's judgment about people was right on. But she had a blind spot when it came to Jake Saunders. For some crazy reason, she thought the boy walked on water.

"What about you, Christy?" Mary Ann asked. "Do you think Jake is *adorable?*"

"I'm glad he asked me to the prom," I answered truthfully. I *was* glad. The fact that I was dreading it didn't preclude me from being happy that he had asked me. For my mother's sake.

"I'd like hot pink nail polish," Mom told Eula as the manicurist pulled her hands out of two small tubs of soapy water. "You only live once—I might as well let my presence be known."

"Mom, enough jokes," I called. It was nice that my mom still had her sense of humor intact, but I couldn't laugh along with her cancer jokes. They made me sad.

"I'm sorry, honey," she replied. "It's just so good to be out of the house that I'm feeling a little giddy."

"That's okay." I was a horrible daughter. How could I deny my own mother even a second of pleasure? She had the right to say whatever she wanted—I just wished it didn't have such a disturbing ring of truth.

Mary Ann gave me a pat on the shoulder. "Your mom is one of the strongest women I know," she said softly. "She'll get through this."

I hoped Mary Ann was right. But deep down, I knew that she wasn't. Still, now wasn't the time to dwell on matters over which I had no control. Instead I would focus on the light in my mother's eyes and thank God that we had this afternoon at the hairdresser's together.

Every minute was precious, and I didn't intend to forget it. Besides, if Mom could still enjoy life to the fullest, then so could I.

I smiled at Mary Ann in the huge mirror that faced the chair. "Don't hold back on that coloring goo," I instructed her. "Let's go for it!"

That's what Mom and I were doing. We were going for it, right here, right now, in a place where women had sought comfort since the dawn of time. The beauty parlor.

"You know, I think I'm going to get a pedicure too," Mom announced. "Let's throw caution to the wind."

I glanced at my mother. She was starting to look tired, but the light was still in her eyes. And as long as that light was there, she was the person I had always known and loved. Cancer couldn't change that.

"You know what?" I said to my mother, who was waving her left hand in the air to make the polish dry faster.

"What, sweetie?" she asked.

"This is one of the best days of my life." And it was true. I just hoped that the *worst* day in my life was still years and years away.

Thirteen

Christy

I ALMOST DIDN'T recognize myself as I stared into the mirror on Saturday evening. The girl I was looking at was *me*—but a brighter, smoother, more glamorous version. I turned my head from side to side, checking out my new haircut for the tenth time in the last hour and a half.

Mary Ann is a genius, I thought. She belonged in the hairdresser Hall of Fame. I hadn't thought there was anything wrong with my hair before Friday afternoon—it had been brown and straight and went halfway down my back. I wasn't the type of person who tortured herself with curling irons and hair spray. My idea of a good haircut was one that required, like, *no* maintenance.

Now my hair fell just below my shoulders, and Mary Ann had layered it around my face to give it shape and movement. Best of all, she had added golden highlights that made my hair shine and brought out the golden flecks in my hazel eyes.

But it wasn't just my hair that looked different. Earlier Mom had come into my room and done my makeup herself. She had gone all out, using powder, blush, lip liner, and lipstick. But the pièces de résistance were my eyes. Mom had coated the lids in a warm shade of dark gold, then used a charcoal liner. When she had finally brushed black mascara onto the lashes, my eyes had popped out like never before. The overall look was natural but, well, stunning—if I did say so myself.

"Let's hope I have a chance to show it off," I said to myself as I pulled my prom dress off its hanger.

For the last few days there had been a nagging worry at the back of my mind that Jake wasn't going to show up for our prom date. True, he had promised. But that had been before that awful night at his house. Since our conversation on Monday we had barely spoken. In fact, I had gone completely out of my way to avoid him. I hadn't even seen the guy since Thursday morning.

I slipped into the dress, then pulled up the long side zipper. Finally I stepped into the high-heeled strappy sandals I had bought for the occasion. Okay. One last look and then it was countdown time.

Once again I stared at myself in the mirror. The dress I had chosen was simple but elegant. It was strapless, made of deep rose silk, and fell almost to the floor. No ruffles, spangles, or beads for me. But there *was* still something missing. I picked up the small pearl earrings my mother had worn on her prom night and carefully put them on. It was the only jewelry I wanted to wear.

Somehow the earrings made the evening seem real. This was *prom* night. It was the event that teenagers built up in their minds for years—a rite of passage in the journey toward adulthood. If Matt were going to be my date tonight, I would probably be laughing giddily as I stashed an extra lipstick in my evening bag. I would be checking my breath five times, making sure I was prepared for our first kiss on the dance floor.

But Matt wasn't my date. Neither was Zach or Joe or Steven. My date was Jake. And all I felt anticipating his arrival (I hoped) at the door was a vague sense of nausea and a major case of nerves. The most romantic night of my life was going to resemble a train wreck.

"Voilà!" I announced as I walked into the living room, where my parents were awaiting my big entrance.

My mom was lying on the couch, covered by a shawl. She had been feeling basically rotten all day, but she had insisted on both doing my makeup and being downstairs when Jake arrived. Now that I saw her face, I was happy that I hadn't put up a fight, trying to keep her in bed.

"Christy, there's only one word to describe you," Mom gushed. "Beautiful!" She held out her hand for me to take. "And that's on the outside *and* the inside."

My dad reached out and took her other hand. "You look just like Rose," he said softly. "I feel like I'm peering into the past."

"Thanks," I told them. "I have to admit, this is the closest I've ever felt to a fairy princess."

"Honey, this is going to be such a magical night. I want you to forget about *all* of your worries and just enjoy it." She kissed my hand. "You deserve to have a wonderful time."

"I will," I promised her.

I didn't care about the dance. Not really. *This* was the moment I had been waiting for. No matter how the rest of the night progressed, I was declaring the evening a success. The look in Mom's eyes was all of the "wonderful" I needed.

As long as Jake shows up, I added silently. The date himself was as important to Mom as the dress, the earrings, and the vintage handbag.

Dad glanced at his watch. "Jake should be here any second," he commented. "I'll get the camera ready."

He got up and left the room in search of the camera. Once he was gone, I tapped my foot nervously, praying that Jake wasn't going to ditch me at the last minute. *He wouldn't do that,* I told myself. *His mom wouldn't let him even if he wanted to.*

Then again, Jake was stubborn. If he had decided that he couldn't stand spending another minute with me and my tears, nobody was going to change his mind.

"Sweetie, is something wrong?" Mom asked. "You seem anxious."

I stopped tapping. "No, I, uh, was just wondering whether or not Jake is going to like my dress," I lied.

"He will, Christy." Mom pulled the shawl more tightly around her shoulders and let her eyes drift shut. "I'm just going to shut my eyes for a minute before he gets here."

I bit my lip as I watched my mother. She was weaker. I was sure of it. This wasn't just one of her "bad" days. She was losing strength day by day.

In the hallway the doorbell sounded. "He's here!" Dad called, walking back into the living room.

Thank goodness, I thought. Jake had come through.

Mom's eyes opened. "Get the door, honey. Dad and I will wait in here."

I took a deep breath and walked to the door. *Here we go,* I thought. *The moment of truth.*

"Hi, Christy." Jake's voice was friendly but distant. Sort of like he was greeting his second cousin twice removed who he'd only met once before.

I wasn't prepared for my physical reaction to Jake in a tuxedo. He looked amazing. He had even gotten a haircut. I stood there, trying to think of something to say.

"Nice to see you, Jake," he said. "Why, thank you. Nice to see you too, Christy."

"Oh, s-sorry," I stammered. "Nice to see you, Jake."

"You changed your hair." He said it as if I had broken some cardinal rule of prom going.

"What? You hate it?" I asked, feeling self-conscious.

129

He shook his head. "No, I, uh, it looks, uh, pretty."

I stood back to let him inside, and when he moved away from the door, I saw a white stretch limo waiting at the curb. "Whoa. Nice ride," I commented. "What happened to Ramona?"

He grinned. "She's taking the night off."

"Thanks for being here, Jake," I told him, mustering all of my dignity. "And thank you for all of the nice touches. It'll mean a lot to my mom."

Jake smiled. "Hey, when I take a girl to the prom, I take her to the *prom*."

"Don't keep us in suspense," my mother called from the living room. "Get in here, you two."

Jake took my hand and pulled me into the living room. "Hey, Mr. and Mrs. Redmond," he greeted them. "I have come to whisk your beautiful daughter to the winter wonderland we're promised the gym has been transformed into."

"Jake, you look incredibly handsome," Mom declared. "I'll be sure to give your mom copies of the dozen pictures we're going to take."

"Please don't," Jake asked. "She'll turn them into T-shirts and hand them out at the next family reunion."

Mom laughed. "You see, Christy?" she said. "I'm not the only overzealous mother in this neighborhood."

In that second all of the anger and resentment I had been feeling toward Jake since the other night seemed to melt away. He had made my mom laugh. And he was here. With a limo. And compliments.

130

And a gorgeous corsage that he was about to pin to my waist. I couldn't remember the last time I had felt so grateful to another human being.

"Stand by the fireplace while you do the corsage," Mom instructed. "It'll be a great photo."

I felt like a complete idiot as Jake and I posed in front of the fireplace. But I couldn't help grinning when my dad yelled, "Cheese." Mom was acting like she was sixteen years old, ordering us into poses and cracking one corny joke after another.

There was the picture of him pinning on the corsage. The picture of me pinning on *his* boutonniere. The picture of us with our arms around each other, facing the camera. The picture of us with our arms around each other, looking at each other. The list went on and on until the roll was finished.

"Have a wonderful time," Mom said when she finally felt satisfied with her photo-album material. "And *don't* think about us." *Translation: Don't think about me,* I thought.

"I'll have her back by dawn," Jake promised as we headed out the door. "Don't wait up!"

As we walked toward the limo, my dad waving in the doorway, I knew what I had to do. I had to apologize to Jake for the way I had blown him off in the library. Maybe we weren't best friends, but he deserved my respect at the very least. There weren't that many guys in the world who would be willing to give up their own prom night just to make their mom's friend happy. He was one in a million.

*　　*　　*

Once we were alone in the back of the limo, my heart started to pound. *It's not because we're alone,* I told myself. *It's because I know what I have to do.*

"I'm sorry for being such a jerk," I blurted out. "You're not a tottering, elf-skinned hedge-pig."

Jake laughed. "Christy, I think that's the biggest compliment you've ever given me." He paused. "But truthfully, I'm just glad you're speaking to me again. I was worried we were going to spend the entire evening in icy silence."

"I've been so confused lately," I confessed. "One minute I'm happy, the next I'm crying." I sighed.

He laughed. "We're seventeen," he pointed out. "We're supposed to be confused."

"So, we're friends, such as it is?" I asked, holding out my hand.

"Friends—such as it is." Jake shook my hand firmly as the driver pulled the limousine into the Union High parking lot.

I looked out the window and saw none other than Wendy Schultz walking into the prom with her date. I opened my mouth to make a snappy comment, then abruptly shut it.

The atmosphere between Jake and me had started to thaw. I didn't want to do anything to change that. Not now, after he had been so understanding about my wacky behavior.

Maybe for one night we can have a truce, I thought. *Maybe we can even have some fun.*

Fourteen

Jake

ONCE WE GOT inside the dance, Christy started to ooh and aah over the decorations. And they were pretty impressive. The Union High gymnasium had been transformed, as promised, into a veritable winter wonderland.

But I barely registered the hundreds of twinkling lights or the tiny tables or even the huge disco ball hanging over the center of the dance floor. My gaze was firmly fixed on Christy, as it had been since the moment she opened the door tonight.

Two words, one girl: *absolutely fabulous.* When Christy had greeted me at the door, I felt like I had been punched in the stomach. I had seen her thousands of times in my life. I had even been aware of her subtle beauty for what seemed like forever. But tonight I felt like I was seeing Christy for the first time.

The way her hair brushed lightly against her shoulders made my fingers itch to reach out and touch her smooth, ivory skin. And when I looked into the depths of her hazel eyes, I felt like I was tumbling headfirst into a pool of lava. *It's just the dress,* I told myself. *You're reacting to a girl in a beautiful, sophisticated, pink . . . creation.*

Except that it wasn't the dress. Christy had been infiltrating my thoughts for weeks. Thanks to her, I hadn't even been in the right frame of mind to go on an actual date with a *normal* girl since I asked her to the prom. That wasn't like me. In fact, it was the *opposite* of me.

When Christy had reached out to shake my hand in the back of the limo, I had felt like I'd been zapped with electricity. Never had a friendly handshake made such an impression. I had been instantly beamed back in time to that night on the sofa in my bedroom. I had been right back at that near kiss.

I knew with one hundred percent of my intellectual capability that Christy and I could never be a couple. We agreed on nothing, and we had raised bickering to the level of high art. It was guaranteed that an extended conversation with Christy was going to reduce me to a blithering, stuttering fool.

That's what my *head* told me. But when I spotted Matt Fowler on the other side of the gym, doing his lame imitation of Ricky Martin, my heart told me something else. I couldn't bear the idea of watching Christy flirt with that stupid guy.

Matt had the personality of a bad used-car salesman.

Sure, he was good-looking. But so what? Ted Bundy had been a charming guy, and he turned out to be a serial killer. Okay, maybe Matt wasn't felon material.

Nonetheless, he wasn't worthy of someone like Christy. Yes, she had faults too numerous to name. But she also had fire and strength and intelligence and wit and an inner light that made her shine even in the worst of times. It was my *duty* to keep her from making the mistake of falling for that guy. As an old friend, it was the least I could do.

"Why don't we dance?" I suggested as Christy stood gazing around the already crowded prom.

"We don't have to, Jake," she responded. "I appreciate the offer, but a deal is a deal. Now that we're here, you're officially off the hook."

I had to play this carefully. "I really think we should hit the dance floor for a couple of numbers," I insisted. "That way you can tell your mom all about it when you get home."

I wasn't being *totally* manipulative. I really did think that Rose would badger Christy for all of the details about her prom experience.

Christy nodded. "You're right," she agreed finally. "And I promise I won't step on your toes unless I absolutely can't help it."

"Deal." I clasped her hand and led her toward the center of the dance floor.

Holding Christy's hand, my palms felt as sweaty as they had the fateful night of our first and only date. Thankfully, I had matured enough to realize that the way to deal with nerves was *not* to insult

135

my date and proceed to make a complete idiot of myself. Instead I would simply take the next opportunity to surreptitiously wipe my palms on my tux pants.

I took Christy in my arms as the band struck up a rendition of "Let's Fall in Love." I half expected her to cringe as I placed my hands on her waist, but she didn't. She put one hand on my shoulder, the other on my waist, and began to move to the music.

"This is nice," Christy commented. "I haven't danced since I went to homecoming with Michael Farley my sophomore year."

Ugh. Michael Farley. Two years above us, the guy had been a walking ego. But I kept my mouth shut. I wasn't about to incur Christy's wrath at this particular juncture by issuing an ill-conceived opinion of her ex-flame.

"Uh-huh . . . ," I answered in a noncommittal voice.

Christy laughed softly. "That guy was the biggest loser. He kept telling me that if I was lucky, he would 'give me something to write about in my diary.' " She quirked an eyebrow. "Lucky for me, I didn't *have* a diary."

"Sounds like a gem." I wasn't going to fall into this trap. I knew girls. They could insult past dates, but far be it from anyone else to chime in on the conversation.

"Anyway, you're a much better dancer than he was," Christy assured me. She paused. "Is it my imagination, or am I sort of talking to myself here?"

"I don't know what you mean." I twirled her around, hoping the touch of finesse would impress her.

"I mentioned Michael Farley, who I *know* you hate, and you didn't even react." She looked up at me, her eyes sparkling. "Is the great Jake Saunders at a loss for words for the first time in his life?"

"I, uh . . . ." I wanted to say something witty. But I couldn't. I had been struck completely dumb by the nearness of Christy's lips to mine. "I don't even remember who he is," I said finally. "Although I do have a vague image of a giant pumpkin attached to a hormonally challenged body."

Christy grinned. "Now, that's the Jake I know and love." She gasped. "I mean, the Jake I *know.* The love part was just a figure of speech."

"Right. Of course." We needed more dancing and less talking. I was getting dumber by the second.

Why? Because this tiny, traitorous part of myself had positively come alive when the word *love* had escaped (and I mean that literally) Christy's mouth. What did it mean?

"If you're quiet because you're concentrating on locating Wendy, she's on the other side of the dance floor," Christy informed me.

Wendy who? I thought. I hadn't thought of her once since we had arrived at the prom. In fact, I hadn't exchanged more than a few pleasantries with Wendy Schultz since that night in my room. That night. That night. That night. Why couldn't I get it off my mind?

"I'll catch up with her later," I told Christy. "I

was actually thinking about something else. I was, um, wondering if you were getting thirsty."

"Are you?" Christy asked.

No! I wanted to scream. *I'm not hungry or thirsty or thinking about Wendy Schultz.* I just wanted to pull Christy close and spend the rest of the night barely moving on the dance floor. I wanted to inhale her perfume and rub my cheek against hers and whisper into her ear.

"I'm fine," I told her. "I really like this song."

So what if I had no idea *what* song the band had just started to play? It was slow; it was romantic; it was good enough for me.

"Do you want to go find Jane and Nicole?" I asked. "They're probably here by now."

I knew how much girls liked to confer at events like these. They could spend hours discussing dresses, makeup, and fashion faux pas. As much as I wanted to keep dancing, I wasn't going to hold Christy here against her will. It wasn't my style.

"I'll find them later. I, uh, really like this song too." She seemed to drop the idea of leaving the dance floor in search of a cup of sticky, overly sweet punch or someone better to talk to. Christy's eyes were closed as she swayed back and forth.

As I studied her sweet, serene face, the truth hit me. The tenderness I was feeling toward Christy had nothing to do with her mother's illness. And it had nothing to do with the fact that we had known each other forever. The truth didn't even have anything to do with her beautiful dress or the intoxicating scent of her hair.

Christy had gotten under my skin. I was falling all over again for this frustrating, somewhat crazy girl. I had been falling for her for a long time, but I hadn't let myself admit it. The idea was too overwhelming, too scary.

It's hopeless, I told myself. Christy and I were a match made in . . . I didn't know where. All I knew was that every time we got together, catastrophe seemed to ensue. *But we're getting along okay right now,* I argued with myself.

Maybe Christy and I had experienced a few rough years. But did that mean we were destined to snipe at each other every time our paths crossed? Again my head answered that question one way, my heart another.

I pulled Christy closer, testing the waters. She didn't protest. She sort of melted into my embrace as if being in such close proximity to my body was the most natural thing in the world.

I rested my head against hers and closed my eyes. Maybe there was hope for the two of us after all. . . .

Fifteen

Christy

"HAVE ANOTHER SUGAR cookie," Jake offered. "It's on me."

I made a gagging motion. "I can't believe I
choked *one* of those down. There's no way I'm
going to try for two."

Jake grinned, snapping the hard-as-a-rock sugar
cookie in half. "This cookie could have been used
as one of a caveman's first tools," he commented,
depositing the cookie onto a tiny paper plate.

I raised my glass of punch. "What about this
stuff? It tastes like strawberry-flavored cough
syrup."

He put his own cup to his mouth and downed
the contents in one huge gulp. "Aaah . . . refreshing!"

"Yuck!" I giggled. Jake's face was slightly contorted,

but he was smiling as if he had just downed a delicious cup of hot chocolate.

"So, what do you say?" he asked. "Are you ready to head back out to the dance floor? I heard a rumor that the band is going to play the hokey-pokey next."

"Let's do it."

It wasn't until Jake and I were wending our way through the dancing couples that I realized how bizarre it was that we were voluntarily going back to the floor for another round of dancing together.

I had been so busy laughing and talking with Jake that I hadn't even thought about the fact that we'd practically had a written contract to stay away from each other once we arrived at the prom. It had seemed natural for us to stick together.

As I continued to follow Jake through the crowd, I thought about what Jane had said. We had grabbed a couple of minutes for girl talk when Jake and Max had been standing in line for the dreaded punch together.

"You and Jake make such an amazing couple," Jane had exclaimed. "I don't know why I never saw that before."

I hadn't known how to respond to Jane's comment. It had come out of absolutely nowhere and landed like a slap on the face. Jake and me? An amazing couple? The notion was ludicrous, absurd, and outlandish—all rolled up into one.

And yet . . . I hadn't come out and said that to her. I had just stood there stuttering until, mercifully, the guys had shown up with our glasses of punch. But with that one sentence my entire night had taken a turn. The power of suggestion was an incredible phenomenon. I simply couldn't look at Jake through the same lens I had been using for the past five years.

"You don't mind if I pull out my *Saturday Night Fever* moves, do you?" Jake asked. "I saw it on cable the other night, and I've been itching to disco ever since."

We had reached the center of the dance floor, and Jake was jumping up and down as if he were a runner trying to limber up.

"Feel free. Just make sure to avoid eye contact with me," I teased him. "I don't want to be seen on the floor with a guy who wishes he were in a white suit and platform shoes."

"All right, all right," he conceded. "I'll save the disco moves for the privacy of my own home."

Jake put his arms around me, and I experienced the same melting sensation that I had earlier in the evening when he had pulled me close. By the time we left the floor in search of refreshment, I felt like a piece of taffy that had been left in the backseat of a car on an August afternoon.

The prom was turning out to be more fun than I ever could have imagined. Correction. *Jake* was turning out to be more fun than I could have imagined. It was like I had stepped into some alternate universe in which Jake and I had never had that terrible date that ended our friendship.

I liked dancing with him. He was graceful—but

not a show-off. And he knew just how to hold me. In fact, I liked dancing with Jake *too much*. It was one thing to feel like we were in the process of re-discovering our lost friendship. But I found myself wishing he would hold me tighter.

I'm attracted to him, I admitted to myself. This wasn't like the other night on his sofa. I couldn't blame my feelings on being upset. I wasn't in tears now, searching for any human connection I could find. This was pure physical attraction.

"Get ready for the dip!" Jake exclaimed. "We're really going to go for it this time."

I braced myself. Jake was a good dancer, but he had dropped me on the floor the last time we had attempted this move. Of course, I hadn't helped matters by losing my footing when my heel caught on the hem of my dress.

"Ready and waiting, Fred," I told him.

Clasping his hand, I took a few steps back. Then I twirled counterclockwise until our bodies collided. Immediately Jake put his other arm around my waist and dipped me so low to the ground that my hair brushed the floor.

From my upside-down position I spotted Matt, dancing several couples away. Matt! I had completely forgotten about him.

"Yes!" Jake yelled, pulling me upright. "The judges would have to give us a ten for that dip—if there were any." He grinned. "Nice job, Ginger."

I laughed. "Fred, without you, I'm two left feet."

As I drifted back into Jake's arms, I knew that it

wasn't the blood that had rushed to my head that was making me dizzy. It was Jake.

It was crazy, but the only place I wanted to be right now was right here with *him*. I had zero interest in going over and saying hi to Matt. I had even avoided making eye contact with him a couple of times already. I was afraid that he was going to remind me of my promise to save him a dance.

You're an idiot, I told myself. At this very moment Jake was probably plotting how to get rid of me so that he could flirt his way through every available girl in the room. He and Wendy Schultz most likely had some synchronized plan that involved the two of them meeting in an abandoned broom closet for a major make-out session.

"Just let me know when you're ready to try the tango," Jake whispered in my ear. "Thanks to my mother, I've had to watch *Dancing with the Stars* all week."

Jake is having fun too, I realized. A guy who wasn't enjoying himself didn't crack jokes and goof around. And I couldn't help but notice that Jake hadn't even glanced in Wendy's direction. Or anyone else's, for that matter. He had been the perfect date since he arrived at my doorstep.

The music slowed, and Jake pulled me closer. "Everybody else is dancing cheek to cheek," he pointed out. "We, uh, might as well go with the flow."

"Yeah, sure," I agreed breezily. But inside, my heart was fluttering and my stomach had dropped to my feet.

I was overwhelmed—with emotions and desire and, strangely, fear. I had never felt this way before. At least, not since seventh grade, when I had spent every waking moment thinking about . . . Jake.

Jake's arms tightened around my waist. We were so close that I could feel his heart beating. Was this real? Was Jake experiencing the same flurry of emotions that I was?

Or is he just being nice to me because he feels sorry for me? I wondered. Was it possible that Jake was trying to make me feel good because he knew that I was going through the worst time of my life? I had thought so the night that Jake and I had almost kissed. I had been sure of it. The pity kiss.

But my heart wasn't letting me believe that Jake was only hanging out with me because of his loyalty to my mother. I had seen the sparkle in his eyes, and I had heard his laughter. Jake hadn't *had* to hold me so close. And he couldn't make his heart beat that way—not if he weren't genuinely feeling *something*.

But this didn't make any sense. This wasn't the way Jake and I related. We were combative and surly and sarcastic.

"I need to go to the ladies' room," I said suddenly, pushing away from him. "I'll be back in a minute."

I needed space. And time to think. I had to sort out these confusing feelings before I started to fall for Jake in a big way. *Except I'm afraid it's too late for that,* I thought. *I think I've already fallen.*

★   ★   ★

I'll think about Jake in a minute, I decided once I was in the girls' locker room. First I wanted to call home and check on Mom.

Yes, she had told me to have a great time and not give her a second thought. But that was like telling me not to breathe. She had been happy this evening, but she had also been in pain. I wouldn't be able to think with absolute clarity until I knew she was okay.

I took my Nokia cell phone out of my evening bag and scrolled through my contacts as I stood in the corner of the locker room. As I dialed our family's phone number, I said a silent prayer of hope. Hope that Mom wasn't in any pain. Hope that she was feeling great. Hope that her cancer had miraculously disappeared while Jake and I had been dancing and drinking fruit punch.

"Hello?" The voice that answered the phone didn't belong to either of my parents. It was Jake's mom.

Why is she there? I wondered. Nobody had mentioned that she was coming by tonight. Jake had told me that his parents had rented a movie and were planning to make homemade pizza.

"Hi, Mrs. Saunders," I said, my heart lurching. "It's Christy. I wanted to check in and see how Mom was doing."

"Christy, honey. Hi."

I felt like I was going to throw up. Molly never called me "honey." "How is she?" I asked again. "Tell me."

There was a pause. "Your dad took her to the

147

hospital," she said finally. "I came over so that I could tell you when you got home."

"Oh no," I whispered. "Please, no."

"They wanted you to enjoy the prom," Mrs. Saunders continued. "There's nothing you can do at the hospital."

"This isn't happening," I said, more to myself than to Molly. "Is it . . . what's going on, exactly?" I asked breathlessly.

"I don't know, Christy," she responded, her voice filled with sadness. "But you might want to . . ."

I didn't hear the rest of what she said. I hung up the phone and sprinted out of the locker room. I had to get to the hospital. Now! My mother could be dying at this very moment, and I wasn't there.

I pushed my way through the gym, tears streaming down my face. I didn't stop to talk to Jake. I didn't stop to talk to anyone. There was no time for questions or hugs or sympathetic gestures. I just wanted to get out of there as quickly as I possibly could.

Finally I burst through the gymnasium door. I slipped out of my sandals as I scanned the parking lot, searching for the driver who had brought Jake and me to the prom.

Suddenly I felt a hand on my arm. "Christy?" a soft voice asked.

I turned my head and found myself looking at Nicole's mystery man. She had finally located him, and they were here at the prom together. I had seen them several times, but they hadn't come over to say hello yet. So how did he know my name?

He was talking to me, but I couldn't really hear what he was saying. I just knew that I saw understanding in his dark brown eyes. Not just sympathy . . . but real understanding.

How could he know anything about my mom? Before I had a chance to even ask him, he explained. His name was Justin, and his own mother had died of cancer last year. He'd seen me in the cancer ward last year. I hadn't remembered Justin until now. Maybe I hadn't wanted to.

I told him that my mom had gotten worse. "Please don't tell anyone that you saw me," I said finally. "I'm not ready to talk about this."

"I won't tell the others," he told me, handing me his prom ticket with a phone number written on it. "Promise that you'll call me if you ever want to talk. I really do know what you're going through."

I nodded and squeezed his hand, vaguely thinking that Nicole had chosen a great stranger as her prom date. I was looking wildly around for the driver of the limo that Jake had rented. At last I spotted him. He was standing next to the limousine. I hiked up my dress and raced to his side.

"I need to get to Memorial Hospital right way," I told him. "It's an emergency."

"Of course," he responded.

I dove into the back of the limo as the driver slid into the driver's seat and gunned the engine. "We'll be there in ten minutes," he assured me.

I closed my eyes. *I'm on my way, Mom,* I told her silently. *Just hang on until I get there.*

Sixteen

Jake

AFTER ABOUT FIVE seconds of standing alone on the dance floor, I realized that it wasn't a place where I wanted to be solo. It doesn't take long for a guy dancing by himself to start looking like a major geek. But I didn't want to find another partner (like Wendy, who had been glancing my way all night) either. I wanted to dance with Christy. Period.

Finally I maneuvered my way off the dance floor, keeping my eye out for Christy as I headed toward the edge of the crowd. Now I stood several yards from the door to the girls' locker room, where I would be sure to spot her the moment she walked out of the bathroom.

I tapped my foot and glanced at my watch. She had been gone almost fifteen minutes. Girls! Once

151

they all congregated in the women's room, they could spend up to an hour gabbing about who knew what.

But I was getting impatient. And from the other side of the gymnasium I could see Wendy slowly making her way in my direction. I needed to find Christy—ASAP.

"Hey, Jenny, was Christy Redmond in there?" I asked as Jenny Leland walked out of the locker room.

Jenny shook her head. "Nope. Sorry."

Great. She had left the locker room. Now what? I scanned the dance floor, searching for Christy's pink dress. But I didn't see her. Suddenly I had a horrible thought. What if Christy had ditched me so she could hang out with Matt Fowler?

It's no big deal, I told myself. It was a free country. Christy could do whatever she wanted. But it *was* a big deal. I didn't *want* Christy to be off somewhere with Matt. I wanted her to be by my side or, more accurately, in my arms.

I started to walk around the perimeter of the gymnasium, searching for Christy. My heart dropped when I saw none other than Matt Fowler standing in a corner. His back was to me, and he appeared to be kissing someone. Christy!

Then I saw a brief flash of mint green. *Encouraging,* I thought. I walked closer to Matt and craned my neck so that I could see who he was kissing. Phew. It was Sandra Donell, his date.

So Christy wasn't with Matt. I continued my

journey around the perimeter of the dance, keeping my eyes peeled for that beautiful pink dress, that shiny head of dark hair. I didn't see Nicole or her date. I *did* see Jane and Max, but they seemed oblivious to the rest of the world—as they had been for the majority of the evening.

I reached my original post near the girls' locker room, and still I hadn't even glimpsed Christy. *Maybe she went outside,* I thought. It was pretty hot in here—I wouldn't mind getting a little fresh air myself.

It was the only explanation. I picked up my pace and more or less jogged to the entrance of the gymnasium. Outside, I inhaled the fresh, sweet air and scanned the parking lot for Christy.

Plenty of people were out there, but none of them was wearing a pink dress. As I walked among the cars and limousines that were parked outside, I noticed that Christy wasn't the only person missing. I didn't see our driver, Ted, anywhere.

I approached a couple of limo drivers who were hanging out next to one of their vehicles. "Hey, have you seen a guy named Ted?" I asked. "Long hair, goatee, black cap?"

One of the guys nodded. "Yeah, Ted. He was here a while ago. But he took off with some girl."

My stomach felt like it had just been twisted into a giant pretzel. "Was she wearing a pink dress?" I asked.

The guy nodded. "Yeah. And she was *hot.*" He grinned. "Sorry, guy. Looks like you lost your date."

I felt like punching him. Instead I turned and headed back to the prom. This was nuts! One second everything was great. The next second Christy had abandoned me in the middle of the dance floor and hijacked our limo.

Why would she do that? I asked myself. Nobody, not even Christy, would do something so blatantly rude. Not unless there was a logical explanation.

Suddenly I stopped in my tracks. Christy *wouldn't* have left the prom without a good reason. I was sure of it. If nothing else, she wouldn't want to explain to her mom why she was home early.

Mrs. Redmond. I got out my cell phone and left the gymnasium, hoping against hope that the pin in my stomach was simply the result of too many sugar cookies. *Please let me be wrong,* I prayed as I dialed and put my free hand in the pocket of my tux pants.

My dad answered the phone on the first ring. When I heard his voice, the pit in my stomach transformed itself into a stabbing knife.

"Dad, is everything okay?" I asked. "I'm at the prom, but Christy disappeared. . . ."

"It's Rose," Dad said, his voice heavy and sad. "She went to the hospital about an hour ago. Christy called home, and Mom gave her the news. I guess she didn't want to take the time to tell you what was going on." He paused. "Mom said she hung up the phone before your mother had even finished speaking."

"I need to go to the hospital," I announced. "I need to be there for Christy. But the limo is gone. . . ."

"We were going to head over to Memorial too," Dad said. "Wait outside, and we'll pick you up in ten minutes."

"Thanks." I hung up the phone, feeling like a total jerk.

I shouldn't have thought for one second that Christy was off with Matt or had decided to strand me at the dance. She wasn't that kind of person.

Now I was going to be there for her. I wanted to be by Christy's side—even if she didn't want me to be.

It was after midnight, and so far I hadn't seen Christy. The waiting room at Memorial Hospital was a depressing place: plastic chairs, two vending machines, that antiseptic smell. I had flipped through a dozen issues of *Time* magazine, but none of the articles held my attention.

I had learned from my parents that Mrs. Redmond's condition had worsened shortly after Christy and I had left for the prom. She had taken an extra pain pill, but it had done no good. Finally Mr. Redmond had called my parents and told them that he was taking Rose to the emergency room. Mom had gone to the house to wait for Christy so she could give her the news.

My mom and dad sat on the chairs opposite me. Every once in a while one of them would doze off. Then they would wake up with a start and ask if there had been any word. Each time the answer was no.

Finally I glimpsed Christy coming down the hallway. I sat up straight in my chair and braced myself for bad news. But her face was a complete blank, almost as if she were suffering from shock.

"Christy!" Mom exclaimed as soon as she saw her. "How is she?"

"She's stable—for now." Christy's voice held a note of resignation that broke my heart. "And they've given her a major dose of pain medication. She's asleep."

Mom stood up and folded Christy into her arms, rocking her back and forth. "If there's *any-thing* we can do, you just say the word."

My mother sounded strong now, in front of Christy, but she had been crying on and off for the past two hours. She had been holding my father's hand so tightly that her knuckles turned white.

"Thank you, Molly." Christy disentangled her-self and brushed a tear from her cheek. "But all we can really do now is hope for a miracle."

And then she saw me. "Jake, hey." She saw that I was still in my tuxedo, and she glanced down at herself. She seemed to have forgotten that she was walking around the hospital in a ball gown. "I'm sorry I left like that. . . . I just had to get here as fast as I could."

I shook my head. "Of course. Don't worry about it."

I wanted to say something else. I wanted to tell her how sorry I was, and I wanted to hug her and kiss her and wipe away her tears. But I felt paralyzed.

"Coffee," Christy whispered. "I think I need a cup of black coffee."

"There's a machine around the corner," I told her. "Let's get a cup."

Now that I had a mission, I sprang into action. I jumped out of my seat and rushed to Christy's side.

Then I took her arm and gently guided her to the coffee machine.

Christy sighed and slumped against the wall as I poured her a cup of hot, black coffee. "You don't have to be here," she said quietly. "I appreciate it. But there's nothing anyone can really do right now."

I set the coffee down on top of the machine and turned so that I could look in her eyes. "This is the only place I want to be right now," I told her. "And not just because I care about your mom. I want to be here for *you*."

Another tear slid down Christy's cheek. I reached out and brushed it away, then put my arms around her. She felt so fragile, I wished I could protect her from everything bad in the world.

"Thanks so much, Jake," she whispered. "It means a lot to me to hear you say that."

"I'm going to be here for as long as you need me," I assured her.

She pulled away and took my hands in hers. "You've been an incredible friend, and I'll never forget it."

Again I took her in my arms and hugged her tight. "You'll get through this," I promised. "I know you will."

I wished more than anything that I had some magical power to make all of this go away. But I didn't. No one did. All we could do now was wait . . . and as Christy had said, hope for a miracle.

Seventeen

Christy

ON SUNDAY MORNING I stood by my father's side as Dr. Ziegler came out to speak to us. She had been my mother's doctor since all of this began, and I had come to trust her. She was always sensitive but honest. I knew she would tell us the truth, no matter how painful.

We had been sitting in the small lounge at the end of my mother's hall since they had admitted her to the hospital and moved her from the ER to the oncology ward. Neither of us had suggested leaving. We had simply dozed off in our chairs until sunlight began to stream through the windows.

"How is she?" Dad asked, his voice wavering. "Is Rose any better?"

Dr. Ziegler shook her head. "I'm sorry, Robert. Rose is very weak."

159

"Is she going to be able to leave the hospital?" I asked. It was the question that would determine everything.

"No, I don't think so, Christy," the doctor answered. "We've done everything we can, and Rose has put up a brave fight. But sometimes these diseases are too powerful to overcome." She paused. "As long as your mother is here, we can make her as comfortable as possible. That just couldn't be done at home. Not at this stage."

"We'll want to be with her twenty-four hours a day," Dad told Dr. Ziegler. "I assume that won't be a problem."

As they continued to speak in hushed tones, I felt my mind leaving my body. I was standing there—still wearing that ridiculous prom dress—but I was watching myself from above. I simply couldn't process this information.

My world was splintering into a million tiny pieces. It was cracking apart, like a precious Ming vase smashing against a tiled floor. The doctor was telling us that it was time to give up the last vestige of hope.

Mom was going to die. Maybe not today. Maybe not tomorrow. But soon. And there was absolutely nothing I could do about it. I couldn't even cry right now. I had to be strong for my dad, and I knew my mom wouldn't want to spend her last days with us being complete basket cases. We had to make every minute count.

I came back into my body and looked at Dr.

160

Ziegler. "Is she awake now?" I asked. "Can I talk to her?"

She nodded. "Rose is awake, and she's quite lucid. I've just had a long talk with her."

So she knew. Mom knew that she was never again going to leave the hospital. A long time ago she had asked us to be straight with her. Dad and I had both promised that we wouldn't hide the truth from her. The doctor had made that same promise, and I had no doubt that she had given Mom the cruel, undeniable facts.

"Can I be alone with her for a few minutes?" I asked my father.

He nodded. "Of course, honey." He put an arm around me. "You go on in. I want to ask the doctor a few more questions anyway."

I stood on my tiptoes and kissed my dad on the cheek. Then I took a deep breath and crossed the short distance to my mother's private hospital room.

Outside the door, I peered through the window and saw Mom sitting up in bed, staring out of the window. She looked contemplative . . . but surprisingly peaceful. I forced myself to smile. I was going to be the first person she saw since she got the news, and I didn't want to be a downer.

I'm here, Mom, I thought. *And I love you.*

"Hi, sweetie," Mom greeted me as soon as I walked into the room. "How are you?"

I walked to her bed and perched beside her so

161

that I could hold her hand. "I'm fine, Mom." I took her hand in mine. "How are *you?*"

She smiled. "Well, I've been better, honey. But I'm glad you're here."

I choked back tears as I squeezed her hand. "We just talked to the doctor. She told us. . . ."

Mom nodded. "We don't need to think about that right now, sweetie." She paused. "I want to talk about you and Dad and anything under the sun that doesn't have to do with cancer."

"Okay, Mom. Whatever you want."

Suddenly Mom put her hand over mine and sat up a little straighter. She looked right into my eyes. "Christy, we don't have a lot of time left together. Promise me, mother to daughter, that from this second forward you'll tell me *everything* that's in your heart. I don't want to waste this precious time discussing the weather or movies or what medication they're feeding me through this tube stuck in my arm."

"There's so much to say," I whispered. "I don't know where to begin."

She grinned. Only my mother could be attached to tubes and monitors and still manage to smile as if she were sitting down to tea with a couple of friends. I knew already that this was how I would remember her. Smiling. Laughing. Loving.

"Let's start with something simple," she suggested. "First of all, I want to say that I'm sorry you had to leave the prom early. I wanted you to stay and enjoy every second—but I should have known that my loyal, dutiful daughter would call home to check on her sick ol' mom."

"I didn't care about the prom," I told her. "To tell you the truth, I didn't even really want to go."

She looked shocked. "You didn't?" she asked. "But you were so excited. You and Jake had such a wonderful evening planned." She paused. "Why didn't you want to go?"

"It's a long story." I sighed, but I couldn't help smiling a little bit as I thought of Jake. "It's not that I didn't want to go to the prom itself. . . . I just didn't want to go with Jake."

I paused, wondering if I should tell her the whole truth. Then I remembered what she had asked of me, and I took a deep breath. From this moment forward, I was resolved to share everything that was in my heart with my mother. It was the only chance I would have to do so.

"The only reason Jake asked me was because he knew how much it meant to you," I admitted. "And I agreed to be his date for the same reason. We wanted to make you happy."

Mom let go of my hand and took my face in her hands. "Christy, I'm so sorry. I'm touched that you two wanted to please me, but it wasn't necessary."

I smiled. "The weirdest part is that I actually *liked* being his prom date," I told her. "We were dancing together and laughing. . . . I felt like I was in a movie."

"I'm glad, honey." Mom smiled, but her eyes had a faraway look. I guessed that she was remembering

163

her own youth and the times she had spent with my father when they were my age.

"Mom, how did you know that Jake and I might belong together?" I asked. "I mean, up until the last couple of weeks, I couldn't stand the guy!"

"Someday you'll have children of your own," she responded. "And then you'll realize that a mother's intuition is almost always right."

"But I don't know how Jake feels about *me,*" I told her. "I mean, I don't even understand my own emotions."

Again my mom smiled. "Christy, growing up is a long, painful process. Maybe Jake is the boy for you, and maybe he isn't." She paused, as if searching for exactly the right words with which to impart her maternal instinct. "The important thing is that you always follow your heart. Don't concern yourself with what other people want or think you should be—and that includes Dad and me."

"But I want you to be *proud* of me," I told her. "That means everything."

Her eyes welled with tears. "Christy, I *am* proud of you. You're a wonderful daughter and a wonderful human being." A lone tear slid down her cheek, but she was still radiating that beautiful, peaceful smile. "All I want is your happiness."

"Thanks, Mom." I leaned down and hugged her tight. Despite her frailty, the warmth of her embrace still had the power to make me believe in myself and in the future.

As we hugged, I thought of the hug Jake had

given me last night when I had gone downstairs to get a cup of coffee and tell the Saunderses about her condition. That hug had also made me feel safe and protected.

Mom had said that all she wanted was my happiness. And I was starting to believe that Jake was a key element to realizing that happiness. But it wasn't something I could contemplate right now.

I was going to focus every ounce of my time and energy on my mother. From this point until . . . the end . . . she was the only person who mattered.

Eighteen

Christy

A WEEK HAD passed since Mom had been admitted to the hospital. I couldn't believe how different this Saturday night was from last weekend. The prom seemed like a distant memory—a haze of twinkling lights, taffeta dresses, and slow, melodic ballads. Now my whole world consisted of doctors, nurses, hospital food, and the constant tests my mother was undergoing in order to have her condition monitored.

I had been to school a few times, but my teachers had been incredibly understanding. Each and every one had told me not to worry about upcoming final exams and term papers. Instead they had arranged to give any necessary assignments to Jane and Nicole, who had come to the hospital every day after school.

Jake had been by at least once a day, entertaining all of us with funny anecdotes about his day in school. And then there was Molly. She had supplied us with an endless number of sumptuous lunches and dinners, both at home and at the hospital.

Home. It seemed almost as far away as the prom. Dad and I had taken turns going to the house to shower and change or catch a few hours of sleep, but neither of us had been able to stay away from Mom longer than was absolutely necessary. Even when she was asleep—which had been most of the time—we had kept a bedside vigil. Neither of us wanted to miss a moment with her.

The days at the hospital had taken on such a familiar routine that I had been lulled into a sense that things had become almost normal again. It had seemed that we would go on like this forever. Mom would be sick, and Dad and I would be there to hold her hand and tell her that we loved her.

But as I looked at Dr. Ziegler's face now, I crashed back to planet Earth. Her eyes told me what I had dreaded hearing for almost two years now. Mom had taken that final turn for the worse. The one that meant the end of her life wasn't only a certainty—it was imminent.

She's been in pain, I told myself. *I don't want her to suffer forever.* But selfishly I *did* want her to keep suffering if it meant that I could hold her and talk to her and look into her eyes.

I looked away from the doctor and gazed at my mother. She was asleep, but it was a fitful, agonized sleep. Even with all of the medication that she was receiving intravenously, Mom was moaning as if she were being tortured.

Dr. Ziegler took off her glasses. "Christy, Robert, we've known this was coming. . . ."

My dad's hands clamped down on my shoulders, as if he knew he wouldn't be able to stand without the support of my narrow frame. "We have known," he whispered, his voice full of anguish. "But somehow I don't think either of us believed she would ever really get this bad."

"I . . . I . . ." There were no words to express what I was feeling.

"You had better say your good-byes now," Dr. Ziegler continued. "There's simply nothing more we can do."

Dad nodded. He went to Mom's left side, then motioned for me to come stand next to him. "We'll say good-bye together," he announced.

With one hand I held on to my dad. With the other I reached out and held my mother's knee. "Mom?" I whispered. "Can you wake up now?"

She groaned in her sleep, but her eyes fluttered open. Since she had been in the hospital, a lot of the time, even when she was awake, her eyes had been cloudy from either pain or pain medication. But as she looked at us now, I could tell that she was lucid.

"Hi," she whispered. "Here are my two favorite people. Let's party."

"Oh, Rose." Dad's voice was barely above a

169

whisper, but he managed to smile as he leaned over to kiss her lightly on the lips.

Mom's eyes were full of gravity as she gazed at us. "I know what's happening," she said. "I can feel it."

Tears streamed down my cheeks, and I had to bite my lip to keep myself from starting to sob. "We're right here with you, Mom. We're not going anywhere."

She nodded. "I want both of you to know how much I love you," she whispered. "I've had the best husband and the best daughter that ever were. It's been a wonderful, fulfilling life."

"I love you, Mom," I told her. "You've been the best mother any girl could have. And you'll *always* be my mother—forever."

"Christy, please do one thing for me," she asked, her eyes filled with tears.

"Anything," I promised, my heart aching inside my chest.

"Remember that all I've ever wanted was your happiness," she told me. "Enjoy every moment of this precious life."

"I will, Mom. I promise." I was sobbing now. I couldn't stop the tears. I didn't even want to.

She turned to Dad. "Bobby, I want the same for you. Be happy. And take care of our little girl."

"I'll take care of her, Rose," Dad vowed, tears pouring from his eyes. He reached out and gently ran his fingers down her sunken cheek. "You can let go now, my love. We know you're tired. . . . Just rest."

As Dad and I clung to her, Mom closed her eyes. In a few seconds her breathing quieted . . . and then it stopped altogether. Beside us a monitor began to beep.

Dr. Ziegler stepped out of the shadows and switched off the monitor. "She's gone."

"Christy . . ." Dad let go of Mom and wrapped his arms around me.

I held tightly to my father, racked with grief. I could hear nothing but a sort of rushing in my ears, and my entire body throbbed with pain. Neither of us tried to hold back our sobs as we stood there, hugging and crying.

The time to be strong had passed. Mom was gone, and nothing would ever be the same again.

On Sunday morning I stumbled downstairs after a sleepless night. Dad and I had come home from the hospital together sometime after midnight. The house had seemed so empty that we had turned on every light. Then we had sat down together at the kitchen table, too tired to cry any more tears. It was almost dawn when we finally went to our rooms.

I had tried to sleep, but it was impossible. Memories had washed over me like, as they say, sands through an hourglass. Mom brushing her hair. Mom helping me pick out a new dress for the first day of second grade. Mom holding me on her lap while I cried because Craig Layborne was picking on me at school.

Sometime after dawn I finally processed the

truth. My mother had died. She was gone, and I would never see her again. I had thought I couldn't cry anymore, but I was wrong. I buried my face in my pillow and let out all of the emotions I had kept bottled up inside for the last few months.

When I had spent myself, I felt calmer. Along with the grief and the pain, I found myself feeling grateful that my mother's struggle was over. She was finally at peace.

I glanced at the phone in the hallway and thought about calling Jane and Nicole to give them the news. But no. I wasn't ready quite yet. I didn't want to say those terrible words aloud—not even to my two best friends.

Now I walked into the living room. This was the last place I had seen Mom before she had entered the hospital. She had been lying on the sofa, laughing and smiling as Dad snapped pictures of Jake and me.

I took a photo album from one of the shelves of our built-in bookcase and sat down on the couch in the exact spot where Mom had been. As soon as I opened the album, I felt transplanted in time, back to an age when my world had consisted of scraped knees, meat loaf, and naps.

The pages of the album were like chapters of my life. Mom had documented our lives on a constant basis. There were a dozen more photo albums on the shelves, and I knew that in the days leading up to the funeral, I would pore over each and every picture.

Looking at the images of my mother was painful, but I also found comfort in the sheer number of memories that we had captured on film. Years from now I would be able to sit down with my children and introduce them to their grandmother through these hundreds and hundreds of pictures.

"She'll never really be gone," I realized. Even now I could feel her presence around me, almost like a warm security blanket.

I flipped a page of the album. There was one of my all-time favorite pictures. It had been taken at my first birthday party. Molly Saunders stood off to one side, holding a one-year-old Jake. She was laughing as I, covered in birthday cake, reached up from my high chair and smeared Mom's face with pink frosting. Dad had told me that *he* had been laughing so hard, he had barely been able to focus the camera.

I reached out and touched my mother's cheek in the photograph. Then I slid the picture out of its plastic encasing. I was going to frame this one and keep it next to my bed, where I could look at it every morning and every night.

Lost in thought, I jumped when I realized that the doorbell was ringing. Part of me wanted to ignore whoever was at the door. But it wouldn't be right. There were other people who had loved Mom, and I knew they would want to share their grief with us on this terrible day.

I set the album aside and heaved myself off the

couch. There was only one person besides my dad that I *really* felt like seeing right now, and he was probably still asleep at this hour on a Sunday morning.

But when I opened the door, I found myself looking into Jake's eyes. I should have known. Jake had proved during the last few weeks that he would always be there when I needed him, and now here he was.

I could tell from the look in his eyes that his mother had given him the news. There was no need to say those dreaded words aloud.

"Christy . . . I'm so sorry." He took a step toward me, his face damp with tears.

I didn't speak. I simply succumbed to the magnetic pull I felt toward Jake. When I was close enough, he reached out and put his arms around me, holding me tight. As I had so many times recently, I allowed myself to let down my guard.

But these weren't the anguished, tortured tears I had cried this morning. These were tears of exhaustion and at relief at finding myself exactly where I needed to be. Even so, I was surprised by the sheer comfort I found in Jake's embrace.

"I'll be here as long as you need me," Jake promised.

I held him tight, feeling like I never wanted to let him go. *Maybe mother* does *always know best,* I thought. She had certainly been right about Jake. He was a special person . . . and he was my best friend.

Epilogue

A Few Months Later, Sometime at the End of August

"GRATED ZEST OF one lemon," I read aloud from the recipe for the springtime shrimp I was making. "Now what, exactly, is 'zest'?"

If Mom were still here, I could have called out to her and asked the question. It was an urge I still had twenty times a day. But now, over three months since her death, I didn't dissolve into tears every time I wanted to ask her a question or tell her a story or simply give her a hug and a kiss.

Sure, I still cried plenty. There were times when both my dad and I missed Mom so much that we would get in the car and go visit her grave just so we could tell her about how our days had gone.

But I had started to laugh again too. And when I wanted to feel close to my mother, I would head into

175

the kitchen to try out a new recipe. She had taught me to make my first pancake, and every time I mastered a new dish, I felt her presence, cheering me on.

And then there was Jake. It was hard to believe that several months ago I had considered him to be public enemy number one. We had been hanging out together all summer, just like we had when we were kids. We had ridden our bikes, gone out for pizza, watched movies, even revisited the diner where our friendship had fallen apart so many years ago. We had toasted each other with chocolate milk shakes (after carefully removing the ketchup bottle from the table) and vowed that we would never again let our pride stand in the way of what promised to be a lifelong friendship.

I hadn't called him an errant, onion-eyed bug-bear even once. Times had changed, and even without Mom life had gone on—just like she had said it would.

With Jake I could talk about my mother without worrying that I was going to bring down everyone around me. Nicole and Jane had provided me with incredible support, but they hadn't known my mom when I was little. They didn't know the same stories that Jake did.

I ran a cheese grater over the rind of a lemon, hoping that I was right in assuming that this would provide me with the "zest" necessary for my recipe. If not . . . well, there was always another dish to try. It wasn't so much the product of my cooking that mattered, but the act itself.

Even Jake had said that he was starting to find cooking to be therapeutic. I had coerced him into making so many meals with me that he had actually begun to know his way around the kitchen.

Jake. Jake. For the past few weeks every thought I had that didn't involve my mother seemed to have one thing in common: *Jake.*

All summer we had been the best of friends. And that's what I had needed. Friendship, with no strings attached. But lately I hadn't been able to stop myself from thinking about *that* night. The night that Jake and I had been sitting on the sofa in his bedroom. The night we had been *this close* to kissing.

I set down the lemon and closed my eyes. In my mind I could see the look in Jake's eyes as he had leaned close. I could almost *feel* his full, red lips on mine. . . .

The fantasy ended abruptly when I heard the doorbell ring. I ran my hands under the faucet, then walked through the empty house to answer the door.

"Christy?" I heard Jake's voice from the other side of the door. "Are you in there?"

My heart began to pound as I opened the door. Jake stood on the front steps, holding a bouquet of wildflowers. Did the flowers *mean* something, or were they just a nice, *friendly* gesture?

"Hey!" I greeted him. "Want to help me make springtime shrimp?"

He grinned. "Actually, I had something else in mind—if the shrimp can wait."

"Okay . . ." I was confused but intrigued. Then I glanced over Jake's shoulder and saw a white limo parked at the curb, just as it had been on prom night.

"What's going on?" I asked. "I—I don't get it."

Jake bowed slightly from the waist. "If you'll do me the honor of accompanying me on a little journey, Christy, everything will become clear."

I took a quick mental inventory of the kitchen. The stove was off. The oven was off. The shrimp was in the freezer. There was nothing there that needed my immediate attention. "Sure . . . that sounds nice."

Jake looked incredible. He was wearing dark blue Levi's and a crisp white T-shirt that showed off his dark, golden tan. I, on the other hand, had flour in my hair.

"You look great," Jake said, his voice low. "Just perfect."

As he took my hand and led me toward the limousine, I felt like I had stepped back into my fantasy. Only this time maybe it was for real.

"Where are we *going?*" I asked forty-five minutes later. "Are you going to leave me in the middle of the forest and have me follow a trail of bread crumbs?"

The limo driver had dropped us off at a trail outside of town, and we had been walking into the woods for almost fifteen minutes.

He laughed. "Patience, my sweet. We're almost there."

My sweet. What a wonderful pair of words. I decided I didn't care where we were going. As long as I was with Jake, I was exactly where I wanted to be.

"Ta-da!" he announced a few minutes later. "We have arrived at our final destination."

My mouth dropped open, and I felt awash in pure delight. We had reached a beautiful, secluded spot in the forest . . . where Nicole and Justin and Jane and Max were sitting on a huge, red-and-white-checkered picnic blanket. Spread out in front of them was an elegant picnic supper. Nearby was a portable CD player and a huge pile of discs.

"This is amazing," I exclaimed. "But what are all of you doing here? What's going on?"

Nicole grinned. "We've all been feeling bummed that you never got to finish your senior prom," she explained. "So we're re-creating that magical night, right here, right now, our own way."

"It was all Jake's idea," Jane added. "He's been working for days to give you your own private 'prom' with all of your best friends."

Tears came to my eyes as I realized how much effort everyone, and especially Jake, had put into making this happen. But they were happy tears, for the first time in a long time. I was overwhelmed with emotion as I looked into Jake's twinkling blue eyes.

"I don't know what to say," I whispered. "Thank you."

He took both of my hands in his. "Just say that you'll have this dance with me . . . for your mom," he said quietly. "The next one will be for *us.*"

Justin pushed play on the portable stereo, and suddenly the woods were filled with the sound of Frank Sinatra.

"I would love to dance with you," I told him.

Then I melted into his arms, and we began to move in the fading, dappled light. As I held Jake close, I felt surrounded by my mother's love. I was sure that she was watching us . . . and smiling.

But it wasn't just Mom's love that I felt. Suddenly I knew that I wasn't the only one who had been remembering the kiss that Jake and I almost shared. He had been thinking of it too. I felt his love as clearly as I heard the music.

As the last bars of the song ended, Jake drew me all the way into his arms. "Christy, this is something I've wanted to do for almost as long as I've been alive," he whispered.

And then my arms were around his neck, and our lips found each other. I felt like my entire being had opened up . . . like Sleeping Beauty when the prince awakens her with the soft touch of his lips.

The kiss deepened, and my body felt like it was on fire. I didn't care that my friends were watching. I was ready to kiss Jake in front of the whole world, if anyone was interested in watching. Deep down, this was a moment I had been waiting for as long as I could remember.

When at last Jake and I broke apart, I became aware that my friends were clapping and cheering. "Finally!" Nicole exclaimed. "I thought you two would *never* get together."

"We've found each other," Jake told Nicole. "In our own time."

"Yes, we certainly have," I agreed, staring into his eyes. "It took a long time, but it was well worth the wait."

I turned to my friends, who were beaming as if they had just won the lottery. "Thank you, everyone," I told them. "Being here, with all of you, it's easy to remember what really matters in life." I paused, gazing into Jake's eyes. "Family, friends . . . and love."

As another song began, Max pulled Jane to her feet, and Justin pulled Nicole to *her* feet. "Can we join the party?" Max asked.

"By all means!" Jake proclaimed. "This is our prom, after all."

I drifted back into Jake's arms as the rest of the group joined us on the "dance floor." This was a moment I would treasure for the rest of my life.

Again Jake kissed me, sending sparks up and down the length of my spine. I hugged him tight, feeling truly happy as I moved my eyes toward the sky.

You were right all along, Mom, I told her silently. *Mother* definitely *knows best.* Then Jake and I kissed again . . . and after that, the evening became a blur of laughing, hugging, and kissing. Just like Mom would have wanted.

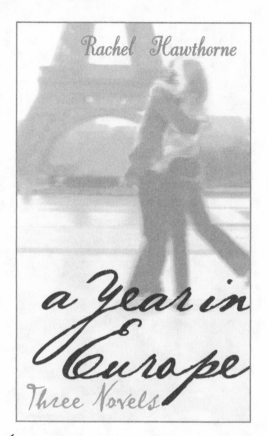

No matter what the season, a trip abroad never goes out of style. Don't miss *A Year in Europe* — three fun novels about three girls from Texas, three beautiful countries, and three sizzling romances with irresistible foreign guys!

Here's a preview. . . .

Robin

KIT MARLIN HAD the most cultured voice I'd ever heard—warm and gentle, sort of like Hugh Grant's. Mine was more like a herd of cattle, which was exactly how Jason Turner had described it.

My mouth grew dry, and my chin tingled. I thought I might be ill. No, no, Princess Diana would never have thrown up in the middle of an airport.

I swallowed to get rid of the stuffed-cotton feel in my mouth. *Remember, you're in London now. Speak like Princess Di.* "I was expecting a female person," I said formally, in a very low voice to disguise my accent.

He leaned forward slightly. "Sorry?"

For what? I wondered. *Keeping me waiting?*

Then it dawned on me. That wasn't what he meant. I'd watched Hugh Grant in enough movies to realize that Kit meant, *Excuse me? What? Come again?*

I cleared my throat and said a little louder, "I was expecting a female person."

He smiled warmly. The most beautiful, welcoming smile I'd ever seen. "Kit is short for Christopher."

My scared-spitless smile evaporated as the reality hit me. Not only didn't I have an English sister to study and imitate, but I had to live in the same house with a guy for the first time in my life. I mean, I'd lived with my daddy, but that didn't count. He was a father. Kit was a . . . Well, Kit was a *guy!*

Sure, he was English and he was cute—to-die-for cute—but he was still a guy, and we'd be sharing accommodations!

If Jason Turner from no-big-deal Dallas thought I was a hillbilly, what was Kit Marlin going to think once he got to know the real me?

"Will you please excuse me a moment while I converse with my companions?" I asked Kit in a low voice.

He furrowed his brow. "Pardon?"

I reined in my impatience. I was certain that talking in a low voice would work once we got out of the bustling airport. Raising my voice just a little bit, ever mindful to keep my words clipped and even, I repeated, "Will you please excuse me a moment while I converse with my companions?"

"Oh, right," he said, nodding. "I'll watch your baggage."

Walking like I was balancing a book on the top of my head, I escorted Dana and Carrie to an area out of earshot. With my back to Kit, I contorted my face into an expression of hopeless despair. As much as I wanted to, I couldn't very well scream in the middle of the airport. "What am I going to do? He's a guy!"

"A cute guy," Carrie pointed out. "And that is so totally not fair. Your first night in London, and a dream guy walks right into your life."

"You're missing the point here! Didn't you hear him talk? He's too English. What do I do now? How am I gonna live in the same house with him? He's gonna think I'm a freak if he hears how I talk and sees how I act." I knew I was rambling, something I did when I was totally nervous—and at that moment I was more nervous than I'd ever been in my entire life.

"He won't think you're a freak," Dana assured me. "He'll like you just like we do."

I shook my head fiercely. "No, no, he won't. Can I stow away with one of you guys and go to Paris or Rome?"

Carrie put her hand comfortingly on my shoulder. "Hey? Aren't you dare-me-to-do-anything Robin?"

"I've only ever lived with my parents," I blurted out. Why couldn't they see what a disaster this was? "Don't dare me to live with a guy!"

"I've got five brothers," Carrie reminded me. "All you have to worry about is making sure that you get a good heaping amount of food on your plate before he sits down to eat because guys wolf down everything in sight. And you just need to check the toilet seat because they always leave it up. Always. It's disgusting."

"I can't do this," I insisted. "He was supposed to be a girl. Kit is a stupid name for a guy."

"As in Kit Carson?" Dana asked.

I glowered at her.

Dana shrugged. "I'm just saying . . . he seems okay with you being a girl. So you can handle this, Robin."

I glanced over my shoulder. Kit was watching me. He quickly looked away.

Carrie leaned close and whispered in my ear, "And he is so totally hot."

I glared at Carrie. "That's one of the things that makes this so hard."

But neither Dana nor Carrie was listening to my pleas for understanding. Instead their eyes were flashing silent *dare yous*. Sometimes it's not a good thing to have friends who know your weakness. I gave a brisk nod. "All right. I can do this. It's not a whole year. It's just a whole school year, which is what . . . one hundred and eighty days?" Wasn't that how Henry VIII counted the time he spent with his wives before he beheaded them—in days instead of years?

"You can do it," Carrie assured me.

"But you're going to have to stop whispering," Dana told me. "And the formal talk? Where did that come from? *Companions?* My grandmother has a *companion.* We're *friends.*"

Carrie nodded. "I have to agree with Dana on this one. You sound too bizarre." She looked past me to where Kit was standing. "He, on the other hand, sounds just like Hugh Grant." She sighed dreamily. "You are so lucky!"

I felt anything except lucky, but I knew that Dana and Carrie were right. I had to stay. Convincing my parents had been a difficult task. If I changed plans now and went to Paris or Rome, they'd have a cow and tell me to come home.

"I'll cut back on the formal words, but not the low voice." I hated to admit it, but *female person* had been a little out there now that I thought about it.

"Oops, there's Miss Lawrence waving at the door. We've gotta go," Carrie said. She gave me a tight hug. "You're gonna do just fine."

I nodded, blinking back the tears stinging my eyes.

Dana hugged me fiercely and kissed my cheek. "Don't cry yet. We're still in the same city, and we'll see you tomorrow." She drew back and smiled. "And tomorrow night we'll all cry when we say good-bye."

Carrie grabbed Dana's arm. "Come on. Let's see if we can talk Miss Lawrence into taking us to a pub tonight."

"She's not going to take us to a pub," practical Dana responded.

"Simply for the cultural experience," Carrie assured her with a laugh.

"Y'all be careful," I called softly after them as they hurried to the cart holding their luggage. So softly that I didn't think they heard me. But I couldn't risk calling out, couldn't take a chance that Kit would hear my real voice.

I watched them say good-bye to Kit before pushing the cart toward the door. I felt like my lifeline was cut when the doors closed behind them.

I wanted to scream, *Wait, take me with you!*

But I had come here to change my screaming ways.

I pasted a smile on my face and walked toward waiting Kit.